The Last Correspondent

ALSO BY SORAYA M. LANE

The Girls of Pearl Harbor
The Spitfire Girls
Hearts of Resistance
Wives of War
Voyage of the Heart

The Last Correspondent

SORAYA M. LANE

LAKE UNION PUBLISHING

Text copyright © 2020 by Soraya M. Lane
All rights reserved.

Published by Lake Union Publishing, Seattle

www.apub.com

Amazon, the Amazon logo, and Lake Union Publishing are trademarks of Amazon.com, Inc., or its affiliates.

ISBN-13: 9781542023573
ISBN-10: 1542023572

Cover design by The Brewster Project

Printed in the United States of America

For Sammia & Sophie.
Your guidance, as always, was impeccable.

I have too frequently received the impression that women war correspondents were an irritating nuisance. I wish to point out that none of us would have our jobs unless we knew how to do them, and this curious condescending treatment is as ridiculous as it is undignified.

Martha Gellhorn, war correspondent,
in a letter to military authorities, 1944

PART ONE

CHAPTER ONE

ILLINOIS, UNITED STATES, JULY 1943
ELLA

Ella turned her face up toward the sun and stretched, her neck still sore from the hours she'd spent at her typewriter the night before. She grimaced as her shoulder groaned painfully, and vowed not to sit for so long without moving again.

There was an envelope poking out of the mailbox and she walked quickly down the steps from her front door to the path, plucking it out and checking to see if it was the only letter. Her heart thudded as she turned it over, hoping to see her brother's familiar scrawl, but instead of finding Brendon's hand, she found the formal stamp from the publication she wrote for.

Frowning, she slid her finger beneath the seal and took out the letter. Why would they be writing to her? Ella tucked the envelope under her arm, quickly scanning the perfectly printed words on the page.

Her heart sank.

Dear Miss Franks,

It has come to our attention that, despite submitting your stories under the name of Ernst Franks, you are in fact a Miss Ella Franks. As you will be well aware, we are strictly forbidden from hiring women as journalists at the United Press, and as such we will no longer be able to publish your writing. Whilst we appreciate the work you have done for us, writing under a pseudonym, we nonetheless see this as a deliberate and fraudulent attempt to conceal your gender and therefore obtain a job with us under false pretenses.

We wish you all the best with your future endeavors.

Ella read the letter again, her eyes traveling more slowly over the words this time, before crushing the paper in her hand and squeezing it until her fingers hurt. Tears formed against her lashes but she refused to let them fall, chewing hard on her bottom lip as she battled her emotions.

I've been fired.

Just like that, for being a woman, she'd been fired. After a year of cleverly turning in her stories as Ernst Franks, and asking for her checks to be made out to simply E. Franks to ensure she could still bank them, it was all over. It seemed so archaic that publications like the *United Press* strictly forbade the hiring of women, but they weren't the only publication, far from it.

Ella walked silently into the house, kicking the door shut behind her and going straight to her bedroom. She stood and looked around at her perfectly made bed, at her desk beneath the window, papers stacked neatly beside her typewriter. At the cigarette discarded in the ashtray with a pen propped against it—a birthday gift from her brother, who believed so genuinely in her talent as a writer despite her *gender*.

It's over.

She dropped the balled-up piece of paper to the floor and stalked toward her desk, standing over it as she breathed heavily, her nostrils flaring as her shoulders trembled. Anger tore through her, pulsated like a living, breathing force.

In one fast movement, she swiped the papers off her desk, batting her beloved pen to the ground, too.

Ella dropped to her hands and knees, chest heaving, her shoulders bunched up as she collapsed. Then, no longer able to contain her emotions, tears ran down her cheeks and fell to the carpet as she rocked, sobbing, guttural noises erupting from her as the weight of her failure consumed her. She may as well have been grieving a loved one, her pain so acute it stole her breath away. She thought she'd been so clever, writing about the effects of war on the local economy, how it was affecting politics, businesses and the everyday person struggling to get by on newly introduced rations, and they'd liked it when they thought her articles were written by a man. But of course no one cared for her reporting skills when they knew her gender. Heaven forbid if anyone had dared to employ her knowing she was a *woman*; then she'd have only been allowed to write about the latest Veet Cream hair removal product or the perfect new Brylfoam shampoo. It made her shudder just thinking about it.

She heard footsteps echo out on the wooden hallway floor and she scrambled up, reaching for her chair to steady herself as her body trembled. She wiped furiously at her cheeks with her fingertips, clearing the salty tears from her skin as they fell to her mouth, and attempting to catch her breath between hiccupping sobs.

"Sweetheart, are you home?"

Her mother's voice was like a warm song drifting down to her room, and Ella took a few more gulps of air before answering her, not wanting her to hear the waver in her tone.

"Ah, just a moment," she stammered.

But she felt her mother's presence without turning, knowing she was already standing in the open doorway behind her. And then Ella heard her drop to her knees, quietly picking up the scattered papers.

She should have bent down to help her, but instead she wanted to scream at her to leave them, to burn them for all she cared. But she didn't. Because this was her mother's house, and because she had no right to be angry with her mother when it was her editor she wanted to scream at. And also because they were in the middle of a war, and her mother would make her feel like a petulant child for being upset over a job given the times they were living in. But despite knowing all that, it didn't make the news hurt any less.

"Ella, I'd like you to come with me tonight," her mother said, touching her arm as she passed. "We need more young women volunteering with the Home Guard, and we have a rifle drill this evening near the university. Please come."

Ella swallowed. Her mother asked her all the time, but usually she had a deadline to wield as an excuse.

"Yes," she whispered, nodding her head as if to convince herself. "I'll come."

Her mother's brows rose in obvious surprise. "You will?"

Ella took the papers from her and dropped them beside the typewriter, glancing up and finally making eye contact with her. "Yes. I will."

"And does this sudden interest in joining me have anything to do with the mess in here?"

Ella's breath shuddered from her lips and she clenched her fists so her mother wouldn't see her hands shaking. "Yes," she said evenly, refusing to shed another tear. "It appears I'm going to have a lot of free time on my hands for volunteering."

Her mother pursed her lips, her eyebrows drawing together as she studied Ella.

"You won't be writing anymore?" she finally said.

"Oh, I'll be writing," Ella muttered stubbornly, "just not for that stupid goddamn newspaper."

"Ella!" her mother scolded. "No swearing in my house."

She chewed on her bottom lip, fingers suddenly itching to type, wanting to belt out a story about the injustice of being a woman and not having a voice, even though she knew no one would publish it. She could almost see the look on her editor's face when he read *that* type of story—not that she'd ever actually write it. She hadn't ever written anything for publication that involved her personal opinions, instead reporting the facts as she saw them.

"And now she's smiling again, just like that," her mother groaned, throwing her hands up into the air. "But there's no getting out of coming with me tonight, do you hear? There are plenty of capable young women there, all doing well with their rifle training. It'd do you good to meet them instead of hiding away in here with that blasted typewriter all day."

Ella stifled another smile as her mother crossed the room and opened the window, smoothing down the bedcovers as she passed.

"How I ended up with a daughter like you," she murmured, and Ella mouthed the words as her mother said them, used to hearing that exact phrase on a daily basis. But it was always followed by a squeeze of her shoulder and a kiss on the cheek, which at least made her think that her mom secretly approved of her work. Or maybe she was just deluding herself.

When she was alone in her room again, Ella opened her drawer and took out a cigarette, knowing her mother hated her smoking in the house but seemingly unable to ever type without at least a few puffs before she started. It was one of her little rituals around her writing, the need to smoke at least half a Lucky Strike until the words started to flow, before forgetting about it and letting it burn down to nothing in the glass ashtray beside her.

She pulled out a fresh sheet of paper, cigarette between her lips, and fed it through her typewriter, the habit calming her as she considered her current predicament. Maybe she'd write that article just for something cathartic to do.

"Darling! It's time for breakfast!"

Ella shut her eyes for a moment, blocking out her mother's voice and wishing she had the nerve to write straight back to the *United Press* and refuse to accept their treatment of her. But that little voice of self-doubt, the one that had almost stopped her from writing under a false name to begin with, was whispering at her that perhaps she just needed to accept her fate. That maybe she hadn't been good enough in the first place.

"Ella! Come along before your eggs go cold!"

She sighed and stood, staring down at her typewriter, desperate to settle her hands over the cool black metal and start tapping out a story, even if it would never be published. But that could wait.

"Coming, Mama!" she yelled back.

———— ⚬⟋⟍⚬ ————

Eight hours later, she was trudging off to meet the group of women her mother had talked about for months now. Her mom had been like a parrot, telling her everything about them and how brave they were, so if she was honest, there was something satisfying about meeting them. Not to mention the fact that she probably should have written an article about them all those months ago.

Ella smiled to herself as she patted the small notebook in her pocket, vowing to scribble notes about the women she met throughout the evening just in case she was able to put a story together.

"Come on, sweetheart, keep up," her mother called out, striding out up ahead.

And then she saw them, and she had to stop her jaw from dropping. The women waiting wore practical, almost man-like coats over their dresses to protect them from the slightly cooler evening wind, but despite their clothing, they were the most beautiful bunch of ladies she'd ever seen, with not a hair out of place and their lipstick perfectly brushed on. And they were all holding guns in their gloved hands.

Ella absently touched her hair, a scarf tied around it, and wished she'd followed her mother's advice and made more of an effort with her appearance. She was used to spending most of her days curled up with her typewriter, and the more she'd worked, the less she'd started to worry about how she looked.

"Everyone, this is my daughter, Ella." Her mother beamed, her shining smile sending waves of guilt through Ella—it wouldn't have killed her to come along before now, given how proud her mother was of her little group.

"Hello," she said, raising her hand and smiling back at the women.

"You ever shot one of these before, Ella?" one of them asked, holding out a rifle.

"Um, well, no actually, I haven't," she admitted, pulling out her pen and paper to start taking notes. "I tend to fight my battles on the page, not with bullets!"

She expected them to laugh, but only her mother smiled at her joke. The others looked more confused than anything. Ella cleared her throat awkwardly, realizing that her mother obviously hadn't mentioned that her daughter was a journalist. Or if she had, it clearly hadn't impressed them.

"I was thinking I could interview you all, you know, as you train and patrol," she said, glancing at each of the ten or twelve women blinking back at her, their expressions impossible to read. "I'm a, ah . . . a writer." It almost felt fraudulent saying it now that she didn't actually have a job. But the stories she'd been writing on the social issues that were arising as a result of the war had all been printed, so technically she was still a writer.

"Or you could just get on with things and learn how to shoot one of these," the same robust-looking woman said, thrusting the gun more forcefully at her this time, clearly not impressed by her suggestion.

Ella stared at the weapon, nodding as she slowly reached out one hand and gripped the wooden barrel with her fingers. "Oh, yes, of course," she said, shooting her mother a quick sideways glance as she took it. "Of course I can, we can always talk later, I suppose," she muttered.

But her voice was lost to the chatter of the women around her, who seemed oblivious to anything other than the work they were doing. She sighed and fell into step beside them, notebook tucked back into her pocket, resigned to the fact there was going to be no more writing until morning. And then an idea struck her, and she almost burst out laughing.

This was what she could write about. The *United Press* might not want her, but surely another publication would be interested in having a woman write about what *women* were doing during wartime? She smiled to herself as she marched, thrilled with her idea.

This way she wouldn't have to pretend she was a man just to get published, although the idea of everyone knowing it was *her*, with no pseudonym to hide behind? Ella gulped. It was exhilarating and terrifying at the same time, but most of all it scared her so much she knew it would take all her nerves to follow through with it. In the past, she'd been so careful to make herself sound like a man through her writing, but if she did this? She wouldn't have to change the way she wrote to sound so formal and robust; she wouldn't have to pretend anymore.

"Ella, stop dreaming and hurry up!" her mother whispered, tugging her arm.

Ella grinned, trotting along to catch up as her head filled with possibilities.

CHAPTER TWO

SICILY, JULY 1943
DANNI

"Bloody hell, are you sure about this, Danni?"

Danni tried to disguise her smirk, thankful for the dark as her English companion gripped the side of the plane beside her.

"We've been through this, Andy," she shouted back. "Just remember your training, and when they say jump—"

The near-deafening rumble of the plane muffled his protests further, and she slapped her hand over her mouth to disguise her laughter at Andy's half-hearted yelp as one of the troops shoved him out the plane door. She should have been terrified; logically she knew that she had every chance of not making it home from her bold decision to parachute directly into conflict, but she was starting to become addicted to the excitement of it all. The men she worked with always claimed whiskey was their poison, but for her it was the adrenalin of her work that made her blood pump like liquid fire through her veins. Poor Andy didn't seem to thrive on it as much as she did, although she was always telling him to stop being so damn British and enjoy living in the moment more.

"Go!" someone yelled at her as more men started to leap from the plane, and she released her hold, smiling to herself when no one dared to push her as they'd pushed her partner. Clearly they'd listened to her when she'd said she'd scream bloody murder, as the Brits liked to say, if anyone dared to lay a hand on her. The plane swayed sideways then lurched sharply, the wind whistling around them and sending spikes of nerves through her stomach.

Silence.

It was the one word that catapulted through her mind as she jumped, the wind whooshing up to meet her ears almost instantly, making her dizzy for a moment as she squinted at the field below. Her fingers itched to hold her camera, but it was fixed safely to her body along with as many flashbulbs and rolls of film as she could carry, and there was no way she could have taken a shot with the ground racing up to meet her so quickly and the light far too dim. She would have to rely instead upon Andy's articulate words to capture the feeling of falling through the sky from a plane, with paratroopers like a sparse flock of birds floating around her as they too rushed toward the ground, being battered by the elements as they spiraled down.

The moonlight was the most beautiful crescent in the sky, but there was barely a moment to admire it before it was time to prepare for landing, as the relentless wind tore at her eyes and skin and sent her into a spin. *Oh no.* Instead of landing on a bare patch of ground, a tree seemed to be racing up to meet her and she struggled to get out of its way, lurching to the side as she wrapped her arms around her chest to protect her camera, but to no avail.

Crash. Danni groaned as she immediately tangled in the branches, with no amount of kicking or flailing doing her any good. She was properly stuck, but at least she hadn't whacked into the ground and smashed all her bulbs.

Damn it! She decided to stay still, dangling less than three feet off the ground, but it may as well have been twenty for all the good it did her. Danni was acutely aware of the danger they faced, that she'd ended up in a tree that could soon be surrounded by the enemy, and she doubted they'd care about her correspondent badge, which was supposed to spare her from being killed. She clenched her jaw, refusing to be drowned in her own dark thoughts.

"Andy!" she whispered, her voice sounding hoarse as she tried to clear her throat. "*Andy!*" she gasped again, more frantically this time as tendrils of panic began to rise in her throat.

She should never have laughed at him. *God.* He'd probably leave her to be shot down by a sniper just to spite her now. Danni gulped. So much for being brave; it wouldn't do her any good if she were taken out before she'd even put her boots on the ground.

Then voices whispered near her, carried on the breeze, and she breathed a sigh of relief. American voices. It was a beautiful melody to her ears.

"Andy!" she hissed again.

And suddenly, as she wriggled and flailed some more, he was there, his eyes glinting in the moonlight, barely visible.

"You called?" he asked.

"Just hurry up and get me down, would you?" she muttered, wishing she hadn't been quite so forthright in threatening any man who laid a hand on her. She could do with more than one pair of hands right now to help her down.

Andy tugged at the branches and lifted something over his head, and within seconds Danni dropped to the ground with an animal-sounding grunt. He was the one man who was never afraid to manhandle her, or tell her exactly how stupid some of her ideas were. She loved Andy to pieces, in a completely brotherly way, although she'd never admit to him just how much she'd come to rely on him.

Oomph.

"Sorry, I should have been more gentle," Andy said dryly.

Danni would have thumped him on the arm for being smart, but she was more interested in making sure her camera had survived the jump. She had it attached to her body and wrapped tightly in a spare shirt like the precious parcel it was; the one piece of equipment she needed to do her job, she protected it as fiercely as a lioness would her cub. She instinctively touched her side, too, checking the bag that was also strapped carefully to her body, and was relieved not to hear the crunch of broken glass.

"You okay?" she asked Andy, once she'd done her checks. "Tell me you didn't enjoy it just a little bit?"

Andy nudged his shoulder into her. "I'll admit, it was kind of beautiful, but it's not something I'm planning on doing again any time soon, especially with a bloody typewriter strapped to me. Next time you come up with a harebrained idea, I'm not buying into it."

She didn't reply, not about to tell him that he always said yes to her. *Eventually.* Although this time she did almost feel sorry for him, given that he'd confessed a fear of heights to her, not to mention the fact that his Remington typewriter was a lot more cumbersome than her camera.

They'd been working together for nearly four years, and they had an unwritten rule that they always traveled together, no matter what, and after so long working side by side, she couldn't imagine it any other way. They could talk about anything and nothing, depending on their mood, and there was no one else she'd trust with her life.

"Tell me again why this was such a great idea?" Andy muttered as they huddled close, walking shoulder to shoulder as they searched for the rest of the 505th Parachute Infantry Regiment.

"Because we're the first to land here," she whispered back. "Which means you have the biggest story to send back to London, and I'm going to have photos that no one else does."

She heard his resigned sigh. "If it makes it past the censor."

Danni patted his back, understanding his frustration at not being able to write what he saw and send it back without it being doctored. Sometimes she'd seen them delete information that was readily available to all, and it made his articles almost impossible to decipher at times.

Over the course of the hour, a small group of them assembled, and Danni was careful to listen and do as she was told. In the past, she'd managed to get away with defying orders and sailing very close to the wind, but this time she needed to toe the line. Not only was she closer to the conflict than she'd ever been before, but she was also the only woman to ever be this close to the front line or to parachute with troops, and she wasn't about to blow it. As far as she was concerned, she'd already pushed her luck as far as it might go.

They'd landed in an egg-shaped area behind enemy lines in Gela, Sicily, and from the briefing they'd received, the troops were expected to close off all roads leading to beaches and secure the drop zone, but Mother Nature was not playing her part. The wind howled around them, the worst possible conditions for landing other than if lashing rain had been paired with it, and she knew that things could turn bad. Fast. Their survival certainly wasn't a given.

"My estimates are that less than a quarter of us have landed where we were supposed to, and that's including these two," the commanding officer said. "The other companies must have scattered all around us."

Danni absently fingered the stitched "C" on her armband that marked her as a war correspondent, wishing that she were holding her camera. But it was no use; it was dark and she wasn't allowed to create any light with her flashbulbs.

"The rest of the 505th have landed outside our drop zone, but our mission remains. We will complete the operation and continue to fight in small groups. We can only hope that the others have banded together where possible, so we can secure Sicily and keep the landings on the beachhead clear."

Excitement rippled through Danni as she surveyed the brave men crouched in a semicircle to her left. She'd spent months in North Africa alongside the troops, and was well used to listening to briefings and being up close and personal with soldiers, but there was something different about being on the ground with them like this, to see them thinking on their feet and adapting. She knew from earlier briefings that Operation Husky was a plan to secure the concrete pillboxes from where the German gunners controlled movement on the roads.

"You two," the commanding officer whispered sharply at her and Andy. "You'll need your wits about you. There're Germans at every turn, so keep your heads down and stay quiet. Follow my commands, and I'll do my best to keep you alive."

"Yes sir," Danni whispered back, and she smiled as Andy leaned into her a little, nudging their shoulders together. He was like the brother she'd never had, and as much as she knew she could survive on her own, she was grateful to have him by her side.

The men started to spread out and she followed, heart beating so loud it sounded as if it were thumping in her ears. As far as she was concerned, being part of Operation Husky was the best experience of her life, even if only minutes earlier she'd been stuck in a tree like a ripe plum waiting to be plucked by the Nazis.

———— ❧ ————

Danni's fingers found the grooves on her Leica camera, and she dropped to one knee to get the shot, relying on the natural light to avoid using her bulbs. It had been a long day, although so had every day since they'd landed, and her feet hurt so badly she was almost too scared to look at them. She knew the blisters would be torturous within a couple of days, but they hadn't even had the chance to take stock and remove their shoes until now. As the men around her started to let their guard down, many of them slumping back, rifles slung across their bodies and their eyes drooping shut, she knew it was her one opportunity to photograph them at ease. These were often her best images, the ones where no one even seemed to notice she was there, and she was grateful that she'd brought her smaller camera on this adventure—having a roll of film was definitely easier than using the double-sided glass plates on her bulkier Speed Graphic, even if that was still her favorite camera to shoot with.

"Is it true you were in North Africa?" one of the younger men asked, his boots kicked off to reveal diseased-looking feet. She couldn't have looked at them under normal circumstances, but behind the lens of her camera, nothing fazed her. It was like her mind shifted gear and nothing was too gruesome to commit to film, as if her lens was a filter that changed the way she looked at the world.

"Yes," she said, smiling as she dropped the camera a little to look at him directly, realizing from his baby-faced cheeks that he was probably barely eighteen years old. "I wasn't supposed to be near the front there, but lines shifted and I ended up a lot closer to the action than I was technically permitted to be." She could almost see Andy laughing behind her—he might have a slightly different version of that story to share; one where he saw her fight tooth and nail to get close to the action. He was naturally more reserved and was usually the one cautioning her, which was why they balanced one another so well.

Danni could tell from the surprised expressions around her that she'd managed to impress the men listening to their conversation. The soldiers she met never expected her to have seen so much of the war.

"I think I like it here better than there, though, to be honest."

"Why, are the men better-looking?" another young paratrooper asked with a grin.

She gave him what she hoped was a withering look, before positioning herself with her camera again and capturing their laughter, heads bent together, clearly exhausted and grubby-faced, but relaxed. She was as passionate about capturing natural moments like this as she was about showing the fighting and realities of war; she'd seen firsthand that war wasn't all blood and conflict. "Actually, it's kind of nice being with Americans again," she said. "The Brits didn't exactly like me being anywhere near the action, but our officers seem more open-minded and tolerant when it comes to women correspondents now."

"How did you get that camera?" another man asked, and she noticed the way he was appraising her equipment.

She moved closer to him, holding the Leica out. It wasn't often she let anyone touch her gear, but the look on his face told her he needed to hold it. Perhaps it was making him think of the past.

"Do we have a photography aficionado in our midst?" she asked, grinning when he turned the lens on her and took a shot.

"I'm guessing you prized this beauty off a dead German," he said, handing it back to her, holding it as someone else might a precious doll. "Because not many Americans have one."

She winked, not about to vocalize just how right he was. After everything she'd seen, she *had* taken it as a war trophy of sorts, but she'd given the dead photographer the respect of developing the roll of film left in the belly of the camera before she'd used it herself.

A noise made her turn, and she lifted her camera as her eye caught a much higher-ranked soldier standing watching her. He raised an eyebrow, a cigarette dangling from his full lips, his eyes narrowing at what she imagined he thought of as an intrusion, or perhaps he disagreed with how she'd acquired the camera. The younger men and lower-ranked soldiers never minded her taking photographs, but she knew his type; he'd probably complain about her being there and she'd have to justify her position all over again. Heaven forbid if he complained that she wasn't wearing the regulation war correspondent skirt—it wasn't exactly a practical outfit to wear when jumping from a plane or trudging behind soldiers for days, and she'd always bucked the trend where skirts were concerned.

Andy cleared his throat beside her, as if warning her not to take the shot, but she did it anyway, positioning her camera and perfectly capturing the American against a pink sky as it swirled toward dusk. She preferred to shoot that way, just relying on her eye and the natural light to get her shots when she could, and she knew there would be just enough light to catch his silhouette.

"Is that why you're not with a British company now? Because they didn't want a woman with them?" another young paratrooper from earlier asked, digging into the dirt with the heel of his boot, his eyes flashing up at her as if he were embarrassed to be talking with her. She understood, though; some of the men were so young, and their flushed cheeks told her how inexperienced they were around women.

It was part of why she wore her uniform, as she liked to call it—so there was nothing for them to stare at, unless they'd never seen a woman in trousers before. She wore sturdy men's boots, pants, a button-up khaki shirt with her "C" armband proudly displayed, a scarf tied at her neck, and a wide-brimmed, Australian hat on her head, long brown hair braided beneath it. Her hat had become misshapen, stuffed into her bag during her jump, so it had certainly seen better days. The one thing that had remained perfectly intact was her red lipstick, which was as much an item of uniform as her trousers were, because she'd had the foresight to tuck that into her bra along with some rolls of film. It was a part of her armor that she never liked to be without, her little ode to her mother, who'd never been seen outside their home without her trademark red lipstick firmly in place.

"You could say that I pushed the boundaries when it came to reporting for the *Daily Telegraph*," Danni said, raising her eyebrows at Andy as he muttered something and laughed. He'd never let her forget that *he'd* had to switch publications too, when she'd decided to work with the Americans instead. Or, more accurately, been forced to work with them. "I managed to switch my accreditation from British forces to US, and I'm now working for *Time* magazine. It seems us Yanks are far more lenient at the moment when it comes to women being close to actual fighting, despite many newspapers back home still not employing women to work for them." Danni shook her head. "It makes absolutely no sense, but almost all publications are so backward around women writing for them. Unless they're writing about cosmetics or perhaps the odd movie review, it's a blanket ban on hiring."

Just as she was about to open her mouth again, a noise that was akin to an eruption of sorts sounded from behind her. She lifted her camera and spun around, before slowly lowering it when Andy cleared his throat again, louder this time, and stood to attention beside her. But he needn't have warned her—she'd have recognized Lieutenant General Patton anywhere. The way he stood, his shoulders impeccably straight as if he had a rod in his back, commanded attention, as did the stern look he was sporting. She only wished that look wasn't directed at her.

"Can someone tell me what the hell this broad is doing on my battlefield?" he barked.

Danni would have had to be deaf, and perhaps blind, to miss the snigger from the officer who'd caught her eye earlier. When she glanced at him again, he looked as amused as if he were watching a film—he was clearly enjoying it.

"*Somebody?*" Patton demanded. "Tell me what the hell—"

"It's an honor to meet you, sir. I'm Danni Bradford, war correspondent and photographer for *Time* magazine." She held out her hand, bravely stepping forward, but he didn't clasp it. Instead he stared at her as if she were an alien. Perhaps, amongst an exhausted, clapped-out array of soldiers, she looked exactly that.

"Major Cameron!" he barked, completely ignoring her introduction even though he was still staring at her, his eyes narrowed.

She swapped glances with Andy, who shook his head as if trying to tell her to keep her mouth shut. Danni wasn't intimidated by the general; he was only doing his job, and like most old, war-hardened men, he wasn't used to seeing a woman anywhere near his troops on the field. She'd also heard that he shared the anti-Semitic prejudices of the Germans he was fighting, and that he had a deep-set disapproval of African American men being allowed to fight, so it was hardly surprising to her that he was prejudiced toward women, too. But she wasn't going to back down.

"Sir, it's my understanding that she was invited to accompany the 505th, along with her colleague there," the man whom she now knew was Major Cameron volunteered. "If you ask me, this ain't no place for a woman though, so I understand your concern."

I'll have words with you later, she thought, feeling her nostrils flare with anger as she glared at Cameron.

He just crushed his cigarette beneath his boot as he watched her, still seeming to find the exchange humorous, or at least that's how it appeared.

"I'm going to give you two minutes to tell me why the hell I should let you stay with my troops, young lady," Patton said, stepping closer to her with such a fierce look on his face that she should have been trembling. But she wasn't, because she'd walked this path a dozen times now, fighting for her right to photograph the war, and not even an overzealous, high-ranking officer was going to scare her.

She had a job to do, and that was to show the world what war looked like; what it felt like; what it smelled like; and that's exactly what she was going to tell him.

If the obvious anger trembling through him doesn't make him explode in front of me first.

"Well?" he demanded.

Danni cleared her throat. *Nothing about convincing Patton is going to be easy, that's for sure.* She had a feeling that for the first time in her life, she might just be up against an impenetrable brick wall.

CHAPTER THREE

LONDON, ENGLAND, JULY 1943
CHLOE

Chloe stared at the letter she'd just written to her brother, tears pricking her eyes as she reread the words one last time. He was going to be furious with her—in fact, he might not ever forgive her—but she knew that this was her chance to leave. If Andy were home, he'd have sooner locked her in her room like Rapunzel and kept her prisoner than let her follow her heart.

She carefully folded the paper and put it into an envelope, scrawling his name on the front and tucking it into her pocket for safekeeping. She'd give it to the lovely old lady next door before she left, to make sure he got it as soon as he returned to visit.

With that done, she smiled to herself and danced across the room to her suitcase, trying her best to forget about Andy. Her case was already brimming with clothes she'd struggled to fit in, and she decided to see if she could find another case to use. She rummaged around in the hall closet and eventually emerged with another, smaller case to put her shoes and cosmetics in.

I'm coming, Gabriel. It won't be long now until we're together again!

Chloe hummed to herself as she finished packing, glancing at the clock and realizing she needed to hurry if she was going to make the train. Sitting on her larger case to close it, she spied the small stack of letters she'd saved and quickly crossed the room to scoop them up.

She sighed and looked down at them, able to recite them all by heart she'd pored over them so many times. Gabriel had written to her when he could, when it was easier for him to get mail out of France, and although his letters weren't full of the outpouring of love that hers were, he'd frequently told her how much he'd enjoyed their whirlwind week together in Paris. She couldn't wait to see the look on his face when he saw her again! It had been such a long time since they'd seen one another—almost three years now—but every letter, every memory, meant the world to her.

Tucking them into her smaller case, Chloe stayed bent over a moment, her thoughts suddenly full of her brother rather than her lover. She knew why—because his fury was going to be immeasurable when he returned, which was exactly why she needed to leave now before he had the chance to stop her.

"Don't you even think about it, Chloe," Andy fumed. *"Nowhere in Europe is safe to travel, and certainly not for a woman on her own."*

"So it's fine for you, but not fine for me?" she asked, exasperated. *"I have traveled before, you know. What do you think I was doing all those years when I was modeling?"*

"Stop being so bloody naïve, Chloe!" he shouted. *"We are at war, and you need to grow up and understand that, instead of arguing with me like a petulant child! This is not some fun, prewar modeling assignment!"*

"I'll show you, Andy," she muttered to herself as she shut her case and picked it up, pushing the memories away.

Chloe glanced at herself in the mirror, at her pouty, pink lips, her softly rouged cheeks, and her carefully curled hair. He'd told her to grow up, and she had. Leaving home and going to France was the most grown-up decision she'd ever made, and nothing was going to make her change her mind.

"Farewell, Andy," she whispered, blowing a kiss in the direction of his bedroom. "Until we meet again."

He always had the best of intentions for her, but she was tired of being told what to do. Which meant it was time to take charge of her life, starting with where she lived and with whom. *The war be damned.*

CHAPTER FOUR

JULY 1943
DANNI

Danni stood silently, her hand steady on the camera as she leaned forward, taking the shot.

Click.

The soldier's face swam before her as he cried out, the light-brown mud slick on his brow as he thrust his rifle forward.

Click.

Another soldier, the perfect picture of calm compared to the other man she'd turned her lens toward, spoke sharply into a telephone. She could see why he'd been chosen for the job, his ability to keep going despite the gunfire around him was invaluable to the rest of his unit. He was lying on his stomach as shots erupted around them, yelling now as the noise amplified.

Click.

She hesitated, her finger pressed lightly against the camera button as she studied her subject, rising from her bent knee to slowly get the shot. Major Cameron was side by side with his men, and she was intrigued by the way he clamped his hand to an injured soldier, taking over the fallen man's position without seeming to think twice about it. She'd heard enough to know they were expecting to encounter not one but two German battalions, but the way the paratroopers had reacted was like watching a well-oiled machine.

She quickly opened the back of her camera and carefully took the roll out, wrapping it in parchment paper to protect it and putting it in her bag, before replacing it with another and closing the camera.

"Get down!" someone yelled, but Danni blanked them out, her eyes locked on Cameron as he continued to take charge. This was what she lived for, *this* was why she was here. She wanted everyone to be able to see the reality of war, and there was no way she was going to duck out of harm's way now. She would capture the moment they secured the beachhead; she had to.

"Danni! Get the hell down!"

She realized that it was Andy yelling at her, his clipped British accent closer to her now. But she still didn't turn away.

"Just one more shot," she whispered to herself, adjusting the light meter and leaning forward, checking her footing before turning her attention to the fighting nearby and wishing for a longer lens. If she could just lean a little closer, if she could just . . .

"Danni!"

Fingers curled around her leg and she kicked, trying to dislodge the hand, but she soon realized she was going to fall if she resisted, and so she dropped to her knees of her own accord before that could happen.

"Dammit, let go of me!" she muttered. "I had it all set up!"

"You're crazy," Andy whispered. "Didn't you hear them?"

She let out a breath she hadn't even realized she was holding. "What? Those insects?"

"Insects? Danni, tell me you're kidding?"

28

She blinked at Andy, trying not to laugh at the pained expression on his face. "What?" The incessant noise had started to drive her crazy, but it wasn't exactly something for him to be that cross about.

"They weren't insects buzzing, Danni, they were sniper bullets whizzing past your bloody head!"

She swallowed, keeping her hands busy on her camera as she digested Andy's words. Sniper bullets? How could she have been doing this job for so long and mistaken bullets for insects buzzing around her head as she took shot after shot?

"Hey, you know me. I'll do anything to get that last shot," she said, trying to sound lighthearted and hoping she'd fooled him.

But she'd been working alongside Andy for long enough to know that she most likely hadn't.

"Sometimes I wonder if you've got a death wish," he muttered, his spare pencil tucked behind his ear as he lay on the dirt, tucking his notebook into his pocket. "You want to know why your editor insists you have a chaperone? *This* is why. Honestly, you can't take photos if you're dead, can you?"

Danni crawled on her stomach beside Andy as bullets ricocheted above them, and the reality of what she'd just been so close to hit her hard. *Did* she have a death wish? She grimaced at the stones piercing her elbows as she fought to cover ground, head tucked down low, bag bumping against her hip. *Maybe there's a fine line between being reckless and being married to a job.*

They'd known there were still Germans in the area—or *the beasts of Berlin*, as the boys seemed to be fond of referring to them of late—but there had been little warning that such an explosive moment of gunfire was about to unfold before them. Danni rolled on to her side, panting slightly and sharing a quick smile with Andy as she looked around them. The side of the cliff was high, and small rocks kept breaking off and shuddering down as gunshots continued to fire.

She tucked one hand inside her shirt, tugging out the little gold cross on a fine chain from around her neck, quickly pressing her lips to it and sending up a silent prayer. She left a smudge of red lipstick on it, but she didn't care.

"You still think that little cross keeps you safe?" Andy asked, dust and sand caking his face and making her wonder what she looked like if he looked that bad.

"Maybe," she said. "Although I started doubting God a long time ago—the moment I started seeing *all this* with my own eyes." She shrugged, wincing as she transferred her weight slightly and put more pressure on her elbow. "But my dad gave me this cross when I was a little girl, and aside from my cameras, it's the one thing I treasure in this world."

"Let's move! And keep your goddamn heads down!"

Danni yelped as her foot was kicked hard by a large boot, followed by her shirt being scooped up at the back as someone hauled her to her feet.

"Get your hands off me!" she muttered.

"Next time keep your damn head down when I tell you to," the voice barked back. "This is precisely why *women* aren't supposed to be close to fighting!"

Danni stumbled forward and caught the fury in Major Cameron's face as he glared at her, but it lasted barely a moment before he marched off, men scrambling behind him. She reached into her bag, checking her flashbulbs, cringing when one pierced her finger. Pulling her hand back she sucked on her skin, the metallic taste of blood making her feel sick; over the past few hours, it felt like she'd swallowed mouthfuls of sand, and her mouth was bone-dry. And to make matters worse, she was down at least one bulb, and she'd barely had enough as it was.

"You okay?" Andy asked.

Danni nodded, although once again, Andy knew her too well to believe her.

"Then let's get moving before we both lose our heads," he muttered.

She ran low, head down, her feet pounding the ground rhythmically alongside Andy's, smiling at him briefly despite it all when he caught her hand and gave it a quick squeeze. This was what she thrived on, what she lived for, and if she were to take a bullet and die alongside the men she followed, then so be it.

"Down!"

Danni obeyed Cameron's call this time, even though he himself kept running, sliding to the ground up ahead. She lay on her side, camera in position, capturing the pain etched on his face as he lifted his rifle as the onslaught continued. And suddenly she didn't care about her bulbs, so long as she could keep her camera safe and keep her lens trained on the fascinating man in front of her. He might act like an ass to her, but she'd seen many officers in her time in North Africa, and she'd never encountered one like him there. Cameron never put anyone else between the danger and himself, taking command of his men and leading by example, showing a fearlessness for his own safety at the same time as being as protective as a bear over his den when it came to his men.

She had a feeling she was always going to hate him on a personal level, that they were going to butt heads every step of the way, but it wasn't going to stop her from admiring him.

The shooting seemed to continue for hours, and Danni and Andy kept making ground together when they could, him scribbling frantically, usually tucked down low to stay out of sight as much as possible, and her literally putting her neck on the line to capture what she could. She knew that, come nightfall, he'd have a flashlight between his lips, trained on his typewriter as he furiously typed up his notes in the tent beside hers.

But as the gunfire slowed, so did Danni's heart rate, and she slumped down beside Andy for a moment. He was so engrossed in his work that he didn't seem to notice her as she bumped into him. She tipped her head back and tried to make herself comfortable on the ground, pushing with her heel at something in her way.

What the . . . Danni sat up, pulling her foot back fast as she realized what she'd been sticking her boot into. She gulped and glanced at Andy, who was still frantically writing and hadn't noticed what she was doing.

There was a foot lying half buried in the dirt, partially covered with the remnants of a boot that had clearly been blown apart. A foot that, possibly only hours earlier, had once belonged to a man, and was now discarded like a piece of trash.

Bile rose in her throat but she quickly lifted her camera, needing the barrier between her and the body part. It changed the scene, *any scene*, made her feel as if she were removed from what she was seeing, documenting *things* rather than reality.

And then she realized everything had gone silent. Danni lowered her camera and looked around, seeing men on the ground—alive but slumped with exhaustion—nearby and in the distance.

"I have to get this back to London as quickly as I can," Andy said, leaping up and then promptly tripping over the foot that Danni had been about to bury.

"What the hell . . ." Andy cursed, as Danni's hand shot out to grab the pencil that flew from his hand.

Andy looked from the foot and back up to her again, but neither of them said another word about it. What was there to say, when they'd both witnessed firsthand the atrocities of war?

"Bloodthirsty barbarians," Andy cursed, holding out a hand to her. Danni clasped it, walking around the body part and almost straight into the chest of Major Cameron.

"You," he said. "Come with me."

Danni followed, camera around her neck as she scrambled to keep up with his long stride. Despite the fatigue etched into the faces of everyone else around her, Cameron seemed immune to the same condition.

———— ❧ ————

Less than an hour later, after being forced to wait to speak with General Patton, Danni wasn't feeling quite so optimistic about working with her fellow Americans as she had earlier.

"Are you going to at least tell me what this is about?" she asked Cameron.

His mouth was set in a straight line as he smoked a cigarette, leaning casually against an army jeep like he hadn't just been in a battle that could easily have claimed his life.

"No," he finally said.

"It's obvious you don't want me here," she said, refusing to back down, almost wanting to see his temper flare if it meant getting a reaction from him.

"Want one?" he asked, holding out the pack of cigarettes to her.

She shook her head slightly, not fond of smoking despite nearly everyone else around her partaking.

"Look, women are supposed to be at home or nursing, not running around in the middle of a war," he said. "This isn't a place for any woman, so don't take it personally when I tell you that you shouldn't be here."

Danni bristled, but she was used to it. "There are plenty of women doing more than tending the home fires and nursing right now, *Major*," she said, trying not to sound like a hissing cat as she glared at him. "There are women working with the Resistance in France, flying planes for the military, and doing everything a man can do. And there are plenty of female war correspondents making their mark, as well. And I, for one, am tired of hearing that a lack of female latrines, amongst other excuses, is a good enough reason to keep us away."

He just stared back at her, blinking, the smile that touched his lips making her want to slap him.

"Call me old-fashioned, but I don't want women in a war zone. Period. Nothing you say to me is going to change that."

"Tell that to the women who care for you when you're sent to a field hospital," she muttered. "That'll make you change your tune."

Cameron seemed to find her outburst amusing, and she was furious that she'd taken the bait so easily. It wasn't like her to be so touchy—hell, the troops in North Africa had joked she had balls of steel—but something about this particular man rattled her.

"There are very good reasons why women aren't allowed near combat," he said, voice lower now, more serious. "We have men break under the pressure every day, so what's to make anyone believe women wouldn't? Not to mention the fact that our men could end up taking risks to protect women in those situations. And besides, you're quite right, it's not as if we have women's latrines, is it?"

"My place is here, documenting what I can, to show the truth of war to the people," Danni said. "I only wish you could show my work the same respect that I pledge to show yours, instead of coming up with a raft of reasons why my gender makes me weaker than you."

Cameron nodded, his smile gone, and dropped his cigarette, crushing it beneath his boot and standing to attention. As she turned and found Patton walking briskly up behind her, his back ramrod straight and his eyes permanently narrowed in an almost cruel way, she realized the show of respect had been for his superior, not for her.

"You," Patton said, his chest rising and falling from the exertion. "I've made arrangements for you to remain with the field hospital. No broad is going to be getting under the feet of my men in battle, you hear me? I have no idea how you managed to get here in the first place, but you won't be staying."

Danni knew when it was worth putting up a fight, and she could see that now wasn't the time. Not yet. "Yes sir. I understand." She fought the urge to glower at Cameron, wondering if this was his doing. His arguments were so outdated, but unfortunately still shared by so many higher-ranking men.

"Because of my good grace, you're not being sent back to London immediately, but if I hear so much as a whisper that you've disobeyed my orders to stay at the field hospital . . ."

"No sir, that won't happen." She was not going to create an enemy of a general, and certainly not one as influential as Patton.

"There's plenty there for you to photograph, and I don't want to hear that you've been anything other than an exemplary guest."

Patton gave her a long, cold stare before, dismissing her, he turned his attention to Cameron. She watched the two men put their heads together as Patton produced a map and spread it out across the hood of the vehicle Cameron had been leaning against.

"I'll stay with you," Andy whispered, having come up behind her. "We can both report from the field hospital, bide our time there. He's right, there'll be plenty to see, and we can figure out where to go next."

Danni scoffed. "So you can report on injuries instead of following the action? Don't be ridiculous. We both know that Patton isn't going to have a problem with a respected male correspondent tagging along, so you should go for it. I'm not holding you back." *Again.* She didn't say the word, but she should have.

Andy grimaced. They both knew she was right about him being welcome. "Still, I'm not leaving you. We're a team."

She didn't argue with him—they *were* a team, and it wasn't the first time he'd chosen to stay with her. Andy had stuck his neck out for her in North Africa, demanding that she be allowed to work alongside him, and if it had been anyone other than Patton calling the shots, she was certain he'd have done the same again.

Raised voices silenced them both, and Danni quietly lifted her camera to capture Patton as he stood glaring at Cameron.

"Sir, with all due respect," she heard Cameron say, his voice lowered. "General Alexander made it clear that we are to head west. Are you certain you want to defy that instruction?"

"And I've told you, we're marching toward Palermo at daybreak," Patton barked.

Danni frowned as she saw the way Cameron looked at Patton, wishing she could have captured the image on film as Patton stormed away. She hated that she wasn't going to be following them, but the photos she'd taken so far had been outstanding, even if she hadn't got that one last shot, and she was prepared to take one step backward given how far she'd already come. Besides, it wouldn't do her any favors if she showed Patton in a bad light. She could send her films back to London from the hospital, and they would be published before anyone else had the chance to beat her to it.

She'd seen firsthand the Allies drive German and Italian forces out of North Africa, and now Sicily was another notch on her belt. Finally, it felt like she was photographing success instead of simply slaughter, and that, at least, meant her struggles had paid off.

———— ◦◦◦◦◦◦ ————

Danni lay on her bedroll and stared up at the star-filled sky. Her boots were heavy on her feet and made it hard to get comfortable, but she'd learned to be ready for anything, and that meant being prepared to leap up from bed and run if she needed to. She sighed, rubbing the heels of her hands into her eyes for a moment. Already it felt like she'd been following the war for so long, and the tiredness that thudded through her body on a daily basis told her just how much of an effect it was having on her. Not to mention what a long day it had been today. The fight had continued, on and on, for so long that the troops had looked like they were going to drop, but it had eventually turned in their favor and that seemed to spur them on, giving them all a final boost of energy to secure the beachhead.

"The memories make it hard to sleep, don't they?" Andy said, his voice low and soft as it came to her on the warm night breeze. "It never seems to get any easier."

"You can say that again," she replied, reaching for her camera in the dark. For some reason she always found comfort the second she touched the cool metal, as if it awakened something in her and made her think about her job rather than the past. She slid her hand against it, through the shirt she always wrapped around it for safekeeping at night.

"It was a tough day today," Andy muttered.

She grunted. "You can say that again, too." Danni shut her eyes, squeezing the thoughts away as she remembered who they'd lost. It was the hardest part of following along so closely with troops—they were no longer nameless casualties of war, but actual human beings. "Anything on your mind?" she asked, as Andy went silent beside her.

"Actually, I was worrying about my sister," he said. "Do you remember I told you that she fell in love with that older man when she was in France?"

Danni laughed. "Trust me, it's not something I could easily forget. She's not still pining over him, is she?"

Andy groaned. "She keeps asking me when I think the borders will open for travelers again! It doesn't seem to matter how many times I try to explain that Paris is occupied by the enemy, so it's not like there's just some arbitrary ban on tourists."

Danni patted his hand. "You're doing a great job. You're probably fretting over nothing; she'll fall in love with someone else well before the borders open."

Andy sighed. "By twenty-two I would have thought she'd understand the mechanics of war more intimately, but it seems I was wrong to make that presumption."

Danni didn't tease him, even though she would have loved to tell him that his sister Chloe clearly knew something about being *intimate*. He'd virtually raised his much-younger sister after their parents had died, and it was the only subject Danni wouldn't ever tease him about. She might be a beautiful model, but Chloe was also naïve and quite the handful, and from what he'd told Danni, Andy did his best to keep her in line when he wasn't on assignment.

"How long have you two been working together?" came a voice in the darkness. She thought it was the young soldier who'd asked to hold her camera the day before, but she couldn't be certain.

"Since before the North African campaign," Andy answered, "so I'd say just over three years. Clearly I did something wrong in another life, because I've been charged with babysitting her ever since."

Danni scoffed and reached out to punch him, but he expertly dodged her arm, despite the dark.

"What he meant to say is that he's been fortunate enough to tag along with me for a good few years now," Danni corrected.

Now it was Andy chuckling, and it made her smile. Despite everything she'd seen, and everywhere they'd been together, their friendship had never wavered. She was lucky to have him, and she hoped he felt the same about her, despite the teasing. Even when they weren't on assignment, the rooms they kept at The Dorchester were side by side, and there wasn't a day that passed when they weren't together. And although he'd never said anything, she got the feeling that she wasn't exactly his type. She'd wondered often, even though he'd never said and she would never explicitly ask, whether she was in fact entirely the wrong *gender* for him to be attracted to. Which was why she didn't care at all if anyone presumed they were together, not if it protected his secret.

"I didn't even know women worked as photographers," the same voice said. "But it's kind of nice having a woman around, you know?"

Danni stared up at the sky, not sure what to say in response.

"I didn't expect to cross paths with a female war photographer either," Andy said, and she smiled as she listened to the way he talked about her, always ready to defend her honor or go to bat for her. "To be honest, I wasn't convinced she should be there either, until I was asked to keep an eye out for her." He chuckled. "Actually, my editor told me it was part of my job description to work with her and make sure she made it back to London in one piece. Now though, there's no one else in the field I'd choose to work with ahead of her."

"Andy, have you been drinking?" Danni teased. "It's not like you to be so nice to me."

"Yeah, yeah," he grunted, and she heard the rustle of him moving on his bedroll.

There were other men scattered around them—her correspondent's card meant she was technically treated as a captain, although she had no official rank, and she was allowed to mess with the officers. Without it, she wouldn't have been allowed near them unaccompanied. She guessed they were all listening now, but given it was her final night with them, she supposed it didn't matter what they learned about her. Men always seemed to be curious about what she did, most not understanding why she was so damn determined to do her job, and if they wanted to listen, then she had nothing to hide.

"How long have you been taking pictures, Danni?" another voice in the dark asked. "What made you want to do this?"

"I've always loved photography, and I actually learned alongside my father when I was a little girl," she said, remembering the little darkroom her father had created for her in an unused part of their garage. "And what else is there to photograph during times of war, other than war itself?"

"It ever too much for you?" the same voice asked. "Being so close to the war, I mean?"

"I've felt that way plenty of times, but we all just have to keep going, don't we?"

She shut her eyes and imagined sleep, although her mind was ticking over too intently to even contemplate shut-eye now. But it wasn't memories of being a little girl trailing around after her camera-toting father that were troubling her, it was the soldier's question. War *had* almost broken her, well before she'd made a name for herself as a correspondent, when she was just starting out and she'd fought to save whoever she could, as if she had the power to do it all on her own.

The man stared at her, tears running down his cheeks. She backed away, swallowing her emotions until they erupted within her, choking her and making it near impossible to breathe, let alone speak. Children behind her, families, thanked her and reached for her hand, patting at her, but she couldn't utter a single word in reply. Because all she could see was the man she'd left behind. And the old woman on her knees wailing beside him, begging Danni to find a place for them, too.

"You promised!" the woman cried. "You promised us you'd take us with you."

They were words that came to her with such knife-deep sharpness in the night, as if they were being yelled directly into her ear, that she often woke bolt-upright and covered in a thick layer of sweat.

"Danni?"

She quickly wiped her eyes, sniffing and clearing her throat. It was always in the dark, the memories invading her thoughts whenever her mind was idle. Or perhaps it was when she was close to other pain, other tragedy, that it somehow crept back into her consciousness.

Andy shuffled beside her and she felt his big hand reaching for hers. She clasped it, holding on tight as the memories passed in a wave.

"We did everything we could, Danni. You know that as well as I do," he whispered to her, instinctively knowing what had upset her. They'd been through it together, so it shouldn't have surprised her, but somehow it always did.

"It doesn't make it any easier to forget," she whispered back.

After she'd fallen into a job at the *Daily Telegraph*, she'd marched straight into the London office and demanded that the editor-in-chief send her to Poland. He'd seemed to appreciate how ballsy she was and decided to test her by sending her there on her first assignment. And that was when she'd first met Andy, when he'd been tasked with ensuring she make it back to London, and she'd instead tasked *him* with helping her secure visas and run refugees from Prague to Belgium, right under German noses. Needless to say, her editor hadn't been impressed with how long she'd taken to return, but it had cemented her friendship with Andy.

A shiver ran through Danni and she wound an arm tightly around herself. She'd known from the moment she'd arrived in Poland that photographing war was her calling, only she hadn't banked on how deeply the human suffering would affect her. There had been so many refugees, and the moment she'd bravely shown Andy what she was doing, and more importantly *who* she was doing it for, they'd become a team. And they'd never looked back.

"Can I tell them?" he whispered, squeezing her hand. She squeezed it back, before slowly letting go.

"In Poland, Danni enlisted me to help as many refugees as we could," Andy told the men around them. "These people, these *humans*, were caught in Hitler's crosshairs, and when the Czechs conceded to his ultimatum, well, there was only so long before those high-risk refugees were caught and dragged into whatever hell he had planned for them. Only, no one knew that a well-connected, determined American woman was waiting in the wings to save as many lives as possible."

There was not a snore, not a snuffle, around her now, and Danni had the sudden realization that all the men were listening to Andy speak about her.

"How many were there?" someone asked.

Danni cleared her throat. "That first group I moved—well, I thought I could move all of them. I was *told* I could move all of them. But the Belgian officials changed their minds, and in the end I only had one hundred and sixty places for one hundred and sixty-two refugees." She shut her eyes and wished their faces weren't so vivid in her mind still. "I think about the two people I left behind every day, but from that moment on, I vowed to show the truth through the lens, the human sacrifice of war that exists at every turn. It's why I'm here, and it's why I keep fighting for my place to be alongside you all."

Andy always told her to be proud of what they'd done, and she was, but the fact that they hadn't been able to save all of them—that pain would never go away, no matter how hard she tried. She steeled herself against the emotions, pulled her camera to her chest, and tried to focus on the familiar weight of it in her hands.

"Danni?" Andy whispered. "You okay?"

She swallowed and pulled her blanket higher up her body, even though the scratchy fabric itched her chin. "I will be."

"Danni, I'm sorry," Andy said, and his hand skimmed her shoulder, the touch instantly making tears prick at her eyes. "I shouldn't have brought it up in the first place."

"Thanks for the bedtime story, but it's time we all got some shut-eye," came a husky drawl.

Danni resisted the urge to snap back a remark, knowing exactly who the owner of that voice was. Cameron's tone was unmistakable, and she wished she knew more about him so that she wasn't on the back foot all the time. Although she doubted he was ever going to do anything other than regard her presence alongside his men with contempt. He'd made that clear when he'd smugly watched her as Patton had given her her marching orders, and it had taken every ounce of her willpower to remember how highly she'd regarded him in the field earlier.

"Sorry for keeping you awake," she muttered back.

She knew Andy meant well, but perhaps he shouldn't have shared what had happened between them. It wasn't so bad for the men to know her truth, but talking about it had brought the memories back, opening a gateway in her mind that she preferred to keep firmly locked.

Danni thought of the troops marching in the morning, hating that she wouldn't be with them to document their progress further. But she had photos to get back to her editor when they reached the base, and that was what she had to focus on. And once she'd done that, then she'd figure out how to get where she needed to go.

Patton and Cameron be damned.

CHAPTER FIVE

PARIS, FRANCE, AUGUST 1943
CHLOE

"Surprise!"

"What the hell?" Gabriel almost stumbled into her, grabbing her elbow and roughly pushing her toward the door. "*Chloe?*"

"Ouch," she complained. "Gabriel, you're hurting me!"

"Quickly, get inside." He fumbled with his key and nudged her forward, far more forcefully than she expected, and she tripped as he quickly closed and locked the door behind them, hauling her cases with him.

"Well, that wasn't exactly the welcome I was expecting," she grumbled as he took hold of her elbow again and marched her up the stairs. "Gabriel! Stop it!"

"Chloe, how, why, *what* the hell are you doing here?" he exclaimed, dumping a stack of newspapers on the table and pushing her down into one of the chairs. He raked his hair off his forehead, sitting across from her, a look on his face that was so far from what she'd anticipated that tears instantly filled her eyes.

"I thought, I thought . . ." She brushed her cheeks as the tears spilled down them and jutted her chin up, so exhausted and overwhelmed by what she'd done that all she wanted was to fall into Gabriel's arms. "I thought you'd be so happy to see me," she sobbed. "I've come all this way, and you're not even excited that I'm here?" Maybe it was the shock of seeing her with no forewarning. *That's* what it must be.

"Oh Chloe, Chloe," he groaned as he bent and opened his arms to her.

She fell against him, holding on to him and sobbing into his chest as his hands ran up and down her back in a soothing motion.

"I've been planning this for so long, and I thought you'd see me and sweep me into your arms. I thought . . ." Embarrassment flooded her cheeks with heat.

"Chloe, how did you even get here?" Gabriel asked, holding her back slightly. "It's not that I'm not pleased to see you again, it's not, but I don't even know how you managed to get to Paris?"

She reached up to touch his face, stroking his cheek, but Gabriel pulled back. *Was* it just the surprise of it all? Or did he actually not want her to be there? She wasn't used to being rejected and even the thought of it stung.

"I was so tired of waiting," she said with a shrug. "One of my old modeling friends is a dancer now, for the Moulin Rouge, and she told me how easy it was for her to travel. Because the German soldiers *love* the dancing girls so much."

All the color seemed to drain from Gabriel's face. "You're dancing at the Moulin Rouge?"

She laughed. "No, *silly*. I just pretended to be so I could get here, and it worked like a charm."

Gabriel stood and started to pace back and forth, looking more like a caged animal than a man who had just been reunited with his lover. It struck her just how different he looked, a shadow of his former self. There were lines bracketing his mouth and feathering out from his eyes, his hair no longer cut neatly as it had been then, stubble over his jaw. Back when they'd first met, she hadn't thought anyone would notice their significant age difference, but now he looked every bit of the ten or more years older than her.

"Chloe, Paris is under German occupation," he said, as if he were speaking to a child. "You do understand what that means, don't you?"

"Obviously I know that, Gabriel. It's why I had to pretend to be a dancer," she said, rolling her eyes. Had he not heard her?

"Chloe, this is serious!" He came back toward her, dropping to his knees and taking her hands in his. "You can't lie to the Gestapo. You can't treat this as a fun little jaunt. France is at war and the repercussions of what you've done could be very, very serious! Not to mention it could cause unnecessary interest in your whereabouts."

She pulled her hands away from his. "Don't talk to me like I'm simple, Gabriel. Of course I know all that."

"Chloe, what if someone recognizes you? You've been on the cover of so many magazines, you can't just pretend to be someone else! The Gestapo could think you're a spy for Britain and then . . ." Gabriel's voice trailed off.

"And then what?" she asked. "What are you trying to say, Gabriel?"

"Nothing, forget I said it," he muttered. "But I'm serious, Chloe. No more lying, not here, not now. It's not safe."

He sighed and stood, walking over to the kitchen and pulling out two glasses and a half-empty bottle of whiskey. He poured one larger measure and one smaller, draining half the larger glass before turning and walking back to her.

"Here, have this," he said, sinking back into the chair opposite her.

She took a little sip, cringing as it burned her throat. "I just don't understand why you're so upset. I thought this was what you wanted, too. You sent me those letters, and after the week we spent together . . ."

"It was a long time ago, Chloe," he said.

"So that's it then? You've changed your mind?" she asked. "Were you just replying to my letters to be polite?" Just the thought of it made her skin crawl, that he might not be as in love with her as she was with him. And after the week she'd endured to get to him, traveling in filthy trains and not being able to bathe, her hair a matted mess at the back from the nights she'd had to sleep with nothing but her case as a pillow. Not to mention having to sweet-talk the Nazi soldiers, which had almost made her stomach turn, just to enter the city.

"Look, Chloe, I'm very fond of you, you know that, but . . ."

Her eyebrows shot up. "But what?" He was *fond* of her? What the hell was that even supposed to mean?

Gabriel looked tired. The skin beneath his eyes was dark. And the way he stared at her, it was nothing like she remembered. Gone were the fine threads he used to wear as well, replaced with very casual trousers and a loose-fitting shirt that had been darned several times.

"Look, it's not that I'm not happy to see you," he said quietly. "But this is a different Paris to the one you visited, Chloe. It's not safe for you here, not anymore."

"But you can keep me safe, can't you?" she asked, pouting at the way he shook his head.

"I don't know, Chloe," he said sadly, draining the rest of his drink. "I honestly don't know anymore."

She started to cry again, big, plump tears that she couldn't control raining down her cheeks.

Gabriel rose and pulled her to her feet, holding her against him, stroking her hair. "Shhh," he whispered, cradling her.

"Do you have someone else?" she asked, leaning back and searching his eyes. "Is that why you don't want me here?"

He shook his head. "There's no one else, Chloe. But these are different times, that's all. I honestly don't think you realize what you've landed yourself in."

When she stood on tiptoe to kiss his lips, he moved and pressed a quick kiss to her forehead instead, more like a brother than a lover.

"Let's get you into bed," he said brusquely. "We can talk in the morning."

She bit down on her lip and gripped his hand tightly as he led her toward the bedrooms.

What have I done? She squeezed her eyes shut as her mind drifted back to Paris in 1940, when they'd had the magical week together that had sealed her fate.

Chloe stood beside Gabriel, a nervous flutter in her stomach as she waited for him to look at the photographs. She wasn't used to worrying about her photos, she'd been a model for years now, but there was something about the editor-in-chief of French Vogue *intimately studying the images that had her all aflutter. And it wasn't just his position of power—the man was handsome in the most classic kind of way, with a thick head of blond hair and the most intense, piercing blue eyes she'd ever seen.*

"What do you think?" he asked.

"You actually want my opinion?" she asked.

"I saw the way you were looking over the layout before," he said, turning to her. "So tell me, what do you think? Perhaps you have an eye for this type of thing?"

She smiled up at him, lost in his ocean-colored eyes. The knowing, secret smile on his face made her blush as she bumped shoulders with him and bent forward. She'd only been in Paris two days, and already she was head over heels in love with the man.

"I think they're beautiful," she replied, so pleased with the whimsical images spread out before her. The photo shoot had been exquisite, with Paris the backdrop to the gorgeous clothes she'd been sent to model, and having Gabriel watching her had only added to the excitement of it all. She hadn't expected him to be so handsome, or so determined to get her into his bed. "And I like the way you've told a story in each image with the different locations around Paris," she gulped, wondering if she'd said the right thing. "What do you think?"

"They're perfect. Exactly what we need to show off the spring collections. And you're right, I wanted to tell a story with these images, showing how strong and beautiful Paris still is."

She beamed, pleased that he agreed with her.

Gabriel leaned forward and seemed to examine one of them more closely. "The couturiers worked fast on these new collections," he said. "The Americans are desperate to buy, but no one knows how long they'll still be able to send shipments with this war raging on, so they're expecting the orders to come in thick and fast."

Chloe shivered at the mere mention of war. It was the reason her brother had begged her not to travel, but it had also made the whole trip that much more exciting. When the editor at Vogue in London had offered her the assignment, she'd said yes in a heartbeat. She'd be whisked home before she even had time to get caught up in the crosshairs of war—or at least that's what they'd promised her. Although she was starting to wish her trip would be extended so she could spend longer with Gabriel.

"Work your magic, ladies," Gabriel said to the team working on the magazine layout. "And you"—he grinned, proffering his arm—"you are coming with me for champagne and the best caviar you've ever tasted."

Chloe waved farewell to the assistant editors they were leaving behind to work, and slipped her arm through Gabriel's, letting him escort her from the building. He was older than her, perhaps by a decade although she wasn't sure, and she loved the way he took command of a situation, the way everyone stopped what they were doing when he entered the room. She particularly liked how his gaze softened when he looked at her, the way his expensive cologne seemed to cling to her as she tucked into his side.

The moment they were out of sight of the building, he caught her in his arms and she pressed against his chest, her breathing fast as he ducked his head to kiss her. Only in Paris, she thought, as she tipped back a little and sighed into his mouth as his lips brushed so gently back and forth against hers, as if they had all day.

"How am I ever going to let you go back to London?" he whispered, his breath warm against her cheek.

"I bet you say that to all the visiting models," she whispered back.

"Never," he said, sliding his hand into hers and pulling her close as they started to walk again. "You, you're something special."

She giggled and let him lead her, and soon they were sitting side by side, thighs brushing, at a little restaurant tucked away from the cobbled street. Chloe observed him as he ordered champagne and lunch for both of them before reaching for her hands again. He touched her so openly, as if he couldn't care less who saw them.

"What if we kept you here for another few days?" Gabriel asked, his hand seductively stroking her thigh. "I want to keep you in my bed just a little longer."

His words took a moment to sink in. "You want me to stay?" she asked.

"I know it's selfish, especially during such tumultuous times, but I'm not ready to give you up just yet."

"I'll have to think about it," she said coyly, stroking his hand as she started to imagine a life in France with a man like Gabriel. Could she stay? Would he have so much fun with her as his plaything that he'd ask her to marry him? Her brother would kill her if she stayed longer, he'd been furious that she'd said yes to the trip at all.

"Indulge me just a little longer, and I'll make it worth your while."

Their champagne arrived and she sipped it, giddy on life and love as she leaned deeper into the intoxicating man beside her.

She loved her brother, she did, but he had his own life, and if she could stay with Gabriel just a little longer . . . She kissed him, already imagining herself naked in his bed again, twisted in his sheets with him, after an afternoon sipping champagne and flirting.

"You're a very hard man to say no to," she whispered against his lips.

Gabriel stroked her face, his fingertips brushing her cheek as he gazed at her, warming her, making her feel like there was no place in the world she'd rather be.

CHAPTER SIX

SEPTEMBER 1943
ELLA

Ella trudged into her room and collapsed on the bed; she was exhausted. For almost two months now, she'd spent most afternoons or evenings volunteering with the Home Guard, and although she wasn't as skilled with a rifle as half the women there, she could at least hit a target and she'd started to enjoy the camaraderie now she'd gotten to know the other women better. Not to mention the fact that they'd finally started to open up to her, talking as they patrolled, which had given her great information for her story. Every morning for the first month, she'd sat at her typewriter and fleshed out the piece she'd been working on, and then she'd started writing about other things women were doing to assist the war effort, but today she was too exhausted to type. She could only hope that her article on the Home Guard women she now admired so much would be enough to reignite her career.

Knock. Knock. Knock.

Three insistent taps echoed down the hallway to her bedroom. Ella groaned and pulled her pillow over her face. Whoever it was, she didn't want to see them. Her father was at work, her mother was out, and the only thing she wanted to look at was the back of her own eyelids.

Knock. Knock. Knock.

"Ugh," she groaned, furiously flinging the pillow off her head as she stalked down the hall, slipping in her woolen socks as she yanked the door open. Who would be knocking on her door so loudly first thing in the morning?

No.

Her heart stopped.

No, no, no.

Ella quickly shut the door again, as fast as she'd hauled it open.

The boy standing on the other side didn't make a noise, and she pressed her back to the door and tried to breathe, feeling like she was fighting for every lungful. Tears sprang into her eyes and she quickly blinked them away. She knew what this meant, who he was. These boys, they delivered the news every morning as soon as the cables arrived. They were the ones who went house to house, the ones bearing information about dead or missing loved ones, and there was no way she was going to hear that news. Not today, *not ever.*

She pressed the heels of her hands into her eyes.

"Ma'am?" the boy called out. "Are you there?"

"Go away!" she called back. "Just please *go away!*"

"I can't ma'am, I have news and—"

Ella brushed her cheeks. *Not Brendon. Oh please, Lord, not Brendon.* It would break her mother's heart. *And my own.*

"Ma'am, it's not what you think," the boy called out again. "Please, I have an important message for you."

Ella took a moment to catch her breath, blowing out one long shuddering exhale before slowly opening the door again, not knowing if she could trust him and wishing she weren't home alone. She stared at the boy, cap in his hand, his eyes big and round. He couldn't be more than fourteen, and she instantly felt sorry for how she'd treated him. It wasn't his fault that he had the worst job of the war.

"Ma'am, I don't have a telegram for you, I have a message," he said.

She gulped. "So my brother's not . . ." The words just wouldn't seem to leave her mouth, hovering without being said, sticking in her throat.

"I don't know anything about your brother, ma'am. I mean, I don't have anything to give you about his whereabouts," he mumbled.

She waited as his eyes finally lifted to hers again, and she pulled her cardigan tighter around herself, cold seeping into her bones.

"There's been a call for you at the post office," he said. "The man didn't leave a name, but he said he couldn't call your number here because of the party line—you know, in case someone else was listening in."

Ella nodded. "Go on," she said.

"He said to come find you and tell you he'll be calling back in an hour. You're to be waiting at the post office for his call, but I don't know anything else."

Ella's eyebrows pulled together as she stared back at the boy. "And he gave you no name or information at all?" she asked. "Nothing to identify himself by?"

He shook his head and then took a step back, patting his bag as if to tell her he had work to get on with. She shuddered as she realized what he was about to do, the families' hearts he was about to break, but instead of pushing the thought away, she wondered if it was in fact a story waiting to be written? Perhaps she could give a perspective to what it was like for the boys who delivered the news, as well as what it was like to see them coming down the road, hands raised to knock on an unsuspecting door?

Ella thanked him and watched as he turned to go, her heart resuming its usual rhythm as she considered just who this mystery man could be, forgetting about her new story idea for now. If it were Brendon who wanted to speak to her, he'd have given his name—and besides, he would far more likely have tried to contact her father. And there were no other men in her life she was expecting to hear from, other than her dad who'd be home by dinnertime. Besides, her father wouldn't have anything secretive to tell her that couldn't be shared on their own phone line. The worst that could happen was that one of their nosey neighbors might hear some family business, but it would hardly warrant a call being dispatched to the post office.

Ella finally shut the door and stood deep in thought, shivering in the hallway even though she was certain it wasn't actually cold. She walked quickly back to her bedroom, deciding against having a rest even though her head was starting to pound from lack of sleep. She undressed and darted into the bathroom where she filled the sink, washing her face and using a facecloth under her arms and around her neck, before taking out fresh clothes and dressing again. She took care to brush and fix her hair, even putting some lipstick on for good measure. Heaven help her if her mother came home before she left—she'd get the shock of her life to see her daughter looking so well-groomed.

Ella looked at herself in the mirror, wondering why she'd made such an effort when it was only a phone call. Rolling her eyes at the woman staring back at her, she went back into her bedroom and collected her notebook, pen, and Lucky Strikes. She was about to have one when she thought better of it, and decided to make herself coffee and toast instead. Her stomach was rumbling and the last thing she needed was to be hungry and exhausted at the same time.

Who's going to be on the other end of the phone line? She sighed and busied herself with spreading butter on her toast. Curiosity killed the cat, that's what her mother would have said. But Ella was a journalist, and without a good dose of curiosity, there'd be no one to write about the damn cat in the first place, she thought with a smirk.

Forty-five minutes later, she was standing in the post office. She smiled at Benjamin, who'd worked there for as long as she could remember, his wiry hair looking like he never brushed it, or perhaps it simply didn't cooperate, and his glasses perpetually sliding down his nose.

"Hello there, Ella," he said with a smile. "Come for your phone call, have you?"

She nodded. "I certainly have."

He was sorting through piles of letters and she stood back and watched. Everything had changed since America had joined the war, including the volume of letters passing through post offices, and the fact that workers everywhere were now either older men, boys, or women. The streets had a strange hollowness without the young men that usually populated them, and it struck her as even more ridiculous that she wasn't allowed to write for print when there were so few journalists even available to write anymore.

The sharp, shrill ring of the telephone echoed through her and she jumped, as Ben answered then waved her over. He patted her hand, much the way her father would have if he saw her looking nervous, and she stepped forward and took the receiver from him, curling against the wall as she spoke into it.

"Hello?" she said, clearing her throat as her voice seemed to catch with a croak.

"Ella Franks?"

"Yes," she said, more confidently this time. "This is she."

"It's Ralph Mountford, editor at the Associated Press. I'm pleased to be speaking to you—or should I call you *Ernst* instead of Ella?"

His raucous bark of laughter made her cringe, and she held the phone away from her ear for a moment.

"How exactly can I help you, Mr. Mountford?" she asked, wondering what on earth he was doing even calling her.

"Look, I'm not going to mince words here, Miss Franks. A colleague of mine gave me the letter you'd written, about wanting to report on women's war issues, and I'll be honest, we need someone like you." He paused. "Your idea has merit, and I loved your piece on the women training with the Home Guard. I think our readers will like it too."

He needs someone like me? She pressed the phone closer to her ear. *His readers will like it?* Did that mean he was going to publish her article? Her heart skipped a beat.

"I'm not interested in archaic rules around female journalists, not when their credentials are good. I need a war correspondent to cover women's issues in Europe, and I think you're just the lady for the job."

Ella couldn't reply. She could barely even breathe. *He what?* She'd written and sent letters to various publications *weeks* ago, fueled by anger at her firing, and inspired by the women she'd met on patrol. But she'd never actually expected anyone to respond to her.

"Miss Franks? Are you there?"

"Yes, sorry, yes I'm here," she managed. "It all sounds marvelous, but I have to ask, why me? Why offer me a job like that when I've never worked as a foreign correspondent before?"

His laughter startled her it was so loud. "Hold up, you're the one who wrote to *me* wanting to write about women in the war!" He laughed again. "Look, it might surprise you, but I can't really send a man to cover women's war issues, and I don't exactly have female journalists beating my door down looking for work. Your letter came at just the right time, and we're planning on running your article on the women from the Home Guard next week. It just so happens that I'm prepared to flout the unwritten rule about employing female journalists, even if my rivals aren't."

Ella leaned into the wall, worried she might actually faint. She could hardly comprehend what he was asking of her.

"And you're certain I'm qualified enough for an overseas posting?" she asked, her hand starting to tremble more from nerves than excitement now.

"Look, do you want the job or not?" he asked. "I'm putting myself out on a limb here."

Ella gulped, trying to imagine what her brother would say, how much he'd tease her if he found out she'd talked someone *out* of giving her a job. She'd heard that the rules around female journalists were more relaxed overseas; it seemed newspapers didn't mind women actually being journalists in England and much of Europe. "When do I start?" she whispered, as butterflies started to beat their wings in her stomach.

"I'll put the formal job offer in the mail for you, but in the meantime, prepare to leave sooner than later," he said. "We'll book your passage for you and cover a small daily stipend on top of your wages, and you'll be expected to start reporting the day you arrive in London. We want you to hit the ground running, so to speak."

"London?" Ella smiled as she leaned more heavily against the wall. She could barely believe the words she was hearing.

"Yes. And Miss Franks?"

She grinned like a Cheshire cat and was grateful he couldn't see her. "Yes?"

"Be warned that there are plenty of men who don't believe women should be covering the war, even if they are writing about women's wartime issues. I admire the boldness of your writing, but it'll be an uphill battle over there, and some won't be as modern in their outlook as I am." He cleared his throat. "But at the same time, men don't want to be covering what women are doing in Europe, so I don't think you'll find you have a lot of competition in that respect. You won't be stepping on anyone's toes, so to speak."

"I appreciate your confidence in me," she said, feigning her own confidence and managing to sound more cutthroat journalist than fluttery-stomached girl. "I won't let you down."

"Good. Well, I'll be in touch soon. Keep an eye on the mail."

She said goodbye and hung up the phone, seeing Benjamin watching her curiously from across the room. Ella wanted to scream and dance she was so happy, but she kept her composure as she smiled at him and two ladies who were now lined up by his desk, before walking sedately out on to the sidewalk.

And then she promptly lost her composure, stomping her feet and squealing as she tilted her face up to the sun.

This was it. This was the big break she'd been waiting for. She hadn't even known it was possible to dream so big!

London, here I come.

The only thing left to do was break the news to her mother.

Ella walked beside her mother, listening as she talked with the energy of a woman who hadn't just spent long hours patrolling through the night. Even though it was only early fall, the wind had been uncharacteristically cool. While her own fingers pricked with discomfort, her body ready to collapse into bed, her mother seemed oblivious to the conditions.

When there was finally a lull in her mother's steady stream of words, Ella spoke up, knowing that her news was going to be about as popular as a lead bullet.

"Mama, there's something I need to talk to you about," she said.

That slowed her mother's pace considerably. She could clearly hear the uncertainty in Ella's tone.

Ella touched her mother's arm, head dropping to her shoulder as they walked. She wanted to absorb the feeling of her, to enjoy the moment before she devastated her with the news, because devastate her she would. Suddenly she felt more like a girl again, instead of a woman about to embark upon the biggest journey of her life.

"It's about my writing," she said tentatively.

She could feel the tightness of her mother's body as she kept her arm looped through hers. And when her mother didn't reply, she knew she just had to spit the words out and get it over with. She would have told her before their shift with the Home Guard, but they simply hadn't crossed paths soon enough for her to do so.

"What about your writing?" her mother asked.

"I've actually been offered a job," Ella said, "as a journalist. A correspondent, to be precise."

"Oh," her mother said with a sigh. "Well, that's what you want, isn't it? I'd say that's wonderful news. Are they being a bit more lenient about women writing now that so many of our men are away fighting?"

"Well, not exactly." Ella hesitated, cringing. "It's in . . ." She paused, swallowing hard. "In *Europe*, starting in London actually. Hence my gender not being such a problem."

The silence that followed was deafening, and she knew when her mother pulled away from her that her announcement wasn't going to be taken well.

"You aren't serious?" her mother said, stopping and staring at her. Her anger was like a silent pulse that Ella could somehow not only feel, but see, as it throbbed between them. "What's wrong with what you were doing? Writing about more local issues and being able to do it from Illinois?"

"Mama, I know it will come as a shock to you—*heavens*, it came as a complete shock to me too! But this is the break I've been waiting for; it's the opportunity of a lifetime."

Once again, she was greeted with silence and tightly pursed lips.

"I received a call, from an editor who's read my work and wants me to be their European correspondent," Ella continued, filling the silence. "I had actually written to a number of publications, trying to find someone to take me on to cover women's war issues, and—"

"Why didn't you tell me? You've been planning this all along and you never said a word?"

"Honestly, I never thought anyone would say yes," she confessed. "And I certainly didn't expect to be sent overseas! I thought I'd be writing local stories about women, not articles on women so close to the actual war."

"You can't do this to me," her mother said. "Ella, with your brother already away serving, you simply *cannot* expect me to give my permission!"

"Mama," Ella said, her voice low, bristling at the very idea that she might need her mother's permission, but knowing she needed that affirmation at the same time. "My writing is important to me. It's not just a fun hobby, it's what I want to make a career from doing. I *want* to see what is happening with my own eyes, and report that to the world. In fact, I feel it's my duty to do so." *I can't do this if she doesn't believe in me.*

Ella hurried beside her mother as she started to walk again, seeing that no amount of talking was going to change her mind.

"Please," she said, reaching for her mother's arm and not letting go of her even as she tried to brush her away. "Mama, I know this is hard for you to understand, but this is what I've been dreaming of doing for so long. You have no idea what it's like to want something so badly, to be so good at something, and be told at almost every turn that you can't do it because you're a woman."

That stopped her mother in her tracks. They both stood, breathing heavily, her mother's chest rapidly rising and falling as she faced her. "No, Ella, I don't know what that's like. Because I grew up knowing that my husband would be the provider, and that my job was to look after our household and raise our children. Clearly I didn't do a very good job of that, did I? I don't know where all these ideas even come from, but it's not appropriate for you to trot off to Europe on your own!"

She may as well have slapped Ella in the face. "Mama, you don't mean that, surely? Is it so dreadful to have a smart daughter who can wield words as well as your group of volunteers can wield a gun? To want more from life than what's merely expected of her?" Ella was almost starting to doubt her own words as her mother gaped at her.

She took her hand and pressed her mother's palm to her cheek, softening as she saw the pain in her eyes.

"I know this is hard for you to understand, but this is a changing world, Mama. I want to write about all the amazing and unexpected things that women are doing. But most of all, I want to make you proud."

"Don't you say that, Ella. You can't win me over with your clever words," her mother scoffed, marching toward home now as if the Devil himself was chasing her.

"Mama," Ella called after her. "*Mother!* Please don't walk away from me. Can't we talk about this?"

Part of her wanted to scream at her mother—that she should be happy for her instead of holding on to some kind of ideal that her daughter was supposed to conform to. But the other part of her was just sad and wanted to fold herself into her mother's arms. Ella wanted to inhale the sweet smell of her perfume mixed with whatever she'd been cooking that day, just like she had as a little girl, when a cuddle had been able to cure anything from a bleeding toe to a broken heart.

"I'm sorry, Ella," her mother suddenly blurted, spinning on her heel, tears streaming down her cheeks as she opened her arms. "Come here. I'm so sorry, my darling girl."

And Ella ran. Just like that little girl she'd been remembering, she fled into her mother's embrace, smiling into her hair as her mom stooped to hold her.

"I don't want to upset you, Mama, but I want this so badly. It's the most exciting thing that's ever happened to me," she whispered. Part of her wondered if she was even capable of fulfilling such an assignment, and as much as she wanted to pretend otherwise, she needed her mother's reassurance now more than ever.

"I know it is, sweetheart, I know." Her mother held her tight and long. "No mother wants her daughter going closer to war, not with our boys already there, but you've got a talent, and you need to use it. I know that."

They were the words she'd been longing to hear. She hadn't needed permission to travel abroad, but knowing she had her mother's blessing meant the world to her.

They linked arms again and, more slowly this time, walked for home, their heads tilted toward one another as their footsteps echoed the same beat.

"Promise you'll write as often as you can."

"I promise," Ella said quietly.

She didn't tell her mother that a letter had arrived that morning, advising that she'd be going by ship before Christmas; or that she knew how tough it would be for a female correspondent to succeed in a man's world. These were things she could tell her after the fact, when she was thousands of miles away across the pond.

"I knew I should have insisted you go to that school for young ladies," her mother muttered as they finally reached home. "Maybe then you'd have been content perfecting your cooking skills and learning how to sew."

"The place that was supposed to turn me into a *lady housewife*?" Ella scoffed, knowing her mother was only trying to provoke her. "I would have been expelled within days."

"You know your father wrote and asked whether he would receive a refund if that happened?"

Ella gasped. "He didn't!"

"Oh, he did," her mother said with a wry smile. "And when they wrote back and said there would be no refunds made in the case of a suspension or expulsion, he quashed all my plans to send you there for fear he'd lose his hard-earned money."

Ella laughed as she leaped up the steps to their door. All these years, she'd thought it was her headstrong refusal to attend that had put an end to the Economic School for Ladies or whatever it had been called, but instead she had her father to thank.

He knows me too well.

CHAPTER SEVEN

LONDON, MAY 1944
ELLA

Ella had the distinct feeling she was going to die. The air-raid siren was so loud it seemed to pierce right through to her bones, and the scramble of people jostling their way down to the shelter was making her feel claustrophobic.

I'm fine, I'm fine, I'm fine, Ella kept chanting to herself as she clutched her typewriter to her chest and followed the procession of people. Her typewriter was surprisingly light to carry around, and there was nothing more precious to her—it had been a gift from her parents before she left, and the shiny red Remington Portable was the most gorgeous thing she'd ever owned. It had sure beat trying to lug her enormous old Underwood across the pond with her.

Oomph.

With her head tucked down as she hurried, she hadn't noticed the person walking toward her, against the crowd.

"Sorry," she muttered.

"Watch it!"

She looked up and stood still as the crowd filed past her, mortified when she recognized the woman she'd stumbled into. "Sorry, I—"

"First air raid?" the other woman asked, sticking out her hand. "I'm Tania."

"Ella," she replied, laughing nervously. "And is it that obvious?"

"Look, plenty of us just stay in our rooms now. They make it nice down there, but there's nothing worse than sleeping rough with all those people, and then coming up in the morning to find your bed with its perfectly fresh, unwrinkled sheets and the coverlet turned down, knowing you could have just slept there all night."

"Really?" The siren was still wailing and, right now, Ella just wanted to get to safety. She'd spent the day in London looking at the devastation that had occurred during the Blitz, and she was well aware that some journalists had coined the current wave of attacks the "Baby Blitz," and it terrified her. The bombed buildings looked haunted, some of them reduced to waste and others almost like dollhouses, with one side blown clean off and giving a view into the domestic scene of a home inside. The last thing she wanted was to be buried beneath a pile of smoking rubble just because she'd chosen fresh, crisp sheets over safety, especially after her voyage had been delayed for so long. She'd almost doubted she was ever actually going to make it to England!

"Really," Tania said as she was jostled sideways. "But if you want to be a patsy and go downstairs, then by all means knock yourself out."

Ella gulped as Tania left, surprised at how abrupt the other journalist had been.

Moving with the crowd again, Ella flashed her green press accreditation card at the person waiting at the door to the basement shelter, and was ushered to a separate area for war correspondents. She looked around, blinking, eyes adjusting to the dim light.

"You press?" someone asked.

Ella quickly pulled out her card again and another woman waved her over.

"Come find yourself a good spot before the others arrive," she said, her smile kind.

"I, ah, met a correspondent named Tania on the way down here. She mentioned that some of the journalists just stay in their rooms now?" She wasn't sure if perhaps *she* was expected to do the same thing.

The other woman laughed and held out a hand. "Marion," she said warmly. "And yes, the die-hards like Tania like to report exactly what it feels like to be in the midst of it all, and they're particularly partial to fresh sheets and a turned-down bed."

Ella laughed and settled into a chair. "It sounds dangerous."

"Ha! Try telling them that," Marion replied. "One day we'll go back up and, instead of finding our beds waiting for us, there'll be a dozen correspondents bombed to pieces in their rooms."

Ella looked around at the corner set up for them, hardly able to believe it. She'd been told that The Savoy knew how to cater to correspondents, and that they provided both a workspace and sleeping quarters for them all in the well-equipped basement, but she'd imagined it would be an exaggeration. It clearly wasn't.

"You look impressed."

A deep, amused-sounding voice made her turn. Ella's cheeks burned as she took in the raised dark eyebrow and warm brown eyes of a man perhaps five years her senior. He was stretched out in a chair as if he were reclining in a library rather than a bomb shelter.

"I am," she said, watching as others moved around the cordoned-off area she was in. "I was expecting something very basic. Have you been down here before?"

His smile made her wonder if she'd said something funny. "Just once or twice," he said.

"Well, I suppose they don't call it the most luxurious bomb shelter in London for nothing," Ella said. "I heard they wanted to keep *The Times* and the *Herald Tribune* staff happy when they moved their offices here. Are you familiar with any of the correspondents based at the hotel?"

"You could say that."

"You wouldn't believe how hard it is lugging this blasted thing around all day," Ella moaned, flustered as she bumped about with her belongings. "Honestly, it might be portable but it's still cumbersome."

"I can only but imagine," he replied.

She settled on a chair, fumbling with her typewriter and bag. When she looked up, she saw that he was still watching her, and it struck her just how handsome he was. The light wasn't fantastic, and as she wondered if maybe she recognized him from somewhere, Marion walked back over, patting her on the shoulder and wagging her finger at the man she'd been talking to.

"Stop teasing the poor girl, Michael," Marion scolded.

"Michael?" Ella's eyes widened in horror when she looked back over at him, wishing the ground would open up and swallow her. "Oh my gosh, you're Michael Miller, aren't you?" In other words, recipient of the best writer of a news story award and one of the most highly respected correspondents in the industry. Not to mention author of a number of bestselling novels. Ella had just started to feel like a real correspondent, and now she'd gone and made a fool of herself.

"I am. And you are?" he asked, leaning forward, hand extended.

She reached out, clasping his palm and hoping hers didn't feel too sweaty against his soft, warm skin. He was dashingly handsome, and his eyes twinkled with humor.

"Ella," she managed, clearing her throat. "Ella Franks."

"So tell me, Ella Franks, how did you end up reporting in London? I can tell from that lovely accent of yours that you're not native to this side of the pond," Michael asked politely, as if he hadn't even noticed how mortified she was. How had she not realized she was talking to a seasoned writer who knew far more than she did about lugging a typewriter around the world with him!

She cleared her throat, trying to recover her composure and sound more confident than she felt. "I've, ah, only been in London a few days. It's a long story, but in short, it involved me writing under a male pseudonym back home, losing my job, and then somehow being offered a role here by the Associated Press reporting on women's war issues in Europe. I thought I was coming here before Christmas, but they decided they didn't need me here as soon as they'd originally thought."

Michael's eyebrows shot up. "You were writing under a *male* pseudonym?"

She groaned. "It's embarrassing, I know, but at the time—"

"It's not embarrassing, it's bloody brilliant!" He leaned toward her, as if she were part of some exciting conspiracy. "Tell me you're not really here to just write about women's issues though? Let me guess, that's your cover before you try to get to the front lines somewhere and report on the action firsthand?"

Ella stared back at him. Clearly he thought she was a lot more gutsy than she was. "Er, no," she said. "I was just excited to get here, and interviewing various women's groups has been very interesting actually."

Michael nodded and collected up some papers, seeming to lose interest in her. But when she spoke again, she noticed that his mouth was bracketed by a smile, as if he'd been expecting her to ask something else.

"Michael," she said quietly.

He put down his papers.

"*Should* I be trying to report from the front?" she asked, hoping she didn't sound ridiculously naïve. She lowered her voice. "I was so excited to be sent here at all that I didn't really consider . . ." Her voice trailed off. *Was* there something wrong with being content writing about women?

"Ella, I'm going to talk straight to you," he said, and she tried to ignore the burn in her cheeks as those intense dark eyes rested on hers. "Just because you're a woman, it doesn't mean you need to settle for writing exclusively about women's issues. When else in your life are you going to be able to see war firsthand, and report back to all those millions of Americans waiting for news at home?"

Ella stared back at him, but as she opened her mouth to speak, more people bustled past and the space around them filled up. Before she could get his attention again, Michael was deep in conversation with another correspondent, and she found herself with Marion on the other side of her.

"Don't let Michael heckle you," the older woman said. "He's a good man, but he's always one to push the boundaries. Doesn't mean you have to do the same, so long as you don't mind his teasing."

Ella nodded. "He does have a point, I suppose. Why bother coming all the way over here and not seeing war?"

Marion's smile was kind. "Look, you'll find the correspondents here a decent bunch. We're competitive, always, but it's a nice atmosphere. We all get along well, and so long as you're up for a drink or two, you'll have a lot of fun." Marion laughed. "Although you Americans seem to work a lot harder than us. Your work ethic puts us to shame."

"So we stay down here until morning, right?" Ella asked, not sure what to say in reply to her work ethic comment. She'd heard the Brits only worked afternoons, but she had no intention of taking it easy while she was in London. And she also didn't want to say the wrong thing again.

"That's right. So make yourself comfy, find a bed, and try your best to get a half-decent sleep," Marion said. "The staff always has linens downstairs here to make sure we can rest properly, and they have a snore warden to make sure no one is kept awake."

"A *snore warden?*" Ella bristled. "Now you're the one making fun of me!"

A deep chuckle from across the way made her look up, and she saw that Michael was alone again. "Trust me, Ella, it's true. One morning I woke to find a hand clamped over my mouth when I didn't heed the *please roll over, sir* warnings."

Ella smiled to herself at Michael's comments, trying not to glance at him again for fear he might notice, as everyone slowly started to quiet around them. She supposed it was commonplace for most of the guests now, especially the permanent residents, but it certainly wasn't a normal feeling for her to be crammed with so many people into a basement. Even if it was a luxurious one as far as bomb shelters went.

Once she was as comfortable as she could be in her makeshift bed, she set her portable typewriter beside her and pulled out a small flashlight she kept in her bag, along with pen and paper. She'd been meaning to write to her mother since she'd arrived but hadn't had a moment to do so, so she decided to make the most of her enforced downtime. Ella positioned the light in her mouth, between her teeth, and propped the pad of paper on her knee.

> *Dear Mother,*
> *Well, I'm here! London is a beautiful place, and it's actually quite possible, despite the rubble and devastation, to see what a glorious city she is, and what it would have been like before the war. The Savoy*

is something else as far as hotels go, although all the other correspondents seem so much more experienced than I am, and at times I feel very much the outsider. I know what you're going to say, that they all started somewhere, but it's hard not to feel a little out of my depth.

Tomorrow I'm to report on the Women's Land Army, so American women can see how the British women are coping during the war and pitching in. And then I'm going to be interviewing nurses and even the Red Cross Clubmobile girls. They sound like an incredible group of women who travel all around the place in trucks, serving donuts and coffee to the troops to help boost morale. I'm looking forward to meeting them, and of course all these women are doing incredible things for the war effort, but it's been suggested by a colleague that perhaps I shouldn't restrict my reporting to only women's issues. I will give it some consideration, and it's certainly made me wonder if I should be fighting for bigger stories. Either way, I promise you I won't take any unnecessary risks.

I miss you and Daddy so much, and I would love a letter when you have a moment to write. Right now I'm in the basement of the hotel in the bomb shelter, which is as luxurious as it gets, but it would still be comforting to read about home.

With all my love

Ella

She folded the letter and sighed, tucking it carefully into an envelope as the room settled around her.

"Ella, in case I don't see you in the morning, be sure to meet us all for drinks early evening tomorrow, before dinner," Marion said in a low voice, leaning over. "There's always a good group of us most evenings, actually, drowning our sorrows over a gin or two." Her laughter was muffled, but Ella heard it. "And Michael will be there too, in case you need another reason to join us."

Ella didn't bother to hide her smile, pleased no one could see her. "Thanks. I'd like that."

Maybe that was how she'd find her footing in London, by learning from the correspondents who'd already trodden the same path she was on. Ella lay beneath the sheets, listening to the low hum of so many people breathing and moving, closing her eyes and hoping sleep would find her.

And maybe, just maybe, she wouldn't mind running into Michael again either.

———— ❧～❧ ————

Two weeks later, Ella downed her gin, the burn in her throat as intense now as it had been when she'd tasted her first one straight after arriving in London. But she didn't care, her breath hissing out of her as she put her glass with a bang on the table.

"This is ridiculous," she muttered. "Absolutely, goddamn—"

"She'll have another," came a calm voice, as a hand closed over her shoulder.

Ella looked up and saw Michael standing there. He looked weary, with dark shadows beneath his eyes and stubble on his cheeks that hadn't been there when they'd first met, but he was still handsome enough to make her falter.

Another gin slid across the bar toward her, along with a glass of golden amber liquid that Ella guessed was whiskey—clearly Michael's standing order. She reached for hers and took a big, hearty gulp. It still burned like hell, but at least it took her attention from the palm against her shoulder.

"Better?" he asked.

She exhaled a breath she hadn't known she was holding. "A little," she replied.

"So tell me what's got you all in a fluster."

Ella almost blurted out "you," but instead she reluctantly passed him a copy of her recently published article for the Associated Press, resisting the urge to roll her eyes. "It's this dreadful article. I can't believe they changed it so much."

"Honey, if it's the censors you're drowning your sorrows over, we'd have commiserated with you straightaway," a slightly raspy voice cooed. "We do that on a daily—hell, *hourly* basis sometimes."

Ella looked up, and then straight down again. Her heart started to pound. *Danni Bradford. The* Danni Bradford was standing in between her and Michael, gesturing to the barman and leaning forward as if they weren't complete strangers.

"Danni, meet Ella," Michael said, holding the paper up so Danni could see it. "Ella, meet Danni. She's just returned from a long stint traveling through conflict zones in Europe."

Ella could barely gasp out "hello" as she tried to snatch back the paper, but Michael was having none of it, keeping it just out of her reach. She'd heard that seasoned correspondents like Danni were often gone for months and months on end, paid a daily stipend regardless of where they were, and filing their stories via wire or physically sending them back to London. She could only imagine where Danni's travels had taken her, and if she were braver she might have asked.

"The censors are bastards," Michael complained. "I'd roast every single one of them alive if I could. I've started to think they're just on some kind of power trip, the way they redact some things so ferociously, and leave others almost untouched."

He and Danni laughed, but Ella just sat in horrified silence as Danni started to read. She was one of the most famous photographers in the world, known for her daring and often risqué shots of the war, and now she was reading out Ella's feminine fluff piece for all to hear. She'd worked for days after interviewing the incredible American Clubmobile girls—the hardest-working, most amazing women she'd ever encountered—and her painstaking work had been trivialized to the point that it was almost unrecognizable. She took another gulp of her drink, shuddering and wishing the ground would open up and swallow her.

"*Lipstick and donuts,*" Danni read. "*How painted lips and a little Southern charm warms every soldier within a mile.*"

Ella reached for her gin again, the words echoing in her mind as she shook her head, mortified. "I can tell you right now that the headline is not reflective of the story I wrote," she stuttered. "I think my editor's changes are worse than anything the censor could have cut. It's mortifying what they reduced my in-depth article to."

Danni patted her on the back. "Look, every correspondent in this room has been where you are now. Is it just the headline or the whole thing?"

Ella sipped at her drink again, realizing that the woman she was so in awe of wasn't laughing at her or belittling her, but genuinely commiserating with her. "The whole thing," she said, clearing her throat and speaking louder. "I wrote this passionate, informative piece on women putting their lives on the line every day, about how brave and incredible they are, and it was turned into some pathetic powder-puff piece."

"*There's nothing a hot cup of coffee and a warm donut can't fix, and that includes the morale of our soldiers serving in Europe. As the war rages on, a group of women known as the Red Cross Clubmobile girls are blazing their own trail, hot on the heels of our men to deliver home comforts just when they need them the most,*" Michael continued to read over Danni's shoulder.

Danni shrugged, like it was no big deal.

"Do you see what I mean? I wrote about how hardworking, smart, and highly trained these women were, how they could maintain their own trucks as well as any male mechanic could, and they make it sound like they're just dollies serving a few cups of coffee in their spare time! These women work twelve-hour shifts, for God's sake, every day of the week."

"There, there," Michael said, but Ella could hear the laughter in his tone. "No need to bring the good Lord's name into it."

Ella was about to sling a barb back about not realizing he was a God-fearing man, but she bit her tongue instead. She knew why it stung to hear him speak like that, because he hadn't thought her reporting on women's issues was important in the first place.

"Is it wrong that I'm so upset about this?" she asked no one in particular.

"No," Danni said, sighing as she pushed her shoulders up into a gentle shrug. "But it comes with the territory, especially when you're reporting on women. God knows that men love belittling us and the work we do, and we just have to take it on the chin sometimes and keep doing what we do best."

"Point taken," Michael said, raising his hands as if in surrender.

Ella chewed over the other woman's words as she sipped her gin, more slowly this time.

"So what do I do?" she finally asked.

Michael and Danni exchanged glances as another man whom she hadn't met before came over to join them. He had sandy-colored hair and bright blue eyes, but he looked worried about something; his mouth turned down and his shoulders hunched forward.

"You do what we're all trying to do," Danni said. "You fight every day to report the stories *you* want to report on, and you try to figure out a way to get to France."

Ella froze. "France?" Never in a million years had she considered that *she* could be going to France herself. Writing about France, sure, but *going* to France?

"You look like a startled little rabbit in headlights," Michael teased, downing the rest of his drink. "You seriously haven't been plotting how to get to France when it all goes down?"

"So it's true, everything that's being said?" Ella asked. "I wasn't sure how much of it was rumor to be honest."

"What do you think?" Danni asked, ordering another drink and passing it to the man who'd joined her.

It was then that Ella looked around, truly looked around, and realized just how full the room was now—it was heaving with correspondents. "Is that why they're all here tonight?"

"While you've been fretting about this *fluffy* story, we've been digesting the latest on the possible Allied invasion," Danni said. "Come on, let's go see what more we can find out. You missed the briefing, but we weren't actually told a lot."

Ella had been out in the field all day—literally—doing a follow-up piece on the Women's Land Army, and Danni was right, she'd been so caught up in typing up her transcript that she hadn't read all the briefings from the day. She mentally scolded herself as she smoothed out the creases in her skirt and collected her drink, following the others.

There was more of a buzz about the place than usual, and although everyone was hideously competitive about breaking stories and keeping information garnered to themselves, it was a fun, welcoming atmosphere. Although she'd put money on it that any information on the possible invasion would be held between very tight lips.

"Keep your eyes and ears open," Michael whispered into her ear, sending goosebumps rippling across her skin. "After enough to drink, even the most seasoned correspondents can end up with loose lips."

She choked, spluttering and trying not to look at *his* lips.

"Danni, we need to talk," the man who'd arrived moments earlier said, pulling Danni aside.

Danni moved a few steps away with her male companion, and Ella wondered what was so urgent. They had their heads bent close, and the man looked agitated. She heard him say something about needing to go home, but she didn't want to eavesdrop.

"You okay?" Michael asked, as if he had no idea the effect he had on her.

"I, ah . . ." Ella turned to look at him, clearing her throat and standing up a little straighter. "I'm a little intimidated, I suppose. And I'm wishing I hadn't had so much to drink."

"Intimidated? Of this lot?" he asked, holding his glass high and clinking it gently to hers. "Don't be. We're all just scrambling for the same stories, and the only thing we're all incredibly good at is drinking. You have just as much right to be here as any of us."

Ella smiled. She'd certainly noticed how much alcohol everyone consumed. They even seemed to prefer gin to cigarettes.

"What do you think that's all about?" she asked, gesturing toward Danni, who looked to be consoling the man about something now.

"Who knows?" he said with a shrug. "Those two are joined at the hip; they've been working stories for longer than most of the correspondents here have even been covering the war."

"Michael, what are your personal thoughts on France?" she asked, deciding not to even pretend to be coy with her line of questioning, and pulling her eyes from Danni. "And more importantly, how *do* we get there to see it firsthand?"

"Sweetheart," he said as he leaned closer, his warm breath touching her skin, his English accent making him sound so exotic and exciting to her. "Despite me joking about before, there ain't no way you're going to see the invasion firsthand. The only correspondents who'll be able to do that will be men, simple as that."

He obviously saw the stutter in her body language, because he scooped his arm around her shoulders and gave her a sad kind of smile.

"It's just the way it is. The powers that be don't want women close to the front lines, and that means there's no way any of you will get accredited to sail with the troops."

"Danni didn't seem to think she'd be kept from going there."

Michael laughed. "Danni doesn't let anyone stop her from doing anything. If you really want to get there, you'll have to be inventive, that's for sure. But my gut feeling is that I'll return and you'll still be here tapping away about the Women's Land Army."

Ella held her composure, even as she bristled inside at his blatant disrespect for her work. She'd damn well show him! She nodded as if it weren't a big deal, but when he turned and moved on to talk to someone else, she marched straight over to Danni, waiting for the other woman's friend to leave and then mustering all her courage. She touched Danni's back and leaned in to speak directly into her ear.

"Excuse me, Danni, but do you think there's any chance of women traveling to Normandy to see the landings firsthand? I was just informed that there's no chance any of us will make it there!"

Danni frowned. "If they go ahead as planned, then no, I don't."

"Surely there's something we can do about it?" Ella said, still smarting from Michael's comments about her tapping away on her *women's* stories.

Danni just frowned. "Look, I'm not happy about it either, but there's always a way to flout the rules. You just need to get creative."

Ella digested Danni's words, liking the confident way she held herself. She had a feeling that Danni played by her own set of rules. Michael might have been the one to light the fire in her belly with his taunts, but Danni was the one she wanted to listen to, and she suddenly knew there was no way she was missing the biggest event of this war.

"Danni—" she started, before the wail of an air-raid siren pierced the air.

For Christ's sake, she thought. But it didn't matter. Going down to the air-raid shelter would give her time to come up with a plan, and figure out exactly how she was going to get herself to France.

Ella tried unsuccessfully to calm her nerves as she waited for her editor to answer her call a week later. She'd been wanting to speak to him for days now, but it seemed the urgent telegrams she'd been sending him had finally caught his attention. And now she was standing, telephone receiver in hand, ready to plead her case.

When they were finally connected, Ralph Mountford's raspy voice came on the line.

"Ella! It's so good to talk to you. How's it all going over the pond, huh?"

"Well, it would be better if you'd print my stories as I file them," she said, summoning every ounce of confidence she could. "I can only imagine what some of the women think about me when they show me how extraordinary they are, and yet the articles bearing my name make them out to be nothing more than a pretty face doing some light lifting!"

"Ella, calm down," he said, his hearty laughter making her want to slam the receiver down on him. "Some of the women's stuff is a little boring for our New York readers, so we just jazz it up a little here and there, that's all. I can see that being in Europe has you chomping at the bit."

Jazz it up? She clamped her hand over her mouth to physically stop herself from replying. She'd scheduled a call with him to discuss France, not to berate him for his overzealous editing.

"But your work is great, Ella. We couldn't be more thrilled with the stories you're filing. Keep it up."

She took a deep breath and dropped her hand. "I want to start reporting on the war itself," she said calmly. "Women, men, troops, and bombs. I want to file stories on the whole lot. It's why I came here and it's what I want to be doing."

"Look, I hear you, Ella, I do, but there's only so much that can be said on the war itself that hasn't already been said. What you're doing for us, you're telling stories that need to be told, am I not right?"

"I know I need to provide a fresh perspective, and I'll still tell women's stories for you because they're important to me, but I want more leeway with the articles I file. I can't be pigeonholed all the time."

"Okay, okay," he replied, his voice crackling slightly over the line. "I'm happy for you to write more—"

"From Normandy," she interrupted, feigning confidence. "I want to be considered to go there. To report for you from where the action is. I know that every publication is only sending one correspondent, and I want to be yours."

"Ella, you know there's a ban on women going to the front lines! You're being unreasonable. There is no way the military will send you an accreditation to go there."

"Ralph, I know you can do something to help me," she insisted.

"Look, the best I can say is that you get yourself on a boat somehow, and I'll publish your stories." He laughed. "And pay you handsomely for them if you manage to achieve the impossible."

"I have your word?" she asked, her heart starting to pick up pace as she pressed the receiver even harder to her ear.

"Yes, but you know this comes with risks," he cautioned. "If you don't get the right accreditation and you go on your own accord, if you—"

"I'll get there," she said, as nervous excitement started to thrum through her. "You let me worry about that."

She had no idea how, she just knew that there was no way all those men were going to see the moment that might be the turning point in the entire war up until now, without her somehow going along too. Not to mention she wanted to prove to Michael that it wasn't just the infamous Danni Bradford who knew how to get what she wanted.

"You stay safe, Ella. Promise me that?"

She smiled, proud of herself. "I'll try my best."

When she hung up the phone, she almost skipped her way to the bar she was so excited. Not to mention she'd never wanted a drink so badly in her life—being ballsy and standing up to her editor like that hadn't exactly come easy.

"Someone looks pleased with herself," a deep, deliciously British voice said. Michael looked up from his notepad as she passed.

"It's been a good day," she said, grinning.

"It has indeed," he replied. "The first of the correspondents received their accreditations tonight."

Ella didn't even bristle at the comment, not letting him see her surprise. She was getting on a ship, she just hadn't figured out how yet. "Good for them," she said, summoning every bit of confidence she had to sashay straight past him.

The excitement and chatter in the bar that night was palpable, and Ella's mind was racing, trying to figure out exactly how she was going to execute her plan. If Michael and the other men were going, then so was she. Even if the very thought of it was making it almost impossible to stomach her drink.

CHAPTER EIGHT

CHLOE

Chloe bristled as she heard the click of the front door unlocking. She quickly shifted to the sofa, wrapping her arms around herself and pouting as she listened to Gabriel's heavy footfalls. Months of being confined to Gabriel's apartment, and she was going stir-crazy. She'd expected to be able to move about the city freely, albeit with a curfew perhaps, but he refused to let her go *anywhere*. And although his apartment had seemed so extravagant and exciting when she'd first seen it three years earlier, she had fast tired of it.

She glared at him as he came into view. "Where have you been?" she demanded.

He sighed as he placed a small bundle of papers on the table. "I'm sorry I'm late," he said, dropping a brief kiss on the top of her head as he passed.

Chloe would have pouted some more, but she doubted he would have even noticed.

"Do you have someone else?" she asked, standing and following him. "Gabriel!" she demanded when he didn't turn around. "You keep sneaking around, you're out all hours, and you don't even seem to notice me!"

She heard his groan as he finally turned. "No, Chloe. There's no one else. How many times do I have to tell you that?"

Chloe folded her arms across her chest. "Well, if it's not another woman, then why do you keep leaving me like this? I thought it was bad being stuck at home in London, but now that I'm here . . ."

Gabriel turned away again, bending down to reach into a cupboard, and before she could demand to know more, he was facing her again. And she could have melted into a puddle at his feet.

"Happy birthday," he said, holding out a bottle like a peace offering.

"You didn't forget?" she whispered, before throwing her arms around him and pressing a kiss to his lips. "I can't believe it! And a bottle of Taittinger? What a treat!"

Gabriel wiggled the cork and it went flying with a loud pop, and she raced to find glasses for them, holding them out with a grin as Gabriel poured. The bubbles fizzed almost to the top, and she happily clinked her glass against his.

"Happy birthday, Chloe," he whispered, before taking a sip.

"This reminds me of our first night together, when we danced in the dark and you kissed me as we sipped champagne," she said, inhaling the sweet smell of her drink as the bubbles tickled her nose.

"To Paris being like that again one day," he said, sounding annoyingly somber.

"Do you think about it often?" she asked, studying his weary face and realizing just how different he looked to the man who'd been the suave editor-in-chief of French *Vogue*. "The fashion industry, I mean. Will you go back to it after the war?"

He sank into one of the kitchen chairs and she did the same, watching as he stared into his glass. "We kept going as long as we could, before it all came grinding to a halt not long after you left after that photo shoot," he said. "All the great designers will flourish again, I'm certain of it, but I don't know if I'll be able to go back to that life."

She frowned. "Why not? Once the war is over, everything will go back to normal, will it not?"

Gabriel gave her an exasperated look. "Chloe, it could take years for Paris to return to her former glory, if she ever does. It's not a given that we'll win this war, and if we don't . . ." His voice trailed off.

She took a sip of her champagne, feeling slightly giddy already. "I heard that Christian Dior left the army and is working alongside Pierre Balmain, trying to breathe life into the fashion industry," she said, repeating what she'd been told in London.

Gabriel's lip curled. "Did you also hear that he's dressing the wives of German officers and French collaborators, too? All in the name of fashion?"

She'd expected him to be impressed by her fashion industry knowledge, and instead he looked insulted. Chloe sighed. "And the other designers? What of them?" she asked.

"Coco Chanel sacked all her employees and has made her views very clear," he said.

"Is it true or a vicious rumor that she hates the Jews and is aligned with the Nazis?" Chloe asked.

Gabriel nodded sadly. "All true." He sipped his champagne. "Another reason I can't imagine my old life ever reigniting."

They sat a moment, and Chloe brushed away tears. "I'm sorry, Gabriel. It's obvious you don't want me here, and now—"

"Shhh," he said, setting his glass down and moving his chair closer. He opened his arms and she clung to him as he held her, his lips murmuring against her hair.

"There's so much I wish I could tell you, Chloe, but I can't," he whispered. "You're a beautiful, fun girl, and I loved the time we had together, but so much has changed, that's all."

"Did you ever think of me as more than a fling?" she murmured back, hearing how needy she sounded and hating it.

Before Gabriel could answer, a loud knock sounded at the door. The insistent rapping of knuckles on wood sent Gabriel shooting out of his chair and tripping over her as he ran toward the stairs. What was it with his carefully worded answers and his refusal to tell her where he was going and who he was seeing? She didn't believe for a second that it wasn't another woman.

"Are you expecting someone?" she called out.

"Wait there," he called back. "Do *not* move."

Chloe's fingers found her champagne glass and she clasped the stem. The look on Gabriel's face, the panic in his eyes as he'd glanced at her, made her heart race. She took a shaky sip and then followed him, standing at the top of the stairs and seeing a woman standing there, speaking rapidly in French. Chloe's French was good, but they were speaking so fast she couldn't make out every word. Anger pulsed through her as she saw the familiar way the woman touched Gabriel. Was this who he was always leaving her to see?

Before she could demand to know who she was, Gabriel had shut the door and was leaping up the stairs two at a time.

"Quickly, pack your things. We have a minute, maybe two."

She stood, dumbfounded. "Who was that, Gabriel? Is she your lover?"

"Shut up, Chloe!" he shouted. "Just get your things. We have to go and we're not coming back."

Tears pricked her eyes again, this time at the harshness of his tone, but she could tell from the frantic way he was moving that he was deadly serious.

"Gabriel, you're frightening me," she cried.

He grabbed hold of her shoulders, his eyes frantically searching hers. "Now isn't the time, Chloe. You need to move, and you need to move quickly."

"What dress shall I take? Where are we going?"

"For God's sake, Chloe, we're not going on vacation. Grab whatever you can. Whatever is left behind, you won't be seeing it again."

As he ran from the room, she followed, grabbing her case and stuffing her clothes into it. She grabbed her hairbrush and makeup, her heart pounding as she tried to close her case and failed. What was going on?

Gabriel pushed past her and threw one of her dresses out as if it meant nothing, before forcing the bag shut. She noticed he was only carrying an overnight bag, a pristine-looking Louis Vuitton, a hint of his former life as a high-flying player in the fashion world.

She followed his lead and took food from the cupboards, filling a bag, then stood aghast as he scooped up a stack of papers and threw them into the fire, setting them alight.

"What are you doing?" she asked.

"Burning evidence," he replied.

"But what—"

"Chloe, I work for the Resistance," he said. "I produce and distribute newspapers for the underground movement, and because of that, our apartment is about to be raided. I've been discovered. We need to leave as quickly as possible."

He stopped at the table and shook his head.

"I'm so sorry, Chloe. But if we don't go now, the Gestapo will find me, and they'll likely kill us both."

Kill us?

She swallowed, staring at Gabriel. At the man she'd fled London to be with, naïvely thinking things would still be the same between them as they had been during that heady week, years ago. He paused and took a quick sip of champagne, and she did the same, still not taking her eyes from him.

"Oh, Chloe," he murmured. "I'm so, so sorry it's come to this."

Gabriel's hand found hers, and she gratefully tucked her palm into his as he rubbed his thumb gently across her skin.

Darkness was their friend and seemed to swallow them whole as they disappeared into the night, until a noise in the silence echoed around them.

Crack.

The unmistakable, singular sound of a gunshot carried to them on the wind, stifling Chloe, making her breath stall in her throat as Gabriel tugged her along beside him. He was relentless, not slowing as he forced her down the road toward the cover of more buildings and then trees.

Without stopping, without seeing, Chloe knew. And when he finally let her look, hidden against him, she saw the body. It was the woman who had been standing at the door; the woman she'd instinctively been jealous of, thinking she was Gabriel's lover. In fact, that woman had risked everything to warn them, to tell them to go while they still could.

They started to run again, her hand tucked tight into Gabriel's, fear like she'd never known before propelling her forward, clutching at her throat, warning her that if she stopped for even a second, the next bullet could—*would*—be for her.

She'd naïvely traveled to Paris thinking it would be an adventure, defying her brother's insistent pleas that it was too dangerous, and now she had the sinking feeling that she was never, ever going to make it home to him.

Oh, Andy, what have I done?

CHAPTER NINE
LONDON
DANNI

"Danni, do you have a minute?"

"Andy!" Danni jumped out of the seat in the lobby and went to throw her arms around him, but the expression on his face stopped her. She could tell just from looking at him that he was the bearer of bad news.

"What is it?" she asked. She'd missed him the week he'd been gone, and she'd been so looking forward to him coming back. "You've got a look on your face like someone just died. Did something happen at home?" He'd left to go to his sister, worried he hadn't received any letters from her in so long, although Danni had tried to reassure him that Chloe was probably just busy and didn't have time for letter-writing. But their assignment had kept them away from England for months, the trip to Sicily taking much longer than planned, and their return travel made almost impossible as the fighting all through Europe continued to intensify. Which meant it had been a long time since Andy had gone home to see her. When they were working, he always stayed at the hotel with all the other correspondents.

"She left me this," Andy said quietly, handing her an envelope. "I waited for her to come home all week, even though I could see some of her things were gone, and then our elderly neighbor returned from seeing family, and she had been keeping this for me." He sighed. "I thought she must have been staying with friends or something, since she never did like living alone, but she's actually gone."

She took it, slipping her finger inside and taking out a piece of paper. Danni glanced up at him before scanning the perfect handwriting.

> *Dear Andy,*
> *I know you're going to be so cross with me for doing this, but I couldn't stand being apart from Gabriel any longer. I wanted to wait to say goodbye to you, but if I'd done that you would have found a way to put a stop to my plans.*
>
> *Being in Paris was the most exciting week of my life, and I can't just wait forever for this blasted war to be over. I've already waited three years! So I decided to make my way back to him. It won't be easy, I know, but I cleverly figured out a way to get there. You're not going to like it, but a girl I knew from my modeling days has just returned from the Moulin Rouge and it sounded amazing! Very naughty, of course, but it does seem fun, and the German officers just love all the girls. I'm certain I can pass as a dancer, so I should be able to get to France without so much as a hiccup.*

Please don't come looking for me. You won't be able to change my mind, and besides, I have no intention of leaving Gabriel when I find him. He'll keep me safe in Paris, so don't worry, and there's always his family chateau near Caen.

All my love, darling brother. I know you'll be furious with me right now, but know that I do love you. Perhaps we can all holiday together in France once the war is over?

Chloe

"Oh, Andy, I don't even know what to say." Danni glanced up at him before scanning the letter one more time. "I can't even believe she'd do something like this."

Andy looked like he was about to pull all his hair out he was tugging at it so furiously. She'd never seen him so agitated before. "I knew something was wrong when I hadn't heard from her, but I had no idea she'd do something like this. She left the letter with the neighbor months ago. I can't believe I was imagining her here safe all that time, and she was gone before we even left that field hospital in Sicily."

"Is there anything I can do?"

"Go to France and drag her back home?" He shook his head. "Honestly, she's so naïve. Imagine thinking she could just travel into a country that's under German occupation like that!" He groaned. "I mean, I thought she'd forgotten about him, or at least put thoughts of running back to him out of her head. She knew I didn't approve, that I thought it was ridiculous to be in love with someone she'd only known a week."

For the first time in her life, Danni was all out of words.

"Where's Caen?" she eventually asked. "Is it anywhere near the beach where you'll be landing?"

Andy nodded and took a folded piece of paper from his pocket. "I've already looked," he said, unfolding it and showing her the map. "It's here. Perhaps an hour, maybe less from the looks of it. And I seriously doubt Gabriel would still be in Paris, so she may well be there."

"Andy, I'm so sorry," Danni said, opening her arms and pulling him close. She held him tight, not usually one to be overly affectionate, but Andy had no other family and his sister meant the world to him. "But in all seriousness, if he's a man with resources, and he has this chateau away from Paris, then it's entirely likely that he's looking after her and she's fine."

"I suppose so, but knowing she could be anywhere . . ." His voice trailed off as he hugged her back, before pulling away. She diverted her gaze, knowing he wouldn't want her to see as he brushed his eyes with the backs of his hands. "She could be dead for all we know, or in a German prison, or—"

Danni stopped him. "Chloe might be naïve, but she's also smart and perhaps more resourceful than you know."

Andy cleared his throat. "Maybe."

"So what's the plan?" Danni asked.

He sighed and took out another envelope from his jacket pocket. "This was waiting for me at the hotel reception."

He showed her a green card and a letter. Danni glanced at it, not even wanting to touch it.

Andy had his clearance to travel to Normandy.

"Hey, all things considered, it could actually be good timing," she said.

Andy frowned. "I'm so sorry, Danni. They've sent all the selected male correspondents accreditation passes today to travel via ship together to Normandy, so we can report on the landings, but—"

She held up her hand. "You don't have to explain it to me," Danni said brusquely. "You're not the one making the rules, and I've known they'd be arriving for all the men any day now."

Inside she was seething, but she wasn't going to vent to Andy. She was telling the truth; she bore him no ill feelings that he'd been given a pass, and she certainly didn't expect him to decline just because she couldn't go. But the fact that some fat, balding old men were deciding who could and couldn't go to France based on gender alone made her blood boil.

They'd been back in London for a week now, and she was itching to get closer to the action. The Savoy had been full so they'd kept their rooms at The Dorchester with at least a quarter of the other correspondents in the city, and she'd been dreading the passes being sent out for days now. If she wasn't able to get back into the conflict areas soon, she could be stuck in London for the foreseeable future.

"At least you might be able to look for her while you're there," Danni said. "And you know, if I was going with you, I'd do anything I could to help you."

He nodded. "I know you would. And if it weren't for Chloe . . ."

She smiled and touched his shoulder, seeing the pain reflected in his eyes. By all accounts he'd been incredibly close to his sister, and she knew he'd do anything to find her. "You'd still be going," she said. "Because you've done so much for me for so long, and I would never hold you back from this."

"Thanks, Danni."

"The best thing you can do is imagine that she arrived safely, and she's happy being reunited with her man," she said. "The alternative is grim, so it's not worth jumping to conclusions until you've exhausted every avenue trying to find her once you're there, right?"

Danni wrapped her arm around him, knowing there was nothing else she could say to make it easier on him.

"Oh, and I have something for you," Andy said. "There was a telegram waiting at reception for you, too, and I collected it for you."

She held out her hand. "Thanks."

"Shall we meet later for a drink? I'll come past your room when the others have finished up for the day, if you'd like?"

Danni smiled up at Andy, laughing when she noticed the small pencil still propped behind his ear. "Yes to a drink. I need a very strong whiskey to drown my sorrows tonight. And if you're looking for your pencil, you might want to look around here," she teased, touching her own ear.

Andy laughed, as good-natured as always, and she realized how much she'd miss him when they parted ways. She'd already missed him the past week, used to him having the room adjoining hers. In the beginning she'd resented his presence, thinking of him as an unwanted chaperone, but as soon as they'd started working together, her concerns had disappeared. Especially after Poland.

"I am sorry, Danni, that you weren't cleared to travel," he said, his eyebrows drawn tightly together as he started to turn away. "Unfair doesn't even begin to describe this whole situation."

She nodded and watched him walk away toward the entrance of the hotel. She stood for a moment, looking skyward and wondering whether she had the nerve to march straight up to General Eisenhower's suite and demand to be given an accreditation in person. It was no secret that he was planning the landings from the generous suite he'd taken over earlier in the year, only a floor above her head, but she also knew that getting on his bad side and making a fuss wasn't necessarily going to help her cause in the long run, especially when he had far more pressing matters to concern himself with than the plight of a single photographer. But still, the thought of doing it, of knowing he was in the same hotel as her, at least gave her some element of pleasure. Maybe she'd happen upon him in the bar later and be able to plead her case, although she hadn't yet seen him in any of the common areas.

Remembering the telegram Andy had given her, Danni opened it and scanned the contents, cursing as she read it.

IN RESPONSE TO YOUR LETTER I AM NOT SUPPORTING YOUR CLEARANCE TO TRAVEL TO THE FRONT. I SUPPORT THE DECISION TO SEND ONLY MALE CORRESPONDENTS. WOMEN HAVE NO PLACE NEAR THE FRONT LINE. GENERAL PATTON

Well, damn. Danni scrunched the paper into a ball, anger welling inside her all over again. She'd been convinced that Patton would be her best chance at getting some form of clearance to travel, even if he hadn't exactly been her ally in Sicily, but nothing was going the way she'd hoped. Patton wasn't her favorite person and she certainly wasn't his, but she'd thought he might have at least realized how good she was at her job after the series of photos from her time in Italy had been published to great acclaim. Not to mention the fact that she'd chosen *not* to send in damning photographs of him arguing with an officer.

Danni made her way up the stairs, liking the burn in her legs as she took them two at a time. There simply had to be a way to get on that boat with Andy, but instead of coming up with ideas, she was drawing blanks.

Once in her suite, she rummaged around for a pen and paper and flopped on to the bed, belly first, to write a letter home. Her poor mother had written her at least half a dozen letters over the past month and she was yet to respond to one of them. Danni stared out the window, sitting up to see better and admiring the view of Hyde Park. Right now, it was almost possible to imagine she was in London prewar, before the Blitz had left a cemetery of buildings in its wake.

She lifted her pen and sighed, determined to write her letter before Andy came looking for her. It had been a long day and she still wanted to freshen up before they went out.

Dear Mother

I'm sorry it's taken me so long to reply, but I do love receiving your letters. I've had such a battle this past month, just work things so nothing for you to worry about, but sometimes my frustrations at being a woman in a man's world are stifling.

Thank you for sending clippings of my photographs, it's always a thrill to know that I'm taking images a world away from you, and yet you get to see what I'm seeing. My editor has given me what the British would call a proper telling off, yet again, at some of my images being too gruesome to publish, but I'm only photographing what I see, and isn't it my job to report on the true horrors of war? As well as moments that aren't so horrific, of course, when I see them. I truly want to be the eyes of the American people.

I'm going out for drinks tonight with some of the boys, including Andy. You'd love him, Mother, he's a lot of fun to be around and he knows just how to get me riled up sometimes. Nothing romantic, of course, he's just a friend, so don't go getting the wrong idea! I like to think of him as the brother I never had.

All my love to everyone back home. Please read this to Father and give him a big lip-smacking kiss for me.

Yours, Danni.

She reread her own words and smiled, imagining the look on her mother's face when it arrived. Danni always vowed to write to her more often, but despite her best intentions it never happened.

Danni placed the letter inside the envelope and quickly addressed it, before looking at herself in the mirror and deciding she really needed to do something with her hair. She was used to wearing her hat when she was in the field reporting, but she couldn't exactly wear one out at night.

She shook out her long, dark brown hair, noticing the streaks of gold that had appeared at the tips. They reminded her of her childhood pony, whose dark mane had always been tinged golden over the summer months. Danni finished brushing out the tangles and did her best to fashion it into something resembling a bun; she was not well versed in the latest hairdos and didn't care terribly so long as it was off her face. Then she reached for her red lipstick, smiling as she remembered her mother giving her the two small cases of her signature color the day before she left for Europe, along with a small glass bottle of perfume. Danni finished her lips and took out the bottle, seeing there was only a tiny bit of the sweet fragrance left. She squirted it on her wrists and then dabbed at her neck, the smell filling her nostrils and instantly taking her home.

A knock startled her and she took a moment to stare at her reflection, almost surprised at the woman staring back at her, with her knowing eyes and serious-looking mouth; the war had changed her, she could see it in her own gaze.

"Just a moment!" she called out.

Danni quickly changed her shirt, and then swung open her door to find Andy leaning on the frame. His eyebrows rose when he saw her.

"What? Do I have something on my face?" she asked.

"No," he answered, his face breaking into a smile. "You just look really nice, that's all."

Danni laughed, almost embarrassed by the compliment. "You don't scrub up so bad yourself."

She collected her purse, glancing at her camera as her fingers itched to pick it up and take it with her. Instead she ran over and tucked the Leica under her pillow, just in case there was an air raid. Her Speed Graphic was safely wrapped in her spare clothes, so that was as safe as it could be.

Andy held out his arm, and she happily linked hers through it after shutting the door to her room.

"Come on," she said. "You're definitely in need of a drink or three."

"Would you believe I met up with some of the paratroopers from the 505th while I was drowning my sorrows waiting for you, and they're going to meet us in the bar downstairs before we move on elsewhere."

"Sounds good to me," she said, letting go of Andy's arm as they made their way down the stairs. "Anything to take my mind off Normandy and yours off your sister."

"How about we don't talk about my sister tonight," he groaned.

"My lips are sealed," she replied. "But feel free to talk about how gutless it is of the American and British governments to stop women from doing their jobs."

"Hey, you'll find a way to get there," Andy said. "If anyone can, you can."

She caught his eye and wished she were as hopeful as he was.

"Well, when you think of a way, make sure you tell me," she teased. "Because right now my options include rowing my own boat across the Channel, or changing course in my career and writing fluff pieces from the sidelines."

Before Andy could answer, they were in the lobby of the hotel, and soon they passed through to the bar. Murky tendrils of smoke hung in the air as Andy opened the door for her, and within seconds they were both being greeted by other correspondents and a handful of soldiers they knew. Danni sighed. It was like joining a big family, being part of the war; and it was why being denied a pass to what could be the most monumental move forward for the Allies was so heartbreaking for her. She cared about the soldiers, about the war itself, about showing the world what she was seeing and what was happening. And she almost felt it was her duty to record what she could on film for the men she'd grown so fond of.

"Danni! Andy!" She looked up and saw the paratroopers Andy had mentioned. She waved back and they made their way over, calling out over the loud chatter around them that came with so many people being in one place at the same time.

"Well, if it isn't our favorite photographer," one of them said, taking a big slug of his drink before giving her a kiss on the cheek.

Danni laughed and patted his back, not wanting to encourage him. "Good to see you too, Fraser," she said, pushing him away just as another of the men enveloped her in a bear hug and lifted her off the ground.

"Hands off!" she demanded, struggling not to laugh as she tried to extract herself. "How many drinks have you lot had?"

"Hey, if you only had two days' leave, you'd be making the most of it too!"

Danni laughed and leaned between them, waving the bartender over and ordering a whiskey.

"Hey, Harry," she said, smiling at his familiar face.

"Danni," he replied with a wink. "You going to try one of my cocktails tonight?"

She shook her head. "Maybe later. You know me, always whiskey."

Harry Craddock, the bartender, was famous for his martinis and other cocktails, which meant he was always trying to get her to change her poison, and though she knew the Londoners preferred gin, she'd become accustomed to the amber liquor when she'd first started working as a correspondent. As she waited, she noticed Michael Miller sitting farther down the bar, at ease amongst the crowd as he scribbled in his notebook. She often saw him propped up at the bar working late into the night.

If he hadn't been writing, she'd have gone over to talk to him. Michael would definitely have some ideas on how to get where she needed to go—that man never took no for an answer.

Andy suddenly nudged her in the side, and she turned around, drink in hand, about to reprimand him when she saw the reason why. Danni took a long, slow sip of her drink as the reason came closer.

"Now yours wasn't a face I was expecting to see tonight."

She smiled, about to retort that, other than The Savoy, The Dorchester was the residence of almost every correspondent working the war, but she held her tongue. "*Major*," she said instead. "Nice to see you again."

Cameron came closer, his dark brown eyes shining. She hated that her gaze danced over his face, taking in his tanned skin, neatly trimmed beard, and recently cut hair. She might not like the man, but he was certainly easy on the eye.

"How did you enjoy reporting on the field hospital in Sicily after we parted ways?"

And just like that, she hated the man all over again.

"Oh, it was wonderful," she said sarcastically. "There's nothing quite like reporting on wounds and interviewing doctors and nurses."

His smile told her that he thought he had the upper hand, and she didn't like it one bit.

"I can only but imagine."

They stared at one another a moment, and she felt like there was no one else in the room. Just this one man, who was so utterly handsome and infuriating in equal parts.

"So tell me, Danni, are you heading anywhere else interesting for work?"

She smiled. "I'm working on it. You?"

He laughed, lifting his drink and sipping, although his eyes never left hers. "I think we both know where I'm going to be headed."

Yeah, like we both know where I'm not going to be headed. She didn't give him the satisfaction of taking the bait.

"I thought soldiers weren't allowed beards?" she said, taking a large gulp of her drink and maintaining eye contact, just like he'd done to her.

"It'll be gone soon," he said, absently stroking it. "I've had a longer leave than usual, and it's been nice having it back."

She hadn't thought about what he might have done before the war, but now her interest was piqued. Obviously he'd had a beard, and although she would never tell him, it did suit him.

"Come on, Cameron. Let's go!"

Another man slapped him on the shoulder and Cameron nodded as he quickly downed his drink.

The men he was with started to walk away, but Cameron surprised her by taking a step toward her.

"Danni, why don't you join us?" he asked. "We're going to an officers' club nearby."

She felt her eyebrows shoot up at the invitation. "You want *me* to come to an officers' club with you?"

He nodded, extending his arm. "What do you say?"

"I say," she said, taking a small step closer, "that I'd rather be where the action is than at some swanky officers' club. And maybe you should try having my back instead of getting me thrown off a job next time—if you'd like me to start joining you for drinks when you're off duty, that is."

If she'd wanted to get a reaction out of him, then she'd done exactly that. His face darkened as he stared down at her.

"Maybe you should try behaving more like a lady and wear a dress every once in a while," he said.

In response, Danni placed her drink down on the bar behind her and took out a cigarette, leaning over one of the soldiers to her left to get a light. When she turned back, drawing on the Lucky Strike, Cameron spun on his heel and marched away from her.

"You have a good night!" she called after him.

Her stomach flip-flopped; she was pleased with herself for taking him down a peg, but at the same time felt guilty for baiting him like that. But he'd deserved it, after the way he'd treated her in Sicily. She was hardly going to fall at his feet just because he set those twinkling eyes upon her—if she did that, half the men she encountered for her work would end up being her lovers.

"I don't know if it's wise to make an enemy out of him," Andy said into her ear. "He seems influential, especially with Patton."

She shrugged and batted Andy away, ready to order another drink. On some level, she knew that he was probably right, but she wasn't about to tell him that.

"So tell me, boys, what's news?" she asked, as someone pulled out a chair for her and she gratefully sank into it.

They talked about everything, from their few days of leave to what they thought might happen over the coming weeks, and just as she was ready to turn in for the night, there was a tap on her shoulder. She turned, not expecting to find the young correspondent Ella standing behind her, looking very nervous.

"Ella, isn't it?" Danni asked.

Ella smiled. "Yes. I wasn't sure if you'd remember me from the other night."

"It's not every night I get to read aloud a piece on lipstick and donuts," Danni said, laughing. "How *did* you get on with your editor?"

She turned away from the men and gave Ella her full attention. There was something she liked about her, even if the poor girl did look like a pretty little rabbit in a lion's den.

"I actually insisted that he send me to Normandy," Ella replied.

"And how did that go down?"

"Well, he told me I could go," Ella said with a grimace. "So long as I made my own way there."

"Of course he did."

Harry came toward them then, and Danni waited as all the men ordered another round of drinks, and then he waved over to her.

"Danni, let me make you my signature White Lady," Harry said. "I promise you'll like it."

She nodded. "Okay, okay, I'll try it," Danni said, gesturing to Ella beside her. "But make it two."

They stood for a moment, and Danni noticed Ella glance down the bar at Michael.

"Have you known him long?"

Ella's cheeks flushed a deep red. "Who? Michael?"

Danni laughed. "I don't see you blushing over any other man."

Ella looked mortified, and Danni almost felt bad for teasing her.

Harry leaned over with their drinks then, and she took them. "Thanks, they look amazing."

Danni took a sip, deciding straightaway that the clever bartender had been right. It was delicious. She gave him a quick thumbs-up, and he winked before turning his attention back to his cocktail shaker.

"Michael's different. He's . . . I don't know." Ella sighed. "I suppose I've never met anyone like him before."

"Well, all I can say is, don't go falling in love with him," Danni cautioned. "He's a great guy, but he's married to his job, and nothing will ever be more important to him than chasing the next story. He'd make a terrible husband."

"How do you know that?" Ella asked.

Danni sipped her drink. "Because he's like me. And I'd make a terrible wife."

"Who'd make a terrible what?" Andy asked, coming to stand beside her, arm slung over her shoulders as he stuck out his hand and introduced himself to Ella.

"The man heading this way," Danni said, exchanging an amused look with Andy as Ella nervously gulped down her cocktail.

"Ella, Danni," Michael said, kissing first Ella's cheek, then hers. Danni smiled and air-kissed him back. "Andy." He shook Andy's hand. "What's happening down this end of the bar?"

"I was just telling this lot what a terrible husband you'd be," Danni said. Poor Ella's cheeks were a deep beet-red now. "And of course what a terrible spouse I'd be, too."

Michael held up his drink. "Marriage would be my idea of a nightmare. I wouldn't last a week with a ball and chain."

Ella spluttered and coughed, holding up her drink as if it were to blame. Andy nudged Danni in the side, reprimanding her, but she just nudged him back and finished her drink, pleased to see that Ella had recovered and was now talking to Michael. She set her glass down.

"You're turning in for the night?" Andy asked.

Danni nodded. "I am. I'll see you in the morning."

"Need me to walk you to your room?"

She shook her head. "No, but thanks for the offer. Enjoy the rest of the night, and try not to worry about her too much, okay?"

He groaned as he kissed her cheek. "Easier said than done."

Danni said her goodbyes and left the others at the bar. There was only one place she wanted to be right now, and it involved her and her work—there was only so long she could be social before she was pulled back to her first love, *photography*. She went to her room and gathered her supplies, taking a bag and making her way to the bathroom. The staff had let her set up in there numerous times before, and she was lucky because there were significantly more journalists than photographers in residence.

Danni started to hum as she worked, fingers light as she turned the space into her very own darkroom. She had the chemicals she needed to make a bath in the sink, and within minutes she was taking the negatives out and preparing to wash them in the warm water.

This part of the process always calmed her: the magical element of seeing the images she'd captured brought to life on the wet paper. Something about it took her back to her childhood, too. Her father had loved her trailing around after him, hanging off his every word and watching the way he set up his shots—she'd learned so much from him when she was a girl. The little darkroom he'd created for her had been their thing, their personal bond that never changed no matter what age she was, because they'd both loved working side by side. Sometimes they hadn't talked, other times they talked the whole time, and they had spent many hours like that.

She stared into the tub of water as the black-and-white picture formed before her eyes. Danni had a string line set up above the bath, and she reached up to pin the image there, the wet paper needing time to dry before she could take it down and study her work. But she could see that the photographs were as good as she'd expected them to be.

Guilt washed through her as her thoughts turned to her dad again. It was always when she was alone in the dark that the lump in her throat grew bigger. Because photography had brought her and her father together, but it had also pulled them apart. They'd fought bitterly about her leaving home to travel abroad, her father vehemently opposed to women being so close to the war. He'd suffered through the Great War himself and still bore the scars, which was why he didn't want his daughter anywhere near the fighting.

When she'd left, at the very start of the war, Danni had left behind not only her family, but her boyfriend too. She had fond memories of Alex, but domestic life had never been her calling, and he wasn't brave enough or bold enough to accept a wife who wasn't prepared to be a traditional homemaker.

Over the years, her mother had forgiven her and now took great pride in collecting her published photographs and collaging them, and her father had come to terms with what she was doing, too. Although they'd been determined to stop her leaving in the beginning, they'd softened dramatically over the years as they followed her success from afar. And their disapproval had only made her stronger, more determined, with a fire inside her that wanted to expose the truth of war. To show the world not only the horrors, but the kind moments and the courageousness of human nature, too.

Danni lifted another photo and squinted through the dark, her eyes well-adjusted to the dimness of her surroundings. When she looked at some of her work, it sometimes took her by surprise. The rawness of what she captured often looked different through the lens of her camera, and although she was able to focus on work when she was out, being alone and seeing the photos come to life in front of her was confronting.

When she was traveling, as she had been in Sicily, it was more common for her to send her rolls of film back to London for them to be developed and chosen without her, but she ached to be following through the entire process herself. It was cathartic to her, and it also let her see what an impact she could make.

Today her photos captured London: defeated yet optimistic, broken but not damaged beyond repair. The gaping holes, rubble, and crumbling stone were horrific, and they painted a picture that required no words, but to her they also spoke of resilience.

Danni finished bathing the negatives and stared up at her work. *Resilience.*

It was what she needed, to make her way to Normandy. *Resilience.*

She smiled as someone banged on the door, clearly wanting to use the bathroom. She suddenly had an idea. Andy wasn't going to like it, but all of a sudden she knew how to get on a ship to Normandy after all.

CHAPTER TEN

BAYEUX, FRANCE
CHLOE

Chloe put the last plate on the draining board and looked down at her hands, horrified at the red, worn-looking skin.

My, how the mighty have fallen. She squeezed her eyes shut and leaned against the bench, refusing to cry. Her mother had died years earlier, when she was still a teenager, but that's what she would have said if she were there now, seeing how her beautiful model daughter had been reduced to a maid.

A noise in the hall alerted her to the men arriving back, and she wiped her hands on the towel and dabbed at her eyes. If they were back, they would expect to be fed, which meant the kitchen was about to fill with tired, dirty men who she was expected to prepare food for.

This was not how she'd expected her first visit to Gabriel's family estate outside of Bayeux to be. She'd pictured a rambling chateau filled with exquisite furniture, with manicured lawns and perfect hedges. She'd imagined maids tending to *her* needs as she lounged about with Gabriel, drinking wine and nibbling on cheese.

Instead, she was the one doing all the housework and cooking in an enormous chateau full of dust, with most of the furniture still hidden beneath protective sheets. And the lawns were a mess—long and unkempt, like everything else about the place. It matched her mood, the way she felt so out of control, her mind a tangled web of worries and thoughts. Not to mention the nightmares that kept her awake almost every night; of the woman who'd come to warn them, the woman she'd immediately been so jealous of when she'd seen her at the door. She'd never seen a dead body before, let alone seen anyone killed so violently or been near gunfire, and she knew she'd never, ever forget her.

"Chloe?"

She forced a smile and turned, seeing Gabriel standing in the doorway. His face was smudged with black, his blue eyes bright against the dirt, and she wished she could take his clothes off and wash them for him. Only, they were long out of soap for the laundry.

"Is everything alright?" he asked.

"I've done my best, Gabriel, but I can't do it all," she said, her voice wobbling. "I can't cook with the best of ingredients, let alone what I have here, and I . . ." Her voice trailed off. She should have greeted him with a warm cup of something, and instead she'd blurted out all her worries.

"Chloe, you're doing fine," he said, coming toward her and reaching out his hands. "I appreciate it all, I promise you I do."

She doubted that very much, but she did appreciate his kindness. He hesitated, looking down at her, but she took the opportunity to step into him, closing her eyes when his arms looped around her. The lust between them had never reignited as she'd imagined it would, and she'd come to terms with the fact that it was never going to be like it had been the last time they'd been together, at least while the war was raging on. But she still craved his touch, yearned for the moments that he held her, when he came to her in the night, when she felt for a small moment as if he wanted her as much as she so desperately wanted him.

"Gabriel, how long are we going to have to stay here?" she asked him.

He sighed, but she didn't let him pull away, keeping her arms tightly around him. She didn't care that he no longer smelled of expensive cologne, or that his clothes were peasant-rough instead of the most expensive cottons and cashmere, she just wanted to be close to him.

"Chloe, I just don't know," he said. She could hear the honesty in his tone, and she could also feel the way he shifted away from her when he heard the other men coming. He cleared his throat and she saw his eyes harden, commanding as he spoke now instead of soft as he'd been with her. And when Gabriel spoke, everyone in the house stood to attention. His deep voice, the powerful way he gave them instructions, was like an alpha version of the editor she'd once fallen for.

"Take something to eat and then we'll go out to rifle-train," he announced. "We need to keep up our skills, make sure we're prepared for anything."

Chloe gulped. She'd gone from being entirely naïve about the war to having a very hard, very fast education in what it was like to live in occupied territory. They'd traveled for days on foot to get to the chateau from Paris, and instead of hiding away—just the two of them—they'd ended up in the thick of the Resistance network.

She still didn't understand how it all worked, and Gabriel kept most of it from her, but she'd started to piece together as much as she could. And the reality was terrifying. Every day she half expected gunfire to erupt, to see Nazis running toward the house and hiding in the long grass, shooting at anything, or *anyone*, who moved. And the more Gabriel tried to placate her, the more anxious she became.

"Gabriel?" she said, as the men dispersed.

He looked at her, his jaw set in a tight line, as if he were lost in thought.

"Gabriel, I overheard some of the men talking this morning, about the Allies landing on the coast. Is it true?" She wrung her hands, nervous as she waited for him to reply, hoping that he trusted her enough to tell her the truth.

"The intelligence appears solid, but we won't know until it happens."

"And am I allowed to know what you're planning? Am I . . ." She paused, forcing the words out. "Am I allowed to help?" She was terrified of being close to his Resistance work, especially when she didn't truly understand what he was doing, but she was going crazy with worry, and she wanted to be useful. And perhaps if she offered to do something, she'd get to spend more time with him, and he might even stop looking at her as if he felt sorry for her.

"The Resistance is all about creating chaos for the Nazis," Gabriel said quietly. "I didn't want you having any part of this, but Chloe, what we're doing, it's crucial to disrupting Hitler's plans in France."

She nodded, her hands trembling as she reached for him. "I understand. I just wanted to know if there's any chance that the Allies are actually coming."

Gabriel led her by the hand, away from the kitchen and closer to the back door. When he spoke, his voice was soft and low.

"We have eyes on the Germans, and every indication is that they don't see this part of the coast as a threat. Hitler believes the attack will come from the Pas-de-Calais region, less than a hundred kilometers northeast of Normandy, but all the information he's received has been part of an elaborate ruse."

"So you need to distract them from seeing it coming," Chloe said, finding her voice. "You need to do your part in making sure they don't know the Allies are heading for Normandy? Is that it?" Could it be that the end of the war was closer, *much closer*, than she'd realized?

He didn't reply, and she opened her mouth to say something else, then shut it again.

"What is it?" he asked, his smile making her blush. For a brief moment, it was as if it were just the two of them in the house.

She took a deep breath. "Gabriel, I want to learn how to shoot a rifle," she said. "I'm scared of being here alone and not being able to defend myself."

Gabriel's eyes widened. "*You* want to learn to shoot a gun?" he asked.

Chloe squared her shoulders, jutting her chin a little higher, trying to pretend she was on a photo shoot, mustering her old confidence. "Yes. I do."

He strode past her and returned with a rifle, throwing it the short distance between them. She surprised herself when, without fumbling, her fingers closed around it, catching it in one swift move.

"Come on, then," he said. "Let's see what you're made of."

Chloe walked beside him, a little thrill rising inside her at getting to spend a moment in time with Gabriel, just the two of them. She would have volunteered to shoot sooner if she'd known it was the way to his affections.

"Hold it like this," Gabriel said when they were standing outside, well away from the house. "You need to have the butt of your rifle tucked in just here, and your front hand needs to support it." He stood so close, warm against her as he guided her arms and nestled the gun into her body.

"Like this?" she asked.

"Just like that," he said quietly. "Now, I want you to look down the sights and line them up with the target. Take a deep breath to exhale, and then relax and gently squeeze the trigger."

Chloe did as he said, letting all the air out of her lungs before squeezing.

Bang.

She leaped back, the pain from the way it kicked into her so intense, she thought she'd managed to shoot herself.

"Did I hit it?" she gasped.

Gabriel was chuckling to himself as he took the gun from her, and when she looked at where he was pointing, heat flooded her cheeks.

"Well, you hit something," he said.

The tree to the left of the target had an apple-sized hole blown into it, and as the men started to file out of the house, she realized she was the source of their laughter.

"Again," she said, staring defiantly at Gabriel.

The soft hollow on the inside of her shoulder was throbbing, and even her cheek hurt from the way she'd been holding the gun. If she'd had a mirror handy she'd have checked to see if she still had all her teeth on that side of her mouth. But she was tired of being useless and afraid. She'd never wanted to learn anything as badly as she wanted to be able to shoot a gun and defend herself.

"You're sure?" he asked, looking amused.

"I'm sure," she replied, standing up tall.

"Well, alright then," he murmured. "But we don't have a huge amount of ammunition, so just one more shot."

Gabriel loaded another bullet for her, and Chloe wished desperately to impress him—with her determination at least, if not her skill. She gripped the rifle tightly when he passed it to her, forgetting about the pain in her shoulder as she carefully followed his instructions.

Boom.

Chloe grinned as she saw she'd hit the target.

"Maybe she is a natural, after all?" Gabriel teased, ruffling her hair as he took the rifle from her.

Chloe lapped up his praise, prepared to shoot targets every day if it brought her closer to Gabriel.

Tomorrow, she thought. *Today I'm going to try to enjoy my day, and tomorrow I'll tell him about the baby.* It was why she'd wanted to learn how to shoot in the first place, because the only thing worse than being defenseless was being defenseless and pregnant.

CHAPTER ELEVEN

ELLA

Ella stared at her reflection in the mirror, taking in her long, golden-blonde hair. She swallowed, reaching for the scissors. It was her means of getting to where she needed to go, but as she picked up the scissors and stared at her long tresses, falling to below her breasts, she knew she'd be heartbroken when she looked at herself after the fact.

It will grow, she told herself, even as she hesitated, the blades against her hair, cringing and trying to decide whether to cut the bulk off first and then hack away at the rest, or . . .

"Don't do it."

Ella jumped, the scissors falling with a clatter into the basin. In the bathroom mirror, she saw Danni leaning against the doorjamb and shaking her head.

Ella picked up the scissors again and slowly turned. "I . . . I didn't realize anyone else . . ." Her voice trailed off. "I thought I had a few moments to myself in here, that's all."

Danni must have been there visiting someone at The Savoy— Ella hadn't seen her since the drink they'd shared a few nights earlier.

"Don't cut it," Danni said simply. "Be proud of being a woman. You need to think of a different way to get there instead of doing that."

Ella had to stop her jaw from falling open. "How did you know that's why I was doing it?"

"How did I know that you were chopping your hair off to make yourself look like a boy?" Danni laughed. "Honey, this hotel is made up of more correspondents than anyone else, and all of us women are trying to figure out a way to make it across the Channel. Of *course* that's why you're doing it."

Ella swallowed. Hard. Danni sure had her all figured out. "It's the best idea I've come up with so far."

Danni shrugged and came over to wash her hands. "They're bastards trying to stop us, but you . . ." she said, her eyes meeting Ella's in the mirror. "You're way too pretty to ever be mistaken for a boy. And that hair is too pretty to hack off, especially if you don't get away with it. And trust me, you won't."

Ella watched as Danni dried her hands. She still remembered seeing an image of Danni in *Vogue* early on in the war, a profile depicting the photographer who'd defied orders and become one of the most respected in her profession, and she'd been in awe of her ever since. Which is why Ella was surprised that she was acting as if there were no possible chance of them getting to Normandy.

"Have you figured out a way?" Ella asked, surprising even herself with her bold question. "To get there, I mean."

"Maybe," Danni said with a conspiratorial smile. "I guess you'll have to wait and see, but it certainly doesn't involve me attempting to change gender."

Ella leaned back against the sink, her fingers searching out the cool porcelain as she examined the woman who was technically her rival, even though she felt as if they were working in completely different leagues. Danni was legendary as the most successful female correspondent in Europe, and as nice as she'd been to her, Ella was acutely aware that they were competing.

"Come downstairs," Danni said. "It might be the last night all of us correspondents are together. The adrenalin here is contagious, if nothing else."

Danni disappeared as quickly as she'd appeared, and Ella was left staring at the door, wondering if Danni was right. She glanced at the scissors again and, after a final look at her hair, she tucked them into her purse, staring into her own eyes for a moment before hurrying from the bathroom to follow Danni. Maybe she wouldn't cut her hair, maybe it was worth keeping it so she could look like herself when she got to Normandy. But Danni was wrong about Ella needing to go downstairs to get caught up in the excitement—she'd already caught the bug, she already knew she had to get there—it was why Danni had found her standing in the tiny bathroom ready to cut her tresses off in the first place.

She made her way down to the bar, looking through the haze of smoke as she tried to locate Danni.

"Ah, there she is."

Ella saw Michael from the corner of her eye, but she waited a moment before turning, relieved that she didn't blush this time.

"I'm pleased you could join us on this final night."

She shrugged. "We'll be seeing each other again," she said, feigning confidence. "It just so happens that I'm going to be covering the war itself, after all."

Michael looked impressed, and she smiled when he ordered her a drink. What she wasn't prepared for was when he caught her wrist, drawing her toward him, his face suddenly so close that she was staring into his eyes.

"That's the girl I've been waiting for," he whispered, his voice as smooth as honey as he dipped his head even closer.

Ella wanted to say something witty in response, but could barely even breathe as his fingers cupped her cheek and his words touched her ear.

"Can I kiss you?"

She nodded as Michael's warm lips brushed tenderly against hers, his mouth moving slowly as he deepened their kiss.

"You know, Danni was right the other night," he murmured. "I'd be a terrible husband. I can barely commit to a brand of cigarettes, let alone a woman. But I do like a good kiss."

Ella stifled a giggle as he turned to get their drinks. He was incorrigible, but it only seemed to make her like him all the more.

"I suppose it's lucky I'm not looking for a husband then," she replied.

Michael passed her a drink and then lifted his own. "Cheers to that," he said, laughing as he tucked her against him; she fit like a glove. Looking up, she met Danni's gaze across the smoky bar. The other woman raised her glass and Ella grinned back at her.

Thank God she'd listened to Danni and kept her hair—without it she might have missed out on the best kiss of her life.

———— ⚜ ————

Ella lurked in the shadows the following night, watching, waiting. The boat glistened in the moonlight, bright white against the more dull, muted greys or camouflaged tones of the other ships waiting in the port. People moved in an almost constant stream, back and forth, taking provisions and loading supplies, the docks heaving with activity.

Which means that now is my chance. Ella knew that if she waited, she might never make it on board the snow-white hospital ship with the green line running along the side and blood-red, freshly painted crosses adorning the hull and deck. She breathed deeply, checking her hair was still tucked neatly beneath her nurse's hat, and stepped out, walking quickly toward the orderlies taking supplies on. She was dressed in the starched white uniform of a nurse, her own clothes hidden in the bag over her shoulder, with her typewriter and supplies in a separate bag that she was lugging in her other hand.

Ella slowed until most of the orderlies had disappeared on to the ship with their next load, and then she walked quickly, her feet taking her down the dock and up the gangway on to the ship. She'd spent hours watching the ships, trying to work out the most logical, fail-safe plan to get on board one of them, wondering if her initial suspicions had been correct; she'd decided they had. Only, instead of trying to disguise herself as a male orderly, she'd managed to track down a nurse's uniform instead. She might not be a nurse, but she was a woman, and she knew there was little chance of any man questioning whether a nurse should be boarding a hospital ship headed out into the Channel.

Now all she had to do was get on to the ship and find somewhere to hide, which she knew might be the hardest part of all. There were only a handful of women on board from what she'd seen, and that meant they'd notice in a heartbeat that she wasn't supposed to be there.

Ella's foot landed on the deck and she glanced around at the provisions stacked everywhere. There were enormous cans marked "Whole Blood," as well as endless amounts of plasma blood and bandages. It was enough to make her stomach churn, thinking of all the men who'd urgently need blood, their bodies ripped apart by the savagery of war.

She kept walking, trying not to move too fast or appear too anxious as she carried her bags along the deck, her eyes darting from side to side, frantically searching for somewhere to hide. And then she saw where the lifeboats were stored. Her heart started to beat fast as she hurried toward them, knowing that in only another thirty seconds or so she could collapse and bunk down until nightfall. There was no way she'd be discovered once she was hidden away, because who would go looking for a lifeboat before they were even sailing out of the harbor?

Ella looked carefully over her shoulder to see if anyone was watching her, then she dropped low and crawled as far back as she could into her hiding place, before leaning against one of the rafts, her head lolling back as she started to laugh. She was positioned between two rafts, perfectly hidden from sight.

I've done it! The thought sent thrills of excitement through her, followed by the desperate feeling that she was going to vomit. She might not be on the official ship with all the male correspondents, which she knew would set sail first thing in the morning, but she was going to see the war firsthand after all, and the thought was terrifying.

She'd come to Europe to be the eyes reporting back to America, and that was exactly what she was going to do. So long as she stayed alive long enough to file her stories, her work would be published for anyone back home to read, which meant that everyone would know exactly how capable a female correspondent could be during wartime. And right in the middle of combat, no less.

Ella squeezed her eyes shut, listening to the lapping waters surrounding the ship as wave after wave of panic suddenly started to thrum through her, replacing her earlier confidence.

What have I done? She'd been so desperate to prove herself to Danni and Michael and all the other correspondents, and now she was a stowaway at risk of arrest? She balled her hands into fists and wound her arms around her knees as she started to rock back and forth.

For hours, she'd been so focused on her plan, on what she had to do in order to get on the ship, and now she was here, reality was setting in. What if she were arrested and sent home? What if their ship was hit and she died at sea, and no one even knew what had happened to her?

Her breath was ragged now and she wriggled forward so she could stare up at the sky, trying to imagine what sort of scene she would see come morning. That was if she didn't lose her nerve and leap off the side of the damn ship and swim for shore before then.

She turned her thoughts to Michael, remembering what he'd told her.

"If you manage the impossible and ever do get to Normandy, or to any other conflict zone, don't be nervous."

"That's easy for you to say!" she scoffed.

"Just think of me," he said with a shrug. *"Just think that you're writing me a letter and telling me what you're seeing. Think of it as a conversation, remove yourself from the reality of it all, and just record it as if you're writing to me."*

She sighed, wishing they'd had more time together, that she could have lapped up a little more of his knowledge—and indulged in a few more kisses—before they'd parted ways. She might never see Michael again, but he'd been nothing short of a pleasant distraction, that was for sure.

CHAPTER TWELVE

DANNI

"Just follow my lead," Danni said, walking slightly ahead of Andy, fingers clutching the camera that hung around her neck. "It's going to work."

"I'm glad you're so confident," Andy muttered, but she noticed that he didn't break his stride, not leaving her side.

"Good evening," Danni said, flashing a quick smile at the official standing on the dock. "We're here to interview the nurses on board the hospital ship that's departing in the morning."

The soldier looked her up and down and then glanced at Andy. It irritated her that he instantly bypassed her and chose to address her partner instead.

"You have your accreditation with you?" the man asked.

"Of course," Danni said confidently, but he took Andy's first, anyway.

"You're not going with the other correspondents?" he asked Andy.

Andy shook his head. "No, my publisher already has a correspondent traveling with the official convoy, so I'm stationed in London for the coming weeks."

The soldier took Danni's small green card then, before studying her face.

"How long are you going to be?" he asked.

"We won't be long, we're just here to interview the half dozen nurses on board and then we'll be off," Danni said. "General Eisenhower himself wants reports on how these women are faring ahead of their voyage," she said in a low voice. "We'd hate to disappoint him."

She waited for Andy to kick her, knowing that he'd be rolling his eyes over her gross exaggeration, but the soldier seemed to stand taller, straighter, as if he were suddenly part of something bigger. In truth, she'd tried to get a meeting with Eisenhower at The Dorchester after writing him an impassioned letter about women traveling with troops, but he'd had no interest in meeting her. She supposed he had a lot on his plate, but still.

"You'll be gone within the hour?" the soldier asked, directing his question at Andy.

"The last thing we want is to get in your way," Andy said smoothly. "We'll be walking back down the docks in an hour, I promise."

He gave them both their passes back and stepped aside. Danni kept her head down, walking quickly, heart pounding; she was used to operating on adrenalin and little else, but this felt different.

"If we get caught . . ." Andy muttered, keeping pace with her and not even bothering to finish his sentence.

"We won't," she said, sounding far more sure than she felt. "Now, let's have a quick look around, and then find somewhere to stow away for the night." She had to sound confident—Andy was convinced he might find his sister if the invasion was a success, and if they didn't make it across the Channel . . . She pushed the thought from her mind, not about to start doubting herself now.

"The things you get me to agree to, Danni," he whispered sharply. "I still can't believe we're doing this."

She didn't reply because he was right, she *did* repeatedly ask a lot of him, but he couldn't deny that it led to great stories for them both, stories that continued to define their careers. Not to mention he could have easily sailed to Normandy without her. But if they pulled this off without being found and arrested, she'd make history.

Danni pushed her thoughts away and looked around the ship as they moved through, surprised at how enormous she was. Despite the orderlies moving back and forth, and the stacks of supplies on board, it felt empty—ghostly almost. It was scrubbed clean, the deck gleaming and the red crosses freshly painted. Even the deck rail was shining as if it had been recently polished. As they explored, she saw hundreds of beds, bare except for the new blankets folded at each end. The supplies were incredible, and so obviously telling of what was to come—how many bandages and how much blood was going to be needed—the stuff of nightmares.

She positioned herself and took a shot, flashbulb going off as she captured the lines of beds.

"Come on, we need to find somewhere to hide," Andy said, tugging her along beside him. "Any longer and someone is going to come asking questions."

She followed because she knew he was right, and soon he'd led her away from the beds and out to the side of the deck. Voices were coming closer and she tucked her camera tight against her body, bags bouncing at her sides, as Andy pointed.

"In there."

If Danni hadn't known him so well, she would have balked at his suggestion, but she followed him without hesitation into the small restroom. When they were both inside, he shut the door behind them, and they collapsed against opposite walls.

"Hey, at least it's clean," she joked, glancing around at their surroundings. "It's like they've scrubbed this ship within an inch of her life in preparation for what's to come."

"They sure have," Andy replied, rubbing his temples with the heels of his hands.

"You're regretting this, aren't you?" she said softly. "I'm so sorry if I somehow pushed you into this. I wouldn't have blamed you for leaving me."

"Just get the whiskey out, would you?" he said. "There's something about risking my neck and imagining being arrested, not to mention ending my career, that's playing with my head, that's all."

Danni snorted. "They have to find us to arrest us, and that's *not* going to happen. We're better than that." But despite her words, her stomach churned—risking her own job was one thing, but she'd never forgive herself if Andy lost his.

Now it was Andy snorting. "Let's just hope you're right. Now give me that drink."

Danni pulled out the bottle of liquor she'd promised him and took a long, deep swig before passing it over.

"Tell me this wasn't the craziest damn idea you've ever come up with," Andy said as he took a sip, and then another and another.

"It *is* the craziest thing we've ever done together," she said, standing and locking the door just in case anyone did come searching for them. "But it'll be worth it. I promise."

Andy laughed. "If only I believed you."

She grinned back at him. "If only."

Despite her excitement at what they were doing, there was a price that came with defying orders. Logically she knew that Andy should be fine, so long as he didn't try to be a martyr if they were caught—she was planning on taking the full weight of the blame. But her? Well, if she were caught before they made it, then her career was most definitely over. She'd be arrested and stripped of all her accreditations and she'd never report on the war again. But if she wasn't caught and she was the only woman to reach France and see the conflict firsthand? If her photographs were published around the world before anyone else's? Then it would all be worth it, even if everything did fall apart afterward.

"You're one brave woman, Danni," Andy said, holding out the bottle to her. "I'll give you that."

She took it and gave him a wink, as they both laughed. "I'll take that as a compliment."

"You damn well should."

The boat swayed slightly then and Danni held her breath, fingers crawling out to touch her camera. Once they were in motion and the ship was heading into open water, they could stop worrying, but until then, anything could happen.

"How are you feeling about your sister?" she asked, to keep her mind from her growing sense of nausea.

Andy gave her a long, steady look. "Would you think I was crazy if I said I wanted to go looking for her myself?"

She shook her head. "No, I wouldn't. In fact, I'd say that I'll be coming with you." Andy had tears in his eyes, and she reached for his hand, squeezing it before letting go. "We're in this together, okay? I know you'd do the same for me, so we do our jobs, get our work done, and then we find a way to get her, by hook or by crook, okay?"

He carefully passed her something from his pocket and she took it, not sure what it was.

"Danni, I need you to take this for me," he said.

She passed him the bottle and went to open it, but his fingers closed over her hand to stop her.

"It's for Chloe," he told her. "If something happens to me, if I can't find her and you—"

"No," she said quickly, trying to pass it back to him. "Give it to her yourself." But Andy's grip on her hand was firm.

"Take it," he repeated. "Just in case. *Please.*"

She relented and nodded. "Fine. I'll take it just to keep you happy. But *nothing*, I repeat *nothing*, is going to stop you from finding her yourself."

"Danni, you and I both know what we're heading into," Andy said. "Neither of us ever knows whether we're going to be coming back from the work we do. I just need to know that if I'm gone, you'll find her."

She didn't reply, because he was right about not knowing.

"There's a photograph of her folded in there, too," he said. "Just in case."

"Just in case," she repeated, carefully securing it in her inside jacket pocket and wishing they hadn't just had what felt like a very morbid conversation.

Andy was silent then, and she cleared her throat.

"So just to be clear, we get to Normandy, we cover the battle, and if we assume that the Allies advance and start to liberate France, then we can make it our mission to find her." She'd been studying maps ever since Andy had told her what had happened to his sister, and she was confident they could make it to the town she could be staying in. It was perhaps a day's walk from the beach where they'd be landing, depending on the conditions, to get to Caen, and if their soldiers were successful, then it was highly likely they could make it to the region and try to find someone who knew of her.

"You always make everything seem possible," Andy muttered.

She took a swig from the bottle. "That's because I'm not used to taking no for an answer."

Hours later, Danni held her stomach, wishing she hadn't consumed quite so much whiskey. It was suddenly like acid in her stomach, gnawing away and making her desperate for solid food rather than the liquid sloshing in her empty belly that had left her feeling queasy as the ship set sail.

"I need to stretch my legs," she told Andy. "Want to come?"

He groaned and she could tell he too was regretting their impromptu drinking session. Not to mention the fact his skin was starting to look green from seasickness.

"I don't suppose anyone can arrest us now that we're on our way," he muttered, standing and then holding out a hand to haul her up, too.

She took it gratefully and then leaned forward to unlock the door, glancing up at him as she slid the lock back, almost expecting someone to be waiting on the other side, triumphantly ready to arrest them. But as she opened the door a sliver and looked out, all she saw was a moonlit sky washing light over the deck. It was an impressive moonlight too—a full, high moon that sat like a big, round white ball in the sky.

"The coast is clear," she said, stepping out and looking around.

It was almost eerily silent, the water lapping at the sides of the big boat the only sound to break the otherwise perfectly quiet night air. Danni wasn't well briefed on how many people were even on board, other than knowing there were only six nurses, which seemed ridiculous for a hospital ship with so many beds to fill. But right now, all was quiet, as if no one was there at all.

She heard Andy move behind her and they stood together, looking around in awe. The boat was such a brilliant, shimmering white that it seemed to shine right through the darkness, and she wondered at how intelligent it was for the ship to be so obvious. International law was supposed to prohibit it from being targeted, of course, but having seen the war with her own eyes for so long now, she knew that didn't afford them true safety from the enemy. They could easily blow them from the water without a second thought.

A shuffling noise made her turn, and she locked eyes with Andy. "Did you hear that?" she whispered.

He nodded, and moved to stand closer to her as they both turned. Something akin to fear sluiced through her; she wasn't used to being afraid, but she was out of her depth on a ship she shouldn't even be a passenger on.

"I heard it again, I think it was over there," Andy said, his voice a low murmur. "Want to go look or just head back and barricade ourselves in until morning?"

Danni was too curious about anything and everything to hide away. Nerves pulsed through her but she held her head high, refusing to give in to the feeling. "Who's there?" she called, sounding braver than she felt. "Show yourself."

Her voice seemed to boom through the darkness into the murky shadowland of the smaller vessels that were piled together.

They were greeted with silence, but just as Danni was about to call out again, something moved. Andy stood in front of her protectively, and she moved right beside him, not about to have him in the line of fire to save her.

"Who's there?" Danni demanded again, impatient now and hoping they weren't about to lose their lives to a German stowed away, ready to gun them down.

And then, just like that, a woman stepped out, her wheat-blonde hair falling over her shoulders as she stumbled out of the life rafts. She held up her hands, as if she thought *they* were going to shoot.

Danni stifled a laugh. "I see you decided not to cut your hair off."

Ella reached up to touch her locks. "I suppose I have you to thank for that."

"It seems you're not the only reckless female correspondent, Danni," Andy said, laughing as he looked between them.

"Do you have any idea what you're in for, Ella?" Danni asked, immediately irritated that Ella was on board. She wanted to be the first *and only* woman to report on the invasion. "What you're going to see, nothing can prepare you for it."

"I . . . I . . ." Ella swallowed, and Danni fought the urge to roll her eyes. The poor girl looked like she was going to cry. What the hell was she going to do when she actually saw men dying around her?

"I hope you've thought this through," Danni muttered. "And what you've risked to come here. And don't think I'm going to be your babysitter, because I'm not." She might have encouraged Ella to find a way to get what she wanted, but she certainly hadn't expected any other woman to *actually* figure out a way to see the invasion firsthand.

"I know what I'm risking, and I have thought this through, I just didn't expect to feel so uncertain once my plan worked," Ella said. "And I suppose I'm hoping that by the time I file my story and get caught, the rules might have changed. Surely they'll see that we deserve our place reporting from the front line just like men do?"

"Wishful thinking," Danni muttered. "I've been playing this game a long time, pushing and bending every rule I can, but nothing ever changes when it comes to old men making decisions that involve women. Not even Eleanor Roosevelt has been able to help us, despite being incredibly supportive of women and all the roles we've filled."

Ella was silent for a bit, and Danni studied her in the moonlight. She couldn't believe she'd had the confidence to stow away. The girl had a nerve, she'd give her that.

"Did Michael know you were going to do this?" Danni asked.

"Michael?" Ella laughed, nervously. "If I'm honest, I think I did this to prove myself to him as much as to myself. I hated that he made light of the work I was doing."

Danni realized she hadn't included Andy in the conversation and stood back, waving him closer. "What do you think? Should we turn her in or let her travel with us?"

Andy stared at Danni, deadpan. "Us turn *her* in? Are you joking? We'd all be arrested if we did that."

Danni swallowed, waiting to see her panic, but she appeared calm—outwardly anyway. She was probably only a few years older than Ella, but looking at her, she felt a decade older. The other woman had an air of innocence about her, and Danni had the distinct feeling that she wasn't going to have the stomach for what they were about to witness.

"Ella, I want you to really think about this before you go ashore," Danni said, lowering her voice. "What you're going to see, it's going to haunt you for the rest of your life. If I were you, I'd stay on board."

"There are millions of people back home who need me to see this for them," Ella said firmly. "It sounds to me like you just don't want me there."

"That's not what I said," Danni said, ignoring her last comment. "You're going to see men in pieces, washing other men's blood from their eyes as a massacre roars around them. The noise will be deafening, and every step you take will change the way you see the world forever."

Ella didn't buckle, and Danni recognized the steely glint in her eyes—it was the same one she had. "The only way to change things is to show the truth to the world. Nothing you say is going to make me change my mind, and I actually have a much stronger stomach than you imagine."

Danni placed a hand on Ella's shoulder and smiled, deciding that she liked the plucky blonde more than she'd realized, even if she wasn't planning on letting her tag along with them. "Well, okay then," she said. "Why don't we try to make ourselves comfortable and get some shut-eye while we can? Tomorrow's going to be one hell of a day."

Ella gave Andy a cautious glance, and Danni gestured toward him.

"He's one of the few good guys, Ella. There's nothing to worry about where he's concerned."

Ella nodded, disappearing for a moment to gather her things, and Danni spoke quietly to Andy while she was gone.

"What do you say we ask her to work alongside us? We may as well all stick together," Andy suggested.

Danni snorted. "Andy, are you going soft on me? Since when do you welcome another correspondent joining us? What happened to us being the first to get this story?"

He shrugged. "She's pretty brave even getting on this boat, and if we don't let her tag along, I'd feel like we were throwing her to the wolves."

"Wolves or not, she's not coming with us."

"Come on, Danni. I think the girl deserves a break. I don't see any other women brave enough to do the same."

Danni held up her hands, anger rising. "No one looked out for me when I was starting out, and if they had, I wouldn't be the correspondent I am today."

"I looked out for you," Andy said quietly.

Danni glared at him. "That was different."

"I don't need a babysitter," Ella said, her voice stronger than before as she appeared behind them. "If that's what you're worried about."

"Good, because I've got no intention of being one," Danni retorted.

Andy stepped in front of her. "If you can keep up with us, you can join us," he said.

Danni groaned. How dare Andy do that to her! "If you're with us, you look after yourself. You fall behind, we leave you. You can't handle it, we leave you. We clear on that?" she said.

"Crystal clear," Ella said.

They all stood staring at one another for a moment, before Danni gestured to the bathroom, ready to retrieve her bottle of whiskey. The effects seemed to have disappeared already, now that she'd had some fresh sea air.

"If I didn't know you so well," Andy whispered into her ear as they walked, "I'd say you're scared of the competition."

She punched him in the arm. "I've never been scared of competition and you know it."

Andy punched her back. "I say we have a drink to celebrate then call it a night," he said. "What do you say, Ella?"

"Sure thing," Ella replied.

They settled down on the deck, their packs the only thing to rest against as they stared up at the star-filled blanket above them and waited for morning to come.

The next day, time suddenly moved so slowly that Danni felt as if she were watching from above somehow instead of seeing it all in real time. She'd forgotten all about her annoyance at Ella tagging along with them—the reality of what they were witnessing had promptly put an end to that. A sleek grey ship slid past them in the mine-swept Channel, seeming camouflaged against the ocean, and Danni lifted her camera and captured the soldiers standing silently on her deck. The captain of their own ship was on the bridge, and she took a photograph as he saluted them, standing like a statue watching as they somberly passed by. No one seemed to see Danni, or if they did, no one cared, because from the moment the sky had started to lighten, as pink swirls signaled the start of a new day, she'd been pacing the deck like a caged animal readying for escape. But as she turned from the khaki uniforms of the soldiers, their faces taut with worry and fear, the sounds of war suddenly permeated the air.

"They're mines detonating," Andy murmured.

She slowly turned and looked first at Andy and then at Ella, who had gone as white as a sheet. But Danni could see that it wasn't the noise but the soldiers passing that had disturbed her new companion, as her eyes tracked the men.

They all moved closer to the railings then, silent as they watched the invasion beginning.

I'm witnessing history here, Danni thought, lowering her camera to simply *see* it all. There were some things that wouldn't translate easily to film, but she knew that this scene would be imprinted on her mind for the rest of her life.

Barrage balloons floated in the air, reminding her of a child's birthday party, only they were so far from being celebratory that she scolded herself for even making the comparison. Because, as she leaned out and looked, taking it all in, the violence of what she was witnessing consumed her. And she couldn't stop thinking that she was on a boat that had no way to defend itself or those aboard it—the hospital ship didn't even have a single rifle on board.

First, she saw the cliffs of Normandy, rising through the mist as if welcoming them, and then, as they neared, thousands of destroyers, battleships, and attack vessels stormed through the water, filling every possible inch of sea. There was no doubt in her mind that the Channel leading to Normandy would have seemed enormous had it not been filled with so many vessels, making the wide expanse of water seem more like a pond brimming with toy boats.

It was mind-boggling, the scene unfolding before her, unlike anything she could have imagined, despite all the horrors she'd seen, all the pain and suffering she'd witnessed.

Suddenly the sky came violently to life, raining bombs in the same way clouds could turn dark and suddenly unleash hail or fierce rain. But this wasn't the might of God or whoever controlled the weather; this intense deluge of bombs was coming from stealthy grey planes that hid in the cover of clouds before discharging their terror. Danni tipped her head back and stared up at the sky, watching the mighty planes soar above them, as the noise of war—the roar of the bombers, and the screams and yells of the men—grew louder, threatening to pierce her eardrums.

A hand touched hers and she looked down to see Ella's palm fitted tight against hers. Squeezing her eyes shut for a moment, she reached for Andy's hand on her other side and said a silent prayer, even though she no longer knew if she even believed in God after what she'd witnessed. She might not want a rookie tagging along, but in that moment, it was kind of nice to have the camaraderie.

And she had the most terrifying feeling that the worst had only just begun.

PART TWO

NORMANDY

CHAPTER THIRTEEN

DANNI

To say that Omaha Beach represented the most disturbing, heart-wrenching display of man-made chaos she could ever have imagined would have been an understatement. Danni felt like her heart was lodged in her throat as she watched troops unload from ships into lighter crafts and then on to the shore, and tanks thumping slowly and steadily forward. She lifted her camera, leaning right over the railings, doing her best to get whatever shots she could. Ella was furiously writing in her notebook, as was Andy, telling the story of what was unfolding with their words, and Danni felt, as she always did, as if she were working in a bubble. When she was capturing a scene in front of her, everything else seemed to fall quiet as she immersed herself in her craft.

But suddenly her finger hovered as she took one last image looking out over the water, her war-hardened stomach churning at the scene in front of her. In one breath, it had seemingly gone from a war someone else was fighting, something she had a heartbeat of separation from, to one that was within arm's reach. Because now she didn't see the invasion; she only had eyes for the first patient being brought to their ship, the nurses a whirlwind of action. At the aft rail, a wooden box that looked like a coffin was lowered on a pulley into the water below, then from a smaller vessel, a stretcher was hefted into the box before it was lifted back on to their deck. Danni inched forward, hearing her own raspy breath as she photographed the pale face of a dying boy. A child more than a man. *And a German one at that.*

And suddenly she knew how important it was to photograph his face, to show the world that the sons of Germany looked just like their own boys.

Within minutes, the water around their ship was alive with the six water ambulances that had been swung down from the ship's side, so different to the first vessel that had arrived with the injured German. These small boats could be lifted back in the same way they were put down into the water, meaning the injured didn't have to be transferred into the hideous coffin boxes, but it didn't make the sight any less horrific.

"You weren't exaggerating when you said this was going to be a massacre," Ella murmured beside her, looking like she might pass out.

Danni glanced at her, seeing both compassion and grit in her eyes, before Ella bowed her head to scribble in her notebook again. The work for the stretcher-bearers was backbreaking, and Danni captured what she could, using the natural light rather than her flashbulbs, as much to save them for later when she might need them as to remain as unseen as possible. And in what seemed like only minutes from that first small vessel arriving, but was probably hours, the ship's crew were assisting orderlies and carrying stretchers. They had to carry the patients down a winding staircase, the converted pleasure ship not designed for moving the wounded, but one thing that did strike Danni was the people; they were like a well-oiled machine—the six nurses, four doctors, and fourteen medical personnel barely pausing for breath as they treated the troops on board.

Danni knew she'd taken enough photos to send home, so, with her camera still around her neck and her bag stowed away in the bathroom, she launched into action. Her medical training was limited, but she had a strong stomach and an even stronger work ethic.

"All hands on deck," she called out to Ella and Andy, not sure if they'd even heard her as she ran alongside an orderly and followed him down below.

The pristine, empty beds of only hours earlier were now filling at a rapid pace, and as her eyes adjusted to the change in light, Danni knew she'd done the right thing in pitching in.

"What can I do?" she asked an ashen-faced nurse as she passed. "Tell me how I can help?"

There was no time to talk, no time to do anything other than desperately work to save as many lives as possible.

"Those that can drink need to be given water and coffee," the nurse called out as she ran, stopping to tend to a soldier howling in pain. The man next to him watched with eyes that seemed dead, silent in his pain as blood dripped steadily from his head. "Some of them haven't eaten in two days, find them food."

Danni nodded, moving quickly through the enormous room to find water. She could see that many of the men had their heads bandaged, and she realized that the only way to get water or coffee into their mouths was to pour it through the small hole that had been left for their lips. Certainly no one seemed to care that she didn't belong there.

"What do we do?" Ella asked, her hand startling Danni as it fell to her shoulder.

"Water, coffee, and food," she said, noticing that her own hands were shaking. She quickly balled them, taking a deep breath and refusing to be rattled by the escalating situation around them.

"You do water," she said, motioning to Ella, "and you do food," she said to Andy as he moved toward them. "And we need to light their cigarettes for them. God only knows they'll need them now."

As Danni started to work, making her way slowly through the beds and offering warm coffee to the men, helping an already exhausted-looking orderly, something changed. A low murmur began between the men, amongst those who weren't as badly injured as the others, and it made Danni smile.

"Here you go," she said to one man, holding a cup for him to drink from, his body shaking so badly that she had to set the pot down and hold his head steady. "You'll feel better once you get some of this into you."

She ignored his filthy feet, the shoes cut away from his skin to reveal ugly blisters and bloody toes. Not to mention the gauze and bandages wrapped tightly around his middle that were seeping a dark red.

"Help me," he whispered.

Danni leaned close, lifting the cup again for him to have another sip. "I'm right here," she murmured. "I'll do anything I can to help you."

He slowly lifted his arm, trembling finger pointing, and as she followed his indication, eyes landing on the close-to-death German boy who'd first arrived on the ship, her stomach lurched.

"Help me kill him," the man whispered, his eyes shining with rage as his body began to convulse.

Danni picked up the coffee pot and backed away, wishing she were brave enough to tell him that that boy, a child of no more than seventeen, wasn't any different from him. He was someone's son, a boy who'd been given no choice but to fight—a perspective she had from watching the war rather than being in it. But instead she stayed quiet, not about to argue with a soldier.

It was hours later when Danni made her way back up to the deck, and as she looked out into the murky water, she realized the enormity of what was unfolding. Those men were only the tip of a very steep iceberg. The dead filled the water, and she watched as crew members leaned over with boathooks, looking for bodies and obstacles. They were scanning for mines and sunken vessels, and Danni picked up her camera again as they pushed at the sand, as the ship battled against the tides to get up to the landing barge.

Danni wiped at her face, sweat slick across her brow, breathing heavy as the crew members from the hospital ship were lowered over the side and began to wade to shore.

Her pulse started to race as she checked her camera was secure around her neck and walked quickly to the bathroom to gather her things.

It was time to go.

"Danni."

Danni turned, smiling when she met Andy's weary eyes. He looked exhausted, and although she hoped she looked more alive than he did, she doubted it.

"You alright?" she asked. "It's pretty horrific down there, isn't it?"

He nodded. "You can say that again. But they're coping well, despite the onslaught."

"You ready to go ashore?" she asked, cringing as more artillery fire sounded out. "We need to go now if we're going to be among the first to land."

Andy moved past her and collected his things, checking his bag was zipped properly, and put his trusty notepad in his jacket pocket with a small pencil.

"Have this," he said, throwing her half a piece of bread, which she caught and started to eat, only now realizing how ravenous she was. Downstairs she'd paused only to take a few swigs of water, but her stomach was starting to rumble. When had they last eaten? She hadn't even thought of taking some of the food for themselves.

"You're leaving?" Ella called out, running toward them. "I thought we were a team?"

Danni exchanged glances with Andy. "We're not a team, but if you can keep up, you can come with us." Given what they'd just witnessed, she knew it was immature to *not* let Ella travel with them, she just wasn't going to make any concessions for her.

"Give me a minute and I'll be ready," Ella said, pushing her damp hair from her forehead. "I just need something to eat before I faint."

Andy threw her his remaining piece of bread and Ella mouthed *thank you* to him. Danni was of half a mind to check she'd had something to drink, but decided against it. She wasn't Ella's minder, and if the other woman was going to make it, she needed to be able to survive on her own and make decisions for herself.

As men yelled and ropes creaked hard as they were pulled, lowering the light vessels back over the side for ever more wounded, Danni, Andy, and Ella made their way closer to the railings.

"Excuse me, but we need to get ashore," Danni said. "Can we go down with this next boat?"

The crew member she'd spoken to stared at her as if she were stark-raving mad. "There's no women there," he said. And as if to make his point, he squinted at her and then gestured to shore. "And it's bloody dangerous out there."

Danni smiled at him, forgiving his decision to speak to her as if she had no idea of the carnage going on around them.

"We'll help with the stretchers," she said. "Come on." Danni picked up one end of a stretcher and Andy took the other, leaving Ella to sweet-talk the sailor.

"We've been assisting with the wounded and we're to go ashore now to see what else we can do," Ella told him.

"Why would you want to go there?" he asked. "I can't stand to see you get—"

Danni listened as Ella quickly cut him off. "We're war correspondents and we're well used to seeing war up close. Now if you'll just let us get in here . . ."

Her voice trailed off and Danni took it as their cue to quickly get in the water ambulance, ready for lowering over the side. When they were finally inching their way toward the water as men above heaved them down, Danni dug her fingers into her camera through her jacket, praying that the one in her bag didn't get wet. She had her Leica around her neck and tucked inside her buttoned-up jacket, and her much larger Speed Graphic along with her bulbs and films in her bag, which was strapped to her back. She knew the only way they were getting ashore involved getting wet, and it was her worst nightmare for her equipment.

"Keep your heads low and walk carefully," the orderly shouted at them as they hit the murky waters with a thud. "Get that stretcher ashore and mind yourselves."

Danni looked at Andy and then at Ella, seeing a sense of calm in the other woman's eyes. She looked steely, reserved, but certainly not scared.

The call came to disembark and Danni threw her legs over and launched into the water. It was like ice, lapping up to her waist, and her teeth seemed to start chattering almost instantly, perhaps from fear as much as the cold.

"Let's go," Andy said into her ear, his voice loud, his grip on her arm firm for the second he stood beside her. And then he was lifting the stretcher toward her and she took the other end of it.

"Be careful," she whispered back, catching his eye.

"Straight back at you," he replied.

"Stay clear of objects and move steadily," the call came. "Do not lose your footing!"

Their conversation was over as they both set to work, the enormity of where they were and what they were about to be part of hitting Danni hard.

Ella was a handful of steps away but they traded glances, before Danni started to walk, minding her footing just like she'd been told, her boots full of water and feeling heavy as lead as her sodden pants clung to her skin.

She was so grateful to have Andy with her. No matter how much she'd grumbled in the beginning, feeling like she'd been given a minder, he'd ended up being her closest friend, and the best partner she could ever have wished for. There was no one else she'd rather be doing this with.

Something bumped into Danni and she jumped, heart leaping as she cringed, expecting something to explode, but as she looked down, bile rose in her throat. The body was maimed, missing an arm as it floated into her, not leaving her as the tide encouraged it to keep bumping against her side.

She vomited into the water then, not able to keep her stomach from heaving as the young man, *a boy*, stared up at her, his mouth distorted and his eyes like bright blue marbles against his blackened face.

Danni leaned to the side and tried to use the back of her hand to wipe at her chin without letting go of the stretcher. It wobbled between her and Andy, and she quickly straightened.

"Sorry," she called out.

"It's fine," he called back. "We can do this."

Ella looked across at her, and Danni shared a small smile with her as Ella nodded encouragement. They were in this together, all of them, but no matter how many photos were couriered back to London or stories filed from the front, no one who hadn't seen it for themselves could ever possibly understand what they were witnessing.

As Danni looked behind her and out farther, she could see that as the tide was changing, more bodies were floating closer to them. Bodies of men who hadn't stood a chance, with families at home praying for their safe return. Bodies like the one that had bumped against her.

"Don't look, Danni," Andy said, just loud enough for her to hear him. "Let's get this stretcher to shore and you can look through your lens instead."

Andy was one of the few people she'd explained her process to, about how different she felt looking at a situation through the lens of her camera instead of with the naked eye. About how she could cope with anything so long as she was working, rather than seeing things as a civilian. And this was one of those moments.

"Andy—" she called back, but her words were stolen from her in one enormous explosion.

Boom!

Danni was thrown back into the water, stumbling as she tried to find her feet, the cold water whooshing up to swallow her. Her face was covered in something, thick splatter that she was frantically trying to push away, and her ears were screaming with noise, even though she knew she couldn't hear anything. The eruption seemed to have happened right beneath her, the blast like nothing she'd ever experienced before.

Arms scooped her up from behind and she didn't fight them, staggering to her feet and hazily seeing Ella as her head throbbed. She could see the other woman's mouth moving now that she was facing her, could see men moving through the water toward them too, gesturing frantically with their hands, but the ringing in her ears didn't stop.

She turned and looked around, disoriented and seeing the shore, looking for . . .

"*Andy*," she screamed, her throat burning from the noise that erupted from her, over and over and over again. "*Nooo!* No!" she cried. "Andy! *Andy!*"

Parts of Andy were strewn through the water, his lifeless face seeking her out, haunting her as she tried to look away and couldn't. She screamed as she wiped at her face again, frantically trying to clean her skin and her hair, realizing it was covered in bits of him, but it was Ella who scooped up water and did it for her as she continued to scream. Her mouth fell open as she started to sob, her body shaking violently. *Not Andy. Please God, not Andy!*

Ella's fingers dug into her arms like claws as she dragged her forward, through the water, toward the beach, leaving the grotesque remains of her friend behind. Danni tripped over her own feet, her boots heavy and her body clumsy, trying her best to walk, knowing that at any moment the same fate could befall either one of them, too. Part of her wanted to drop and let the water sluice over her and take her last breath, but the other part wanted to fight against the pain and the feeling of desolation, like a wild animal refusing to surrender to death.

"Let go of me," she screamed, wanting to go back for him, not believing that he was gone. But Ella never let go.

". . . undetonated mines . . ." Danni heard as her hearing slowly came back and she tried to put together what was being said around her.

". . . wouldn't have seen it coming . . ."

"Let go of me," she whispered this time, not able to fight even though she wanted to.

Danni looked up, her hair dripping, her nose impossible to breathe through as she gasped through her open mouth and stared around the beach. The massacre might be over, but there were dead and dying men littering the sand, just like they'd filled the water, and as the medics and doctors who'd come ashore with them—and been witness to Andy's death—ran to tend to them, she dropped to her knees. Her fingers curled around the damp sand.

For once, no one cared that she was a woman. No one cared that she was there at all. And the one person who did give a damn, who'd risked everything to travel with her, was dead, blown to pieces in the water right beside her.

Danni felt Ella's hand on her back, and forced herself back up to her feet. She unlaced and tipped out her waterlogged boots before putting them back on again, not caring that her pants were sodden and clinging to her legs like a second skin.

"Danni," Ella said, and although her voice was faint, she could hear her now. "Danni, I'm so sorry."

Danni blinked at Ella, the landscape whirling above her as if she'd had too much to drink. She steadied herself and took a deep breath.

Andy is gone. Andy is gone, and I have his letter. She touched her pocket. *I have to keep going. I can't stop.*

"Danni, we can find somewhere to—"

Danni spun around as Ella's words died away.

"We?" she started, her voice sounding as waterlogged as her boots felt. "*I* need to get to work. It'll b-be dark before we know it, and I'm not—I'm not having this all be for nothing," she stuttered, pushing down her grief, her anger.

"I don't care if you don't want me, Danni. I'm sticking with you, whether you like it or not."

Danni didn't have the energy to fight her. She forced out the words, "Well, there's no *we* if you can't keep up."

"Fine. But, Danni, you've just lost Andy, you can't . . ."

Ella was staring at her as her words faded away, studying her in what Danni could only imagine was disbelief, but when Ella

147

took her hand, she didn't, *couldn't* pull it away. She took a big breath, knowing that her entire body was shaking as she tried to act calmly, rationally, like someone whose entire world hadn't just been shattered.

"We can mourn later," Danni said, even as emotion shuddered through her, trying to force its way out. "You have a story to write, and I'm damned if I'm not going to be the first photographer to show this battle to the world."

She knew what Ella must think of her, that she was stone-cold and heartless, but she also knew what Andy would have wanted, and that was for her to do what they'd come to do.

A stray tear streaked down her cheek and she brushed it away with the back of her hand as her ears continued to ring.

This is for you, Andy. It's all for you now.

They scrambled up on to a road, the pebbles enormous, the size of a man's balled fist, their feet sinking deep into them, the rocks scraping their skin even through their trousers and boots. Danni stumbled but protected her camera, hand hovering over it as she prayed that it wasn't damaged beyond repair from the water. The case should have protected it, but she wouldn't know until she stopped.

She was numb. She couldn't truly feel anything, see anything, hear anything. But as she looked up, at the sun lowering in the sky, it brought her back to the present. Night was fast closing in, and with that came a sense of urgency: they had to keep moving, it was a race against time to find somewhere secure for the evening. Or as secure as anywhere could be during war.

A large machine was working to clear the road, its shovel moving deep into the stones, and Danni let Ella go first, following carefully behind her over a white line of tape that marked where it was safe to walk, where the mines had been cleared. Danni shuddered and swallowed hot saliva as it rose in her mouth just thinking about mines, the image of Andy's last smile, his last words, etched in her mind.

She looked up as she walked, her feet moving carefully as if she were balancing on a tightrope instead of a white line on the ground, and squinted through the dust. It was like a haze, as if fog had fallen around them with the onset of night, but she could see now that it was caused by the line of tanks and trucks that were slowly but steadily making their way forward.

"Danni, up ahead," Ella said, and Danni looked where she was pointing to.

The blood-red insignia was like a beacon, and Danni summoned the willpower to keep on moving toward the Red Cross tent.

CHAPTER FOURTEEN

ELLA

It had been thirty-six hours since they'd arrived on Omaha Beach, and it had been a blur. A blur of bodies and artillery fire; blood and sand; a reality that was almost impossible to digest. And during everything they'd witnessed, Danni had displayed a steely grit that didn't reflect at all what she'd been through, although physically Ella could see the toll it had taken on her. Danni was shivering right now, even though it wasn't cold, and her eyes no longer looked like they belonged to her; whereas before they'd always been bright, now they were blank and dull. Worst of all, Ella had no idea what to say, how to comfort her, or even how to tell her that it was okay to grieve for Andy in front of her. And she was starting to worry that Danni hadn't mentioned what had happened.

Ella swallowed and fixed her gaze in the distance, not wanting to go back to that dreadful moment in her memory. Andy had been kind and talented, the sort of man that hadn't been afraid to support women, and the way he'd died would haunt her for the rest of her life. And if she felt that way after knowing him such a short time, how was Danni coping?

"I think we need to rest," Ella said, forcing herself from her thoughts.

"How are your feet?" Danni asked, her voice hoarse. Ella didn't know if it was from emotion or from the dry grit that seemed to be lodged in her own throat all the time.

Ella sat down, stretching out her legs and gingerly unlacing her boots. They hadn't taken them off since . . . Her mind stretched back. Her boots had been on her feet since well before she'd boarded the ship, which meant she hadn't removed them in almost three days. Even when they'd gone back to the ship that first night, carefully making their way before dark on an ambulance boat, she'd collapsed without taking care of her feet. Her socks were still damp, never having had the chance to dry out properly, and she carefully pulled her foot out and peeled her sock down. The pain was deep and throbbing, just like the pain in her stomach from so long without proper food, and the thump in her head from lack of sleep.

She cringed when she saw her skin, the blisters deep and her skin raw. Her feet didn't even look like they belonged to her, but she removed her other boot all the same and stuck both feet out for some welcome fresh air.

"Can you imagine being at home, and soaking your feet in a warm bath?" Ella asked, smiling over at Danni. "My mother would make me put them in salt water and then lather them up with salve. I'd look a fright, but they'd start to heal quickly."

Danni didn't say anything for a moment, and Ella wondered if she'd done the wrong thing by talking about home. But then Danni looked up, and Ella let out her breath.

"If my mother saw me now, she'd plant her hands on her hips, sigh, and give me a lecture about it being my own fault for trying to live in a man's world."

Ella flexed her feet, sat back, and closed her eyes. Her fatigue was genuinely bone-deep, and now that she'd stopped moving, she wondered how she'd ever haul herself back up again.

"Your mother disapproves of your choices?" Ella asked, eyes still shut, hoping that if Danni opened up a little about home, she might feel able to bring up Andy.

Danni made a grunting sound, and when Ella forced her tired eyes open, she saw Danni stretching out her own infected-looking feet.

"My mother is my biggest fan now, and she keeps scrapbooks full of my published photographs that she cuts from papers and magazines," Danni eventually said. "But she certainly wasn't supportive in the beginning, especially when I left my boyfriend behind and forfeited marriage for a job. Moving to Europe with barely fifty dollars to my name wasn't exactly a popular decision, although I like to think it's paid off."

Ella let Danni's words wash over her, imagining what it must have been like for her. She'd at least traveled with a job offer that afforded her a level of security, but Danni had risked everything when she'd crossed the Atlantic for something unknown.

"Do you ever regret it?" Ella asked.

Danni shook her head, and Ella watched her through narrowed, tired eyes. "Not for a second. It's what I was put on this earth to do."

She didn't doubt it. Danni was more committed to the job than anyone.

It had been a long two days. The night they'd come ashore, when they'd stumbled into the Red Cross tent, they'd been greeted by two medics who'd looked like they had no idea what was going on. Or perhaps they'd been too shocked after what they'd witnessed. Regardless, Danni and Ella had wasted no time in instructing them on how to get the wounded to safety—the hospital ship they'd arrived on would be heading back across the Channel before morning, so time had been of the essence. And so they'd moved back and forth to the beach, helping as best they could, until night had fully fallen and there was nothing left to do but wait until morning again.

But with the sounds of shelling in the distance, and the sky lit up regularly with aircraft fire, there was little sleep to be had.

"What do we do if there's a bombing?" Ella had asked a group of soldiers as they'd waited for a water ambulance to come back and collect them.

"You can dive into a foxhole," one of the men had answered. "But you'd do just as well closing your eyes and praying for the best."

"Bloody Omaha," another had muttered. "This place is the stuff of nightmares."

And he hadn't been wrong. Ella had thought she was prepared, but nothing had even remotely prepared her for the horrors she'd witnessed, and she could understand now why Danni had been so hard on her on the boat.

"Danni, if you want to talk about what happened . . ." she started, voice low as she tried to broach the subject.

Danni shot her a sharp stare. "He's gone, Ella. End of story."

"But—"

"No buts," Danni said, turning her back to Ella. "But I did make him a promise, and I intend on keeping it."

"What did you promise him?" Ella asked.

"That I'd find his sister, no matter what," Danni said, with such conviction in her voice that Ella didn't doubt her words. "She might be living not far from here, and I'll move heaven and earth to find her."

Ella sighed and leaned back. If she weren't so tired she might have pushed her further, but if she knew Danni, she'd just walk off and leave her, never to be seen again, if Ella pried too hard.

Four hours later and after far too short a rest, they were at the field hospital, and Ella took out her typewriter, sitting outside at a make-shift table that she'd scavenged. The tent she was positioned beside was huge, surrounded by many smaller tents which housed the nurses and, farther from that, soldiers, forming an encampment much bigger than she'd ever envisaged. It was only a few miles from the fighting, and Ella was barely managing to block out the not-so-distant sounds of gunfire and the whir of planes as they came and went.

She'd scribbled her story already on paper, but she needed to type it up and get it past the censor before she could transmit it. Nerves made her tremble as she flexed her fingers—she was scared of filing her story and being discovered; she was nervous of whether or not her writing was good enough, given she'd never reported on the *actual* war; and she was even more terrified that a rogue German sniper might put a bullet through her head any time she stood up and moved. She pushed that thought away, as it only brought on worries about her brother and who could be aiming a rifle at him.

But as she listened to the groans of injured men and the far-off sound of artillery fire and aviation support, she knew she had to be brave. The male journalists would be ashore soon, she imagined, which meant she was only just holding on to her advantage. And she had her secret weapon too: Michael's words kept ringing in her ears, telling her to pretend she was writing a letter to him when she was composing her articles. It soothed her, seeing his smile and bright eyes in her mind. As her fingers started to fly over the keys, she knew that his trick had worked, and for that she was immensely grateful, as it made it much easier for her to push away her nerves.

OMAHA BEACH—THE WOUNDED
AND THE WINNERS

ELLA FRANKS

The brave troops landing at Omaha Beach on the morning of June 6, 1944, never stood a chance. It was a bloody massacre like no other, and for hours it seemed certain that D-Day was going to be a failure to all of those watching on and receiving the casualties. On board a hospital ship that was equipped to take four hundred patients, we watched in horror as soldier after soldier was ferried to us, the small contingent of doctors and nurses working with precision and dedication to miraculously save all but one life that day. It was all hands on deck, from the crew members hoisting men and pitching in wherever they could, to three war correspondents serving coffee, holding cigarettes, and feeding our starving troops. We were the first correspondents to set foot on land, and the only correspondents to watch the invasion unfold.

But the reality of going ashore was something even more confronting. By afternoon the shelling had ceased, and it was obvious that the battle had turned in the Allies' favor, so we made the perilous journey through the water, battling the tides, making our way past leftover floating mines. Lives were lost as easily as a flower can be trodden into the earth, and as tanks rolled up the rocky roads to continue their assault and gain ground, there were bodies strewn everywhere, left on the beach amongst the fallen tanks and vehicles. With the tides came a floating army of the dead, their bodies washing back and forth, a reminder of the cost of victory.

As we lay in wait, listening for overhead bombing, there was a sense that we were finally coming closer to victory. And the following day, as we looked out at a further onslaught of American and British troops ready to descend, it was obvious that the Allies would stop at nothing to win this war. The Germans were surprised, and their Luftwaffe stood no chance against the might of the Allied warplanes, outnumbering them by more than one hundred and ending their retaliation before it could even begin.

Thousands of American troops died at Omaha Beach between the hours of dawn and afternoon that first fateful day—however, many survived and many more have been brought back to England by hospital ship. Had Allied troops not kept landing in waves throughout the day of June 6, we surely would have been defeated. Because, although the German troops were surprised, their determination cannot be underestimated.

Ella stopped typing and reached for her pack of Lucky Strikes that had miraculously survived, despite getting damp. She lit the end with a match and placed it between her lips, enjoying the first inhale as she glanced sideways at Danni, who was fiddling with her camera, her negatives safely stored and kept dark in her bag.

She reread her words, not knowing when the story would be printed and knowing she would need to write a much longer, blow-by-blow article covering what had happened, but she needed to get this one sent for a start. They had been told the wire dispatches were bad and that there could be long delays, but so long as she'd written it and it could be sent as soon as practically possible, there was little else she could do.

"How are you getting on with your article?" Danni asked.

Ella shrugged. "Honestly? I feel like my words are stifled because I'm trying to write in a way that will avoid censorship."

Danni dropped to her haunches beside her and appeared to be glancing over her words. "You know, Andy struggled with this, too," she said. "He often said that I was lucky because I didn't have to battle censorship as journalists did."

Ella studied Danni, surprised that she'd suddenly mentioned him after being so cross earlier when she'd brought him up.

"Danni, what happened to Andy . . ." Ella said, thinking that perhaps she was ready to talk about it. She knew she had to keep on trying, even if Danni always seemed to shut her questions down.

"Don't," Danni cautioned, her tone clipped. "Thousands of men were lost, and I don't want to think about any of it. Not until we're long gone from this damn beach. Once we're done here, once I've found his sister, then I'll mourn him."

Ella understood, loud and clear. But it didn't mean she wasn't going to keep trying to get her to talk about it. And she also needed to find a way to press her further about this promise she'd made.

"Is your camera working all right?" Ella asked, knowing that if there was one thing Danni would like to talk about, it would be her work.

"I'm worried about my larger one, but there's nothing I can do. I had it all wrapped up and packaged with the film, so I'm crossing fingers and praying."

Ella nodded.

"Actually, I'm not praying," Danni suddenly said, her voice harder around the edges now.

"You're not?"

"I grew up going to church and faithfully believing there was a higher power, but the more I see of war, the more I stop believing. I mean, how could a creator allow this to happen? Allow good men to be slaughtered by the thousands? I just can't understand it."

Ella stared at her typewriter, digesting Danni's words. She was right—they were feelings she'd had herself, especially the longer she spent seeing this war firsthand.

"I suppose I *want* to believe," Ella admitted. "I mean, this war has shattered everything, and it would be nice to think that . . ." She sighed. "I don't know, I just want to think there's someone up there who can help us, I suppose. And I have a brother fighting, too. I guess I need to believe that there's someone looking out for him."

"You never told me you had a brother," Danni said, looking perplexed.

"You've never told me about your family, either," Ella said.

Danni nodded. "How about after all this, once we're back in London, we take the time to get to know one another properly over some cocktails at The Savoy."

Ella laughed, feeling closer to Danni than she ever had before. "Deal."

"Hey, can I tell you something that'll really make you smile?" Danni asked, and Ella almost saw a flicker of the old Danni there, the unflappable one who'd equal parts terrified and impressed her.

"Sure."

"All those correspondents who were so smug about being chosen to come here? They watched the entire thing from the sea, miles back and peering through their binoculars." Danni shook her head. "Can you imagine how cross the likes of Michael Miller and Ernest Hemingway will be when they find out?"

"You're serious?" Ella grinned, the first time she'd felt truly happy since the day she'd smuggled herself on to the boat. Michael would be spitting tacks!

"I am," Danni said, her smile less bright now. "The remainder of the correspondents will come ashore by tomorrow, which means we need to do everything we can to get my rolls of negatives sent back and your stories filed today. You need to give them whatever you can, Ella. This is your big chance."

"To get arrested?" she scoffed. "I have the feeling that they'll come for us the second they see my name."

Danni shrugged, as if it weren't a big deal. "They can't stop us, Ella, and besides, no one's going to arrest you here. They'll wait until we land back in London; they haven't got the resources or time to look for us now. And no matter what happens, we'll find a way to keep on following the war, no matter what. We knew the risks when we decided to come here, and we have to make the most of being here."

Ella was stunned that once again Danni was speaking as if Andy hadn't died, as if she wasn't affected by what had happened to him, but she guessed that was Danni's coping mechanism.

"What in *God's* name are you doing here?"

Danni's face changed from warm to cool; very, very cool, as if a cold breeze had blown straight through her features. Ella's friend stood, hands planted on her hips, and glared at a very handsome soldier who was standing within a few feet of them.

His inky dark hair was combed and slicked back, looking as fresh as if he'd just arrived for dinner. But his uniform told a different story, and she knew in an instant that despite his perfect hair and razored face, he'd no doubt been through hell just like the rest of the men they'd met.

"I'm here in a professional capacity," Danni said, sounding as prickly as a porcupine.

"A *professional* capacity?" he repeated. "Do you think I'm stupid? No female correspondents were permitted to travel, and as far as I was aware, those correspondents who were permitted have only just been allowed ashore!"

Danni smiled and stepped forward, and it was all Ella could do not to laugh. The woman was confident, if nothing else—she'd give Danni that.

"Cameron, I saw the landings unfold firsthand, and I not only photographed them but assisted with the wounded," Danni said. "Not to mention the fact that my partner was blown to pieces right in front of me." The rawness in her voice sent shivers across Ella's skin.

"Which is exactly why you're not permitted to be here!" he roared. "Danni, you need to start—"

"What? Obeying your orders? Because I thought I made it abundantly clear to you that I'm not interested in following rules if they're prejudiced against women."

Ella watched as they stood glowering at each other, feeling as if she were witnessing a sparring match; they didn't even seem to notice she was there. Danni's nostrils flared and the man's face went a deep red, a vein in his forehead starting to bulge.

"There are many reasons women aren't allowed here, which you well know, and I have no other option but to report you." He crossed his arms. "Dammit, Danni, you've given me no choice but to turn you in!"

"Or you could turn a blind eye," Danni said quietly. "Because you know that I've photographed one of the most important moments of this war to date. Those images deserve to be seen by the world, Cameron. If you stop me, then you stop the world seeing what you've all done here."

He looked like he was ready to snap.

"And who the hell is this?" he said, gesturing at Ella.

Danni swept her arm back, her smile back in place. "This is Ella. She's a correspondent for the Associated Press."

He stalked closer to them, but his eyes, his *words*, were only for Danni.

"This is not the end of our conversation," he muttered. "You are to stay close to the Red Cross tent. If you want *me* to respect *you*, then you need to start respecting me."

"And if I don't?" Danni asked defiantly.

His shoulders heaved, his voice deep and low when he finally spoke. "Then you'll find yourself on the next boat out of here, with police waiting for you on the docks. And mark my words, you'll face the full extent of the law."

"Yes sir," Ella said, stepping in front of Danni. "Message received, loud and clear. We will most certainly respect your orders."

He gave Danni a long, slow stare before stalking off toward the tents, and Ella gulped as she watched him go, wondering what history he had with Danni. But before she could ask, Danni's sharp tongue lashed out.

"Why the hell did you agree to his terms?" she fumed.

"Because it beats being arrested," Ella answered.

"That man isn't my keeper, and I don't take kindly to being threatened. I also thought I made it very clear to you that you were to stay quiet and keep up if you wanted to tag along with me," Danni said. "Come on."

"You know what?" Ella snapped back. "You might not want me here with you, Danni, but you've got me whether you like it or not. As far as I can tell, we're better off together."

Danni's nostrils flared slightly. "Is that right?"

"Yes, as a matter of fact, it is." Ella scooped up her things, cringing as she realized she had to put her damp socks back on over her sore feet again. But she didn't for a second let Danni see her pain.

Danni picked up her camera and stalked off, leaving Ella to scramble after her.

"Where are we going?" she asked, exasperated.

"In search of a story."

"But what about—"

"Screw Major Cameron and his orders," Danni said. "No one tells me what I can and can't do."

Ella had a feeling she was going to regret ever agreeing to team up with Danni—she seemed so much more impulsive and prepared to take risks with Andy gone—but at the same time, she'd never felt so empowered. Danni was a rare kind of woman, and even rubbing shoulders with her was making Ella feel like anything was possible.

Unless Danni's soldier friend finds out and gets us both thrown back on a boat to England.

Ella quieted the thoughts in her head and marched after Danni, hurrying to catch up. And for a moment she wondered what Michael would think of what she was doing. It lit her face up with a smile, the idea of him being proud of her, and she only hoped she had the chance to see him again one day.

CHAPTER FIFTEEN

DANNI

Danni opened her eyes and her head throbbed immediately. It always seemed to throb these days; from lack of sleep, from the incessant sound of shelling that echoed in her ears even when the air around her was silent, and from the conversations that kept playing through her mind whenever she was still. She'd barely slept, too afraid to shut her eyes, scared of the dreams that might haunt her. And when she did sleep, she woke shaking, terrified of the dark, terrified of her own thoughts.

Because when I shut my eyes, Andy comes to me.

She clenched her hands into fists so tightly that her nails dug sharply into the soft center of her palms. The memory was visceral, sending waves of violent emotion through her, emotion that she endured silently for fear that anyone would think she was weak. She told herself constantly that everyone around her had lost someone, that this, *this*, was why they thought women the weaker gender and didn't want them on the front lines. But she knew it was a lie—she'd witnessed with her own eyes the torturous, ripping pain and emotion of the men around her. And every time Ella tried to get her to talk about what had happened, it was like the scab being picked off a wound.

Over the past few days, they'd inched farther inland as the field hospital moved to keep up with the changing front lines so they could provide immediate medical support and urgent surgeries to the injured troops. Consequently, it had been a struggle for them to get their work transmitted back to London, but she'd never expected it to be easy, and the fact that she'd managed to report back before the likes of Michael Miller had even made it to shore had pushed her to keep on trying. They'd largely been ignored by anyone of significance, the fighting too intense for anyone to care that two women were quietly taking notes and capturing images of the fighting. But she knew that she was going to cross paths again with Cameron, and she wasn't looking forward to it. He seemed fixated on putting an end to their campaign, and it appeared he was as pig-headed as she was about being right.

And what no one else knew was that it wasn't just work to her, it was personal. As soon as the Allies inched farther forward again, she planned on leaving the camp and moving heaven and earth to find Chloe. It was the first time in her life that something was more important to her than her photography; she was going to stop at nothing to find Andy's sister.

"What I wouldn't give for a mattress," Ella moaned next to her.

Danni turned and watched as Ella stretched. They'd been sleeping rough since they arrived, getting rest whenever they could, but the reality was very little shut-eye and very, very bad coffee. And there was only so long they could get away with drinking the coffee at the temporary hospitals. They were lucky that the weather was holding, because she could only imagine what it would be like when the dirt turned to mud as rain sloshed around the tents and soaked through everything.

"It looks like the 51st Field Hospital is setting up," Danni said, indicating farther afield as she temporarily pushed Chloe from her mind. They were only a few miles inland from Omaha Beach now, still stationed with the troops and medics at the new site, and they were planning on reporting from the clearance hospital, if they were amenable. Danni and Ella had already spent time with the nurses when they'd arrived, which was the only reason they'd managed not to starve—because the medical personnel had taken pity on them.

"Do you think they'll still let us stay in their tents with them tonight?" Ella asked. They had nowhere permanent to camp, since technically they weren't supposed to even be there, and they were simply moving locations with the doctors and nurses.

"Matilda was clear that they'll all be doing twelve-hour shifts, so the tents are only half full each night, with the rest of the girls working all through the dark hours."

"Well, let's go see if we can be useful," Ella said. "They were certainly more interested in helping us when they realized what we'd done on D-Day."

———— ⚬⚬⚬ ————

Later that day, and doing her best to stay out of the way, Danni looked up from her camera, stretching her back out. Whether they found a tent for the night or not, it had been worth remaining with the hospital. Ella had spent the day writing and interviewing those soldiers who could talk, while Danni had walked quietly amongst the beds and peered into temporary surgical rooms, doing her best to accurately photograph and document what the conditions were like. But the fighting was slowly moving even farther away, at least five miles from Omaha Beach now, and she knew that somehow they needed to make it to the front to see it for themselves.

A loud thump and a commotion near the entrance to the hospital made Danni turn, and her eyes widened as she saw a familiar figure standing there, his arm looped tightly around another soldier as he dragged him alongside. The other man's left leg had a tourniquet above his knee, his pant leg ripped to shreds, head hanging as blood seemed to drip in a constant slurry from his mouth and ears.

Danni moved silently forward, taking in Cameron's blackened face, his eyes bloodshot, his body quavering under the weight of the injured soldier. As two orderlies ran forward and a nurse sprang into action, relieving him of the burden, she watched as he reached out for the closest bed, bracing himself, his body trembling.

"You carried him all that way?" The quietly spoken question came from Ella, standing behind Danni, but she didn't turn to look at her. Her eyes wouldn't leave Cameron's face. For someone who prided herself on seeing through the exterior, of being able to capture the truth in any situation, she could see that she'd misread the man in front of her. Instead of looking into his eyes and observing him, she'd been caught up in what he was stopping her from doing.

And now she was seeing the raw man beneath the uniform, and she could see clearly that, as much as he hindered her from doing her job, he was still a worthy subject to photograph. If she could capture him as he was right now—strong yet broken, tough yet compassionate—then she'd have something incredible to show for it.

Danni lifted her camera, her movements as slow as she could possibly make them. The lighting wasn't ideal, but she wasn't going to startle him with a flashbulb. She slipped her feet forward, just a few steps, and clicked. Cameron's face was so smeared with dirt and blackness, his eyes wide, and his shoulders were bowed just enough to show a broad man slightly stooped from exertion.

"Put the damn camera away," he grunted.

She didn't straightaway, but she lowered it once she'd taken a final shot of him glowering at her, not wanting to aggravate him.

"Excuse me," Cameron said as a nurse passed. "Is he going to make it? The boy I brought in?"

She frowned. "He'll live, but he'll surely lose the leg," she said. "You saved his life bringing him all that way though."

The pain of the nurse's words radiated off him as he stood to full height again, the moment of vulnerability passing. But Danni was grateful she'd seen it, that she'd been able to capture it. And she could almost hear the thoughts in his head, wondering if it had even been worth saving a boy who was now going to be sent home a cripple, confined to a wheelchair for the rest of his life. It was also a reminder of how she'd seen him in Sicily too.

"Major, could I have a word?" Danni asked.

"You may not," he replied brusquely, turning away from her.

She didn't take his refusal as an answer and followed him anyway. She caught Ella's eye, but her friend didn't move.

"Sir, I wanted to ask if there's any chance of me having access to a jeep?" she called after him.

That got his attention. Cameron spun around, his heel digging sharply into the dirt as he whirled to face her. "You want a *jeep*?" he said. "What the hell for?"

Danni nodded, keeping it businesslike, not having *any* intention of letting him in on her plans to find Chloe. As far as he would know, it was so she could get closer to the action for her work. "Yes, to enable us to be closer to the front lines—"

He threw his hands in the air. "How many times do I have to tell you that you're not permitted anywhere near the fighting? Or anywhere else but here for that matter! It's bad enough that we have women this close, and if I didn't have so many men in my care, I'd be marching you on to a ship bound for England myself!" He glowered at her. "This is your commanding officer telling you categorically that you may not have privileges, including access to a jeep!"

His shoulders were heaving with each breath he took, and despite his anger, she felt the sudden urge to offer him her handkerchief to wipe the grime from his face. It was enough to make her wonder if she'd gone soft in the head.

They stood, staring at one another, Danni refusing to back down despite the way he was glaring at her.

"Have you considered what's going to happen to you when you finally return?" he asked. "Has this been worth losing your career over?"

"Yes," she said, not needing time to consider her answer. "Whatever my punishment, it's been worth it. Of course it has." *Except for Andy.* She'd take it all back if it meant saving Andy.

"Major Cameron!" yelled a soldier, who looked like he was literally shaking in his boots as he stood in front of Cameron and gave him a rushed salute. "I have an urgent telegram for you, and there's also a telegram arrived for a Danni Bradford."

Cameron took the one extended to him and gestured at Danni. "You can give it to her yourself."

She took it, eyebrows drawn together as she looked first at Cameron, who was more interested in his own telegram than her standing there, and then back at the folded paper in front of her.

DANNI YOUR PHOTOGRAPHS WERE RECEIVED AND THE FIRST IMAGES FROM THE LANDINGS PUBLISHED. HOWEVER WE HAVE DECIDED YOUR IMAGES ARE TOO GRAPHIC FOR FUTURE PUBLICATION. WE HAVE WARNED YOU BEFORE AND HAVE NOW DECIDED TO TERMINATE YOUR CONTRACT. YOU ARE NO LONGER IN OUR EMPLOY.

Danni read the words again and again, the paper starting to shake in front of her. Finally, she folded it and hastily placed it in her pocket before Cameron could have a chance to read it. But when she looked back up at him, he still seemed immersed in whatever his own telegram said.

"It seems the wire transmissions of my photographs made it back to London," she said, keeping her voice even despite the lump in her throat.

Cameron nodded, but she sensed he'd received news every bit as bad as hers, and was trying every bit as hard as she was to disguise it.

"Would you reconsider letting me use a jeep?" she tried one last time. "Please, Cameron. It would mean so much to me."

"It would be wise not to ask me again," he replied, and with his face still blackened and his hands stained with another man's blood, he marched off and yelled at someone, before getting behind the wheel of a jeep. "And it's *Major* Cameron to you," he said as he left, sending dirt spraying behind him.

Danni shook her head. If he weren't such an asshole, she'd almost like him.

"I'm starting to think that you enjoy poking the bear." Ella came to stand beside her, hand raised to shield her eyes from the sun. "He's never going to give us a jeep. We're not even supposed to be here, for God's sake."

"I certainly do not enjoy *poking the bear*," Danni snapped. "And there's no *we*. I'm taking the jeep on my own."

"No, you're not," Ella said. "If you get clearance, I'm going with you."

Danni sighed. "No, you're not." Then she unfolded her telegram and passed it to Ella, deciding it was so much easier to let her read it than telling her.

"What's this?" Ella asked, before falling silent beside her. "Oh, Danni, I'm so sorry. What a blow it is to receive this."

Bitterness tiptoed through Danni's body as she took it back and promptly discarded it, tearing the telegram to pieces and letting it flutter away around them.

"They want to show a version of war that isn't real," she said, staring angrily at the dust cloud in the distance left in Cameron's wake. "I vowed to show the truth, and I'm not going to change that just because an editor sitting in a comfortable office chair doesn't like it, while a generation of young men are being butchered before my very eyes. Maybe I should have sent them a photo of Andy's body blown to smithereens to see what they thought of that!"

She could feel her shoulders heaving with anger, her breath coming in rapid pants. And when she looked back, she could see the shocked, horrified look on Ella's face. She hadn't meant it, of course she hadn't meant it, but to be sacked on top of everything else—it stung.

"What are you going to do?" Ella asked.

"I'm going to do what I came here to do," she replied. "I'm going to photograph the war as I see it, tell the truth with my camera, and I'm going to find another editor to send my rolls of film back to." Danni watched as two planes soared noisily through the airspace above them. "I'm going to start with *National Geographic*, I'm sure they won't be scared of showing the truth. Nothing's going to stop me because this is my job and I won't take no for an answer." She didn't tell Ella about the letter, or the fact that it was burning a hole in her pocket. Andy had trusted her to find his sister if he couldn't, which meant she had two jobs to do in Normandy—two jobs that she would stop at nothing to fulfill.

"Why don't we send them to *my* editor?" Ella suggested, folding her arms tightly across her chest. "We can submit my stories and your photographs together. It makes sense, don't you think?"

Danni stared at the pieces of telegram that remained, slaughtered, barely a memory of the words she'd read only minutes earlier.

"They'd be crazy not to accept photographs from you," Ella continued.

"I agree. Now let's see if we can get some rest," Danni said. "I'm heading out in a jeep tomorrow or the day after, to document the *actual* war." *And start the search for Andy's sister.*

Ella baulked. "What are you talking about? Did I miss something? Did Cameron give you clearance?"

"No, he did not," Danni said. "But when's that ever stopped me?"

———— ✷ ————

The following night, Danni had barely had a wink of sleep, although she had consumed her fair share of gin. It was strong and tasted like liquid fire, but it had warmed her belly and she wasn't about to head to bed when she could be listening to the stories of those who'd survived.

And if she was enjoying it, Ella was absolutely reveling in it. Danni smiled at her across the way, both sitting and leaning against the outside of the tent, their legs brushing the dirt and their arms resting on their knees. Ella was talking to two of the nurses they'd befriended, and it was nice to see her so relaxed after the last few days of horrors.

"We heard there were some ladies visiting," came a slurred voice.

Danni looked up, the moonlight her only tool to see with. She had a flashlight nearby, but she wasn't about to blind some poor soldier with it.

"I've long given up on being called a lady," she replied, standing up and brushing off her trousers.

She soon saw that there were two men, one holding a bottle of liquor by the neck, and she glanced from it to their faces. She was used to dealing with men, all types of them and in all types of situations, too, so the fact that they were looking at her like they wanted to devour her wasn't going to scare her. She had a handful of women behind her, having a quiet drink before they turned in for the night, exhausted, and a couple of men who she was certain would help her if she needed them.

"What's that you got there?"

"This?" she asked, touching her camera. "This is a Leica. A German camera, actually."

One of them reached for it, lunging at her, but she sidestepped and managed to avoid contact.

"Show it to me," he slurred.

"I took this from the body of a dead Nazi," she said, stepping back. "And *no one* touches my equipment."

They laughed. And in that moment, as the women's hushed conversation behind her turned to silence, as she let down her guard a little, not thinking they were going to do anything more than mildly annoy her, the soldier without the bottle swiped her camera from her hand.

"You bastard!" she swore, tripping as she leaped forward to catch it.

"Gotcha!" the other said, leering as he wrapped an arm iron-tight around her waist and fumbled for her breasts.

Danni was less concerned about herself than her camera, watching as the other soldier swung it around, so close to her but not close enough to reach.

"What the hell is going on here?" A voice cut through the commotion, and Danni recoiled as she saw Ella standing with Cameron beside her.

"Let," Danni gasped, "go of me!" She snapped her arm around, twisting at the same time as she kicked hard, straight-legged, into the soldier's crotch, felling him, before setting her sights on the one with her camera.

Only, Cameron beat her to it. He was standing over the soldier, who instantly handed him the camera.

"Get out of here," Cameron snarled at him. "And take that idiot with you."

Danni held out her hand and took her camera from him, panting from the exertion of it all.

"Thank you," she said. "But I can fight my own battles." *The only other person I let fight for me is Andy*. It was Andy she'd expected to come to her rescue just then, until it had dawned on her that Andy was no longer there for her.

"So I can see," he muttered, but she was certain she could hear the humor in his tone.

She pushed thoughts of Andy from her mind, not ready to think about him yet.

"Have I convinced you that I can look after myself if you lend me a jeep for the day tomorrow?"

Cameron laughed. She'd actually got a laugh out of him, which she was going to take as a win given how he'd reacted the last time she'd asked him. Her fingers locked around her drink again and she took a small sip, hoping he didn't notice just how rattled she was from what had happened. For a second, just a moment in time, she'd expected Andy's warm hand to take hers, to pull her back to safety, to just be there for her. But he wasn't, and the loss of him was suddenly a gaping hole beside her.

"Danni, I saw firsthand that you could handle yourself in Sicily," he said, his voice softer now. "But rules exist for a reason. The fact that I don't want you here has nothing to do with how good you are at your job."

"I like to bend rules," she said, trying not to look at Ella making a dramatic face and throwing her hands up in the air behind Cameron. She clearly didn't approve of Danni badgering him again.

"Look, I think you and I got off on the wrong foot," he said. "Not to mention I've had a hell of a day, a hell of week, to be honest, and I've lost a lot of good men."

"How about a truce then," Danni suggested, passing Cameron her drink and receiving a grateful look from him. She looked over her shoulder as she heard groaning, and watched as the soldier she'd kicked limped away. "We have a drink, talk, and start over." She took a deep, shaky breath, wishing she wasn't feeling so out of control, wishing she could order her thoughts. "To be honest, I've had a rough few days, too, so I have no interest in arguing with you."

Cameron's shoulders relaxed and, as she sat down, he dropped to his haunches beside her. "Deal. But no amount of talking is going to make me give you that jeep. I want to make that crystal clear from the beginning."

Danni fought the smirk waiting to spread across her lips. *Oh yes, it will.* She knew she was being reckless, that Andy would have stopped her from doing something so dangerous, but there was a little voice in her head saying that maybe he wouldn't have. That if it was for his sister, he'd have stolen a damn jeep too. And the photo of Chloe was burning a hole in her pocket, reminding her constantly that she had more than one job to do in France.

She breathed deep, inhaling and exhaling a few times in an attempt to pull herself together, to be her usual self in front of Cameron.

"So tell me," she said, as they sat together in the dark, slightly away from the others. "Was the soldier you brought in yesterday someone important to you, or would you save the life of any soldier working under you?"

He grunted and slowly sipped the drink. "I'd do the same for any of my men, and I'd expect the same from them," he said. "I wonder sometimes if there's going to be a family left in England or America that isn't going to be broken by this war. I'd walk on blistered feet across hot coals if it meant I could save someone's son." He took another quick sip of gin. "Or someone's brother."

The way he said *brother* made her pause. His jaw hardened, visibly so, and then he lifted his drink to his lips again.

"Have you lost a brother to this war?" she asked quietly.

His big shoulders heaved with the exertion of his breathing. "I have."

"I'm sorry to hear that," she said, taking the gin when he held it out to her.

"When we both received telegrams yesterday, it was the news I'd been waiting for."

Danni passed him back her cup and watched as he drained the rest of it. She almost cringed for him, imagining what it must feel like in such a big gulp going down to his stomach.

"He'd been missing, presumed dead, and they just, well . . ." He cleared his throat. "His death has finally been confirmed. That's the news I received."

"I'm so sorry for your loss."

Cameron nodded. "Thank you."

"I . . ." she started, the words sticking in her throat. "I lost someone I was very close to this week, too. He was like a brother to me."

"Andy, wasn't it?" Cameron asked, his voice low. Something about telling him felt easier than opening up to Ella, perhaps because she knew what he'd lost, and what he'd been witness to. "I remember him from Sicily, too."

She nodded, furiously blinking away tears. Whenever she thought about Andy, she tried to redirect her thoughts to Chloe, to looking for her, which meant she didn't have to think about him. She hadn't talked about him at all until now, barely even acknowledged that he was gone. "We'd worked together a long time, and he was killed right in front of me."

"I'm sorry, Danni," he said. "I'm truly sorry for your loss."

Cameron stood, and as she craned her neck to look up at him, he held out a hand to pull her to her feet. She took it, palm clasped to his, and realized just how long it had been since she'd touched a man. *Truly* touched a man.

His breath smelled faintly of the gin he'd just consumed, mixed with tobacco. His hand was warm against hers, skin slightly callused in a way that she imagined most higher-ranking officers' hands wouldn't be, but Cameron didn't strike her as being characteristic of most men.

"The months of not knowing was nothing compared to finding out about my brother," he said, voice like gravel as he ground out the words. "But to see your friend killed that way, you're not only dealing with grief, you're dealing with trauma from what you witnessed. Go easy on yourself, Danni."

Danni wobbled on her feet, well used to drinking straight liquor after all her years as a correspondent, but perhaps not used to going without food at the same time. She was light-headed, dizzy almost, as Cameron's mouth moved closer to hers. How did he understand her so well?

"You know, you're one hell of a woman," he murmured. "I don't think any broad has ever driven me half as crazy as you do. You're the strongest, bravest damn woman I've ever met."

She looked up at him, sadness making way for longing—something she hadn't felt for a man in a very long time. "The first day I set eyes on you, I thought you were the most arrogant man I'd ever seen." The image of him with a cigarette dangling between his lips as he languidly puffed and watched her was still imprinted on her mind.

"And I thought you were the most reckless, irritating woman I'd ever encountered."

Danni laughed. "And now?"

"My opinion hasn't changed," he replied, moving even closer, their boots touching now, bodies so close she could feel the heat radiating off of him. "Maybe I'm just starting to have an appreciation for reckless women."

Her lips parted, her posture softening when one of his hands pressed to the small of her back, his mouth moving to hers in a slow, warm kiss that made her tingle all the way to her toes. Just when she thought she was broken, that nothing could stop her feeling numb and raw from what had happened, from the thing she'd borne witness to, Cameron made her feel something other than pain again.

His hand stroked up and down her back before his fingers pressed flat against her to move her forward, chest to chest, and she circled her arms around his neck as he kissed her again. They were in the middle of a war, only miles from where the nearest battle was being fought, and yet he kissed her as if they were standing in a sun-drenched field with not a care in the world.

When their lips separated, she leaned back in his arms. "All these years I've done this job, and I've never let myself get this close to a man for fear it would compromise my reputation."

His laughter was a low rumble in his chest. "And yet here we are."

"Here we are," she repeated, shaking her head. "For anyone to see, I might add. And with a man I wanted to murder less than a day ago."

Cameron smiled and his lips brushed hers again, and for the next few moments she lost herself to his touch and the warmth of having the arms of a man around her. "I think we need to end this before it goes any further," he said, cupping her face, callused thumb stroking her skin.

"Maybe we shouldn't."

He stared down at her, and she brazenly stared back, heart racing.

Cameron pulled her against his chest, holding her tight. "Damn you, Danni," he muttered, his lips against her hair. "I don't even have my own tent right now, but if I did . . ."

She held on to him just as tightly, suddenly needing the contact, craving that feeling of someone holding her and protecting her, taking care of her after so long of steadfastly taking care of herself. Alone.

"Let's sit a while longer," he said, lowering them both to the ground and keeping his arms around her.

She stared up at the stars as tears welled in her eyes, the pain of losing Andy finally overwhelming her, impossible to keep down any longer even though only moments earlier she'd felt the exact opposite of pain. If Cameron knew she was crying, he never said, he just kept his mouth against her hair, her head against his chest, and his arms looped protectively around her.

This is going to make what I have to do so much harder, she thought. But there was no way to avoid it.

She was taking a jeep whether he granted her permission or not. The next time she saw him, he could be having her arrested for defying orders, which meant she had to enjoy basking in his arms while she could. Because no matter how much she liked him, how much she was drawn to him, her work was everything to her, and she couldn't let anything stand in her way. And the promise she'd made Andy was one she'd willingly die for if it meant following through on his wishes.

"You never did say what your telegram was for," he said.

"Oh, nothing important," she murmured, brushing tears from her cheeks before he saw them.

And she guessed that he believed her, as she placed her hands on his strong forearms, her shirt catching on the roughness of his jacket, trying to pretend that these stolen moments with him were enough to last a lifetime. Because he'd never forgive her when she defied him, which meant that this might be her one and only night in his arms.

Danni stared at the sky blanketing them from above, at the twinkle of tiny stars seeming to wave like a million fireflies, and wondered if Andy's sister Chloe was looking up at the same beautiful sky, too. Danni could always go on foot, which would mean not alerting Cameron that she'd snuck away from camp, but she didn't know how far she might have to travel yet if she couldn't find Chloe between Bayeux and Caen. And besides, if she encountered German troops in the area, she'd far rather be in a jeep so she could flee danger more quickly.

"Danni, I'm heading in to catch a few hours' sleep," Ella said, startling her as she stepped in front of her with a few nurses in tow. "Do you want to come with us?"

She'd almost forgotten they weren't alone; the moment she'd found herself caught in Cameron's arms, everything else had temporarily faded away. "I'll catch up with you soon."

Ella started to move away, but Danni quickly called out to her. "Ella?"

"Yes?"

"It's nice to have you here. I should have told you that nights ago," Danni said, her voice lower, more gravelly than usual.

"You're welcome."

There was silence for a moment. The truth was, she'd taken her anger out on Ella, and it wasn't fair. If Andy hadn't died, then Ella would have been an irritation, but she'd done nothing other than offer support and companionship since then, and she was clearly good at her job. Much better than Danni had ever expected.

Danni leaned back into Cameron's chest again, eyes shutting as she gave in to the delicious feeling of the alcohol swimming through her and a man's body against hers, and the faint sounds of war that continued to echo in the distance as she slowly drifted to sleep.

CHAPTER SIXTEEN

CHLOE

Chloe had been waiting all morning for Gabriel to arrive back, and now, as she waited for him to come into the bedroom, she knew that she had to tell him. She'd been trying to find the words for days, but every time she'd seen him she'd simply lost her nerve.

She sat, staring out the window at the garden, eyes scanning the forest as they often did, convinced she would see German soldiers crawling through the trees at any second. The worry kept her up at night sometimes, thinking about how easily they could be discovered.

"Chloe?"

Gabriel said her name as he pushed open the door. It was awkward between them still—they shared a bed most of the time, and had a close bond in that way—but he rarely talked to her about what he was doing or what was happening. And most of the time she felt that he was happy to have her body close by, without wanting the same kind of connection that she yearned for.

"Is everything okay?" he asked.

She stood and turned to face him. She just needed to tell him before she lost her nerve again.

"Gabriel, I'm pregnant."

He looked as if she'd slapped him, his face shocked and suddenly drained of color.

"You're certain?" he asked, his eyes widening as he stared back at her.

"Yes, I'm certain," she said, placing her hand protectively over her stomach.

He started to pace then, and she stayed sitting on the bed. She'd had weeks to come to terms with it, but Gabriel was clearly going to take some time to digest the news.

"What am I going to do with you now?" he suddenly asked, appearing to be talking more to himself than to her. "We can't keep you here, it's not safe."

"But, Gabriel, I thought this would make you want—"

"What?" he asked, shaking his head. "You thought I'd suddenly be able to stop what I'm doing and play family with you?"

She recoiled, and Gabriel seemed to realize how much he'd hurt her, quickly taking her hands and holding them tight.

"What we're fighting for, it's bigger than you or me, Chloe," he said, staring into her eyes and making her feel like he was willing her to understand. "It doesn't matter how you or I feel, or what happens between us; my commitment is to the cause."

"And it's more important to you than your child?" she asked. Had she been so stupid to think that her being pregnant would make him love her? Would make him want to protect her above all else?

"Yes," he whispered. "I'm sorry, Chloe, but it is."

She looked away, back out the window, not wanting to look at him any longer.

"Chloe, if we don't fight, if we don't cause disruptions and blow up railway lines and feed the enemy incorrect information, our child won't even have a world to grow up in. No child in France

181

will, or at least not a world that I'd ever want a child to know, controlled by a man who spreads hate and evil wherever he goes."

"So, what? I just hide away here forever?"

"No," he said sadly, lifting her hands and kissing her knuckles in the warmest display of affection she'd ever received from him. "Now I have to find a way to get you out of France."

"What do you mean?" She snatched her hands back, moving away from him. "You can't be serious, Gabriel. You're going to send me away?" She shook her head. "No, absolutely not! I can shoot a gun now, I can make the food, I can—"

"It's not enough, Chloe. Can't you see that?"

He started to pace again, and she backed up to the window, leaning into the glass.

"The Allies are making good ground near the coast, the Normandy landings were a huge success, and I expect that they'll be slowly liberating towns along the way as they progress."

Her heart was racing and she felt like she could barely breathe. "Doesn't that mean things will change then? That things will go back to normal soon?"

"No," he said, stopping in the middle of the room. "It'll mean that we all need to move on, to help the Allies' advance, and I can't have you coming with me if you're pregnant." He looked defeated. "And I can't leave you here alone, either. I'm responsible for you, Chloe, and I've tried my best to look after you since you came, but you've left me with no other option now."

Chloe didn't reply. What could she say? It was obvious he'd made his mind up, and nothing she said would likely change it. Which meant she was going to be sent home to London, pregnant and unwed. The thought sent a painful shudder through her body.

"You have to go, Chloe. It's for the best," he said. "I need to get you and the baby out of here."

"It's for the best that I leave you? That our child has to grow up without a father?" she sobbed, arms wrapped tightly around herself even though it gave her little comfort. "I can't believe you're even suggesting this!"

"I'm sorry, I . . ." He ran his fingers through his hair, and she could see how torn he was. "If there was another way—"

"But there isn't," she said for him, sadly. "Is there?"

"Hey, we could always use you as a courier for the Resistance." He was teasing, but his joke only hurt her more. "No one would suspect a heavily pregnant woman of transporting contraband or messages for us, would they? Or one with a newborn."

Chloe shook her head, wanting to slap him for even suggesting it, but at the same time knowing that if she did stay, that might be her fate. Perhaps she *would* have to become more involved, and where would that leave their child, then?

"What about after the war, Gabriel?" she whispered. "Will we—"

"We can't think about that right now," he said brusquely. "We don't know when that'll be or what will be possible, and maybe things will change, but the priority is getting you and the baby out as soon as we can."

"But Gabriel, surely . . ."

His expression broke her heart. "That's not something I can answer right now, Chloe, so please don't ask me again."

"I should never have come, should I?" Chloe asked, staring up at Gabriel and willing him to tell her she was wrong. But she could tell from the look on his face that she wasn't.

"No, Chloe, you shouldn't have." His shoulders stooped, the first time she'd seen him look anything other than strong and commanding since they'd arrived at the chateau. "I'm sorry if I led you on, if I encouraged you with my letters. I loved the time we had together, Chloe, but what we had was never supposed to be more than an affair." His sigh was deep. "I couldn't see that back then—times were so different and we had so much fun—but now it's clear to me that I should never have kept writing to you. I'm sorry, Chloe, I'm so sorry."

His words hurt, but over the past months she'd developed a much thicker skin. And Gabriel was right, she could see that now. She'd taken his kindness in writing back to her as him feeling the same way about her, but unlike her, he'd never been in love. To him, she'd been a fling to enjoy; a visiting model whom he'd lusted after. And to her, he'd been her first in more ways than one.

She bit down hard on her lip, but it still didn't stop the tears. Gabriel held her against his chest until her sobs subsided, but when he reached down and tilted her chin up, she saw something in his eyes that surprised her.

Gabriel's lips crushed gently against hers, moving back and forth so tenderly, his hands warm and firm to her back.

"I am going to miss you," he whispered. "If it's any consolation, that is."

Chloe clung to his shirt, her fingers clutching at the soft, worn fabric as she searched his eyes.

"I'm going to miss you, too."

If the Allies were advancing as fast as Gabriel believed, it wouldn't be so long before he'd find a way to send her across the Channel. Despite it all, she would have stayed with him until her last breath if she could have, but she knew that he'd do everything in his power now to find a way back to London for her.

Chloe held her head high as she walked away from him, forcing her feet to move, refusing to break down and beg him to change his mind. Gabriel had been nothing but kind to her, tolerant on so many levels, but he'd made it very clear that she had to leave, and she wasn't going to embarrass herself by refusing. She needed a moment alone with her thoughts, to collect herself, now that he'd made himself clear.

"Chloe, wait!" he called.

She stopped, heart racing, waiting for him to say he needed her, that he wouldn't let her go even if he could, that he'd changed his mind. But all he did was reach out a hand and press it to her stomach, cradling her belly as he stood so close she could feel his warm breath on her cheek.

"You'll be a wonderful mother, Chloe," he whispered.

She nodded as the tears she'd tried so hard to wish away started to stream down her cheeks, then, fists clenched, she walked away from him, knowing that when she turned, he'd be gone. They had a bridge to detonate, she knew that much, which meant she was alone in the chateau again.

Andy, I just want to go home.

For the first time in her life, her brother wasn't there to catch her when she fell. If only she'd listened to him, she would have still been safely ensconced in their house in England, waiting out the war. Her only consolation was that he'd be there waiting for her when she returned. He might have taken up residence at The Dorchester during the war, which meant they wouldn't see a lot of one another, but if she needed him, or the baby needed him, she knew he'd drop everything to look after them.

CHAPTER SEVENTEEN

ELLA

Ella collapsed on to the ground, her body feeling as heavy and ungainly as a sack of flour. She'd spent hours working on her final story about the landings, and she was exhausted. Her only saving grace was that Danni was off photographing the troops, which had given Ella a reprieve from her mad idea about stealing a jeep. Thankfully she hadn't mentioned it again, and Ella was hoping she'd either realized how harebrained the idea was, or that her time in Cameron's arms had softened her ambitions in that regard.

She shut her eyes and enjoyed the sunshine as it bathed her skin. Even if she had all day to snooze, which she didn't, she doubted it would be long enough to make so much as a dent in her sleep deficit. She couldn't even remember the last time she'd rested properly.

"Sleep is for the dead," she muttered to herself, remembering the way Danni had spouted the saying at her only the day before when she'd complained of exhaustion.

Thump. Something kicked at her boot and her eyes flew open.

"Watch it!" she said, drawing her foot in.

Oh Lord.

"How the hell did you make it here before me?"

Michael was standing over her, his face hard to read as he watched her with one eyebrow arched. Ella sat up, blinking as her vision blurred from the bright sky above.

"I thought I'd told you I was going to find a way to get here," she said, wishing her heart wasn't racing quite so much at the sight of him. But she was impressed with how quickly she'd managed to quip that back at him.

"You didn't just arrive today, did you?" he asked.

She laughed. "No, Michael, I actually witnessed the landings with my very own eyes. I came to shore the same day the troops did."

Ella could have knocked him over with a feather he seemed so shocked; his mouth dropped open and he looked down at her as if she'd just announced she was an alien.

"I'm sorry. You what?"

"Unlike you, I managed to make my way here to see the actual *action*," she said, taking great pleasure in for once having the upper hand. She sat up a little straighter, shielding her eyes from the sun. "And I wasn't the only one."

She smiled to herself as Michael looked around, his typewriter bumping against his hip, another pack on his back. She'd wondered if she'd cross paths with him, but she'd been so busy working with Danni, they hadn't seen any of the other correspondents until now.

"Who else was here?" he asked. "Don't tell me you've already sent work back to London?"

Ella pushed herself to her feet, feeling truly confident around Michael for the first time. He'd laid down the gauntlet for her, and she'd shown him that she was more than capable of doing what needed to be done.

"Danni Bradford was the other correspondent here on the day," she said. "It seems that she and I had the same idea for how to get here."

"Ha," he said, shaking his head. "You little devil, I honestly didn't think you had it in you. But you know what?"

Ella held her head high, refusing to fade in front of him even if looking into his eyes wasn't for the fainthearted. "What?" she asked.

"You did something amazing being here that day. As loathe as I am to admit it, you being here means the world has a true, firsthand account of the landings, and for that I take my hat off to you."

Ella stared back at him, brimming with pride at his words. "Thanks, Michael. That means more to me than you'll ever know."

"I suppose that bloody Andy scooped me in the story stakes too, did he?" Michael asked. "He and Danni are one hell of a team. I'm actually surprised they let you tag along."

Ella glanced past Michael and saw Danni approaching, and she quickly stepped in closer to him, wanting to tell him before she reached them.

"Michael, Andy didn't make it ashore," she said, her voice low. "He was . . . well, he stepped on a mine and—"

"Well, well, well, if it isn't Michael Miller."

Michael gave Ella a long, alarmed look, before turning around to Danni.

"Bradford, good to see you," he said, clearing his throat. "I gather I've been beaten to the punch by you two ladies."

"That you have, Miller," Danni said. "It's been one hell of a time, but I hear you spent the first few days relaxing and watching it all unfold from afar?"

He laughed, but Ella could see how much it pained him to admit it. "I saw it all happen just fine," he replied.

They all stood for a moment, before Danni gestured to Ella. "I'm off to see if I can't twist Cameron's arm one last time," she said. "Did you file your story?"

"I did," Ella replied. So much for thinking she'd given up on the idea. "Good luck with Cameron."

Danni slapped Michael on the back as she left them, and the second she was out of earshot, Michael's hand brushed Ella's arm.

"Does she know?" he asked.

"About what?" Ella wished she weren't so acutely aware of his touch.

"About Andy? Those two were thick as thieves, and yet she's acting so normal."

"Oh, she knows," Ella said, sighing. "We were both there. He was talking to her one minute, holding the other end of a stretcher they were carrying, and the blast sent her flying. It was the most horrific thing I've ever seen."

Michael frowned. "But she seems—"

"Fine?" Ella asked. "Trust me, I know. It's like she's blocked the entire thing out. I want to shake her sometimes just to make her feel it. She was in shock for the first few minutes, it was horrendous, but then she seemed to pull herself back together and she's been acting like it never happened ever since."

"Did he have family?" Michael asked. He ran his fingers through his hair. "I honestly can't believe he's gone. He was one of the finest."

"I know," Ella said sadly. "He has a sister, I know that much, but she's somehow missing in France. Danni hasn't told me the whole story, other than the fact that she's going to try to find her as some last promise to Andy. She thinks she might not be far from here."

"I see."

Ella looked at the ground, scuffing her boot in the dirt, not sure what else to say. She might have beaten Michael this time, but he was a seasoned journalist and she could only imagine how superior his work would be to hers now that he was here. It was kind of surreal, seeing Michael in France, surrounded by a sea of khaki-colored tents that dotted the landscape far and wide, their surroundings so different from the hotel in which they'd met. Months ago, she couldn't have imagined it was even possible that she'd be so close to the war, and yet she could hear the booms and cracks of fighting as she waited for Michael to say something.

"Are you coming to the afternoon briefing?" he asked. "You can tag along with me if you're not invited? Or I could take notes for you. Those things are always a drag, but sometimes there's a good snippet of information."

She laughed. "Are you actually going to vouch for me if I come with you?"

He shrugged. "Sure. Of course I am."

Ella was secretly thrilled that he was treating her as his equal, and she loved how relaxed he was about it all, so at ease in the work he did. But instead of letting on, she tried to act as if it were no big deal. "So, are we going to that briefing or what?"

"We are. And after that, I think we need to share a packet of cigarettes and have a *very* strong whiskey, so you can tell me all about the past couple of days."

Ella picked up her bag and tapped her nose. "You're not going to charm my secrets out of me that easily, Miller," she said. Even though, deep down, she knew that Michael could most likely charm anything out of her if he tried hard enough.

"You like having the upper hand, don't you?" he teased.

"Maybe I do." She also liked her newfound confidence that seemed to come from knowing that she had one up on him.

"It suits you," he said.

"What does?" Now she could feel the all-too-familiar blush rise up her neck and bloom in her cheeks.

"Whatever the hell has put that fire in your belly," Michael said with a wink.

Ella smiled to herself as she walked alongside him. Had she changed that much? But when she thought about it, she knew he was right. Standing up for her rights, witnessing the landings, refusing to let Danni go on without her, it had forced her to believe in herself, if only for the simple fact that failure hadn't been an option.

"It's good to see you, Ella," Michael said, giving her a nudge with his elbow, followed by a devilish smile that made her think about the last time she was close to him, about how it felt to have his lips against hers.

Do not think about kissing him. Do not think about kissing him, she repeated in her head.

Ella gave her best impersonation of an experienced correspondent as she coolly replied, "It's good to see you too, Miller."

They walked the rest of the way in silence, and as they neared the tent hosting the correspondent briefing, she lost Michael to the small crowd.

And then she saw Danni, who appeared to be in yet another heated discussion with Cameron, and promptly forgot all about Michael as she headed over to try to diffuse the situation, wondering whether Cameron might finally snap, throw Danni over his shoulder, and march her straight on to a ship headed for England himself.

"What do you say we have that drink right about now?"

Ella laughed as Michael spoke directly into her ear. She was sitting at a makeshift desk outside one of the Red Cross tents, but as she moved to look back at him, the overturned crate she was sitting on tipped.

"Gotcha," he said, catching her around the waist as she tried to steady herself.

Ella grabbed hold of the table, cheeks burning as Michael's hands stayed connected with her.

"You can take your hands off me now," she said, clearing her throat as he backed away and turned over a crate to make his own workstation.

He sat down, eyebrows raised as he leaned a little toward her.

"What are you working on?" he asked.

She angled her typewriter toward herself. "You go and find your own story, Miller."

He laughed. "I'm not interested in your story," he said. "I'm interested in having that drink with you."

Ella folded her arms. "I have a lot of work to get through, and I know full well that if it were you working, you'd not set it all aside for me." She tried to be brusque with him, even though the idea of spending time with Michael was heavenly. But she had her work to focus on, and Michael Miller was not the man to sacrifice anything for; he'd made it clear he wasn't looking for a relationship, let alone a wife.

"I'm not so sure about that." Michael winked. "How about I go find that whiskey for us, and I'll come back when you've finished." He grinned. "Or you could come to the men's quarters and use our facilities. We have quite a good setup."

She refused to bristle at the fact the men had such good facilities. "I'm just fine here in the fresh air," she said, not wanting to think about the spacious tents and workbenches that were supplied for the men. She'd even heard a rumor that, as the fighting advanced, they'd find houses for them to work from. No one cared at all if she and Danni even had so much as a tarpaulin over their heads at night!

"Suit yourself," Michael said. "I'll keep my fingers crossed that those dark clouds don't bring rain."

Ella glanced up, frowning at the sky and then realizing he was only teasing her. She turned back to her typewriter, grinning to herself as she finished her story and pulled it from the reel. It took her a few minutes to scan her words, beaming at her report on the latest action, casualties, and conditions for the medical personnel.

"I wholeheartedly agree. The nurses are doing a splendid job of keeping up morale."

"Michael!" she gasped, spinning around and glaring at him. Her crate teetered again, but she managed to steady herself this time without him having to assist. "You should know better than to read another journalist's work," she scolded.

Michael held up his hands, which were full of mugs and a bottle, making him look all the more guilty.

"Sorry, I couldn't help myself," he said. "But I do come bearing gifts."

Ella sighed. "You're very hard to be cross with for long."

"Whiskey?" he asked, perching on the other upturned crate again.

"Okay, but just one," she cautioned. "I still have to send this back."

He grinned. "How about two, and I'll help you to send the story, so we'll get it back faster."

Ella gave him what she hoped was a withering look, although he didn't seem to care as he poured the alcohol into two cracked mugs and then passed her one.

"I propose a toast," he said, holding his mug high. "To you managing to beat me to Normandy."

Ella clinked her mug against his, unsuccessfully hiding her smile. "To me beating you." She laughed. "Now that has a *very* nice ring to it."

Michael reached into his pocket and pulled out a packet of cigarettes, and she leaned forward when he offered them to her, taking one out. When she looked up, he flicked his lighter, eyes never leaving hers as he moved closer to her.

Ella inhaled, not lowering her eyes. It was like he was testing her, waiting for her to falter, but after everything she'd been through over the past few days, she refused to succumb.

"I wasn't wrong when I said there was something different about you," he said, drawing on his own cigarette and leaning back a little.

Ella puffed again, and took a sip of her drink before answering him. "Do you like the old me or the new me better, then?"

His laughter was warm, and she liked the way his eyes danced in time with his smile.

"Ella, I liked you just fine before," he said. "But I do like that challenge in your gaze now. It suits you."

"I feel different, if I'm completely honest with you," she admitted, taking another sip of her drink and trying not to grimace at the burn in her throat. "I thought I understood war, but I know now that you can't truly understand it until you see it firsthand."

Michael nodded, suddenly looking a lot more somber. "I'm afraid to tell you that it never leaves you," he said. "The things we're witness to, they take a piece of you, and it's hard for anyone else to understand it."

They sat a little while longer, smoking and drinking, before Michael leaned in closer to her, as if he were about to let her in on a secret.

"I'm heading to the front tomorrow," he told her. "So if I'm honest, it's why I wanted to sit here with you a while."

"All the male correspondents are going?" Ella asked, swallowing a lump in her throat.

It wasn't Michael's fault, he was only doing his job, but it still hurt that they were cleared once again, and yet she and Danni couldn't so much as secure a jeep.

"If you want me to ask if you can join us, I will," he said. "You've proven yourself, Ella. Besides, if we're really competing, then I'd rather we had the same advantage."

"You would?" she asked, surprised.

"Sure I would!" He laughed. "I'd still beat you, of course, but at least everyone would know I can beat you fair and square."

Ella went to punch him, trying hard not to laugh, but Michael caught her wrist, and his grin faded to a softer smile.

"What are you doing?" she asked, trying to pull her hand back. But he didn't let it go.

He shuffled forward on his crate, still holding her wrist, and she saw the way his eyes dipped to her mouth.

"You see, I've thought a lot about that time I asked you for a kiss back in London," he said, his voice lower now. "And I can't stop thinking about how much I'd like to ask for another."

Ella should have been flushed and nervous, but as much as her stomach was flipping at being so close to him, all she wanted to do was close the distance and give him exactly what he wanted.

"Perhaps it's the whiskey talking, but I think I'd like that too," she said.

Michael's hand left her wrist and cupped the back of her head. Ella leaned closer, staring at *his* lips now, knowing that if she didn't kiss him, she'd always regret it.

His mouth pressed warmly to hers, and she closed her eyes, losing herself to the sensation of his lips moving in time with hers. She stroked her fingertips down his cheek as they kissed again, his hand sliding down her back, not caring who might see.

When he finally broke off the kiss and pressed his forehead to hers, she let out a little laugh that made him chuckle straight back.

"Thank you," she whispered.

"I think I'm the one supposed to be thanking you."

She shut her eyes for a beat before bravely returning his stare. "Thank you for giving me something to smile about. I needed it."

Michael stroked her hair and then kissed her forehead, and she eventually let him draw her up to her feet. They stood for a long moment, before she finally cleared her throat, dragging her gaze from him.

"I really need to get this story filed," she said.

"You sure you don't want me to do it for you?" he asked. "For the sake of convenience? It would be so much faster for me to wire it for you."

She shook her head. "No, thanks. I'm just fine doing it myself." From another man, it would have been condescending, but from

Michael it felt supportive more than anything. But truth be told it *did* upset her terribly that it was so easy for the men to get their work back to London or New York. Her stories physically going by pouch back to London weren't exactly getting anywhere fast.

He leaned in again and caught her fingers as he kissed her one more time. "Keep on doing what you're doing, Ella. You're damn good at this correspondent gig, in case you didn't already know."

"Stay safe, Michael," she whispered, hating that she was falling so hard for him when her mind was screaming at her to steer well clear of him, that all he was going to do was break her heart.

"Ella, this is what I do," he teased, touching her chin in a familiar kind of way that made butterflies flutter in her stomach. "I'll be fine. In fact, I'll be coming to see you with more whiskey within a day or two, I promise."

She nodded, knowing he was probably right, but worrying all the same.

"You just keep your head down and make sure you do come back," she said, teasing him back but also being deadly serious. "I want that second drink, Miller."

Michael just laughed as he backed away, winking as he turned, and as much as she wanted to drink in the sight of him, to commit his kisses to her memory forever, she knew he was probably like this with all the women he encountered. *A girl in every port*, that's what her mother would have said about a cad like Michael.

Ella folded her arms around herself, staring after his familiar frame until he disappeared into the enormous Red Cross tent that dominated the landscape in front of her.

She stretched then sat down, smiling to herself as she read over her work again. It had been an awful few days, but she had a feeling that that little moment with Michael was enough to see her through the darkness. Even if she was trying hard not to fall for his charms.

CHAPTER EIGHTEEN

ELLA

"Ella, have you heard?"

She looked up from her typewriter, squinting at Danni. The sky was cloudy but it was still bright to her eyes, especially after spending hours hunched forward over her work.

"Heard what?" she asked, yawning.

Danni's face was white, and Ella realized that something was wrong as Danni reached for the table.

"That tour of the front we were so annoyed about missing?" Danni said. "There were two correspondents badly injured."

Ella's heart dropped with a thud in her chest. "Michael was on that tour," she said. "Is it him?"

Danni's knuckles were white as she gripped the table, and Ella had to hold the other end to stop it from flipping. "I don't know anything else, I just . . ."

Ella stood then, reaching for Danni. Her skin was starting to look distinctly ashen. "Danni, are you alright? Take my seat a moment."

But Danni shook her head and pulled away. "I'm fine, it's just a shock, that's all."

Ella wanted to tell her that it was no wonder she was in shock after what had happened to Andy, and now this. But instead she bit her tongue and reached into her bag for her flask. It was half full with gin, and it wasn't like she drank it often.

"Here, have a good swig of this," she said.

Unlike her words of comfort, Danni was happy to take the gin. "Thanks," she muttered.

"Do you mind if I go and check the field hospital?" Ella asked, panic rising. "I just have this strange feeling about Michael now, and I want to make sure he hasn't been hurt."

A correspondent Ella recognized from London jogged over to them then, and Ella took in his blackened face and frantic eyes.

"Danni," he called, going straight past her. "We lost one."

Ella didn't wait to hear more. "Look after my typewriter!" she yelled at Danni, and she ran as fast as she'd ever run in her life toward the hospital tent.

———— ❧❧ ————

Ella stood at the entrance to the huge clearance hospital tent, her heart racing as she gasped for air. She'd run the entire way, turning down offers of assistance from the soldiers she'd passed, and now she was trying to catch her breath and regain her composure before she went in.

Please let him be alive still. Please let it not be Michael.

"Can I help you?"

A nurse appeared at her elbow, adjusting her hat, and Ella quickly reached out to her, recognizing her immediately.

"Florence! It's me, Ella. The correspondent?"

The other woman broke out into a smile and gave her a quick hug. "I thought you were long gone. Where have you been?"

"It's a long story, but I was told two correspondents were injured today," she said, barely able to believe the words she was saying. "Michael Miller, he's a fellow journalist, and I need to know if he was one of them."

"Honey, I'm just starting my shift and the name isn't familiar, but come with me," Florence said. "If he's here, I'll find him for you."

The hospital was a whir of activity that looked like chaos until Ella actually stopped for a moment to watch, and saw that the frenzy was more organized than it first appeared. She stood still and stared around her, waiting for news, and when she heard her name being called she sprang into action.

"Ella," Florence called. "Over here."

She walked carefully, not wanting to be a hindrance as doctors and orderlies moved quickly around her.

"You've found him?" she asked, her breath coming in rapid gasps as she studied the nurse's face. "I had this awful feeling that I'd get here and he'd be gone." Her voice faltered and she reached to hold on to an empty bed beside them.

"I have found him, but Ella . . ." Florence paused, her face falling.

"What is it? Am I too late?" she asked as her hands started to shake so violently that she had to fold them under her arms. "Please," she gasped. "Tell me I'm not too late?" *Has Michael already died?*

Florence's arm wound around her as she started to guide her forward. "Honey, you're not too late, it's just that his injuries, well, they're unique. You need to be prepared."

Ella gulped, nodding, her head moving up and down without her wanting it to.

"Just take me to him," she whispered. "I can handle it."

Florence stopped her, fingers still firmly clutching her shoulder. "He's just over there, Ella. But it's his eyes," she said in a low voice.

"He's all bandaged up and the doctors don't know if he'll ever regain his sight."

Ella trailed away from Florence, feeling the moment the nurse's fingers dropped from her shoulder, as she walked toward the metal bed with a man lying on it, his eyes covered with an enormous bandage that obscured his face beyond recognition. Light brown hair that *could* have been Michael's stuck up above it, and her breath caught as her feet kept moving toward the man. The man who'd stolen her breath at the hotel bar in London, and permanently stamped himself in her thoughts after kissing her.

It's him.

As she inched forward, as she took step after step toward the man she'd been so desperate to impress with her writing, she started to cry.

"Michael?" she whispered as she took one of those beautiful hands in hers and dropped low, lips to his fingers. "*Michael.*"

She felt the pull as he instinctively tried to withdraw his hand from her hold, surprised at her touch, but as she whispered his name, over and over, his fingers suddenly clasped hers tightly.

"Ella?" he whispered back, sounding confused. "Is that you?"

Ella nodded as tears slid down her cheeks and into her mouth, gulping as she tried to stop them. She knew he couldn't see her nodding, even though his head was raised, and she held his hand to her face as she struggled to find the words. How could this have happened to someone as strong and vibrant as Michael? They'd been together only yesterday!

"It's me," she whispered, crying into his hand. "It's me, Michael. It's me."

"Oh, Ella, what are you doing here? I don't want you to see me like this."

"I thought . . ." She took a deep, shaky breath. "I'm just so glad you're alive." She squeezed his hand. "Michael, what happened to you?" she asked.

His hand lifted a little and then pulled away from hers. "Things turned to shit, that's what happened," he muttered. "One minute we were a safe distance away, watching the war unfold, and the next a bloody bomb detonated beside us."

She swallowed, trying to push away thoughts of what had happened to Andy right in front of her, and how lucky Michael was to even be alive still.

"So, can I get you a whiskey?" she asked, trying to tease him like old times and bolster his spirits. "I'm sure I can rustle up something to take the edge off."

But it was clear Michael wasn't going to play along. He made a noise in his throat, turning his body away from her. "You need to go, Ella. This is no place for you."

She stepped back, surprised. "Michael, you don't mean that! Surely?"

He turned, his heavily bandaged face angled away now as he crossed his arms, rejecting her fingers. "Get out of here, Ella. I'm not going to ask you again. I'm not a journalist anymore, so just go."

She sighed, brushing away her tears, pleased that he couldn't see her. "No," she said defiantly. "And that's the most ridiculous thing I've ever heard. You're one of the most respected journalists covering this war!"

"No, Ella, not anymore I'm not." The catch in his voice almost reduced her to tears.

"Don't say that. Please, that's a horrible thing to say," she pleaded.

But even without his eyes, even without him being able to look at her, she could feel the weight of his angry gaze somehow.

"Can you not hear me? Get out, Ella! Get the hell out of here and don't come back!"

Ella stood and stared at him, waiting for him to apologize, to beg her to stay instead.

"I know it's hard, Michael, but there's no reason to—"

"What?" he snapped. "There's no reason to what, Ella? Right now I'm wishing I were dead, that I'd died instead of ending up a goddamn useless idiot who won't even be able to write again."

She sucked back a breath, trying to stay calm, knowing that it wasn't him, that it was the pain and the shock of it all making him behave that way. "Michael, you're not useless," she said softly. "Please, Michael—I, we . . ." She took a breath, whispering now. "Over these past weeks, I think I've fallen in love with you. I don't care if you've been injured, I'm just so grateful that you're alive." She reached for his hand, but he pulled it away from her.

"I'll never forgive whoever it was for dragging me back here," he muttered, turning his back. "I don't want your pity, I don't want your sympathy, so piss off and leave me to wallow in peace."

"Michael! I've just poured my heart out and you—"

"For God's sake, Ella. We had a bit of fun, that's all. Now go."

"Fine, if that's what you want, I'll go," she said, hating how her voice cracked as she forced out the words.

Ella stumbled backward then, knocking into an empty bed behind her, his cruel words ringing in her ears as she turned her back on Michael and wished like hell she'd never come looking for him in the first place. She'd thought she could help him through his pain, she'd wanted him to know how she felt, and he'd just thrown it back in her face as if her words, her *feelings*, meant nothing.

CHAPTER NINETEEN

DANNI

"Danni, stealing a jeep isn't a good idea," Ella pleaded, running along beside her the next morning. "Please, you need to think this through."

"Oh, I've thought it through," she said, jangling the keys and moving around Ella as she tried to block her way. "I made Andy a promise, and whatever happens, it's the one thing I'm going to do."

"How did you even get those keys?" Ella whispered.

"I've been watching for days now, looking to see where they put them when the jeeps aren't in use," Danni said smugly. "It's amazing what you can find out just from being alert."

The day before, she'd sent photos from near the front lines back to London while Ella had gone in search of Michael, but until some other advance was made, she was planning on spending her time looking for Chloe. Nothing, other than a Gestapo bullet, was going to stop her.

"Danni, please," Ella said, taking hold of her arm in a viselike grip.

Danni tried to shake her off, but Ella wasn't letting go.

"If you'd just pause for breath and perhaps talk about what happened to Andy, maybe—"

"Maybe what?" Danni retorted. "He's gone, and the one thing I can do is honor his memory and find his sister. If I don't go now, then when?"

Ella's grip softened, but she still didn't let go. "I'm coming with you then, whether you like it or not," she said. "I just want to make sure you've thought through the—well, the ramifications of your actions. What if this is the end to your time in France?"

Danni shook her head and finally loosened Ella's grip, too. "I've lost my closest friend and my job, Ella. It can't get any worse."

Ella folded her arms, standing in front of her again. This time, Danni didn't try to push past her.

"I'm sorry, that was insensitive, given what happened to Michael and the other correspondent," Danni said. "But it doesn't change my mind. How is Michael coping?"

Ella looked skyward and Danni realized she was fighting tears. "He's badly injured, but his tongue was as sharp as a barb."

"He'll just be furious that he's out of action," Danni said. "He'll come around."

They stood for a moment, staring at each other as their chests rose and fell with each breath.

"Danni, you're one of the most talented war correspondents the world has seen," Ella said. "I just want to make sure that you're absolutely certain you want to defy Cameron's orders like this."

Danni was doing more than defying his orders, she was betraying his trust, but she'd already come to terms with that. No matter how strong her feelings were for him, doing this for Andy was worth the risk.

Danni nodded. "Thank you, but I'm fine with my decision. Now can you *please* move."

"It doesn't matter how mean your words are or what you say, you're not doing this without me," Ella said. "So long as that's clear, then we're good."

Ella stepped back, but Danni could hear Ella following her almost immediately. Soon they were in the jeep, and she started the engine, ignoring Ella, pleased to hear the steady rumble as she put her foot down and skidded south toward Bayeux.

———— ∞∽∾ ————

They drove largely in silence for almost thirty minutes, with only the rumble of the engine sounding out between them. Danni drove slowly now, fighting sometimes to keep the vehicle straight as she surveyed their surroundings. She wouldn't admit it to Ella, but she was kind of grateful for the company, and for Ella's map-reading skills. They'd passed through the town of Bayeux, and after showing Chloe's photo around without success, they were now edging slightly farther east where the larger chateaus were toward Caen, and she was praying they weren't going to come across a German patrol or roadblock. Thankfully they were heading into a rural area, which was hopefully taking her closer to where Andy's sister might be, and farther away from the enemy. Although she knew that was wishful thinking.

"Look," Ella called, pointing to where the trees became more dense.

Danni slowed when she saw something up ahead, her pulse racing as she immediately considered spinning the jeep around and racing back in the direction they'd come. But she refused to listen to that voice of self-doubt in her head.

"What is it?" Ella asked.

Danni narrowed her eyes, squinting as she tried to figure out what she'd seen. And then her blood ran cold.

"We need to stop." She turned off the engine, leaning over and picking up her camera from the back seat as she forced herself to leave the car. She glanced left, shivering when she realized she'd automatically looked to where Andy had always been when they'd been in the field together.

"I won't be long, but I need to document this," she said to Ella, looking around and noticing how picturesque this part of France was, despite all the destruction and terror only a few miles in the opposite direction. It made the scene she was photographing that much starker: bodies against a woodland backdrop. It looked too pretty to be a scene of death.

The bodies up ahead were those of two German soldiers, and as she looked at their faces through her lens, it struck her, as it had on the hospital ship, how similar they were to their own soldiers. Young men cut down in their prime, unwilling bodies fighting in a war that they most likely wanted no part in. It was a story she wanted, *needed*, to tell—that either of those men could have been the son, brother, or boyfriend of someone they knew—and when it came down to it, they were all the same. And the way the sun was filtering through the trees, like shards of white light, amongst the eerie feeling of the woods, the shot was just too perfect not to take, especially when it didn't even require a flashbulb to capture it. It was almost staged it was so stunning, and she knew what an impact a photograph like that would have.

"Don't be long," Ella said, opening her door and following. "I have an uneasy feeling about all this."

Danni wasn't about to let Ella tell her what to do, but if she were honest, she was feeling nervous too. She took a long, deep breath and held her camera at a different angle, her fingers finally ceasing to tremble as she worked.

"Danni, over there," Ella said, pointing when she looked up. "There's another body."

They both walked quietly across the ground. The wooded area wasn't dense with trees; there was easily space to move and the canopy was relatively high, meaning there was light filtering through instead of making it seem daunting and dark. The ground was covered in a soft bed of pine needles, and Danni inhaled as she carefully stepped forward, not wanting to make a noise. For some reason it seemed disrespectful to the deceased men if she didn't stay as quiet as possible.

"This one's in plain clothes," Danni said as she stood close to the body. "A Resistance fighter, do you think?"

"Could be," Ella replied. "It's impossible to tell who won this skirmish. I wonder if it was just them or if others were involved?"

"I'd guess that there would have been others, but then maybe they just came across one another by accident," Danni said. "Or I suppose it could have been a Resistance ambush of some sort, taking down small patrols of German soldiers?" The idea of more German soldiers being around sent a shiver through her, and she knew they were being reckless staying out in the open for any longer than they needed to be.

"Maybe," Ella said. "It's surreal stumbling across them like this, and knowing they were still alive such a short time ago. Imagine if we'd come across the actual fighting?"

The other man was dressed in simple peasant clothes, a rifle cast down beside him. Danni held her camera up again, clicking as Ella scribbled notes beside her, wondering as she so often did about the loss of human life from this war, the toll of men on both sides who were never going home to their families.

Danni was aware that Ella was staying close, but she wasn't in her way and it was actually nice not to be alone.

"I'm usually so immune to all this, but seeing these men dead today . . ." She gulped, turning her back on the scene she'd been shooting and suddenly fighting for her breath. "Lord, I don't know what's come over me."

Ella's hand fell on to her shoulder. "You've held it all in, Danni. We've both been through a lot this past week."

"Yeah, we have, huh?" She sniffed and wiped away her tears, thankful that Ella removed her hand from her shoulder but still stayed close.

Danni looked around, considering the countryside, absorbing the look and feel of where they were, and then turned to take a candid shot of their jeep, doors open, and seemingly abandoned amongst the trees.

"Let's get out of here," Ella said, and glancing back, Danni noticed a shiver run through her. "There could be more soldiers in the area, and the last thing we need is to be captured and interrogated."

"Ouch!" Danni fell, her ankle twisting painfully beneath her as she stumbled forward, landing heavily on her hip. When she looked back she could see it was a tree root snaking up and across where she'd been walking. Pain shot like fire through her ankle and foot, and when Ella rushed over to help her, she could barely stand, even with assistance. She'd been so busy looking through her lens she'd forgotten to mind her footing.

"Danni, what's happened?" Ella asked. "Is it twisted?"

She grimaced as she tried again, unsuccessfully, to put weight on it. "I think it's worse than a sprain," she said. "I don't even know how I'm going to get back to the jeep."

As she leaned on Ella, she looked down and saw a grenade lying amongst the pine needles, and a shiver ran through her as she realized how close she'd come to landing on it, and just how dangerous it was for them to even be in the area.

"Come on, I'll help you," Ella said. "Just keep your arm around my shoulders and I'll hold your waist."

Danni grunted, but grit her teeth and kept going despite the intense pain shooting up her leg and down across her foot. She kept hold of her camera, lowered now, and did her best to hobble alongside Ella without putting too much weight on her. "Thanks, Ella," she said quietly. "I know I'm a lot to handle sometimes, and Lord only knows how Andy did it day after day, but I do appreciate having you around."

Ella just bumped hips with her, and it made Danni laugh, even though she wanted to cry at the same time from the pain. It surprised her how close she felt to Ella all of a sudden. They'd been through a lot in a short time together, and it was only now dawning on her just what a great friend Ella could be. *If I let her.*

"I'll drive," Ella said, taking Danni to the passenger side when they got back to the jeep.

Danni held on to Ella and the side of the vehicle as she pulled herself in. She sat for a moment, dragging her foot so as not to hurt her ankle more, before moving her other leg up and shutting the door.

Ella was in the driver's seat now and turned the key. Nothing happened. Ella tried again, and Danni's pulse started to thump at her neck as panic set in.

"What's wrong?" Danni asked.

"The engine won't fire," Ella said. "It's like there's nothing there." Ella's eyes were wide when she turned to her.

"Try again," Danni said.

Ella did, four more times, but the result was the same. "I don't think we're going anywhere in a hurry."

Ella moved closer beside her, and they both looked around. Suddenly Danni felt more vulnerable than ever as she realized they were sitting ducks in the middle of a conflict zone.

"What could have gone wrong? Could it be the fuel?" Ella asked. "It started up just fine back at base didn't it?"

Danni swallowed hard and turned to look at Ella. "Ah, well, the thing is, the only one I could take without getting caught was one waiting for repairs."

Ella stared back at her before her eyes widened even more, her face looking like it was about to erupt with anger.

"You brought us all the way here in a jeep that wasn't even in good working order?" she hissed. "Danni! I trusted you!"

Danni frowned. "It's not like I asked you to come with me," she said. "And obviously I didn't expect this to happen. I mean, I gave it a quick once-over, and nothing obvious was wrong with it. I thought it must have been one they'd fixed and were waiting to

209

put back in service." *Was I mad taking the jeep?* Her mind started to whir as she realized the situation she'd put them in.

Ella let out a noise that sounded more feral animal than human, getting out of the jeep and marching around the front of it. Danni's heart started to pound even harder, suddenly terrified of being alone, so used to having Andy with her and now relying so heavily on Ella, even if she hadn't wanted to admit it.

"What are you doing?" Danni called out.

"Coming around to get you," Ella huffed. "I'm not sitting here and getting shot just because you were stupid enough to steal a broken vehicle!"

Danni kept her mouth shut as she opened her door and held on to Ella, positioning herself so she could limp along beside her.

"Any idea how far we are from the town?" Ella asked.

"Maybe half an hour's walk from here at the speed I can go?" Danni suggested, breaking out in a sweat as she tried to put weight on her foot and walk. "But there could be houses well before then, dotted around the woodland area."

She could feel the anger pulsing through Ella, so she stayed quiet and just focused on moving. It was slightly better the more she walked, although she knew she was pointing her foot at a strange angle just to limp along. Despite her pain, she owed Ella an apology. What she'd done was reckless, if not downright stupid, but even though she'd known that, she'd pushed common sense away and done it anyway. She bit her lip, trying not to cry. She didn't usually make rash decisions; she made decisions that were often pushing the boundaries, but were well thought-out. Danni knew she'd been making blind decisions in her desperate bid to find Chloe, and it was starting to make her wonder if she weren't going a bit mad.

"Ella—" Danni started, before digging her fingers into Ella's side to stop her.

A rustle behind them, too close, made her turn, words dying in her throat.

"Ella, quick, hide!" Danni ordered, her voice a sharp whisper as she thrust Ella forward, watching her stumble toward the closest trees. "Stay there," she hissed.

She turned, fear freezing her in place as the rustle became the one thing she was more scared of than death itself.

"Don't move," she whispered to Ella, lifting her hands to show her surrender as she moved slowly backward. "You stay hidden, no matter what."

I should have listened. Danni gulped as a man moved out of the trees, his gun raised and his eyes never leaving hers. *I should never have taken the damn jeep.*

The man wasn't a soldier; instead he was dressed in the same simple clothes as the dead man she'd photographed before. But he didn't look any less menacing than a soldier, the way he had his gun trained on her.

Her ears pricked as he clicked the safety off his rifle.

"Keep your hands where I can see them," he said in French-accented English that told her it wasn't his first language. "And tell her to come out."

Danni gulped, shutting her eyes. He must have been listening to them to know they weren't native French speakers.

"Come out!" he shouted.

She knew there was no way out of this. If she screamed at Ella to run, then he'd likely shoot her, and they had no way to defend themselves.

"Ella, come out," Danni called, wishing the earth would open up and swallow her as she heard Ella's footfalls.

"Who are you?" he demanded. "And why are you here?"

Ella had come to stand beside her, and Danni shuffled even closer. "My name is Danni Bradford, and I'm a war correspondent," she said. "This here is my friend Ella Franks, and she's also a correspondent."

"Y-you can tell by the stitching on our arms," Ella said in a small voice, angling her arm. "The 'C' stands for 'correspondent.' I'm a journalist and Danni is a photographer."

The man lowered his gun an inch or two as she spoke, studying them with what appeared to be disdain.

"You're both American?" he asked.

They nodded at the same time.

"What are you doing here? Why aren't you at the American camp?"

Danni glanced at Ella.

"We wanted to report on the area around Normandy," Ella said quickly.

"And we're looking for someone," Danni added.

The man's eyebrows pulled together. "Who are you looking for?"

"May I?" Danni asked, gesturing to her pocket.

He nodded, but he trained the rifle squarely on her again.

Danni pulled the letter from her pocket, taking the carefully folded photo from inside it. "This woman," she said. "Her name is Chloe. Have you seen her?"

He took a step forward, staring at the image a moment before nudging his gun toward her. His face gave nothing away.

"Why are you looking for her?"

Danni swallowed hard. "Because she is the sister of my work colleague, and he was determined to find her."

"How did you get this jeep?"

"We, ah," she started, considering lying and quickly changing her mind in case it cost her her life. "We took it without permission from the American camp, at the, ah, at the field hospital a few—well, quite a few miles back. We took matters into our own hands. To find this girl."

"You stole it?" he asked.

Danni's eyes met his. "I did."

"Turn around," he commanded.

Danni was shaking now as she hobbled on the spot, reaching for Ella's hand. Ella was making little whimpering sounds and Danni could barely stand it. First Andy had died because of her, and now Ella, too? She bit down hard on her lip, fighting tears as she waited for the worst.

But the crack of the man's rifle never came.

"Stay still," he said, putting something over Danni's face. She jumped at his touch, but as she realized what he was doing, her breathing started to slow.

"What is this?" Ella asked. "Please, if you're going to kill us—"

"Keep the blindfolds on," he said. "You walk ahead of me."

Big hands went around her waist and Danni grunted as she was lifted clean off her feet. He must have seen how badly she was limping.

"Don't talk, just walk," he ordered.

Danni cringed as he held her over his shoulder like a sack of potatoes, and she hoped that Ella didn't fall and hurt herself too. The only upside was that he hadn't shot them. And if he wanted them dead, why bother to blindfold them and take them somewhere else?

Unless of course he wanted to get information out of them, in which case their day was about to get a lot worse. She considered screaming, demanding to be put down, but she'd seen the dead soldiers with her own eyes, which meant that her other option was being found by the Gestapo.

If her instincts were correct, this man had to be a member of the French Resistance, which would not only make for a good story, but would mean he wouldn't kill them at all.

Or so she hoped.

CHAPTER TWENTY

CHLOE

Chloe stared from the window as Gabriel returned, gasping as she saw that he was carrying someone, and marching another ahead of him.

What do they have around their eyes?

She ran down the hall and burst through the front door, about to ask him what on earth was going on, when he set the person down and tugged the cloth from her eyes. He had two women with him!

"Gabriel! What's going on?"

He raised an eyebrow at her, as if to silently reprimand her, and she clapped a hand over her mouth. Was she not supposed to say his name in front of strangers? Chloe gulped. Were they prisoners of some kind?

"Gabriel?" the woman he'd been carrying said, rubbing at her eyes and blinking. The change between dark and the bright sunlight was clearly making it hard for her to see. But then the woman's eyes widened. "*Chloe?*"

Now it was her blinking. Chloe took a few tentative steps forward, but Gabriel held up his hand to stop her.

"How do you know—"

"Oh my God, *Chloe*! Ella, it's Chloe!" she cried to the other woman.

The woman speaking hobbled toward her, but Gabriel's hand went to his gun and his command was short and sharp.

"Don't move," he shouted.

The woman froze, looking between the two of them.

"Time for questions. How do you know who she is?" he asked. "Why did you recognize my name?"

The woman smiled. "Because Chloe's brother Andy was my colleague and friend for years," she said. "And I've been staring at a photo of Chloe for days now, the one I showed you back there in the woods, wondering how on earth I was ever going to find her." She laughed. "And here she is. I can't believe it. What were the chances of this even happening?"

Chloe felt like she was stuck in mud. She couldn't move a foot. "You know my brother? You're a friend of Andy's?"

The woman stepped forward, but Chloe saw the way she anxiously looked at Gabriel, raising her hands, a camera in one of them, as she moved.

"I'm Danni," she said. "I don't know if Andy ever talked about me, but—"

"*Danni?*" Chloe squealed, launching forward and opening her arms, grabbing hold of Danni in a hug that almost toppled her over. "I'm so sorry, I just . . ."

They stared at one another.

"Andy wrote to me so often when he was away for work, and he was always telling me about you, so I already feel like I know you so well," Chloe said. "I can't believe you're here. Where is he?" She looked expectantly past Danni, staring at the other woman and then at Gabriel. "Where's Andy? You two are always together in the field, aren't you? And you must be here for work, right?"

Chloe's eyes shifted between Danni and Gabriel.

"Where's my brother?" she asked again.

But she knew, the second Danni reached for her hand, the way her face seemed to crumple whereas only moments earlier she'd seemed so excited to see her.

"Danni?" Chloe asked.

"I'm so, so sorry, Chloe," Danni murmured. "But your brother, Andy, he's gone."

"Gone?" she repeated. "What, as in back to London?"

She saw Gabriel moving closer in her peripheral vision, but she didn't take her eyes off Danni.

"Chloe, he's . . ." Danni paused, the pain on her face palpable. "Andy didn't make it. He was killed during the landings. He loved you so very much. I'm so sorry, but that's why I've been looking for you, because I promised Andy—"

"No!" she cried. "No, no, *no*! There's been some kind of mistake. Andy can't be dead, he's . . ." She looked at Danni, who limped toward her, her mouth set in a grim line, her eyes full of pain. And then Chloe threw her arms around her, sobbing against her shoulder.

It couldn't be true, could it? How could Andy, her loving, larger-than-life, capable big brother, not be alive?

"He was," Danni said, her voice catching. "He was . . . well, he was like a brother to me, too. I know that'll sound strange but—"

"It doesn't," Chloe whispered. "It doesn't sound strange at all, I know how much he loved you."

They stood for a long while, before a large hand touched Chloe's shoulder and pulled her away.

"Let's finish this inside," Gabriel said, his gun relaxed at his side now, although she noticed he still looked anxious. "It's safer for us to be hidden from view."

"You're with the Resistance, aren't you?" Danni asked him, as Chloe kept hold of her arm. "Is that why you were in the woods?"

He nodded. "It is. You stumbled into a covert mission to track down a small group of Germans who've been getting too close to the house. They're getting closer and closer all the time."

"You lost a man today, didn't you?" Danni asked.

Gabriel's jaw tensed, his eyes fixed on something over Danni's head.

"We did."

Chloe could see how tense he was, and she understood now. He hadn't told her they were worried about German soldiers getting so close, but she'd felt the anxiety between the men earlier in the morning. And now she wasn't sure whether to feel sad about losing a man or just grateful that it hadn't been Gabriel shot down. What on earth would she have done without him? She swallowed hard. She hadn't even thought about that possibility before, not really.

"I photographed him, and the two dead Germans," Danni said. "It's why we stopped there."

Gabriel nodded and gestured toward the house, and Chloe turned to the other woman, who'd stayed silent throughout the exchange.

"This is Ella," Danni said. "She knew Andy, too."

"Hello, Ella," Chloe said, holding out a hand even though it was shaking. "It's so nice to meet both of you."

With Danni hobbling between them, they walked through the door Gabriel was holding, and for the first time in months, Chloe suddenly didn't feel so alone. In shock, yes. Devastated by the news she'd just received. But surprisingly, *suddenly*, not alone.

———— ⌒◯⌒ ————

"Can I make you both a coffee?" Chloe asked, hovering between Danni and Ella in the kitchen.

Gabriel had left the house immediately, and she hadn't asked where he was going or when he might be back.

"Chloe, why don't you sit," Ella said, her smile warm as she stood and gestured toward the chair. Chloe saw her gaze drop, just for a second, before lifting again. "This is a lot to handle, especially in your, ah, *condition*."

Chloe instinctively touched her stomach, smiling shyly at Ella. She hadn't been around other women for months now, and she doubted most of the men living in the house would have even noticed. But Ella had guessed straightaway, obviously seeing the gentle curve of her otherwise slender frame. Even Gabriel hadn't realized until she'd told him, although it wasn't like he'd taken much notice of her body since they'd arrived at the chateau.

"I, well, I'm fine," Chloe stammered. "Honestly, can't I make you something?"

"You're *pregnant*," Danni said, suddenly standing and then swearing when she put weight on her foot. "I . . . I . . ."

"Danni, why don't you rest for a bit," Ella said, shooting Chloe a quick look that she didn't know how to decipher.

"I'm fine, Ella, I'm fine, I just . . ."

"You just need a minute, I think," Ella said, going to help Danni. "Is it okay if I take her through here?" She looked over at Chloe.

"Yes, it's fine, of course," Chloe said. "I'll get the coffee on."

She turned to boil the water. Had she done something or said something to upset Danni? She stared into the water, waiting for it to bubble, as the most overwhelming feeling hit her.

Andy is gone. Her brother wasn't going to be there in London waiting for her when Gabriel sent her home; he wasn't going to be there to pick up the pieces and care for her; he wasn't going to be able to make everything right as he always had in the past. It made her feel selfish for expecting so much from him before.

She leaned forward, elbows on the kitchen bench as her breath shuddered out of her in a heart-wrenching sob.

"Chloe?" Ella put a hand on her shoulder. "It's a huge shock, what you found out today. I'm so sorry."

"I can't believe he's gone," Chloe whispered. "It just hit me that I'll never actually see him again."

"And seeing you hit Danni pretty hard, too," Ella said, her voice low.

"So it wasn't something I said?" Chloe asked, turning back and wiping at her cheeks.

Ella's face was kind. "Of course it wasn't something you said. It's just that, after Andy died, Danni seemed to cope with it by focusing on finding you. She was determined to fulfill her promise to him, and suddenly being here with you, well, I think it's all come crashing down on her." Ella sighed. "I think she's finally starting to grieve instead of blocking it out."

Chloe let out a trembling breath as she turned back to the bubbling water. "I'll get us that coffee," she said.

"No, you'll sit down, and *I'll* get us that coffee." Ella steered her back toward the table, pushed her down into one of the seats, and took over making their hot drinks.

"So Danni and Andy, they were very close. Were they—"

"No," Ella said, laughing. "They were more like brother and sister, or at least that's how I saw them." Ella spun around then, her eyes wide. "Sorry, you being his sister and all, that didn't come out right."

Chloe smiled sadly. "It's fine. It's nice to hear about them. I'm glad she was there when . . . it happened."

"They were so dynamic together, which I suppose came from working together for so long. And to be honest, I wonder if that's also what's making this so hard for her, seeing how similar you look to Andy in real life, far more so than from the picture he had of you. It must have hit her hard seeing that resemblance."

Chloe nodded, deciding to change the subject away from Andy, for fear of breaking down in tears. "So, are you a photographer as well?"

Ella shook her head. "No, I'm a journalist. It's how I met Danni, and your brother, although I'm sad to say I didn't know him for long."

"You met him here?" Chloe asked as Ella passed her a cup.

"Well, I first met him in London, briefly, and then on the ship over here I actually got to know him better," Ella said, sitting at the table across from her. "He was a wonderful, kind man. It was him who invited me along, actually. But since the landings, it's just been me and Danni, and without Andy, Danni's had no one to keep her in check. I've done my best, but I don't think I'll ever be as good at reining her in as he was."

Chloe raised an eyebrow. "Does that have something to do with how she ended up thrown over Gabriel's shoulder?"

"Let's just say that Danni likes to photograph everything, to show the true picture of war, and she's the kind of person who takes risks when she needs to. And she's also the type who fulfills a promise." Ella paused. "She wasn't going to let anyone stop her from finding you, which is how we ended up out here alone."

Gabriel came into the room then, and Chloe realized she was nervous.

"Is everything alright here?" he asked.

Chloe quickly stood to make him a coffee.

"I'll, ah, give you two a moment and go and check on Danni," Ella murmured, keeping her head down as she rose and left the kitchen.

Chloe's hands trembled as she started to heat the water again, suddenly overcome with emotion with Gabriel so close.

"Chloe, I can make it," he said. She heard the shuffle of his boots behind her, felt the heat of his body drawing near.

"It's fine, you've had a long day and—"

"Come here." It was a command more than a suggestion, and as his arms circled around her, it didn't take her a second to spin around and cling to him. "I'm so sorry, Chloe. I know how close you were to him."

She cried and hung on to Gabriel, finally finding the comfort in his arms she'd been craving all this time.

"I just can't believe that I'll never see him again," she said, muffled against his chest. "It doesn't seem real that he's gone, even though I know he is."

Gabriel stroked her hair, his lips against the top of her head as they stood for one long, touching moment together, alone in the kitchen. Then the muffled noises of men arriving back at the house and boots being kicked off reached them.

He cleared his throat and stepped away, his fingers brushing briefly down her arm. "They can't stay here," he said. "We'll give Danni a day or two to recover, and then they need to go. It's not safe to have them with us, in case someone is looking for them, so we're going to have to keep an even closer guard on the house while they're here."

She nodded, sniffing as she stared back at him. "Of course. I'm sure they'll understand."

She saw his gaze drop to her stomach, a look crossing his face that she hoped might be something close to love, and then he was gone, as if their moment wrapped in one another's arms had never happened.

CHAPTER TWENTY-ONE

DANNI

Danni had thought that the day Andy had died was the hardest of her life, but she was starting to think that had nothing on being the one to break the news to Chloe, or being witness to the aftermath of it. That night, she'd been lying awake, remembering Andy's face and imagining the look on it if she were able to tell him that she'd found his sister. It was the one thing keeping her going, stopping her from crumbling to the floor, just knowing how relieved he'd be that Chloe was safe. But then she'd think about the way Chloe's face had fallen as she'd delivered the news, and it broke her all over again.

And she was getting the distinct feeling that Gabriel wasn't as invested in Chloe as Chloe was in him. There was something about the way Chloe looked at him, full of such longing and hope, whereas Gabriel was clearly much more preoccupied with what he was doing for the cause than with his personal relationship. It was an attitude she could understand, because it was how she'd always felt about her work, about how important it was for her to keep photographing the war no matter what she had to sacrifice. She'd seen it in his eyes when she'd stopped to photograph him before dusk, and she'd taken some great shots that she knew would be of interest to many editors back in London—of Gabriel standing outside with the men, and of them leaving with their rifles slung over their backs, looking more like a group off for a spot of hunting than potential combat fighting. It was such a stark difference to the uniformed men fighting on either side, and she wanted to show people back home what the Resistance looked like. It had certainly been an unexpected bonus of finding Chloe.

She sighed as she considered Chloe again. Danni's goal hadn't extended much further than finding her and making sure she was safe; but she was overwhelmingly starting to realize that her responsibility where Chloe was concerned might be growing, not ending.

"Penny for your thoughts?" Ella said, coming into the kitchen.

Danni looked up. "I'd prefer to talk about anything other than my thoughts," she replied.

"How about we test that foot of yours out then?" Ella suggested. "At least that'll give us something to do."

Danni's ankle now sported a thick bandage that Chloe had applied the night before, although she hadn't the heart to tell her that it hadn't helped her pain at all. She couldn't see the point in making a fuss when there was nothing anyone could do to help her, and she was loath to hurt Chloe's feelings.

"It's not great, to be honest," she confided. "But I'm keen to see how far I can get."

"I have a feeling we're going to have to move on soon," Ella said. "I can see the way Gabriel keeps looking at us."

Danni nodded. "I know exactly what you mean. I'm not sure he's exactly happy to have us here."

She stood, using the table to brace herself, as Ella came around and took her other arm. Pain shot straight through her ankle, but she pushed past it, teeth clenched together as she ambled along.

"How does it feel?"

"Like hell," Danni groaned. "But the more I move, the easier it becomes, sort of."

They went outside to the back of the chateau, and the sun felt good on her skin as she shuffled along, realizing she could move well enough if she turned her foot out.

"What do you make of Chloe?" Ella asked. "She wasn't as confident as I expected her to be, given her modeling days, and she seems so young somehow."

Danni nodded. "I agree. I wonder if all of this has knocked the stuffing out of her, even before the awful news about her brother," she said. "Andy always said she was so vivacious and full of life, but I have a feeling things aren't maybe as she expected with Gabriel."

"What are we going to do?" Ella asked. "Can we really just leave her here with a baby on the way? I mean, she's living in a house full of transient Resistance fighters! It's hardly suitable to raise a child here."

"I know," Danni said. "And even thinking of her giving birth here, with no access to a medical facility or anyone to help her through the ordeal . . ." The thought of Chloe doing something so traumatic alone sent a shudder through Danni's body. "There's no way I can turn my back and leave her, not now."

Ella cleared her throat, and Danni glanced over her shoulder to see Chloe approaching. She was grateful she hadn't come close enough to hear their exchange.

"I thought you girls had left," Chloe said, looking worried as she hurried across the grass toward them. "I came downstairs and—"

"I wouldn't leave you," Danni said, hoping Chloe could hear how much she meant it. "And look at me! It's not like I can go anywhere in a hurry."

Chloe's smile was sweet and almost a little shy as she came to stand beside them.

"I haven't had female company in a long time," she said. "The thought of not having you both here is awful, to be honest."

"Would you come with us?" Ella asked. "When we leave, I mean. If you don't want to stay here, that is."

Danni traded glances with Ella, as Chloe looked back at the house, clearly anxious.

"I . . . well, it's complicated," Chloe said, touching her stomach. "Gabriel would prefer I wasn't here, but he's the father of my child. I don't want to stay, but I don't want to leave, either. And with Andy gone, I just . . ." Chloe looked close to tears.

"I know it's a hard decision to make, just know that we're here for you," Ella said quickly, and Danni was pleased it was her having the conversation with Chloe. She was all choked up just thinking about Chloe not having her brother and potentially having to leave the man she loved behind, too. She seemed painfully naïve.

"It might be sooner than you were planning," Chloe said. "Gabriel needs you both gone by tomorrow, if Danni's up to it."

Danni's eyebrows shot up. "He does?"

"Something about it being too dangerous for you to stay here," Chloe said. "He doesn't tell me a lot about the work he does, but he sounded worried. He might talk to you when he gets back."

"Did he say where they were going today?" Danni asked.

Chloe shook her head. "All he told me was that he would be gone until dusk, and that he'd find out what was wrong with your jeep while he was gone."

"I see." Danni frowned at Ella, wondering what she was thinking about the situation they'd found themselves in.

"I suppose we just sit and wait then," Ella said. "There's no harm in making the most of being together while we can, don't you think?"

Danni forced a smile and nodded, wishing she could have discussed the situation directly with Gabriel, and cursing her injury. But from the look on Chloe's face she was as nervous as could be, so Danni needed to pretend she was happy to wait it out.

"Danni," Ella said, taking her arm as they started to walk back toward the house, "why don't you tell Chloe about some of the adventures you had with Andy? I for one want to hear more about how you parachuted into Sicily."

Danni saw the almost childlike expression of anticipation on Chloe's face, and knew that Ella was right. As painful as it might be, telling stories about Andy was probably the easiest way to pass the time with Chloe, even if it was going to be hard for her.

"Let's sit here, in the sun," Danni suggested, desperate to take the weight off her foot and rest.

"I'll make us coffee," Chloe suggested, running ahead to the house. "Don't start talking without me!"

"She's clearly desperate to be of use," said Ella. "Poor thing."

Danni couldn't reply as bolts of pain were shooting through her foot, and it took all her willpower not to cry out. Ella reached out to her, and Danni let her help her down to the grass, letting out a sigh as she reclined, shutting her eyes for a moment as she tilted her face up to the sky.

"You're in a lot of pain, aren't you?" Ella asked.

"It hurts like a—" Danni laughed. "You wouldn't like me to say the words."

They sat for a few minutes in silence, before Ella spoke again.

"If Gabriel manages to fix the jeep, do you think we should offer to take Chloe with us?" she asked. "Or is that just asking for trouble? I have a feeling she'd be safer if she came with us."

"I have a feeling he's going to ask us," Danni said in a low voice. "But yes, we need to offer. It's not safe for her to be here, anyone can see that. I dread to think what would happen if she's still here to give birth, and beyond."

Ella's smile was so kind as they sat together, and Danni used her good foot to nudge against one of Ella's.

"You never did tell me about Michael," she said. "Other than to tell me how sharp his tongue was. Was he not pleased to see you?"

Ella looked away, and Danni decided not to push her on the subject if she didn't want to talk. "You could say that," Ella said.

"He's a stubborn mule, that one," Danni said. "Give him some time, let him lick his wounds a bit."

Ella smiled sadly. "You know, I want to hate him, but I can't. There's something about that man that gets me all twisted in knots. I just have to hope you're right, and he does come around. I'd hate to think I was never going to see him again."

Danni returned her smile, seeing how Ella was trying hard to be brave. "You know, I never did apologize for dragging you into this mess," Danni said. "I don't find it easy to say sorry, but I am sorry, Ella. I need you to know that."

Ella nudged her foot straight back. "I'm a big girl, Danni, and I chose to come with you that day. But you definitely should have told me the jeep was a dud."

They both laughed, despite it all, and Danni leaned into Ella, shoulder to shoulder.

"You've turned into one hell of a friend, Ella," she said.

"Ditto," Ella replied as Chloe came back out, carrying a tray full of steaming mugs of coffee. "I wouldn't want to be doing this with anyone else."

Danni grinned. "Me neither."

CHAPTER TWENTY-TWO

CHLOE

"Chloe, you know you have to go with them, don't you? This is our best chance to get you out of France."

Gabriel's question shouldn't have come as such a surprise, especially as Ella had suggested it earlier that day, but it still caught Chloe off guard.

She braved a quick glance at Gabriel and saw the way he was watching her. Concern was etched on his face, but there was also a coldness there that made her so sad.

"I thought you might have changed your mind," she said honestly.

"Chloe, why would I have changed my mind?" he asked, and for the first time she saw the anger inside him, a burning anger that seemed to be for her and her alone.

"Because I'm having your baby!" she cried. "Because you might have finally realized how much I need you. How much *we* need you. Because you've seen how much I'm hurting, and that I don't have *anyone* to go home to now."

As her emotions started to paralyze her, he seemed to become calmer, more stern even, walking toward her and standing close, without touching her.

"Chloe, it's as if you're still a child," he whispered. "You don't seem to understand the horrors of war, even now. Even after all that has happened, you're still holding on to a fantasy of what the world looks like." He sighed. "Of what *we* look like. And I hate that you don't have your brother to care for you, but it doesn't change anything. You still need to go, and I think, deep down, you know that."

She blinked, staring back at him, knowing that he was right. She'd accepted her fate last time they'd spoken about it—but now, without Andy waiting for her, it seemed like the cruelest of punishments.

"I just wish things could be different," she said, her voice wobbling. "I wish Andy was waiting at home for me, to look after me and the baby. Or that something would change so we could stay with you."

"Chloe, right now we need to focus on our country, on saving everyone from an evil that's taking over the world. It's about so much more than just us. And I'm trying to do what's right, for you too." His voice lowered. "Please don't think I'm not trying to do right by you and the baby, Chloe."

She nodded, glancing up as Danni limped into the room. She must have heard Gabriel's raised voice.

"Is everything alright in here?" Danni asked, her expression one of concern.

Gabriel took a moment, before giving Chloe a long, sad look.

"I'm sorry," he said, keeping his back to Danni as if she weren't even in the room, as if she hadn't just asked him a question. "I'm so sorry, Chloe, but there's no other way."

"I understand." And she did. As much as she was fighting it, she did understand. She had just thought that when it came to the final decision, he might have tried to come with her, to look after her, instead of making her go without him. But she had Danni and Ella now, and they couldn't have been kinder to her, so she had to trust in their friendship and believe that everything would work out for the best.

"And Chloe," Gabriel said, brushing his fingers against hers for just a moment. "I fell just as hard for you in Paris as you did for me. I want you to know that. Unfortunately, so much has changed since then."

His words meant everything to her, but the touch was as fleeting as the glance he gave her, and she had the strangest feeling that it might be the last time she'd ever touch him.

Danni had been watching her closely, but as Gabriel turned, Danni's focus shifted to him.

"Danni, you had a leak in the fuel tank, but it's been repaired so it should run just fine now. If I get you fuel for the jeep, and send some men to cover you on your walk back there, will you take Chloe with you tomorrow?" Gabriel asked. "The latest reports I've had are that the route should be clear, for now at least, and I think it's the safest way for you to get back to your camp."

Chloe wanted to scream at him, to run up behind him and beg on her knees not to send her away. But instead she stood, watching, listening, as close to defeat as she'd ever come.

"Of course," Danni replied. "I would give my life for hers, Gabriel. You can trust me to get her back to camp, and if you hadn't asked, I would have offered before we set off anyway."

"Good," he said. "We leave in the morning then, and I'll have my best snipers with me to keep eyes on you."

Chloe took a few steps closer, wishing Gabriel spoke to her as his equal as he did to Danni. But then, Danni was something else. She was strong and capable, so at ease with who she was and why she was there. Chloe could see why Andy had been so fond of her, and she found strength in Danni. She knew that if anyone could take care of her, Danni could.

"The situation is changing by the hour here," Gabriel said, flicking a quick glance back at her, even though his body was angled toward Danni. "The Allies are clearly continuing to advance well, which means they're flushing out pockets of German soldiers. It's making it a very dangerous region to be in, but there's no safer way for you to travel, and it's sure as hell not safe for you to stay."

"You think we're about to be in the thick of it?" Danni asked. "Is that why you want us gone so quickly?"

Gabriel frowned. "That's exactly what I think. It's more volatile here right now than it's ever been, and I want Chloe gone and safely back at your base by nightfall tomorrow."

"I understand," Danni replied.

After he left, Danni came closer to Chloe, and she saw the change in her face, the way it softened now that Gabriel had gone.

"You okay?" she asked.

Chloe shook her head. Danni took her in her arms, holding her tight.

"He wants me gone," she cried.

"No, Chloe, he wants you *safe*," Danni whispered. "And there's a big difference between those two words."

"You don't understand, he never wanted me," she confessed, shaking. "I came all this way, thinking he was in love with me, thinking he'd be over the moon to see me, and instead I was just a fling that he'd long since forgotten about."

Danni shushed her like a mother comforting a child, rocking her until her tears started to quiet.

"If you were just a fling, he'd have abandoned you long before now," Danni said, stroking her hair from her face. "Most men would have done that, but he hasn't. So that means something, doesn't it? He's kept you here with him even though he probably shouldn't have, and the times we're living in aren't normal, Chloe. Everything has changed."

Chloe's breath shuddered out of her. She hadn't thought about it that way before. "I suppose so."

"After the war, you can find him, Chloe," Danni said. "But he needs to know you're safe so he can focus on his work here, and that's something I can do, to help both of you. I promised Andy that I'd find you, and I couldn't live with myself if I didn't do everything in my power to help you out of this situation."

"You really think I can find him after the war?" Chloe asked, stroking her stomach.

"Of course I do," Danni replied. "Now, tell me, how many months along are you?"

Chloe smiled as she thought about the baby growing inside of her. "I'm not exactly sure; I've lost track of the days since I arrived in Paris . . ."

Danni waited as Chloe tried to work it out.

"I think perhaps five months?" Chloe said.

Danni nodded. "Well, you'll have plenty of time to settle in back home in London before the baby arrives, won't you?"

Chloe nodded. She didn't even want to think about going back to their house alone, of raising a baby without Gabriel or her brother in her life.

"I'm going to be there for you, Chloe. You hear me?" Danni reassured her. "Anything you need, you only ever have to ask."

"Thank you, Danni," she whispered, as Danni slung an arm around her shoulders.

She might be losing Gabriel, but she'd found a friend in Danni, and in Ella, and if nothing else, at least she had them. She shut her eyes for a beat, silently thanking Andy in her mind. She was certain, without a shadow of a doubt, that her brother had somehow sent the two women to her.

"You heard Gabriel before," Danni said. "We're leaving in the morning. So you need to get a good sleep, and at sunrise we'll head off for the jeep and hope to hell we can start it."

"And if we can't?" she asked.

"Then we walk, I suppose."

Chloe gulped, staring up at Danni, and then slowly looking out the window at the view she'd been staring at for weeks now. It was time to say goodbye to it all, and even though she'd hated every second of living at the chateau, the idea of leaving still hurt.

"You know, what Gabriel and the others are doing, what the entire Resistance network is doing, it's been instrumental in turning the tides of this war," Danni said. "If nothing else, you can hold your head high and know that the father of your child made a real difference. He's a brave man."

Chloe nodded, letting Danni's words wash over her.

"And he's right, he can't do this with you here," she said softly. "It's the same as the work I do. We need to focus exclusively on what's in front of us. It's too hard for him to be torn between you and what needs to be done."

"You know, I used to work, too," Chloe said.

Danni sat on a chair and Chloe walked to the window, touching her forehead to the glass.

"Andy said you were a very well-known model. He was very proud of what you'd achieved."

Chloe smiled. "I loved every second of my modeling days. It's how I met Gabriel, actually."

Chloe turned at Danni's laugh. "I know that, too. Andy told me all about it, and the look on his face when he showed me your letter." Danni shook her head. "He was furious!"

Chloe looked out the window again. "I knew how much it would hurt him, but I was so determined to leave and come here. I was a fool, but at the time it didn't seem so stupid."

"He was very proud of you," Danni said. "And he loved you dearly. He wouldn't want you to torture yourself about what you did. Perhaps you might go back to your work again one day?"

Now it was Chloe laughing. "Not a chance. I'll be far too old by the time the war is over, and I just . . ." She sighed. "I just can't see it anymore."

"Something else then?" Danni said. "You don't have to stop dreaming just because—"

"I want to be an editor, actually," Chloe said, surprised that she'd confessed it to Danni. "I mean, I *used* to want to be an editor. I loved modeling, but there was something about opening a magazine and seeing all those images that made me wish I was the one choosing them. I'd wanted to tell Andy for so long, but I suppose I wasn't sure if I was capable of doing something like that." She sighed again. "It was one of the reasons I felt such a connection to Gabriel back then, other than how dashingly handsome and charming he was. I felt like he could see me in a way that no one else had before, and I know that sounds stupid but . . ."

Danni was silent and Chloe's face flooded with heat.

"That was silly, I shouldn't have even said anything," she mumbled.

Danni rose and came up beside her, their shoulders brushing as she stared out the window, too. "There's nothing silly about it," she said. "In fact, it's admirable. Andy would have been so proud of you, and I know for a fact that he would have moved heaven and earth to help you achieve your dreams."

"You really think so?" Chloe whispered, looking into Danni's dark brown eyes; eyes that were swimming with tears.

"I know so," she whispered back. "Now, let's get some sleep. Tomorrow's going to be a long day."

CHAPTER TWENTY-THREE

DANNI

It felt like weeks, not days, since Danni had taken the jeep, and she half expected the vehicle to be gone as they made the long journey on foot back to where they'd abandoned it. But Gabriel had assured them it was still there, he'd checked it himself, and she knew that when they made their way into the next clearing, they'd almost be there.

Thinking about Gabriel sent a shiver of goosebumps down her spine. Seeing the way Chloe had looked at him, like a little girl desperate to be told that she didn't have to go, and the way he'd stoically kissed her forehead and nodded that it was time to leave, had been hard to watch. And she knew that Andy's worries about his sister hadn't been unfounded. Chloe was beautiful and engaging, but she'd also been incredibly naïve coming to France, even if her mode of getting there had shown initiative.

Danni almost screamed with relief when she realized how close they were, her legs ready to give way. If the jeep were gone, she doubted she would be capable of another step forward past that point. Now she just had to hope and pray that it would start, otherwise it was going to be a very long, and potentially dangerous, walk home. Not to mention their feet would be covered in fresh blisters—on top of the blisters that had never had time to heal from the moment they'd arrived in France—and she could already imagine how painful it would be to remove her boots and socks when they finally reached camp. Gabriel had insisted there had been a leak in the fuel tank and that was the cause of the engine not turning over, but she wouldn't believe it until she tried it herself. She'd checked the fuel gauge the day they'd left and it had shown they had half a tank, so it must have been faulty, which was why she was feeling so uneasy about it all.

What the hell had she been thinking, stealing a jeep and deciding to go off course during a bloody and very real war? It was a miracle they were even alive, let alone attempting to make it back to where they'd come from. But if she hadn't come, she couldn't have saved Chloe, and that's what she had to hold on to, and when she glanced back at her, she knew it had been worth it.

"I'll get her out of here, Andy," she whispered to herself. "Don't you worry."

"What do you think will happen to us?" Ella's question pulled Danni from her own thoughts, and for that she was grateful. "When we get back, I mean?"

"I think there are a few options, and two of them are grim at best," Danni replied, running her fingers down her thick braid and tugging it over her shoulder as she tried *not* to think about rogue German snipers in the woods. She missed her hat; she usually always had it with her, but she'd managed to lose it back at the jeep when they'd first encountered Gabriel. Her only token that hadn't been lost or damaged was her red lipstick, tucked safely in her brassiere throughout it all.

"Can we stop a second?" Chloe asked. "I feel like I'm about to collapse, my head is starting to spin."

While Ella fumbled for water for Chloe, and they all paused for a moment, Danni took a moment to lean against a tree and rest her ankle, setting down the fuel container they'd been taking turns to carry. Panting, and with tendrils of hair plastered to her forehead, she took her lipstick out and ran it over her lips, used to applying it without a mirror. It made her lips feel moist instead of dry and cracked, and it also made her feel like herself; her lipstick reminded her of who she was, where she came from, and the fact that she was still a woman even though she was working in a man's world. Her legs might have been shaking, but miraculously her hands weren't.

"So, tell me these options," Ella said as they both slid down and sat in the shade of the tree. The sun was beating down and the breeze wasn't enough to cool them after their long walk. Not to mention the nerves that had pulsed through Danni every step of the way and made her sweat much more than usual, even though she knew Gabriel and some of his men were nearby.

She took a piece of bread that Ella passed her, taking a grateful bite and chewing it before answering. She'd barely eaten since the night before, and she was as thirsty as could be, too.

"I think the worst-case scenario is we don't make it back," she said, nibbling at the chunk of bread to try to make it last longer. "We could be taken out by snipers or a Nazi ambush, the jeep could blow out a tire or hit a mine—"

"How about the other options?" Ella interrupted, raising her eyebrows and nodding her head toward Chloe. "The less morbid ones, perhaps?"

Danni wondered whether she should just admit that none of the options were good, but Ella's desperate expression stopped her, and she realized how sensitive Chloe might be to what she was saying. Ella was used to dealing with these types of situations; Chloe wasn't.

"There's no reason we can't make it back," Chloe interrupted between her own mouthfuls. "Gabriel's covering us, so what could really go wrong?"

Danni grimaced, wishing she were as naïve and positive about the outcome. "Sure, of course, we'll be fine," she said, not even managing to convince herself, let alone Chloe. "Anyway, let's talk about something more upbeat, shall we?"

"If you could go home for just a day, what would you do?" Ella asked.

Danni changed position in an attempt to relieve the ache in her leg.

"I would just want to sit on our veranda with my daddy, sipping iced tea and talking, while my mom cooked something delicious," Danni replied, hating how it took the breath from her just answering one question. "I can almost smell her cooking now."

"I'd want the same," Ella said. "Just to be at home, talking and eating with my family." She laughed. "It's funny, isn't it, how desperate you can be to leave home and spread your wings, and then once you're gone, all you can think about is how nice it would be to go back. Even if just for a day." She glanced at Chloe. "What about you?"

"I'd do anything for one day at home with my brother," Chloe whispered. "Even a few hours would be worth it."

Danni's skin turned ice-cold, the memories hitting her like a powerful blast as Chloe spoke about her brother.

"You okay, Danni?" Ella asked, reaching out to her.

"Sorry, Danni, I didn't mean to . . ." Chloe's voice trailed off.

Danni took a deep breath, pushing the memories away as she stood. She was about to reassure Chloe, when a sudden noise made her falter.

"Ella, Chloe," she whispered. "I think we've been followed."

Crack.

Danni's eyes widened in the instant that everything changed. She turned, almost in slow motion, and looked directly into the eyes of a German soldier standing near a tree, his gun raised and aimed straight at her, the curl of his lips telling her that he had no qualms about shooting a woman, before he squeezed the trigger.

"Danni!"

Chloe's scream was so sharp it was like another gunshot erupting beside her. Danni felt her foot slip from under her as her body quivered like an arrow and then shuddered to the ground, doubling over, crumpling in a heap as an intense warmth spread through her before turning into a burning-hot, searing pain.

"*Danni!*" She heard Chloe scream again, or perhaps it was Ella, only this time she seemed so much farther away.

And as her eyes started to slide shut, she saw him lift his pistol again and everything went black.

CHAPTER TWENTY-FOUR

ELLA

"*Danni!*" Ella screamed, the sound of the blast still ringing in her ears as she watched her friend collapse, hitting the ground as blood seeped through her shirt.

And then she saw him. She saw the crude smile, the way his eyes lit up as he trained his gaze on Ella now and raised his pistol again, his stance easy as he slowly pointed it at her.

Ella looked down at Danni, the front of her shirt as red as her lipstick, eyes shut, her body no longer moving, then lifted her head and defiantly stared at the Nazi who was about to fire.

I'm going to die.

She tried to stay strong, to not slip into morbid thoughts, but it was impossible not to imagine the worst.

Boom.

The blast echoed out, reverberating around her, sucking the air from her lungs, louder than the crack of a pistol.

Boom.

The blast sounded out again, and as she slowly opened her eyes and glanced down, she realized it wasn't her. She hadn't been shot.

Ella cried as she looked up, the horror of thinking she was about to die, that the gunshot was going to steal her life, sending her body into shock.

As her eyes focused, as she managed to grasp what was going on, she saw Gabriel standing there, reloading his rifle, the dead German at his feet, and Ella realized the woods had come to life around them.

"What's happening?" she heard Chloe scream.

"You need to get out of here, I don't know how many there are!" Gabriel yelled back. "We must have come across a group of them returning from fighting the Allied forces!" More men appeared, the same men who'd been at the house, and Ella had the terrifying feeling that they'd somehow ended up in the middle of an ambush.

"Danni," Ella cried, hands hovering above Danni's shoulders as she listened to the exchange between Gabriel and Chloe. What could she do? There was so much blood, it was soaking through her clothes now, and Ella pulled at her shirt, ripping it off as buttons went flying. She yanked at Danni's sleeves, trying to move her, her hands wet with blood as she attempted to maneuver her unresponsive friend.

"Danni," she begged. "Please wake up. I can't do this without you!"

Danni was limp in her arms, and Ella lowered her back down again as she tied the shirt tightly around her midsection, trying to stop the bleeding from her stomach and hoping she was doing the right thing. What were you supposed to do for a gunshot wound? Was she supposed to stop the bleeding or try to get the bullet out? Her hands hovered, desperate to do the right thing and wishing she knew what that was. Danni's leg was bleeding too, but not as badly as her abdomen.

"Help!" Ella cried out, her bloodstained hands shaking violently as they gripped Danni's shoulders. "Chloe! Help me!"

Danni made a noise then, a gurgle that sounded like she was choking, and Ella dropped over her.

"Danni!" She shook her shoulders, her tears falling over Danni's face. "You're not leaving me, Danni. Stay with me!"

Danni opened her eyes then, but Ella knew that it wasn't looking good, that the chances of them making it back to camp were almost non-existent now.

"Start moving!" Gabriel screamed at them. "You've got to get her out of here. I'll be right behind you, but you have to move!"

CHAPTER TWENTY-FIVE

CHLOE

Chloe's breath felt like it was being ripped in and out of her, catching in her throat before finally making its way to her lungs. She kept her arm tightly wound around Danni as they dragged her in the direction of the jeep, careful with every step of their boots as they moved through the wooded area.

"I don't think she's going to make it," Ella whispered.

"She's going to make it," Chloe whispered back determinedly.

Ella made a noise that sounded like a sob, and Chloe steeled herself against it, refusing to think that they couldn't save Danni. If there was one thing she could do for Andy, to repay him for caring for her for so many years, it was to save his friend, and nothing was going to stop her. Not even a baby inside her who seemed to be making it impossible for her to breathe deeply and walk at the same time.

"Danni," Chloe said. "Danni, can you hear me?"

Danni made a small moan, and it gave Chloe the power to keep going, to push through the cramping pain in her stomach and force her feet to move, step after step after step.

"Danni, my brother was so careful who he let close to him, because after our parents died, it was just me and him," Chloe said, her breathing raspy now as she tried to add talking to her existing exertions. "So the fact that you two worked side by side for so long tells me that you were one of the very few people he trusted in this world."

Danni made a faint noise again, and Chloe knew she needed to keep talking. It might be the one way to keep Danni semiconscious.

"He was a brother like no other, and it wasn't until I was here, alone and feeling lost, that I realized just how amazing he was," she said, ignoring the tears that had started to stream down her cheeks. "He always protected me, he did everything for me, and I have no idea how I'm going to survive without him."

"You're already surviving," Ella said. "As far as I can tell, you're one of the bravest, strongest women I've ever met."

Chloe let Ella's words wash over her. All this time, all these months, she'd felt so powerless, but hearing Ella say that filled her with strength. She supposed she had been brave today, but it had been a long time coming after existing in Gabriel's shadow.

"How much longer?" Ella gasped.

"Not far," Chloe said, seeing Gabriel in her peripheral vision. "It's just up there, through that cluster of trees." She wished he was beside her, close enough to touch, but she knew that he was staying farther away to protect them. What if he hadn't been there before? She gulped. They might all have been shot.

"Died," Danni whispered.

They stopped walking for a moment, and Chloe leaned into Danni. "What did you say?"

"*Died*," she gurgled again. "Tell how . . . he died."

Chloe glanced at Ella, who gave her a sad look as they resumed walking, both groaning as they hefted Danni.

"She wants me to tell you how he died," Ella murmured. "I didn't want to tell you, I wanted it to come from Danni, but I know she's struggled with how to say the words . . ." Ella's voice drifted away for a moment.

"Tell me." Chloe's voice was hoarse now, and her throat dry, desperate for water. Her whole body bristled with adrenalin, waiting for the woods to come alive with soldiers.

"We were coming into shore," Ella said. "Andy had stowed away with Danni to make sure she could get to Normandy, since women weren't supposed to come, and after helping all morning on the hospital ship, we came ashore. I could hear him keeping Danni calm, telling her they were going to be fine, and his calmness kind of rubbed off on me too, took my nerves away. Only Andy didn't make it out of the water that day."

"My fault," Danni gasped. "Andy," she whispered. "My fault."

Chloe cried then, holding Danni's hand tight. "It was not your fault, Danni," she told her. "You hear me? It was *not* your fault, and even if it was, then I forgive you. I promise you, I forgive you."

Ella was lugging the fuel container in her other hand, and Chloe couldn't imagine how hard it must have been for her—she felt like she couldn't take another step herself and she was only supporting Danni.

"There it is," Ella announced. "It's not far now."

"I can't keep going," Chloe gasped. "I'm going to sit down over there with her, and you come back for us when the car's running. I just can't hold her any longer." Her arms were burning from the exertion and she dragged Danni to the closest tree to lean against in the shade.

"Please God, let it start," Ella muttered, as she left them and ran ahead toward the jeep.

Chloe looked down and saw that Danni had already lost consciousness again. This was not looking good.

Ella was standing by the jeep now, filling it up with fuel, and Chloe wished she weren't so far away so she could still talk to her—she could hardly risk shouting and giving their position away. But she knew there was no way she could manage to lift Danni on her own, let alone take another step while propping up her weight.

The minutes dragged on as she watched Ella get into the jeep. Nothing was happening. *Shouldn't she be driving back by now?*

"Shit," Ella screamed, audible even from where Chloe was sitting. "Shit, shit, shit!"

Chloe listened as Ella howled with frustration, then suddenly she heard the jeep's engine start. Before promptly dying again.

She shut her eyes, so exhausted, wondering how they would ever get back to the American base, when she heard the ignition start up again. At the same time as a single shot rang out, echoing through the forest.

"What was that?" Ella called out, running back toward her now. The terror of where they were and what was happening was like an electric current in the air.

"Stay down," Chloe whispered.

Another shot rang out, then another.

"Quickly, we need to get her in the jeep!" Ella cried.

And then a voice cut through the air, a voice that Chloe knew intimately, and one she'd never forget for as long as she lived, it was full of such pain.

"Run, Chloe!" Gabriel yelled. "Run, my love, and don't look back!"

Chloe cast a quick glance at Ella, who looked like she was a fish floundering out of water, unsure of what to do, before they quickly bent and tried to scoop Danni up between them. Chloe didn't even know if the jeep would start again, but they had to at least try to get to it.

Gunfire erupted then, before they'd even taken a step, an endless stream of shots that sent a wave of terror through her.

We're not going to make it.

Time stopped. Nothing moved. And then the man she loved so much she'd left everything behind for him, came into view again. All she could see was Gabriel's pain as he opened his mouth, running fast behind them.

"Go!" he screamed. "You have to run!"

As he turned away from her, as she looked at his strong silhouette, she saw the German soldier stop, saw him position himself, saw the soldier's gun slowly lift as he prepared to take aim.

Her scream cut through the air as Gabriel fired, at the same time as the soldier did.

"Go!" he yelled again, and this time she didn't hesitate, running fast with Ella as they fought to carry Danni between them. But the pain in Chloe's stomach was almost crippling, a searing-hot burn that ran along her hard, contracted skin and curled around her back, only there was no time to stop.

Chloe's feet wouldn't move as she turned to glance back at Gabriel, tripping over herself, a silent scream sounding out in her head as she saw Gabriel ricochet from a bullet and then drop to his knees. Every bone in her body wanted to launch back in the opposite direction and fight for him, but she couldn't. She had no weapon, no means to protect herself, and she would be signing her own death warrant if she went anywhere near him. Danni slipped to the ground beneath them as Chloe suddenly stumbled.

Chloe's skin was slick with sweat as she supported Danni under one shoulder, Ella doing the same on the other side as they took a step. But then with no warning, just like that, her feet gave way beneath her and she collapsed. She couldn't stop it, and when she tried to get up again, she slid forward and landed in a pile.

Her vision swam and the pain in her stomach intensified, moving higher now.

She touched her belly, her hand resting there, needing to feel her baby, but she pulled back when she felt something sticky. Blood covered her palm, and as she looked down, nausea rose in her throat at the dark pool of blood there, covering the front of her coat.

"I . . ." she murmured, as bright lights seemed to flash like bulbs in her vision, adding to her confusion. "I think I've been shot."

She tried to think, tried to remember, but her brain wouldn't focus. *Had* she been shot? How did she not know? Is that why her stomach had been hurting so badly?

"Chloe?" Ella cried, only she sounded miles away. "Chloe! I'm not losing you, too! Get up!"

She reached for Ella's hand but couldn't seem to find it, and suddenly there were arms going around her, and she heard Ella grunt as she collapsed beside her. Chloe wanted to tell her to keep going, that she could walk herself, that they needed to save Danni, but as she opened her mouth, she suddenly couldn't figure out how to say a word. And as Ella shook her shoulders, blackness swelled inside her eyes until everything disappeared and her body gave in to the searing-hot pain throbbing through every inch of her body.

CHAPTER TWENTY-SIX

ELLA

"You need," Danni gasped, holding her side, "to leave me."

Ella stood, trembling as she stared at Danni, slumped on the ground, and then at Chloe, red seeping through her coat.

"No," Ella said. But as the word came out of her mouth, she knew Danni was right. She was standing in the middle of a forest, perhaps surrounded by more Germans if they continued to advance. Hell, maybe she was about to be caught up in an all-out war, and she couldn't just stand there.

If she did, they'd all be dead.

"Go," Danni whispered.

Ella saw her mouth move, saw the pain she was in trying to force the words out. Ella dropped to her knees and tried to lift her. "I'm not leaving you, Danni!" she cried. "You're coming with me."

"Can't take . . ." She groaned. "Both of us. Save her."

Ella tried to haul Danni up, but ended up slipping back down with her. Tears streaked down her cheeks as she sobbed, fighting for every breath as her lungs seemed to constrict.

"Go," Danni whispered. "Save her. And baby. I'm not . . ." She moaned. "Going to make it."

Ella shut her eyes for a second, trying to think of another way, trying to figure out what she could do. But Danni was right, she wasn't going to make it. They both knew that; not that knowing it made it any easier. She heard noises and knew that she only had seconds to make a decision.

Danni groaned. "Go."

Ella saw her fumbling and reached over, helping her. She took out Danni's pack of Lucky Strikes, about to light one for her, but then they both heard the yelling of men, sounding far too close. It was now or never.

"Go," Danni whispered, the pained word only just audible.

Ella helped her to shuffle back against a tree trunk, then pressed a long, heartbreaking kiss to Danni's dirt-stained forehead. "I love you, Danni. I'm so sorry. I'm so, so sorry," she sobbed, as she stumbled backward and spun around to haul Chloe up into her arms.

"Come on, Chloe," she cried. "Come on, you need to help me."

Ella hadn't known what strength she had, what she was even capable of, until she had Chloe in her arms. She pushed through the screaming pain in her muscles and half dragged, half carried her the short distance to the jeep, stopping only to manhandle her up and into the vehicle. She was going to go back for Danni, she had to; she couldn't just leave her there.

But then gunshots echoed behind them and she glanced back, just once, seeing Danni slumped over and the figures of soldiers crashing through the trees.

I have to leave her or we're all going to die.

She knew then that she'd never, ever forget the sight of her friend left for dead, for as long as she lived. Ella leaped into the jeep as louder gunfire sounded out behind them, turning over the engine, praying for it to start.

"Come on," she cried, sobbing as she turned the key hard. "*Please.*"

She looked over her shoulder and saw the soldiers advancing, guns raised.

"Start, dammit!" she cried, just as the jeep spluttered into life.

CHAPTER TWENTY-SEVEN

DANNI

Danni tucked her camera tight to her side, groaning with pain as she tried to find her lighter. Her last Lucky Strike was trembling between her lips, the packet fallen to the dirt beside her, and she cried out as she tried to shift her weight.

"Come on, you bastard," she swore, feeling her body slump over even farther, unable to right herself. She was tucked tight against a tree, and she'd tried to shuffle around it, as far out of sight as possible, but then her body had just seemed to give up. She was thankful for the long grass around her that she hoped would disguise her. If she could only stay still enough, she might not be seen.

She managed to get hold of the lighter and flick it. She coughed and tasted blood in her mouth, but she managed to keep the Lucky Strike balanced as she lit it, her hand shaking so much she almost touched the flame to her face.

The coughing became more of a gurgle, and she let her eyes fall shut again, knowing there was only so long before she faded away.

The crack of gunfire and the yells of men swam around her, but she was no longer scared. The end was coming, and it was what it was. She'd always said she'd rather die doing what she loved than as a wizened old lady, and it seemed she'd gotten her wish.

I'll see you soon, Andy.

The sound of an engine starting up made her want to look up, but she could no longer open her eyes, let alone lift her head. And as the cigarette slipped from her mouth, her only wish was that she'd made Ella take her camera.

Now those photos that meant so much to her would never be seen. The photos that showed both faces of the war, and the unique shots she'd taken of Gabriel and his fellow Resistance fighters, would be lost forever.

Danni prayed for Ella and Chloe as she slipped sideways, the hard ground seeming to rise to meet her as she fell.

CHAPTER TWENTY-EIGHT

ELLA

The tires on the jeep suddenly spun, and they took off like a rocket. Ella kept her foot down hard, dirt flying up around them as she drove away from certain death, waiting for a bullet to connect with her or one of the tires. Her bloodstained hands were shaking so violently she could barely keep her grip on the steering wheel, as the jeep bumped along the rough track with Chloe's body flopping around, unconscious beside her, her head lolling back at an unusual angle.

Danni had been driving last time, it had always been Danni in charge, and now Ella had no idea what to do, or whether she was even doing the right thing. But what other option did she have? Ella drove as fast as she possibly could to get them back to base. She glanced over at Chloe and her stomach churned, feeling sick at the amount of blood seeping through her coat.

She's not going to make it.

Emotion clogged her throat as she grit her teeth and stared straight ahead, furiously blinking away tears as she pressed her foot even harder on the accelerator. Chloe might be lurching around in the seat beside her, but the faster she drove, the more chance she had of saving her, and she was *not* going to lose Danni and Chloe in the same day. Not on her watch.

She sobbed at the thought of what she'd done. How could she live with leaving Danni for dead like that? And suddenly she thought of Michael, wishing that he was beside her, wishing that he wasn't injured and that she could have spent more time with him, reporting with him. But instead, in a way, she'd lost him too.

The surroundings looked vaguely familiar to her now, and she turned abruptly to avoid a tree when she realized that she needed to turn left to get back to where they'd come from. She knew roughly where to go, and she could only hope that the Allies were continuing to push the Germans inland, rather than in the direction she was driving.

"Stay with me, Chloe," she said, yelling to be heard over the rumble of the jeep's engine. "You stay with me, do you hear? Stay with me!"

Her mind was a jumble of thoughts—should she pull over once they had some distance from the fighting, and try to stem the blood flow some more? Should she get her as stable as she could and keep her still? Or was she doing the right thing in pushing on and trying to get her to doctors who could actually save her? Ella only had basic first-aid training, and just looking at all the blood and knowing Chloe was pregnant was too much for her. How on earth could she try to save her with only her bare hands and no medical supplies?

"We're getting closer," she said, not sure if Chloe was even conscious to hear her. "You'll be in the capable hands of a surgeon before you know it."

So long as they don't turn us away. What if they have too many soldiers to work on and don't care about Chloe?

Ella gripped the steering wheel even tighter, knuckles bright white from clenching so hard. There wasn't time for thoughts like that—she had to believe that someone would help them, otherwise what had it all been for?

It felt like she'd been driving for hours when she finally saw the familiar olive-green military tents ahead that marked the field hospital, and she slowed as armed soldiers held up their hands at her.

"Stop!" they yelled, as she reluctantly braked, pushing her sweat-damp hair from her forehead as she leaned out the side.

"I have an injured British citizen here," she cried. "Please let me through, I need to get her help."

"How did you get this jeep?" One of the soldiers frowned, a cigarette hanging from his lips.

"Please, just let me through. She's pregnant," Ella begged. "Major Cameron will vouch for me."

That seemed to make them stand to attention. The soldier dropped his cigarette, crushing the end of it beneath his boot.

"He loaned you this jeep?"

Ella just nodded, not wanting to get him into trouble. "Come with me if you need to, but I have to get her to the hospital. *Please.*"

They waved her on and she stomped on the accelerator, sending dust flying in a billowing cloud as she drove fast toward the big hospital tent, forcing herself to slow down so as not to hurt Chloe further.

"Come on," she cried. "We're here, Chloe. Come on, wake up, please!"

She leaped out of the vehicle and ran around to the passenger side.

"Help!" she screamed. "I need help out here!"

Ella found a renewed strength as she hauled Chloe out, taking her full body weight as she half dragged, half carried her from the jeep.

"Help!" she screamed again. "Someone! Help me!"

An orderly appeared and then went running back for a stretcher, calling for more assistance, but Ella didn't stop, refusing to wait even a moment in case it was the difference between life and death for Chloe.

"I didn't go through all that to let you die on me," she whispered, her body screaming out at her to stop as she used an almost superhuman strength to carry the other woman. "We're so close, Chloe. We can do this. Hold on, for your baby."

Two men suddenly closed around them and took Chloe from her, lifting her on to a stretcher, just as Cameron appeared, his face ashen-white when he saw her.

She watched as nurses cut the clothes from Chloe's body, the fabric falling away, modesty no longer a concern as they started the fight for her life.

Ella lifted her hand to push her hair off her face again, but all she did was smear something sticky across her skin, and in that moment she knew it was Chloe's blood. Tears mixed with blood mixed with sweat as she stared at Cameron for a long, stuttering moment. She tried to open her mouth and not a word came out.

"Danni?" he asked. "Where's Danni?"

Cameron's eyes frantically searched her face. Ella started to shake again, her body convulsing as she slid to the ground, her fingers digging into the dirt. She looked down and saw that her fingernails were a mix of red and brown, and she felt the overwhelming need to scrub herself clean, to wash away all the awful things that had happened to her that day.

"Ella."

She shut her eyes, rocking back and forth, trying to breathe, trying to focus on something that wasn't blood and death and pain.

"Ella! Answer me!"

She felt like she was in a tunnel and someone at the other end was calling her name, faintly at first, and then louder. And then her shoulders shook, rough hands jerking her back to reality.

"Ella! Where's Danni?" It was Cameron again, and he was bent over her, his eyes finding hers the moment she opened them. "Where's Danni? What happened? Who is that woman?"

She stared up at him. *Danni. More pain, more blood, more bad decisions.*

"Ella, how did this happen? Where's Danni?" he yelled. "I need to know where Danni is."

Ella sucked back air, filling her lungs, adrenalin suddenly surging through her as she saw the panic in Cameron's gaze.

"We had to leave her behind," she managed, clearing her throat as his hands went still on her shoulders. "That woman, she's . . . she's Andy's sister. She's pregnant. Danni went looking for her."

"Is Danni alive? Where is she?" he demanded. "What the hell happened?"

"She's gone, Cameron," she answered. "Danni's gone."

"What the hell do you mean *she's gone*?" he said. "Where the hell is she?"

"We had to leave her," Ella stammered. "We had no other choice."

"Ella, is she alive? You need to tell me where Danni is." He had hold of her shoulders again, shaking her.

Ella shook her head. It was pounding, like someone was slamming away at her brain with a sledgehammer. "There was so much blood and she made me do it. She made me! It was her or Chloe, and she never would have forgiven me if I'd left Chloe behind." Her voice was more sob than stream of coherent words. "I had no other choice."

Cameron lowered to his haunches, his hands settling over hers. She looked down and stared at his fingers, his palms warming her ice-cold skin.

"Ella, you're in shock," he said quietly. "You've witnessed something terrible, and I know it's hard, but you need to help me. I need to know where Danni is."

Something about the way he was speaking to her settled her, made her think more clearly, and as he stood, still holding her hands, she rose with him.

"She can't have survived it," Ella whispered.

"Can you tell me where to find her?" he demanded. "Where did you leave her, Ella?"

"I think so," she whispered. "But I don't think—"

"Tell me everything you can," he said. "Dead or alive, I'm bringing Danni back."

She mumbled directions to him through her tears, and as quickly as Cameron had found her, he was gone.

"You need to get out of here," someone scolded her as she stood, alone, trembling in the middle of the hospital tent. "A nurse will come for you when she's stable."

Someone else bumped into Ella and she stumbled as she moved out of the way, spinning around, suddenly confused about where she was supposed to be and where she should go.

I need to write. It seemed the only logical thing to do, the only thing she could keep busy with as she waited for news of Chloe. She had a duty to tell the world what had happened. She needed everyone to see what they went through, what it was like living in a war zone, the risks they had to take to get the story and save one another's lives. And that included Michael.

She needed to go and find him, that's what she needed to do, and she wasn't going to let him push her away again. She'd just left Danni for dead, a woman who'd become like a sister to her over the past week, and she was damned if she was going to let him wallow in self-pity and not be thankful for being alive.

Besides, it had been Michael who'd told her to imagine she was having a conversation with him if it all became too much; to imagine writing to him. Well, the man was within walking distance, and she intended on *actually* talking to him instead of pretending.

She started to run then, as tears streamed down her cheeks and her body shuddered. She was going to start with Michael, and she wasn't going to stop writing until his story, Andy's story, and Danni's story were told.

"Michael Miller," Ella declared, her voice shaky as she marched up to his bedside with her pen and notepad in hand.

"Ella?" he replied, turning slightly to face her. She desperately wanted to throw her arms around him and tell him how much she cared for him, to stop his pain as much as her own. But after the way he'd rejected her last time, she wasn't going to so much as touch him.

She didn't care that he couldn't see her or that the last time they'd been together he'd pushed her away; she'd come for a reason and she wasn't backing down. If he told her to leave, then she would, but only after she got what she needed.

"I need to interview you, Michael," she said, pulling over a low stool.

"Interview me? Ella, what are you even talking about?" he asked. "I'm not your latest subject matter, for Christ's sake."

Her hands were shaking, and she pressed the pencil to the paper so hard she made a hole in it. Now she understood why Danni had been so determined to keep going after Andy had died, why she'd refused to talk about him and had thrown herself into her work. The alternative was to fall to the ground in a heap and sob, and if she did that, she doubted she'd ever be able to rise again. Suddenly, her work was all she had.

"Ella, what are you doing? I thought I made it clear that I didn't want you here, or anywhere near me."

Ella shook her head. "Don't give me that, Miller. I'm here and I'm not leaving," she said. "I will *not* let you speak to me like that, or tell me what to do."

"Look, I shouldn't have spoken to you like that the other day, but the truth is, you need to forget about me, alright?"

She squeezed her eyes shut for a beat, pushing it all away, trying to stop the noise in her head. She kept seeing Danni, seeing the way she'd looked up at her, defeat in her eyes for the first time since Ella had known her.

"I will not," she said. "You're the one who told me to report on the real war, and you were the one who told me to imagine I was talking to you to help me cope. So here I am."

"Ella—" he started, but she cut him off.

"Full name," she said, choking as she forced the words out. "I need your full name and how long you've been a correspondent."

"Michael James Miller," he said. "But I'm not a journalist anymore . . ."

"Your loss of eyesight does not stop you from being a journalist," she retorted. "Now, you're going to tell me exactly what happened to you that day. Don't leave anything out."

He looked exasperated, even though she couldn't see his eyes, as he folded his arms.

"For the last time—"

"Just tell me!" she demanded, glancing sideways and realizing that she was making a scene. Ella took a long, slow breath and then exhaled. "I'm doing a story on the dangers faced by war correspondents and the reality of the work we do, and I'm not taking no for an answer. I want the world to see what we go through, what we face. I need to do this, Michael. *Please.*"

"Ella—"

"Don't," she interrupted. "Do not give me that line about not being a journalist anymore. I'm telling your story, whether you like it or not, because if the shoe were on the other foot, you'd make me do it. And because I've lost Danni. She's gone. So that's why I'm not interested in you feeling sorry for yourself, Miller." She sucked back a breath, her heart racing as she tried to push away the image of Danni sitting slumped, alone. "You're alive and you have a story to tell. And Danni isn't. So the least you can do is help me tell hers."

He was quiet a moment, before finally speaking again.

"Okay," he said, his voice a low murmur.

She lifted her pencil, gripping it tight to curb the shaking. "And don't think I've forgotten about your behavior the other day. When you're ready to apologize to me properly, you can buy me a goddamn martini, but until then, I'm asking the questions and you're answering them. Got it?"

"Oh, I got it," he said, pushing himself up in the bed. "Loud and clear. Ask away."

But Ella's hand was shaking so violently now she couldn't even make out her own scribble on the page.

"Deep breaths, Ella. Don't you go back to being that shy girl reporting on fluff stories; you can do this, you hear me? You're a seasoned reporter now."

She cleared her throat, listening to him, knowing she should be cross with him for teasing her like that, but also knowing that he was doing it for her own good.

Michael reached for her hand then, and she clasped his.

"Ella!" came a shouted command that seemed to reverberate through the tent.

She looked up and saw Cameron standing there, his face contorted with emotion.

"I'm going to find her now, Ella," he said. "I'm not leaving her out there alone." Ella just nodded, not knowing what to say.

"Even if she's dead, I'm not leaving her there alone." Her heart broke all over again as she heard the choke in his voice.

"Cameron, if you find her, can you salvage her camera?" Ella asked. "She had photos on there, photos we took the day she stole the jeep, and I want to send them back for her. They were important."

He nodded. "I will. I promise you, Ella, I will."

It was her biggest regret, other than leaving Danni in the first place—not taking her camera and promising to have every last image published.

Ella followed him outside and saw a jeep waiting, the engine running with two other soldiers in the back.

"I trust these men with my life, and they're coming with me," Cameron said, as he jumped behind the steering wheel, the jeep lurching away as she stood and watched.

I'm so sorry, Danni. He loved you so much and now you'll never know.

She would never, ever forget the pain etched upon Cameron's face in that moment. If only she'd been able to get Danni back to the jeep, if only she hadn't twisted her ankle, if only she hadn't been shot . . . Ella gulped. Was there a chance Danni could still be alive?

She shook her head and shut her eyes, remembering the blood. They'd left Danni for dead. There was no way she could have made it, and Ella knew it.

"Ella?"

She turned and found Michael there, holding on to a nurse for support as he stood in the open doorway of the hospital tent. She wiped away her tears and went back for him, thanking the nurse and taking his arm herself to lead him back, even though he fought against her hold.

They were silent until they reached Michael's bed and she went to help him in. He pushed her hand away, roughly, and she stood back, even though it killed her to see him fumble over such a simple action. She resisted the urge to tuck him in, sitting on the edge of the crumpled bed instead.

"You ready for me to tell you about the day I was injured?" he asked, his voice gruff, as if he were embarrassed that she was seeing him like that. And she vowed then not to help him, not to pity him for a moment, because that's why she'd almost lost him before.

Ella sniffed and picked up her pencil. "Yes."

"Alright then." He took a deep, shuddering breath. "I was too close to the action," Michael said. "I was tucked down low, and a bomb went off. The blast sent me flying, and when I came to, I couldn't see a thing."

"What was it like, when you were out there? When it first happened?"

Michael lay back, and she focused on keeping her breathing calm.

"It was horrible," he said. "I will never forget the smell of gunpowder, the screams of other men as they fell. I was in so much pain, but then it turned to shock, I suppose, and then panic set in when I opened my eyes and everything was black."

She nodded and wrote, forcing her fingers to keep gripping the pencil.

"We have a job to do that no one can really understand, not unless they've walked in our shoes," Michael said, sounding more somber than she'd ever heard him. "The desire to show the truth, to see everything with our own eyes and try to write words that convey the action as well as the emotion. It consumes us."

"And is it worth risking everything for?" she asked, as emotion clogged her throat again. Because she could be asking Danni this—she *wished* she were asking Danni this.

"It *is* worth it," he said. "In the end, we do what we do because we love it, and because we make it our life." He cleared his throat.

"And sometimes it feels like nothing else is as important as the next story, even if later we realize how narrow-minded that makes us."

Ella pressed her pencil to the page and looked up then, wishing she could touch him, wishing she could take the comfort from him that she craved.

"I am so sorry about the other day, Ella," he whispered. "I'm sorry if I hurt you, but we both know what this job is like." He paused, his voice lower now. "And I can't stand for you to see me like this. It's just not me, or it sure as hell isn't a version of me I want you to see."

She wrapped her arms tightly around herself, wanting to shield herself from him, but at the same time wanting to throw her arms around him and never let him go.

"We need to give it everything, we need to live and breathe it, and the last thing I want is for you to be pitying me instead of giving it your all," he said. "I suppose I don't know who I am if I'm not a correspondent—but you? You have a life, a career ahead of you to look forward to."

Ella kept gripping her pencil. "I'm a big girl, Michael. And for the record, I've never felt pity for you. Pain at your injury, of course, but never pity, not for a second." She shook her head. "You know, I meant what I said the other day. I was falling in love with you, Michael, and your injury wouldn't ever have changed the way I felt. Your attitude did that all on its own."

She didn't wait to hear what he had to say. There was only one thing she wanted right now, and that was to keep writing her story before she collapsed under the weight of it all. And then she was going to sit outside that hospital tent and wait for news of Chloe, even if she had to wait all goddamn night.

CHAPTER TWENTY-NINE

DANNI

The woods were blissfully quiet, and Danni let herself droop, swaying slightly as she fought not to collapse again completely. It had been a huge effort to haul herself back up when she'd regained consciousness, and she doubted she'd have the strength to do it again. She was grateful for the silence, like a blanket around her. She didn't ever recall listening to silence before, or appreciating it, but for now it was a relief to just be still and quiet. There was barely a rustle of leaves around her as she sat, or maybe she just couldn't hear anything anymore. She wasn't sure.

She listened to the rough inhale and exhale of her own breath, imagining Ella and Chloe getting back to camp, wishing she could have spent more time with Chloe before the end.

But I found her, Andy, she thought. *I found her, and Ella will take care of her. If anyone can, Ella can.*

But as her thoughts turned from Andy, she suddenly saw Cameron, standing, watching her. His eyes telling her that she should never have gone. What she would have given to have another night with him, and to tell him she was sorry for breaking his trust in her. She'd been so desperate to find Chloe that it had overshadowed her usual sense and judgment, and without Andy to counsel her, she knew she would have stopped at nothing until she'd found her.

Danni's mind drifted then, losing sight of Cameron and Andy, grasping at her memories, trying to claw them back, but everything was starting to fade. Her breath was making a labored drag, followed by a hiss as she exhaled, and as her eyes shut tighter and her chin tipped down, she wondered just how many breaths she had left.

"Danni!"

Danni opened her eyes, just a sliver, her lids too heavy to do anything else, at the sound of her name. But she must have been imagining it. There was no one calling for her. *Of course there's no one calling for me.* She gripped her camera, making sure it was tucked against her body. It was hard and rigid, but it gave her as much comfort as a teddy bear would a child.

"Danni!"

She heard the call again. She must be hallucinating. Her body was on fire. It seemed to alternate between fire, ice cold, and then a weird sensation of nothingness, which she thought might be shock. But as she tried to sit up a little, her body hunched over and her shoulders slumped, it was like her entire body had flames shooting rampantly across it.

But now everything was silent again, and she knew that death was surely waiting for her, the darkness ready to pull her closer.

"Danni! Where are you?!"

Cameron? Now she knew she was hallucinating. There was no possible way she could be hearing Cameron's voice.

Tears rolled down her face as she slumped again, unable to sit up taller even if she'd wanted to. Death was taking a lot longer than she'd imagined it would. When the bullet had hit her, it was as if her body had sliced in half with the shooting pain; a pain that got worse with every step. Maybe it was simply that she no longer had any concept of time, the minutes stretching on like hours, the hours like days. Still, the relief of death was taking a long time to embrace her. She'd thought once it was dark, it would all be over, but as nighttime started to creep across the sky, dimming everything around her, nothing had changed.

The sound of an engine sent a spasm of fear through her. She started to tremble, waiting for the shots, hearing movement. *Oh God, there's more of them.* She wanted to scream, wanted to run, but the only noise she could make was a grunt, and she couldn't move even if she tried.

Please, Lord, please don't let them take me. A bullet would have been one thing, but if they took her . . .

"Oh God, *Danni!*"

Cameron? Was it him? Or was she slipping further away from reality? She was sure she could see the movement of a flashlight wobbling, but she couldn't keep her eyes open any longer.

Arms closed around her, someone was touching her, and she didn't have the strength to fight it.

"Danni, you're alive!" His hands were so warm, and she leaned into him, remembering what it felt like to be in his arms even though she couldn't move or tell him.

"Danni, I've got you," he said. "Danni, I'm here."

She tried to open her mouth, but nothing would come out, and suddenly she realized how thirsty she was, her lips cracked and dry as they struggled to move. Even breathing required a herculean effort, the push and pull of air going in and out of her lungs seeming almost impossible.

"Sweetheart, I'm going to get you back to camp," Cameron said, his voice all around her as his hands gently touched her face, his palm against her cheek. "Danni, you stay with me. That's all you need to do. Just stay with me! I'm not losing you, not now."

She shut her eyes more tightly as he scooped her up against his chest, as if he were carrying a newborn child, as if he could protect her from anything. Every movement, every bump, sent even more spasms of pain through her body, pain that consumed her to the point she wished she were dead, but Cameron was steadfast and ever so gentle as he cradled her. If these were her last moments, then at least she was in his arms.

"I love you, Danni," he whispered as he walked, his lips against her forehead. "I love you so damn much."

I love you too. But the thought slipped away as she felt her body go limp.

"Quickly!" he yelled. "She's alive!"

It was a battle just to stay conscious and not give in to the pain, but being in his arms, if it was the last thing she ever experienced, was worth it all.

As Cameron tucked her against his body, he let out a single sob; the most guttural, pained noise Danni had ever heard. She opened her eyes just a fraction, one painful lift, to see his face contorted as he rushed her to something, maybe a waiting vehicle, and she glimpsed a soldier standing with a gun held high.

Something was rumbling, perhaps an engine running, but she didn't even try to look as Cameron held her tightly, like he might never let her go. And then suddenly she was being hoisted up high.

She cried, the noise bursting from her as more pain ricocheted through her.

"Drive!" Cameron yelled, holding her firmly again. She knew he was trying to buffer her against the biggest bumps, but every single one still hurt so much it only made her continue to hope death would find her faster.

Danni wished she could tell Cameron it was her time, that she wasn't scared anymore, that it was okay. That she just wanted the pain to end.

"Go faster!" Cameron shouted. "You need to drive faster!"

All this time she'd held her camera, the only thing she wanted with her at the very end, but even holding on to that felt too hard now.

"You do not give up, Danni," Cameron whispered to her. "This is not the end, do you hear me? I'm not losing you, not after we've come this far."

But Danni knew. There was no way she could survive her injuries. It had been too long. She'd lost too much blood. She could feel herself fading in and out as the jeep bumped along the track.

And then her fingers slipped, and she felt her camera sliding from her grasp.

"T-t-take," she mumbled, the word almost impossible to force out.

"What?" he asked, leaning in close. "What are you trying to say?"

"Take," she tried to say again, managing to drop her gaze to her hand.

"I got it," Cameron said, letting go of her with one hand and catching her camera. "No matter what happens, Danni, I'll make sure your films get back to London," he said, holding her tight but still not managing to shield her from the bumps as the jeep jerked sideways. "I'll get your camera to Ella, I promise. I'll make sure it's safe. Your work will not be for nothing, do you hear me?"

She kept her eyes shut tight, not able to look up at him even if she wanted to, not wanting to hear the pain in Cameron's voice, to wonder what could have been between them. Once, all she'd wanted was to tell her story with pictures from the battle lines, to die in the field doing what she loved if she had to go. But now, all she wanted was to go home.

"Try and hold on, Danni," Cameron pleaded, his voice gentle now. "Ella is at camp, they made it back safely, and Chloe's in surgery. She's going to need you when she gets out."

They made it. They're back at camp. They're safe, Andy. They're safe.

"You've got a lot to live for, sweetheart," he whispered. "And this is not going to be the last time I hold you in my arms."

She wanted to smile, to pat his hand and tell him everything was going to be okay, that she loved him for coming for her. But all she could do was shut her eyes and listen to his words as they echoed around her.

If only I'd told you I was falling in love with you when I had the chance.

CHAPTER THIRTY

CHLOE

She was so cold. It was like she'd been out in the snow for hours, but for some reason she felt like she was starting to move closer to a warm, crackling fire. Waves of warmth reached out to her, and she kept her eyes shut, suddenly seeing Gabriel. She tried to reach out her hand, but she couldn't lift it. And then she realized it was only a memory, so vivid it may as well have been yesterday.

"It won't always be like this," Gabriel said, *stroking his fingers against her arm.*

"I hope you're talking about the war and not about being in bed, because I happen to like this."

He smiled and leaned forward, his lips soft as he kissed her. She held the sheet, covering her breasts, modest still in the daylight, even after the night they'd had.

"This war, it'll change everything," Gabriel said, *"but it won't continue. Hatred will never succeed long-term, humanity simply won't allow it."*

She believed him—why wouldn't she? The war would never reach Paris. It couldn't. There were too many people prepared to stand up against the Nazis.

"I'm so pleased you came to France," Gabriel whispered. "It's such a shame it's only for a few days. Maybe I should keep you?"

She giggled, leaning against him and stroking her fingernails up and down his chest. Was it wicked that she was having such a wonderful time with a man every moment that she wasn't working? He was charming, funny, and intelligent, and she'd never been so happy in her life before.

"Maybe I'll let you." She smiled. "But I know you're just saying that to keep me in bed with you."

Chloe turned in his arms and studied his face, mesmerized by his ocean-blue eyes and tanned skin, enchanted by the way he studied her.

She'd come to Paris to work, and somehow on the day she'd arrived, she'd fallen in love, too.

Chloe shivered as the picture disappeared from her mind. She felt a tugging at her body, pulling her, and she tried to resist even though she couldn't see who was touching her. Something was making a loud noise and she could hear someone calling. Were they saying her name? She tried to open her eyes, tried to move, tried to open her mouth, but slowly the coldness came creeping back.

She was cold now. So, so cold.

"Stay with us!" someone cried, and Chloe stifled a cry as hands pressed against her chest.

The pain was razor-sharp, spreading, taking over her body, and the voices above her seemed to disappear as she tried to fight the intense burning in her stomach.

Darkness swirled around her then, and she had the overwhelming sensation that it was time to go to sleep. A whooshing noise was like a lullaby to her, drawing her in, and she started to give in to it, letting go of whatever was holding her back. She could almost feel fingertips holding her, trying to restrain her, to stop her from moving away, but she couldn't stay any longer.

And then she saw him.

The little boy had golden curls, hair the exact same shade as Andy's. Chloe watched as the boy turned, laughing as he looked at her over his shoulder, giggling and running, holding his hand out. But someone else took it. *Andy* took it.

Chloe wanted to reach out, wanted to take both their hands, wanted to call out to her brother, but he was moving farther and farther away. And as he let go of the child's hand, *her child's hand*, bright blue eyes that were the exact same shade as Gabriel's met hers. And then Andy shook his head.

"Stay," he said. "It's not your time."

"We're losing her!" she heard someone yell, as she drifted back, seeing a blurred figure bent over her, until it was too hard to stay awake. Too hard to try to focus on what was happening.

The little boy smiled then and opened his mouth, and Chloe felt herself finally catching up to him, palm outstretched, as the warmth she'd been searching for finally engulfed her, and her brother disappeared from sight.

CHAPTER THIRTY-ONE

ELLA

The side of the tent was all that was propping Ella up. She'd slid to the ground, her legs like jelly as she'd collapsed, as Danni had been taken from Cameron's arms, the medics swarming around her.

She knew that, for the rest of her life, she'd never forget the sight of Danni, unconscious, her body appearing lifeless as she'd been put on a stretcher and rushed to surgery. She'd seen the doctors shake their heads, seen the heartfelt sympathy in the eyes of the nurses, and known instinctively how low the odds were. *But she was alive.* That was a miracle in itself; that Cameron had gone back for her and somehow willed her to live. She would never forget hearing the frantic sound of his shouts coupled with the screeching of tires that had sent her running from the tent she'd been in, to see Cameron with Danni in his arms.

Since Danni had been rushed into surgery, Cameron had paced for what seemed like an eternity, before finally joining her, his body heavy and warm against hers, his black boots, covered in dirt, extending out in front of him. Somehow, at some stage, his hand had found hers, and despite never having been physically close with him before, she'd clutched it, holding it in her lap as if it were the most natural thing in the world to do. Because they were both waiting for news, and he was the only other person who could possibly understand her pain.

They never said a word, and every time Ella looked up at the clock, another tiny part of her heart seemed to break away. With every passing minute, every hour, she knew that the chances of Danni or Chloe surviving were becoming impossible at best.

And if she were honest with herself, the guilt she felt at leaving Danni, at believing she was a lost cause, was starting to consume her. She'd chosen Chloe, and her unborn child—Danni wouldn't have had it any other way—but she still felt the pain and guilt at having chosen one woman over the other.

"They're coming," Cameron croaked, stumbling to his feet, still holding on to her as she scrambled up beside him.

The two doctors were pulling the surgical masks from their mouths, and she saw the way they glanced somberly at one another as they walked toward them. As she and Cameron waited, clinging to one another for strength, all she could focus on was the blood staining their gowns, splattered all over them as if they'd just murdered someone instead of trying to save a life. For some morbid reason, she wondered if it belonged to Chloe or Danni; *or both of them.*

As the doctor on the left opened his mouth, Ella's legs went from under her. Cameron reacted swiftly, catching her, breaking her fall and helping her back up, his arm tucked firmly around her.

"You were the one who brought the young British woman in earlier?" the doctor asked, his eyes bloodshot as he blinked at her.

She wondered then how often he was actually forced to deliver bad news, when none of the men he operated on had family members waiting—so unlike the reality of surgery in the civilian world.

"I am," she croaked.

"She lost a huge amount of blood, but—"

Ella's body convulsed, her mouth opening but no words coming out, as Cameron scooped her up again and kept her upright.

"But?" she whispered.

"But we managed to save her."

"And her baby?" Ella whispered, cringing as she waited for the news.

"Still where it should be. It's a miracle really, but the baby's heartbeat is still strong. There's no reason to think the baby won't be fine."

"Major!" a nurse yelled, running toward them, her face pink and her eyes wide. "Major Cameron!"

Ella stared, struggling to breathe as she grabbed hold of Cameron's hand, holding on to him as if her life depended on it.

"She's alive! Danni made it through surgery!"

Pain and sorrow gave way to a brief moment of exhilaration, as Cameron gasped beside her and the nurse threw her arms around him, parting him from Ella.

"She's alive?" Ella whispered. "*Danni made it too?*"

"She's alive," the nurse said, touching her cheek like a mother would a child's. "She's very much alive, although it was touch and go there for quite some time. I'll keep you both updated as she recovers."

Cameron turned to her and opened his arms, and Ella stepped into his embrace, holding on to him as he sobbed, her own cries muffled against his shoulder. Sadness blurred with happiness with relief.

"She's alive," he murmured. "I can't believe she made it."

"Cameron, she made it because of you," Ella cried. "You're the reason she even had a fighting chance."

Ella finally let go of him, finally ready to trust her own legs. Cameron's face told her that he was about to leave, although it was the surgeon behind her clearing his throat who held her attention.

"Is there something else?" Ella asked. Had she misheard? Was Chloe still in surgery? Had she not understood what he was trying to tell her?

"Ma'am, we can't keep an expectant mother in a field hospital," the surgeon said.

"What are you trying to say?" she asked. Her voice was quavering, as was her body, but she had no intention of letting Chloe down. Not now, not after all they'd been through.

"I have to ask if you can contact the father? We noticed she wasn't wearing a wedding band, but—"

Ella squeezed her eyes shut, trying to block out the image of Gabriel standing there as bullets ricocheted through his body. He'd given his own life without a second thought to try to save Chloe's. She took a deep, shaky breath.

"The father is recently deceased," she managed.

"I see," he replied.

Ella held her head high. "She has nowhere else to go."

"You look after her as long as she needs medical treatment," Cameron said, raising his voice. "And that's an order."

Ella turned to thank him, but despite their closeness as they'd waited together, his face was bracketed with determination instead of grief now.

"You're leaving?" she asked.

"We've secured all the beachheads, and now we move on to Caen," he said. "We're going to take every last German bastard down, and I fully intend on leading the charge."

And after what she'd seen of him as he'd fought to save Danni, she didn't doubt him for a second.

CHAPTER THIRTY-TWO

ONE WEEK LATER
DANNI

To say that Cameron was unhappy with her would have been a gross understatement. It wasn't often that Danni was genuinely humbled by something, but facing that mountain of a man as he stood before her was one of the hardest things she'd ever done. Even bandaged and bleeding, sitting on the edge of a hospital bed and recovering from being shot, she knew she had a lot to answer for. *And apologize for.*

"Of all the crazy, harebrained ideas you could have come up with . . ." he said, pacing in front of her now as she sat shoulder to shoulder with Ella on the bed.

"Cameron, if I may—" Danni interrupted, rising and trying to stand taller even though her injured leg made it almost impossible.

"You may not!" he replied as he turned sharply on his heel and strode toward her. "You've shown a blatant disregard for your own life and those of others, but dammit, Danni, I can't reprimand you."

She blinked at him, promptly sitting back down. "You can't?" she asked. She'd been expecting a lecture, or punishment even.

"Sir, I'm sorry to interrupt."

They all turned to the soldier standing to Cameron's left. Danni hadn't even noticed him approach, but he looked like a frightened rabbit as he shifted from foot to foot.

"What is it?" Cameron barked.

"Ahh, I was told that there might be a-a-a Miss Ella Franks here," he stuttered nervously. "I've been asked to find her."

"That's me," Ella replied.

"Sir, there's a correspondent at the clearance hospital who says it's imperative that he sees her before he's shipped out," the soldier said, still addressing Cameron instead of Ella.

Ella sat up a little straighter, and Danni stifled a smile, knowing exactly who it would be.

"Who is it?" Ella asked.

The soldier never took his eyes off his superior. "His name is Michael Miller," he answered. "Sir, with permission?"

"It's fine, she can go," Cameron allowed, waving his hand to dismiss them.

Danni watched as Ella hurried alongside the soldier. No matter how much her friend denied there was something going on with Michael, her response just now had shown how much she cared for him.

But her thoughts promptly disappeared when Cameron began to speak again.

"Danni, you stole a jeep despite my *express* orders that you weren't to go anywhere without my permission," he fumed. "I was ready to send out a goddamn search party, and then when Ella came flying back into camp . . ." He shook his head. "It's why—"

"Why women aren't allowed near the front lines?" she interrupted.

He shook his head and took a step forward. "No, Danni, that's not what I was going to say." Cameron's eyes never left hers. "It's why I wish you'd confided in me, so I could have helped you. If I'd known what you were doing, I'd have tried to come up with something; I'd have understood why you were so relentless about having access to a vehicle."

"You would have helped me?" she asked, not even bothering to mask her surprise.

His face softened into an expression that broke her heart, and she saw why he was so angry, that he genuinely would have helped her if she'd told him.

"Christ, Danni, just come here, would you?" he murmured.

Cameron opened his arms and she managed to stand and embrace him. His arms were tight around her, holding her firmly, his chest comforting as it rose and fell with each breath he took. She would have stayed there all day and night if she could have, holding on to him and pretending that she hadn't almost died, but knowing that if it hadn't been for him, she'd never have lasted another hour. As the noise of war—explosions and gunfire—sounded nearby, she stood in his bear-like hug, not wanting to be anywhere else in the world, even if she could have.

"Let me look at you," he said, his tone so soft she could barely comprehend it was from the same man. Cameron stroked her face gently with his thumb. "Lord, Danni. When I found you, when I saw you like that . . ." Pain made his voice crack, and she heard the rawness of his emotion. He'd been away fighting since she'd woken, so today was the first time she'd seen him since he'd saved her.

"Berlin's finest sure know how to take a girl down," she replied, hoping her quick response would make him laugh, or at least smile.

"Danni, you were *shot* and left for dead," he whispered, stroking down her arms now. "And yet you managed to survive. What you endured, it was horrific, but you survived and I am so glad that you did."

"When you put it like that . . ." she joked, but Cameron was having none of it. Like her, he knew that the reason she was joking was because, if she didn't try to make light of it all, she'd be in an emotional heap on the floor.

"Danni, you defied all odds to make it." He shook his head. "It was touch and go there whether you were going to pull through, and honestly I didn't know if there was even a chance they'd be able to save you when I arrived back with you."

A tremble started, first in her knees, and then it made its way up her body. As Cameron kept talking, one of his arms holding her still, her entire body started to shake and she reached out to him, fingers kneading into his shoulder as she clutched at him. She'd been stoic for so long, but now it was like everything that had been holding her together, the glue that had kept her patched up, was disintegrating.

"Danni?" he asked, his voice sounding hollow and far away. "*Oh, Danni.*"

She swayed under his touch, but when he moved back, perhaps to call for help, she only held him tighter, leaning into him and letting him cradle her as emotion rocked through her chest.

"I'm sorry," she whispered. "I'm so, so sorry I put you through that. I'm sorry I broke your confidence in me, that I lied to you."

Cameron was truly a mountain—he stood so solid, so strong, as she wept like she'd never wept before.

For Andy; for the decisions she'd made; for her brush with death—for it all. And through her emotion, Cameron never spoke nor moved a muscle, other than to increase the pressure of his palms against her back, as if sensing how badly she needed his presence.

Finally, he stroked her shoulder before standing back and clearing his throat. "Danni, what you did, finding Chloe, it might have been reckless, but it was also incredibly brave," he said. "She never would have survived the Allied advance if you hadn't found her, because the safe house where she was living was overrun by Nazis."

Her heart sank. "It was?"

"But because of what happened that day you were shot, the Germans were caught off guard, and it ended up being quite the win for the Resistance." He lowered his voice. "And for us."

Cameron's fingers intertwined with hers.

"Danni, whatever I've said in the past about women working here, I take it back," he told her. "I will never like women being so close to the war, but what you and Ella have done, being so brave to come here and report back on the landings, the work you both do, it's made me see things from your perspective."

"You have no idea how much that means to me," she said honestly. "But now it's my turn to apologize." Danni took a deep breath. "I put you in an impossible position. I was so desperate to be the first at everything, to prove myself and push the boundaries, but I pushed too far. After losing Andy, I think I just spiraled, because I was so desperate for his life not to have been taken in vain, and to find his sister."

Cameron's eyes were soft as he looked back at her.

"What am I going to do with you?" he murmured, leaning forward, gently pressing his forehead to hers. "You're going to be the end of me."

Danni wished they were anywhere else. She wished that she wasn't about to take advantage of Cameron's feelings for her, to ask him to do something that could jeopardize his career *again*.

Maybe it was because they were living in a life-or-death situation, heightened by the fact they had no idea what the next day, week, or month would bring, but she would have done anything in that moment to hold Cameron close and disappear from it all.

"Cameron, I need to ask for your help," she finally said, looking down at his hand in hers and liking the way their palms fit together.

"Why do I think I'm not going to like this?" His sigh was low and deep.

Danni grinned at him.

"The night before I took the jeep," she started.

"Trust me, it's a night I remember intimately," he said with a wry smile.

Danni knew she was blushing, but she refused to acknowledge it. Since when did her cheeks flush for a man!

"I should have told you about Andy's sister then."

He laughed. "Yeah, you should have. But how about we leave that in the past now, huh?"

She ran a hand down his arm. "Well, that night I betrayed your trust, so this time I thought I'd ask you for help, instead of hatching up my own plan."

"Go on then," he said.

"Well, first"—Danni smiled—"I need you to help me send negatives back to London for me. To *National Geographic* and to *Vogue*."

Cameron's eyes never left her. "And why can't you transmit the negatives yourself?"

Danni swallowed and met his gaze. "Because I, ah, lost my job. It just so happens that I no longer have an editor to send to."

"I'm sorry, what?"

She smiled as sweetly as she could.

"Danni! You know the rules; you have to be attached to a newspaper to be a correspondent here! You can't just be here of your own accord. When did this happen?"

"The rules state that I'm not allowed to be here, period. So as far as I'm concerned, I was defying the rules anyway." She cleared her throat. "And it was the day we both received our telegrams. We weren't exactly on the best terms then. And besides, even if I could send them, I'd have to do it physically in a pouch back to London. The male correspondents can transmit them by wire, which means that, if you authorized it, *you* could perhaps transmit them for me?"

He ran his fingers through his hair, spinning away from her on his heel and seeming to survey something in the distance, before turning slowly back.

"So, let me get this straight," he said calmly, quietly. "You want me to put my neck on the line to get photographs back to London, as well as sending Andy's sister? Because that's the next thing you're going to ask me, isn't it?"

"Cameron, she's British," Danni said. "And it's not like we can just leave her here, is it?"

"Danni, you're asking me to do something—"

"*Extraordinary*," she said before he had the chance to finish his sentence. "I'm asking you to do something extraordinary, to help me. Please, *please*, say you'll do it?"

"It means that much to you?" Cameron asked. "It's worth risking my neck for? To send her home on a hospital ship instead of finding her somewhere safe to stay in France?"

"Yes," Danni replied.

"I'll try," he said. "Of course I'll try for you."

She slid her hand down his arm until her fingers caught his, knowing from the way he looked down at her, the way his fingers clenched around hers the moment they made contact, that he felt the same way about her as she did about him.

"Cameron, there's something I've been wanting to say to you, since the day you saved me."

He looked at her and she almost lost her nerve, not used to admitting her feelings.

"I heard you, what you said to me, when you didn't think I could hear," she said.

He had always struck her as so unflappable, but as his cheeks colored pink, it gave her the confidence to go on. She doubted he was used to opening his heart, either.

"Danni, I—" he started, but she interrupted him, not wanting to lose her nerve.

"I just wanted to say that I love you too," she whispered.

His smile told her everything she needed to know, and Danni stood on tiptoe, pressing her lips to his and clasping the front of his jacket. She ignored the pain throbbing in her head and the ache in her stomach, losing herself to the feel of strong arms wrapped around her, and lips as warm as hot cocoa on a winter's day dancing against hers.

CHAPTER THIRTY-THREE

ELLA

"You sent for me?" Ella asked, rubbing at her eyes as they adjusted to the light in the hospital tent.

"I did," Michael said, sounding smug.

"What's this?" Ella asked as she stood by his bed.

"It's your martini."

"What on earth are you talking about?"

"You specifically told me that when I was ready to apologize to you, I was to buy you a martini," Michael said. "Now that was quite a tall order in a war zone, but it just so happens that I had some favors to call in."

Ella moved closer and took the glass jar from him, laughing as she studied it. The drink looked dubious, but she took a sip anyway, cringing at the sting of liquor so early in the day.

"So you're ready to apologize, are you?" Ella asked, wishing she'd asked for chocolates or even cigarettes instead. She didn't even really like martinis all that much, but he was right—in her fury of the moment, she had told him to buy her one. Except she'd thought that might be in London, not while they were still in France.

"I am," he said. "I was an absolute ass, as in the stubborn-mule kind rather than someone's bottom."

She tried so hard not to laugh that she snorted, clamping her hand tightly over her mouth. This was the Michael she'd missed, the Michael she'd wished she could have back again, and she instinctively sat down beside him, wanting to be close to him. If only he'd been like *this* when she'd confessed her feelings to him.

"You *were* an ass," she agreed. "But I appreciate the gesture."

She grasped his hand, and as if he could sense how emotional she was even without seeing her, he pulled her down and she carefully placed her head on his chest. All she'd wanted to do the last time she'd seen him, and the time before that, was to touch him, and the feel of him against her was as warm and tender as she'd hoped.

She was so tired, her body exhausted from what she'd been through for the past two weeks, and she had the sudden urge to curl into a ball with him and sleep. To just feel his heartbeat against her ear, the curve of his body beneath her hands, the warmth of his touch. Once, it would have taken months to fall for someone, but the war had changed everything; it had heightened every emotion and made time seem like a limited commodity.

"Tell me what you've been doing," he said, stroking her hair as if he'd done it a hundred times before, instead of this being the very first time. "I need something to take my mind off things here."

"It's a long story," she said, squeezing her eyes shut as she spoke.

"I happen to have all day," he said dryly.

And that's when she knew that Michael would be fine, his quick wit making her laugh through her tears, despite it all. From that first night she'd met him in the bomb shelter, he'd teased her, and she hoped that he never went back to being that man who'd admonished her and told her to go.

The words suddenly spilled from her—she was desperate to share what had happened with him. "I've been frantically covering the liberation of Bayeux and Caen this week, and I'm probably going to be arrested and my career will be over soon, but Danni is definitely out of the woods now and Chloe—"

"Whoa!" he said, his hand sliding down her hair and then resting on her back. "What happened to that timid little Ella who wasn't brave enough to report on the actual war? You've been covering the liberation?"

Ella sat up and stared down at Michael, her hand hovering before touching his cheek, the small section of it that wasn't covered by bandages exposing his soft skin. She should have wanted to slap him, but instead she just laughed. His dry humor was one of the reasons he'd equal parts infuriated her and made her want him when they'd first met, and it was just nice to have that version of him here when she'd thought he was lost to her for good.

"She's changed," Ella whispered. "I followed the war, just like you told me to, and it changed me."

"I know," he said softly. "I saw it that day I arrived in Normandy and found you lying on the ground. It's why I didn't want you to see me injured, in case it scared you from doing your job or made you feel as if you had to care for me."

He was right, it had scared her, but it hadn't stopped her. "I think you underestimated how strong I've become," she replied.

"I can see that now, but I wasn't so sure then."

They sat a beat, silent, until she finally found the courage to ask what she'd been holding in. "Michael, do you know any more about your eyes? Is there any chance you'll regain your sight?"

"Honestly, no one seems to know," he said sadly. "Either that, or they just don't want to tell me."

She held his hand up to her mouth, willing herself not to cry as she pressed a kiss to it. And not because she pitied him, but because it was so damn sad.

"On the bright side, I'm in need of a very capable assistant," he said, teasing her, the lilt in his tone telling her that he was trying to cheer her up, despite all he'd been through himself. "I've been working on a novel in my head, and if I'm blind *and* effectively useless given the work I do, I suppose you'll have to type it for me. If you're looking for a job, that is?"

"You won't be *useless*," she gasped, holding his hand so tight she had to force herself to let go.

"I love your optimism."

"Look, you're going to see again," she said, trying to sound positive. "You can see the best specialists in London and—"

"Stop," Michael said calmly. "I'm planning on taking this day by day. I'll find a way to deal with whatever happens. The day I got injured, I'd have killed myself if I could have found a gun. But I've promised myself to find a way to tell all the stories, from these men in here, no matter what." He paused. "So even if I can't see, will you let me sit beside you at the typewriter while we work together? I think we'd make quite the formidable team."

"I think so too," she whispered. She actually didn't care if he couldn't see, she just wanted to be in the arms of a man who lifted her up, who challenged her and made her believe that she could do anything.

"Because I understand, Ella, if you can't—"

"Finish that sentence and I swear to God, Michael," she swore, "I'll hit you, blind or not!"

Michael started to laugh then, a deep belly laugh that made her giggle straight back at him, and instead of moving away from him, she curled into his side, her upper body covering his.

"You're going to get in trouble being up here," he said, his lips against her hair, the most intimate caress she'd ever felt.

"I don't care," she murmured. "I've had one hell of a day."

He started to stroke her hair and she smiled against his chest.

"What are you thinking about?" he asked.

"You really want to know?"

"Try me."

She took a deep breath, mustering all her courage. "I'm thinking about the fact that I'm falling in love with you all over again," she whispered.

"Well, I wouldn't worry too much about that last part," he whispered back. "There might be two of us suffering from that particular ailment."

Ella grinned as she digested his words. The first time she'd told him, he'd broken her heart, but she was so pleased she'd been brave enough to tell him again.

Michael's lips touched the top of her head again, and Ella nestled in close to him, finally giving in to the overwhelming urge to sleep after so many days of fighting it.

———— ✑∾✑ ————

"Morning, sleeping beauty."

Ella slowly opened her eyes, stretching as she blinked and came to her senses. *Michael.* It all came racing back to her, and even though embarrassment shot through her, she still reached for him—him not being able to see her made it easier somehow, less intimate.

"I can't believe I'm still here," she murmured, brushing a quick kiss to his jaw and hoping no one was watching them. But from the low wolf whistle that rang out nearby, she realized that had been wishful thinking. "I haven't slept like that in weeks," she said, gently pushing herself up and trying not to hurt him. She realized she'd never even asked him if he had other injuries, but instead of complaining he'd stoically lain still all night so she could rest.

"Ella, I'm sorry to interrupt," came a soft female voice.

"Hi, Florence," she said, smoothing her hair down and wondering how crumpled and sleepy she must look as she got off the bed. "I hope you didn't get in trouble for letting me through here yesterday."

"It's fine," Florence said. "And you know I'd never ask you to leave, but Matron Clarke has just started her shift and she's hell-bent on getting you out of here, and I just wanted to warn you."

"Go," Michael said.

Ella turned, taking Michael's hand as he reached toward her, clasping it tight as Florence stepped closer.

"Look, I shouldn't be telling you this, but he's being sent back to London soon," she told Ella with a kind smile. "The worst cases are sometimes airlifted out, but he's been marked to go on the next hospital ship so they can see about his eyes."

Ella digested her words, wondering what her next move was.

"Ella, I can't see, but I think I can hear that brain of yours ticking over."

Florence left them and she turned back to Michael, tenderly stroking his face with her fingertips, tracing around his bandages.

"I don't know what to do next," she said. "Do I leave with you, or do I stay and see if I can keep working until someone stops me?"

"You stay," he said, linking their fingers. Michael's full lips parted in a smile. "I'd love nothing more than for you to come with me, but you need to stay. I'd never forgive myself if I kept you from your work. If you have unfinished business here, you need to stay. This is your chance to make a name for yourself, and I'm not going to be the reason that doesn't happen. You can meet me in London soon enough."

Ella leaned over him and inhaled the scent of him, spreading her fingers across his legs as she tried to memorize how he felt. "Thank you."

Tears started to slide from beneath his bandages, and she felt useless, hands fluttering, wishing she knew what to do for him.

"Don't cry," she begged, her whispers frantic. "Please don't cry, Michael, not for me."

They held hands, palm to palm, clasped tight, as she sat on the edge of the bed facing him.

"I don't want to be the reason you don't get to follow your dreams. My work has consumed me my entire adult life, and I'm only seeing now, excuse the pun, what I've missed out on."

"I'll stay with you then," she told him, pressing her lips to his fingers. "I can work in London, report there instead, if I'm allowed to."

"No. One day you might regret it," he said. "So just go, but promise you'll come back to me once it's all over."

His words were soft yet forceful, and she stared at him, trying to commit every part of him to memory as she stood. She nodded and bent over him, pressing her mouth to his as tears curled around their lips.

"I promise," she whispered.

"Ella, did you ever finish that story? The one about correspondents you interviewed me for?"

She smiled. "I did, but I want the timing to be right. I'm going to wait until I'm sent back to London, and find an editor who'll publish the full story without redacting any of it. It means too much to me."

Michael nodded; she knew he'd understand.

She carefully, slowly, extracted herself from him, taking tiny steps backward before finally turning away and walking through the rows of men in the makeshift hospital, staring at the daylight through the door.

She had a job to do, even if doing it made her heart feel like it was breaking in half, like she'd turned her back on the first man who'd ever made her heart beat like it was about to pound straight out of her chest.

Ella had no idea whether she had hours or days or weeks before she would be forced to answer for her actions, but until that final moment, she was going to write every story she could. And if the Battle of Caen was her last piece of correspondence, then so be it. At least no one could say she hadn't fought till the bitter end.

CHAPTER THIRTY-FOUR

DANNI

Danni looked at her two bags, packed and ready for her voyage back across the ocean, hardly able to believe that her time in France was over. But before she could wallow over her wings being clipped, Chloe appeared, limping, her hand held protectively over her stomach.

"You ready to go?" Danni asked.

"Ready as I'll ever be."

She studied Chloe, seeing the resemblance to Andy as her face lit up with a smile. But instead of making her sad, it comforted her now, knowing that the one thing he'd wanted more than anything in the world was to make sure his sister was safe.

"Chloe, before I forget, I have something for you," Danni said.

Because of everything, she hadn't given Chloe the letter that she'd kept safely stored with her Speed Graphic camera. She carefully took it from the bag beside her and passed it up to Chloe. They'd been kept in separate parts of the hospital as they both recovered, and it was only now they'd been able to even see one another.

Chloe stared at her hand, not moving for a moment, but Danni continued to extend it until eventually she took the paper from her.

"I can't believe you kept this for him," Chloe said, and the wobble in her voice made Danni swallow down her own emotion.

"He loved you so much, Chloe. I know he'll be resting easy now that you're safe."

"What have I missed?" Ella asked, appearing in the tent, face flushed as if she'd been running.

"I just gave Chloe the letter from Andy," Danni said, as Ella came to perch beside her.

"Oh, right." Ella looked between them. "Well, it seems it's a day for giving things, because I have this for you."

Danni burst out laughing when Ella thrust a very squashed, misshapen item at her.

"My hat! Who would have thought it'd survive."

Ella looked triumphant. "One of the men found it in the jeep apparently, and I thought you might want it as a keepsake, even if you can't wear it anymore."

Danni leaned against Ella, wondering why such a lovely woman had stuck with her when she'd been so reluctant to have her around in the beginning.

"Thank you, it means a lot."

"And I've had more good news," Ella said. "My brother was injured and there's shrapnel in his leg, so he's been sent home. But he's safe and he has all his limbs, so that's something to be grateful for."

"That's wonderful, Ella," Danni said, but they both fell silent when Chloe cleared her throat and spoke up.

"Do you mind if I read it aloud?" Chloe asked.

Danni shut her eyes, taking a deep breath and forgetting everything else as she waited to hear Andy's final words. "Of course not."

Ella wriggled closer to her and took her hand, as Chloe's soft voice sounded out.

"Dear Chloe.

If you receive this letter, then it means I'm gone, but the good news is that it means you're alive. There's only one person I'd ever trust to deliver this letter to you. Firstly because she's like a dog with a bone and would travel to the ends of the earth to find you, and secondly because she's my best friend. I know you'll love Danni, and I only hope that she can share with you all the amazing times we've had together over the years, and become as loyal a friend to you as she has been to me. If you want to get her talking, take her for cocktails, and she'll soon be telling you all sorts of tales.

Chloe, I can't tell you how much I've missed you since you left, and although you always told me how much you loved Gabriel and wanted to return to him, I'm sure you can imagine how worried I've been during such turbulent times. I've seen so much that it clouds my judgment sometimes, and makes me overly protective of the people I love, namely you. I'm sorry if I stifled you as I tried to protect you, but without our parents here to care for us, I suppose I felt like a father to you. Please give my blessing to Gabriel and tell him that I wish I'd met him. I hope you go on to have a wonderful, happy life filled with children and prosperity. I would have loved to be an uncle, and can only imagine what I'll miss out on.

Goodbye, Chloe, from your loving brother, Andy."

Danni held her hand to her face, trying not to cry as she imagined him penning the letter. She wished she knew when he'd written it, when he'd poured his heart out on paper, and wondered if she'd been oblivious to what he was doing at the time. If only she could have been there for him more, as he was always there for her.

When she finally looked at Ella and then Chloe, she saw there was not a dry eye between them.

"He sure had a way with words, didn't he?" Ella said, breaking the silence.

"That he did," Danni agreed.

"When I get back to London, I want to find a way to honor him," Chloe said, sitting down beside her. "He was such an inspiration to me, and if there's some way I can use my modeling contacts or find a way to showcase his work, it's what I want to do."

Danni tucked her arm around Chloe, holding her close. "If there's something I've learned over the past few years, it's not to take no for an answer. Whatever you set your mind to, you can do it."

"Hear hear," Ella said.

"Danni, do you remember I told you about how I've always wanted to work as an editor?" Chloe asked.

Danni smiled. "Of course I remember."

"Well, do you think it would be crazy of me to contact the editor at *Vogue* in London when we return? I know I'm past modeling now, and even if I wanted to I don't feel like that same girl anymore, but I loved being part of that world. It was one of the things that drew me to Gabriel. It'll be one of the things I want our child to know about his father."

"I don't think it's a stretch at all," Danni said. "And if there's anything I can do to help you, please just ask."

"I know what you mean about feeling like a different girl," Ella said. "I can barely remember who I was before all this."

"Thanks, girls," Chloe whispered as she folded the letter in half. "I can certainly learn a lot from everything you've done."

"Danni, did you get a chance to say goodbye to Cameron?" Ella suddenly asked.

She smiled. "I certainly did. I wasn't leaving without setting eyes on him one last time. He's one hell of a man."

Ella nodded. "You can say that again."

"We've promised to meet at The Savoy, once this is all over," she said. "So long as I haven't been deported back to America by then."

"Keep the faith, Danni," Ella said. "That man would walk over burning hot coals to get to you."

"I know," she said, seeing Cameron's face in her mind as she'd wrapped her arms around him for the last time. "And he's had a complete change of heart about female correspondents too, which honestly made my day."

"It's time to leave, ladies." A stern voice interrupted them.

Danni looked up and saw a nurse waiting for them. It was time for the trip down to shore, where the hospital ship was waiting to transport her and Chloe to London.

"I'll see you soon, gorgeous," she said to Ella.

Ella enveloped her in a warm hug, holding on tight, before she stepped back and hugged Chloe.

"I'll see you both soon, too," Ella said, clearly trying not to cry.

Danni didn't know whether she'd be arrested on arrival, or whether she'd be sent directly for surgery to remove more shrapnel from her hip, but all of a sudden she didn't care. She'd delivered Andy's letter, and Ella and Chloe had survived, and that mattered more to her than whatever her fate in London might be. And now she had the voyage back across the Channel to be in Chloe's company, spending every hour telling her tales of her brother's bravery as she forged a friendship of sorts with the woman whom Andy would have gladly given his life for.

And in a way, he had.

CHAPTER THIRTY-FIVE

LONDON, THREE WEEKS LATER
CHLOE

Chloe sat, back ramrod-straight, in the Bond Street offices of *Vogue* magazine, one hand resting on her round stomach. When she'd returned to London, she hadn't expected to miraculously ignite her modeling career after her absence, especially given her current condition, but she had decided to make contact again. Perhaps it was Danni rubbing off on her, but something about what she'd seen in France had lit a fire of sorts inside of her.

"She will see you now," a young woman said, indicating the closed door down the end of the hall. Despite being bombed during the Blitz, the building was still magnificent, and in moments like this it was almost possible to believe London wasn't at war. On the inside, she couldn't see any damage, and it took her back to when she was a younger woman going to her first meeting at *Vogue*.

"Chloe! It's so good to see you again!"

Audrey Withers was a larger-than-life character—even before she'd been made editor, there had been something about her that Chloe had always been drawn to on the occasions they'd met. Chloe took in her perfectly coiffed hair, pearls, and skirt suit, and then stepped into the arms Audrey was holding wide.

"Darling, you've had quite the ordeal," Audrey said, shaking her head. She gestured for Chloe to sit in one of the chairs, before sitting back in her own seat. "And look at you now! As beautiful as the last time I saw you!"

"It's been an interesting few years, that's for sure," Chloe said, jangling like a bunch of keys she was so nervous. She touched her stomach, conscious of how different her figure looked now.

"Do you remember that day?" Audrey asked, reaching for a frame and passing it to Chloe.

She smiled sadly as she looked at the photograph. It was her, a lifetime ago, on the last photo shoot she'd done before leaving for France. Her cream suit was perfectly tailored, her matching hat perched on her head at a jaunty angle as she gazed up at the sky.

"That building was one of the first to be bombed," Audrey said, her voice soft as she reached for the photo and set it back on her desk. "I keep that here as a reminder of what we have to look forward to one day. But our magazine isn't only about fashion now, although we do still show women how to utilize their existing wardrobe to look fashionable, of course. But we are the voice women look to for guidance on all matters, which means we have a duty to accurately portray the war." Audrey paused. "We are influencing women's lives, and to do that, I need the best people working for me, now and during the transition to peacetime." She sighed. "If we ever win this darn war."

Chloe nodded as Audrey leaned forward.

"What would you say if I asked you to become one of my assistant editors?" Audrey asked. "I want you to work on the war content with me, and it just so happens that I've had clearance to employ another former model of ours. Did you ever work with Lee Miller?"

Chloe smiled at the memory. "I certainly did."

"Well, she's becoming quite the accomplished war correspondent," Audrey said. "Truly inspiring, that woman is."

Chloe sat up straighter. "I would be honored to work with you in any capacity, Audrey."

"I just have one other question for you."

She smiled. "Of course."

"Is it true you're a close friend of Danni Bradford's? I hear she may have some unseen images from Normandy?"

Chloe grinned back at Audrey, and the older woman gave her a wink as she started to laugh.

"It just so happens I am," Chloe said. "But if I'm to secure Danni's photographs, I need to know that you'll publish the raw truth of war. If I can't be bold here, then it's not the job for me."

Excitement thrummed through her body as Audrey sat back, arms folded across her chest.

"It just so happens that I like bold," she said. "And I hate the bloody censor, even if I do toe the line."

"But, Audrey, I should mention the obvious here," Chloe said, gesturing to her middle region. "I know it doesn't make me the ideal candidate, having a baby on the way, but I do have someone organized to help me during the day once the baby arrives, and to be honest, I have to support myself so I need to work."

Audrey leaned over and touched her hand. "You don't need to explain yourself, Chloe. I loved working with you before, and I know I'll love working with you again."

Chloe couldn't stop the grin that spread across her lips. "Then the only question I have is, when do I start?"

"Monday, first-thing," Audrey said. "And bring those rolls of film with you."

Audrey held out her hand and Chloe clasped it. Andy would be so proud to see her standing in the glamorous Bond Street offices of *Vogue*, but oddly enough it was Gabriel who filled her thoughts as she walked away from the most influential editor in London.

You're here with me, Gabriel, she thought as she waved goodbye to Audrey and passed down the hall, smiling at the pretty woman sitting at the front desk. Never in a million years had she thought she'd be working at *Vogue* magazine as anything other than a model, and during her darkest times in France, she'd even doubted she'd ever make it back to London. But Gabriel had given her a love for editing in that brief time she'd had with him in Paris, when she'd had the chance to see him work and been asked her opinion on the layouts; it had shown her another side to the world of fashion and magazines. And as she felt their baby move and stretch, she pressed her hand to her stomach, knowing a part of him was going to be with her on this journey.

She only hoped that if Gabriel was looking down on her, he was sitting with Andy, seeing that she was making a life for herself despite it all. He'd made the ultimate sacrifice for her in the end, forever a hero in her eyes, and because of that it was easier to remember him as the man she'd fallen in love with in Paris, when she'd been just a girl, and he'd been the man of her dreams.

CHAPTER THIRTY-SIX

LONDON
DANNI

Danni stood up as tall as she could, even though it still sent spasms of pain through her side. She was propped against the bar at The Savoy, with two soldiers standing facing her, their expressions grim. She refused to look anything other than defiant as they treated her like a war criminal, even though her only crime had been defying biased gender laws and trying to do her job: to report the truth to the world about the war. She'd been waiting for them to come since she'd arrived back in London, but the matron at the hospital had refused them entry while she was recovering from one of her two surgeries to repair damage to her abdomen and then to remove further shrapnel from her leg. And so they'd tracked her down within hours of her release from hospital. Naturally, she'd headed straight for the bar at The Savoy, keen to catch up on the action.

"Miss Bradford, you are hereby stripped of your military accreditation, and forbidden from working as a foreign correspondent," the older of the two soldiers said. "Your passport must be sur-rendered, as must your ration card, and as soon as you are fully recovered from your injuries, it will be returned to you under the most stringent of conditions, for the sole purpose of your return to the United States of America."

She passed them her passport and card, nodding curtly, as if to dismiss them. But it appeared he wasn't ready to stop speaking just yet.

"Do you understand the gravity of the crime you committed?"

Danni raised an eyebrow without meaning to, and she was certain her face showed her disgust. "If you're asking if I'd do it again if given the chance, then yes, I would."

His nostrils flared with obvious annoyance, but he kept his composure. She knew it was wrong to goad him, but she'd always been unfailingly truthful, and she wasn't about to stop that now.

"Miss Bradford, you're lucky you're not being detained," he said. "You put yourself and soldiers at risk—"

"I'm well aware of what I did," she hissed, no longer able to claw back her anger. It rose within her, bubbling like a volcano about to erupt. "I should have been afforded the same rights as male correspondents from the very beginning, and instead I'm being reprimanded for standing up and demanding to be heard."

She pressed her hand to her side, feeling dizzy as the pain spi-raled further up her body. She was under strict instructions not to push herself, not to experience any stress during her recovery, and already she was reaching boiling point.

The soldiers both looked unimpressed, and certainly unmoved by her sharp tongue.

"Do you understand that you are prohibited from working as a correspondent again?" he continued. "If you do so, you will be arrested immediately."

She inhaled, clenching her fists. "I do," she said through gritted teeth. Now she just wanted them gone.

"Then we wish you well with your recovery," the second soldier said. "God speed."

She ignored both of them, leaning over the bar as if their words meant nothing to her and ordering a whiskey. Her only regret was not already having a glass so she could throw it at their retreating figures.

"You look like you could use some company."

"Ella!" Danni's frustration disappeared as she saw her friend standing there, blonde hair loose around her shoulders and a smile so sweet that it lit up her entire face. "What are you doing back here?"

Ella crossed the room, opening her arms and giving Danni a big hug. "I was called back by my editor, but not before I managed to report on more of the liberations throughout France."

"Did you hear me get my marching orders just then?" Danni asked.

"I heard enough," Ella said, giving her a wink and leaning across the bar to order a gin. "But then, I've heard it all before, so it didn't exactly come as a shock."

Danni stared up at her, seeing the grim line of her mouth and realizing she meant it. "They've already done the same to you?"

Ella sighed. "Yes. Heaven only knows how long I'll be allowed to stay in the country." She paused, lowering her voice. "Do you still think about that day when we landed in Normandy?" Ella asked. "I have alternate nightmares about what happened to Andy and the day I almost lost you as well as Chloe." Her voice went quiet then, barely louder than a whisper. "Sometimes I just can't stop thinking about all that blood, about how we managed to survive at all."

Danni's body went cold and she fought against the shiver that sent goosebumps across her skin. "Sometimes I wake up and my sheets are soaked in sweat, and my heart is pounding so hard I think I'm about to have a heart attack. So yes, I know exactly what you're talking about."

They stood silently for a moment, and Danni was grateful she had Ella to talk to. It wasn't often she had a shared war experience with another woman, and, other than Andy, she'd never truly had anyone to confide in who knew what she'd been through, what she'd seen and could never unsee.

"But being here, just feeling the energy in the bar, the excitement between the correspondents, it brings back the good memories, too." If she shut her eyes, she could almost see Andy beside her, standing with a drink in hand as he had when they'd laughed and talked with the paratroopers all those weeks ago. When Cameron had irritated her so much she'd rather have punched him than kissed him.

"Danni, look over there," Ella suddenly said.

Danni turned, her eyes widening when she saw a familiar, beautiful woman walking toward her, tapping along in her high heels despite being very pregnant. "Chloe!" She ignored her pain as she moved toward her, opening her arms and receiving the warmest of embraces in return.

"Ella! You planned this, didn't you?" Danni scolded. "Why didn't you tell me she was coming?"

"Because Chloe wanted to surprise you with something," Ella said, and Danni watched as she exchanged glances with Chloe.

"What are you two up to?" she asked, at the same time as Chloe took a magazine out of her bag and passed it to her.

"*Vogue* magazine?" Danni asked. "Do you have a story in here, Ella?"

Chloe laughed. "You wouldn't believe it, but I'm working as an assistant editor there now. And my first job was to pull something amazing together for their war coverage."

Danni glanced up at Chloe before opening the magazine, instantly recognizing the photographs that Cameron had wired back to London for her. "Oh my God," she whispered. "You published them? Well, I forgive you for not visiting me, you've clearly been very busy!"

"Oh, she did more than just publish your photographs," Ella said, leaning over her shoulder and turning to the next page. "Chloe published my story about Andy, Michael, and you, the full piece that I wrote from Normandy on war correspondents. It's like nothing you've ever seen before in *Vogue*. This girl came back from France with a fire burning inside her, and she pushed to turn this into something larger than either of us could have imagined."

"I can't believe it," Danni whispered, staring at the photos she'd taken just before they'd found Chloe in France. "They're the most graphic images I've ever submitted. I'd started to think they were never going to be published."

"I'm just so pleased we can show the world what a sacrifice so many war correspondents make to document and photograph the war," Chloe said, beaming at Danni. "When I think of Andy . . ."

Danni quickly reached for her, feeling the same pain at seeing Andy's name in print, at seeing the photos that felt like a lifetime ago.

"I dedicated the story to him," Ella said. "It just felt right."

"It means a lot to me, seeing Andy's name," Danni said, not even trying to hide her tears now. "I don't think anyone who hasn't experienced war would have realized what it's like out there, but seeing his name and knowing that you wrote a story about his contribution to the war, it's just so amazing to see."

They stood together for a moment, all huddled around the magazine as Danni flipped through the pages.

"Have they allowed any female correspondents back to France?" Danni asked Chloe.

"They have, but they're not allowed near the front lines. They have the women in tents near the field hospital, and they're not allowed any of the same privileges as the men still."

Danni snorted. "That's ridiculous. More of them will start going AWOL now, and then the powers that be will learn their damn lesson about trying to disadvantage us."

"Lee Miller reported back recently, saying that the tents are disgusting and located right beside the latrines, and the rain has caused the dirt to turn to mud," Chloe said as they all took a seat at the bar. "The men have been billeted to beautiful old chateaus with running water. They have censors on site and they can transmit their articles themselves. They're being treated like royalty while the women are fighting for every inch of ground they have."

"You've commissioned Lee Miller?" Danni asked, impressed.

"We have. I wish it were you, Danni, but to know that a woman is going to be writing and photographing the war for us, it feels like a huge step forward. She's already sent us her first negatives from the towns the Allies have liberated."

"I've never been scared of competition," Danni said, waving at the bartender to get his attention. "I think it's wonderful that she's been employed by *Vogue*. And I'm so proud of you for getting the job there. Let's have a drink and you can tell me all about it."

"On that note, I have to go unfortunately," Ella said. "I have to pop in and see Michael before visiting hours are over, but I'll see you both again soon."

"Actually, you might not hear from me for a while," Danni admitted, turning to face Ella.

"You're not doing anything stupid, are you?" Ella asked.

"Let's just say that I haven't had my last byline yet. I might head for Italy, or even back to France."

Danni saw Ella exchange glances with Chloe and they all laughed.

"Danni, I know you won't listen to me, but it will be almost impossible for you to travel."

She winked. "Where there's a will, there's a way, but they're not sending me home to America, that's for sure. I'll find a pilot to bribe if I have to, and besides, I'd like to get back to a certain officer, and I'm sure he'll find a way to keep me near him."

They all laughed again, and Danni grinned at the image of Cameron she had in her mind, smiling at her, his eyes crinkled as they'd said their final goodbyes. There was no way she was going home without seeing him again.

"You've been one hell of a friend to me," Ella whispered, kissing Danni's cheek. "Even if we never see each other again, I'll never have a friend like you in this lifetime."

"Same here," Danni said. "I'll never forget what we went through together, and what you did for me."

CHAPTER THIRTY-SEVEN

ELLA

As she walked into the hospital ward, Ella smiled when she saw the familiar golden-brown, wiry hair in the bed closest to the window. It had only been a few weeks since she'd last seen him, but it felt like a lifetime ago.

She stopped dead when he turned, raising a hand and waving to her, his one brown eye as bright as his smile as he fixed his gaze on her.

"Michael?" she cried, hardly believing her own eyes. "*Michael!* You can see me!"

She'd forgotten just how beautiful his eyes were, how much they sparkled, until that moment when she saw him looking at her again for the first time. His right eye was still bandaged, but his left looked as beautiful as ever.

"Glad to see you're still looking so gorgeous," he teased.

Ella stopped at his bedside, taking his hand and holding it tight as she stared at him and he stared straight back at her. She felt more self-conscious now, but she pushed the thoughts away, refusing to revert back to being shy around him after everything they'd gone through together.

"When did this happen?" she gasped. "What did they say?"

"The surgeon doesn't think my sight will ever come back in my right eye, but I'm just happy to be able to see at all."

Ella sat and tucked her legs up on the bed beside Michael, just as she'd done at the field hospital in Normandy.

"It's a miracle, isn't it?" she laughed. "It's an absolute bloody miracle!"

"You know, I might need you to bring my typewriter in," he said, and she had no idea whether he was teasing or not. "Unless I can borrow your portable? I recall mine was blasted off my body in France."

Ella laughed. "What happened to us writing together? Is that over before it even began?"

Michael leaned over and kissed her, his mouth warm and sweet against hers. "Darling, we'll be writing together for the rest of our lives, make no mistake about that. Can't you just see us, side by side, hunched over our typewriters, lighting Lucky Strikes and writing up a storm?"

"For the rest of our lives, huh?" Ella dropped her head for another kiss, gently touching her lips to his. But he was right, she could imagine them, elbows bumping as they tapped furiously at their typewriters together.

"Actually, Ella, there's . . . well, there's something I'd like to ask you."

She sat back, smiling down at him. "And what's that? You want me to write your articles for you while you take all the credit?" she teased.

"Actually, I wanted to ask if you'll marry me?"

Ella almost fell off the bed, and she would have had Michael not caught her arm to steady her.

"Marry you? Michael, I . . ."

He ran his fingers down her arm and caught her hand.

"If all of this has taught me anything, it's that I was so caught up in my work that I almost didn't see what was right in front of me," he said. "I can't think of anything I want more than for you to be my wife, Ella."

She clamped a hand over her mouth, staring down at him. He wanted to marry her?

"Yes," she gasped. "Yes, Michael, I'll marry you."

He grinned and pulled her down for a kiss; a long, slow kiss that had been worth the wait.

"I don't have a ring for you yet, but as soon as I'm out of here, we'll go shopping together."

She smiled against his mouth as she kissed him again. She could lock lips with Michael Miller for the rest of her life, and she doubted she'd ever believe that the worldly, enigmatic journalist she'd been so smitten by was actually hers for keeps.

EPILOGUE

LONDON, OCTOBER 1945
DANNI

"Ohh, let me look at him!" Danni reached out to Chloe, desperate to take the wriggling baby from her arms.

She'd only seen Chloe's son once, having evaded authorities and gone on to cover the liberation of Paris and then the concentration camps throughout Europe, and she was desperate to spend some time with the pair of them.

"Isn't it wonderful that Ella organized this?" Chloe said, as Danni admired her elegant jacket and hat as they stood in the entrance of The Savoy. She certainly looked the part of *Vogue* editor. "I've been telling baby Andy for days that he finally gets to spend some time with both his aunts."

Danni beamed as she held out her arms to him, touching his pudgy hands and looking at his inquisitive, bright blue eyes. "He's an absolute darling," she said. "I just can't tell who he gets those eyes from? They're so like his uncle's, but . . ."

"Gabriel's too," Chloe said as she set him down. "He has parts of both of them, or at least I like to think so."

"His thick blond hair is definitely from his papa," Danni added. "He comes from some very strong men." She smiled down at him. "You have a lot to live up to with a name like Andrew, you know."

"Ella!" Chloe suddenly squealed, and Danni pulled a silly face at Andy as he looked up at his mother's shrill noise. He giggled and started to toddle off, with his mother in hot pursuit.

"It's so good to have our intrepid traveler home," Ella said, hugging Danni.

"Michael," Danni said, giving him a quick kiss on the cheek. "It's so good to see you both."

"Brings back memories being here, doesn't it?" Michael asked, and Ella flushed as he gave his new wife a nudge in the ribs.

"You two are gorgeous," Danni said with a sigh. "Come on, let's go and order something good to eat, shall we?"

"Ahh, can we just wait a moment, Danni?" Ella asked. "Chloe needs to do something."

"No I don—"

Danni saw Ella give Chloe a swift kick, and knew then that something was up. "What's going on?" she asked.

Ella shrugged and Chloe flushed, as if she'd been caught out.

"Ella, what—"

"Hello, Danni."

Cameron.

Danni's heart just about leaped out of her chest as she spun around and saw the only man in the world who could make her knees go weak, standing in front of her. He was dressed in uniform, his hair combed perfectly off his face, shoulders as broad as she'd remembered them, and his beautiful brown eyes locked on hers.

"Cameron!" she said, out loud this time, as she started to walk toward him before breaking into a run. "I can't believe you're here!"

He took her into his arms and swung her around off her feet, lips colliding with hers as she clung to him.

"You've got Ella to thank for this," he murmured as his lips left hers.

"Ella?" she asked, turning around, hands still on Cameron as she looked at her friend, who was smiling very smugly beside Chloe and Michael.

Cameron let go of her then, dropping to one knee as she silently watched, hardly able to believe what was happening.

"Danni Bradford," he said as he took her hand, "you're the most courageous, smart, beautiful woman I've ever met. Will you marry me?"

"Yes!" she gasped. "A hundred times, yes! Now get up off the ground and kiss me again, will you?"

Her friends laughed behind her as she tugged Cameron up, holding on to the front of his jacket as she claimed his mouth again.

"Danni," he said, holding her back, his eyes searching hers. "I want to marry you today, in front of your friends, before you're sent back to America."

"I'm sorry, *today*?" she asked.

"It's why everyone's here," he said softly, caressing her cheek as she blinked up at him. "I wrote to Ella and asked her to help me get you here. I was worried the authorities would find you and send you packing before I got to you otherwise."

She laughed. "Hold on, so you were *that* certain I'd marry you that you organized everyone to be here to witness it?"

Now Cameron was the one laughing. "After everything we've been through together, yes," he said confidently. "Yes, I was. In fact, I even arranged to have a military chaplain here too." Cameron indicated over his shoulder and Danni saw another man in full uniform standing behind him.

"Yes," she said, stroking Cameron's face. "Yes, Cameron, I will marry you today, in front of the people I love the most in the world." She shook her head, hardly able to believe it. "Even though I swore I'd never get married and I don't even know your first name!"

Everyone laughed, and Cameron bent close to her, touching their foreheads together. "Robert," he said. "My first name is Robert. And as for the marrying part, well, I wasn't so sure I'd ever marry either, and yet here we are."

She breathed deeply as they stood together, his body strong as hers started to tremble. How was this even happening? A few minutes earlier, she hadn't even known Cameron had been sent back to London, and now she was about to marry him.

"We don't have to do this," he whispered. "If it's too soon . . ."

"It's not too soon," she said, taking his hand and standing tall. "The war is over, we're all here, it's perfect timing."

He beamed down at her. "Then let's get married."

Little Andy started to clap his hands together and she bent to scoop him up, cuddling him as he squirmed and babbled for his mama. She looked at her friends, and at the man beside her, and the only thing that could have made it more perfect would have been having Andy there to walk her down the aisle.

Cameron tapped a knife against his wine glass, and Danni turned away from Chloe, her thigh against her husband's as she tucked herself closer to him.

"I'd like to propose a toast to my new wife," he said, giving her a conspiratorial smile as he stood.

The rest of the table fell quiet, other than Andy, who was wriggling on his mother's knee.

"Some time ago in Sicily, I met a woman who absolutely took my breath away," Cameron said, chuckling. "And not in the way you'd expect. This woman, *Danni*, she was infuriatingly confident and brave, and although I didn't know it at the time, they were the qualities that ultimately made me fall in love with her."

Danni reached for her napkin and dabbed at her eyes.

"Danni," he said, looking down at her. "I wish I could take away the pain you went through in Normandy, and I wish Andy could have been here today, because I know how much he meant to you. I love you more than you will ever know."

She stood then, taking his hand and leaning into him, head to his shoulder as she tried to muster the words she needed to say.

"Without you, I wouldn't even be here today," she managed. "I never thought I was the marrying type, but you changed everything for me, Cameron. So thank you, for everything."

She turned to him then and stared into his eyes, smiling up at him. Her hand rose, shaking as she cupped the back of his neck, and as he lowered his mouth to hers, she whispered to him, "Thank you for saving me."

He paused, grinning down at her, his arms cocooning her. "Danni, I was never, ever going to leave you behind. Just like I was never going to leave London without marrying you first."

And as their friends started to talk again, the noise level in the restaurant rising with the clinking of cutlery and happy chatter about the war finally being over, she lost herself to Cameron's kisses.

"I think it's time for us to retire to our room, *wife*," Cameron whispered in her ear.

"What a wonderful idea, *husband*."

Cameron took her hand and kissed it, before drawing her close.

"Don't you even *think* about running off and leaving us," Ella said, eyeing them suspiciously and making them both laugh. "We've still got dessert to come, and at least another bottle of champagne before you lovebirds can go."

Danni grinned and pulled Cameron back down to his seat with her. Somewhere between France and London, Ella had gotten to know her far too well. But she wouldn't have had it any other way.

It is necessary that I report on this war. I do not feel there is any need to beg as a favor for the right to serve as the eyes for millions of people in America who are desperately in need of seeing, but cannot see for themselves.

Martha Gellhorn, writing to military authorities before the Normandy invasion

READER NOTE

As with all my novels, the essence of each story is rooted firmly in history. I love writing about strong women during World War II in particular, and shining a light on some of their amazing accomplishments. Researching and writing about female war correspondents, both journalists and photographers, gave me an incredible opportunity to show another fascinating part of women's history.

There are parts of *The Last Correspondent* that are entirely fiction, such as the scene where Danni jumps with paratroopers during Operation Husky early in the novel. There was in fact a female photojournalist who learned to jump with paratroopers, and who was a great inspiration for Danni's character, but she did not jump into Sicily specifically. Likewise, when Danni and Ella sneak on to a hospital ship and land at Normandy, this is based on fact but is, in fact, fiction. In truth, only one female war correspondent hid on a ship in order to make it to Normandy (being the *only* correspondent to be there on the day to witness this moment in history unfold), but for my story I wanted Danni and Ella to be there together. And in case you're wondering, it is true that all the accredited male war correspondents were stuck at sea in the Channel, peering through binoculars on D-Day! This was a small but important part of history that I found particularly fascinating.

Going back to Operation Husky though . . . there was in fact a contingent of paratroopers who jumped into Sicily in terribly windy conditions that meant they all scattered as they landed. This was a crucial success during the war, as the paratroopers created initial confusion, which allowed the amphibian invasion to successfully follow. The American troops did meet two German battalions on the island, as depicted in the novel, and successfully went on to secure the beachhead from the Germans. After that, General Patton marched toward Palermo, despite being instructed to head west. If you're interested in this part of the war, I urge you to read further about Patton's disagreement and power struggle with General Harold Alexander (later known as Field Marshal Sir Harold Alexander), and the way Patton was determined to prove that Americans were more advanced and capable than their British and Canadian counterparts! It makes for interesting reading.

I also wanted to share that there was a very accomplished war correspondent (photographer) who had previously worked as a model before picking up the camera and working for British *Vogue* as a photographer instead. She was loosely the inspiration for Chloe when I first started dreaming up characters for this story, although Chloe's character changed significantly along the way to make her distinct from the other women. Of note, it is also true that when women correspondents were finally allowed to go to Normandy, they were not allowed near the front lines and were confined to tents beside the field hospital in horrid conditions. Their male counterparts were billeted in beautiful old chateaus with running water, whiskey "as good as on tap," and the ability to directly wire their stories back to London and New York! The female correspondents had to send their work back to London manually in a pouch, which was said to be as slow as going by carrier pigeon.

If you would like to read more about the female war correspondents during this period, both journalists and photographers,

I encourage you to start with the incredible women who were so inspirational to me in my research, and who I've provided short biographies of below. Their respective bodies of work are truly inspirational!

Martha Gellhorn is perhaps best known for being the third wife of Ernest Hemingway, but she was also an incredible writer and war correspondent in her own right. She is considered one of the greatest war correspondents of the twentieth century, having covered almost every major world conflict during a career that spanned six decades. Martha was also the only woman who landed in Normandy in June 1944, which made her a huge inspiration for Danni in this novel. Martha took her own life at the age of eighty-nine, suffering from cancer and nearly blind. It is widely reported that she swallowed a cyanide capsule.

Elizabeth "Lee" Miller was a famous fashion model turned photojournalist. During World War II, she became known for covering the liberation of Paris, and the concentration camps at Buchenwald and Dachau. She worked closely with British *Vogue* editor Audrey Withers, who published some of her most graphic photos near the end of the war. She saw her job as "documenting war as historical evidence," and to "provide an eye-witness account" of the casualties of war. Lee advanced with the Allies from Normandy to Paris, and she also traveled with troops to Munich, eventually breaking into Adolf Hitler's apartment! Once there, she stripped off her filthy clothes and muddy boots and soaked in his bath, and she even photographed herself doing it!

Perhaps my favorite photojournalist from this era is Dickey Chapelle, who was an American correspondent during World War II, and continued to photograph conflict right through to the Vietnam War. Dickey was confident, plucky, and fearless when it came to her work, and she learned to jump with paratroopers and regularly traveled in the field with troops. Sadly, one of the many firsts she is known for is being the first female correspondent to be killed in action. When she was covering the Vietnam War, she was hit by shrapnel when a land mine exploded, killing her instantly.

Other inspirational female war correspondents include Margaret Bourke-White, who was the first foreign photographer permitted to photo-document the Soviet five-year plan; Marguerite Higgins Hall was also a prolific correspondent, reporting on World War II, the Korean War, and the Vietnam War, writing for the *New York Herald Tribune* and *Newsday*; and there is also the infamous Marjory Collins, a photojournalist who covered World War II, and as a true pioneering trailblazer, called herself a "rebel looking for a cause."

ACKNOWLEDGMENTS

As usual, I would like to express my eternal gratitude to the team at Lake Union (Amazon Publishing) for continuing to publish my novels and for being so incredibly supportive of my career. In particular, I would like to mention my longtime editor Sammia Hamer, who has been so incredible to work with on all of my books. Special thanks as well to Sophie Wilson, who also helped to sculpt this novel. I'm starting to think I couldn't write a novel without these two incredible editors! I'd also like to thank my copy editor Gillian Holmes, proofreader Gemma Wain, my author support team—Nicole Wagner, Bekah Graham, Hannah Hupfer—and the rest of the Amazon UK team, as well as my agent, Laura Bradford, for everything she does for me.

On a personal note, I would like to thank my ever-supportive family. Thank you to my mother, Maureen, for all the childcare and incredible meals; my father, Craig, for being my constant cheerleader; and of course to my husband, Hamish. I'm very lucky to live in a house full of boys—they are great at making me leave my laptop and enter the real world when I'm busy with my stories—so huge thanks to not only my husband, but also to Mac and Hunter. And I really should give my crazy-annoying beast of a dog—Teddy—special thanks for forcing me out of the house every day to stretch my legs on walking adventures!

As an author, it's hugely important to have a great support crew, and I also need to give a big shout-out to Yvonne Lindsay for writing with me every day and being so supportive. Also to Natalie Anderson and Nicola Marsh for being my lifeline every day too—our emails mean the world to me.

But my biggest thanks goes to you all—my readers—for continuing to support me. I read every review and every message you send me, and it truly means the world to me connecting with you on social media and via email.

Finally, I would like to say a special thanks to Greg Bramwell for his kindness in explaining vintage cameras and photography processes to me! His wisdom was invaluable to me in my initial research for this novel. And to Sharon Scurr, for her excellent idea on how Chloe could smuggle herself into France!